PRAISE FOR THE NOVELS OF
MICHELE ANDREA BOWEN

HOLY GHOST CORNER

"Thoroughly enjoyable . . . a funny, juicy story with plenty of Scripture thrown in to keep us humble."
—**NightsandWeekends.com**

"Filled with delightful characters."
—*Southern Pines Pilot*

"I loved the setting of Durham, North Carolina, and the characters that she so deftly brought to life."
—**MyShelf.com**

"Awesome . . . will have you laughing, crying, and praising all at the same time." —*Birmingham Times*

"Coupled with quirky characters, HOLY GHOST CORNER tells a tale of love almost missed and opportunities overlooked." —**RoadtoRomance.com**

"Peopled with hilarious characters . . . A lighthearted and humorous look at the issues facing today's black Christian woman." —**BookLoons.com**

UP AT THE COLLEGE

"This storyteller is at the top of her game." —*Essence*

more . . .

"Bowen's soulful girl-next-door style keeps this love story current, fun, and grounded in realism."

—*RT Book Reviews*

"Offers an entertaining mix of humor, morality, and steamy relationships as well as an intimate portrayal of academic politicking and college sports." —*Booklist*

"[Bowen] presents a picture of life . . . that is both humorous and faith-based . . . fans of Bowen's early novels will find *Up at the College* equally funny, touching, and well worth reading."

—ArmchairInterviews.com

"Christian romance readers will enjoy Michele Andrea Bowen's fine contemporary." —*Midwest Book Review*

SECOND SUNDAY

"Fresh, passionate, and laugh-out-loud funny."

—*Dallas Morning News*

"Strong . . . Humorous . . . Conspiracies, drama, and political intrigue abound. Bowen deftly balances romance, church politics, and spirituality and offers lessons on a myriad of issues including the power of love and forgiveness and the strength of community. A funny, honest drama." —*Greater Diversity News* (NC)

"Bowen's writing humorously explores familiar terrain for anyone who has witnessed church politics. [This] book contains important messages about redemption and love—that we are imperfect people who serve a gracious and merciful God." —*Black Issues Book Review*

1988 → 2014.
① Joninas etc...
② Cindy Crawford
stalking DMM.
③ Nigger Bitch since 2008
⑥

㉖ of
being
Stalked.

Also by Michele Andrea Bowen

2014.

CHURCH FOLK

SECOND SUNDAY

HOLY GHOST CORNER

UP AT THE COLLEGE

Threshows —㉒ on Me.
Confidential Care
㊵ on me.

HOLY GHOST CORNER

Michele Andrea Bowen

GRAND CENTRAL
PUBLISHING

NEW YORK   BOSTON

This book is a work of fiction. Names, characters, places, and incidents are the product of the author's imagination or are used fictitiously. Any resemblance to actual events, locales, or persons, living or dead, is coincidental.

Copyright © 2006 by Michele Andrea Bowen
Reading Group Guide copyright © 2008 by Hachette Book Group
Excerpt from *More Church Folk* copyright © 2010 by Michele Andrea Bowen
All rights reserved. Except as permitted under the U.S. Copyright Act of 1976, no part of this publication may be reproduced, distributed, or transmitted in any form or by any means, or stored in a database or retrieval system, without the prior written permission of the publisher.

Grand Central Publishing
Hachette Book Group
237 Park Avenue
New York, NY 10017
Visit our website at www.HachetteBookGroup.com

Grand Central Publishing is a division of Hachette Book Group, Inc.
The Grand Central Publishing name and logo is a trademark of Hachette Book Group, Inc.

Printed in the United States of America

Originally published in hardcover by Hachette Book Group
First trade paperback edition, June 2008
First mass market edition, April 2010

10 9 8 7 6 5 4 3 2 1

This book is dedicated to my daughters,
Laura and Janina.
Also, with a special dedication to my grandmother,
Mrs. Jeffie Hicks, a.k.a. "my Da Da."

Acknowledgments

Thank you, Lord, in the name of Jesus Christ, my Lord and Savior, for blessing me with the opportunity and ability to write and publish another novel.

Thank you, Hachette Book Group USA for publishing this book. It has been a blessing to work with all of the wonderful people who have helped me bring each book to fruition and then get them in those stores.

Readers, it has been three years since I have published a new book and you all never failed to encourage me with kind notes, hugs, prayers and well wishes, and continued support of my first two novels, *Church Folk* and *Second Sunday*. God bless all of you.

And I "ain't got nothin' but love" for my family and friends who support me and keep me lifted in prayer. While I can't name everybody, I have to give a few shout outs.

To my mother, Minnie Bowen, I love you and appreciate all that you do to encourage me and my writing. I know you know how much I miss Daddy.

To my cousins and aunts and uncles, with just a few words to lift up the incredibly "crunked" and, more importantly, anointed gospel CDs that my first cousins, Jonathan and Jason Nelson, have released.

To Laura and Janina's grandparents, John and Mildred Spencer, who always make sure that everybody they know reads my books. Granddad Spencer, I would not have been able to create the Rhodes, Rhodes, and Rhodes architectural firm if I had not had the pleasure of watching your illustrious career as a highly respected architect.

And I can not end these shout outs without giving a special "hollah" to Ava Haskins Brownlee and Kenneth Brownlee, who are my sister and brother in the Lord, and make me wonder if we were "separated at birth." Ava had my back in prayer and stood on the spiritual battlefield with me to fight off the fiery darts of the adversary. Ken listened patiently as I talked about the characters as if they were real people, and gave me the space I needed to "debrief" whenever I finished intense periods of working on this project.

Then, there is my church and church family, St. Joseph's AME Church in Durham, North Carolina, where my brother in the Lord, Reverend Philip R. Cousin, Jr., the Senior Pastor, and my sister in the Lord, first lady, Angela McMillan Cousin, have built a powerful, Holy Ghost–filled ministry.

Last but definitely not least, thank you to my uncle, Bishop James D. Nelson, Sr. and my aunt, Mother Bessie Nelson, who demonstrate what a Holy Ghost–filled marriage and ministry is all about. Tell the folks at Greater Bethlehem

Temple Apostolic Church I have been tremendously blessed whenever I have attended service at "super church."

> *Let everything that has breath and every breath of life praise the Lord! Praise the Lord!*
>
> PSALM 150: 6

Chapter One

THERESA ELAINE HOPSON WAS FEELING LOW, THOUGH it was one of those perfect mid-November Durham afternoons—a sunny, fifty-degree, Carolina-blue-sky day. It was a pine-tree-smelling day, a shopping day—the kind of afternoon when no sister could resist dropping by Theresa's store, Miss Thang's Holy Ghost Corner and Church Woman's Boutique. To Theresa's ever-growing numbers of satisfied customers, Miss Thang's, as it was affectionately called, was the most perfect today's-black-woman-friendly store in the Triangle cities of Raleigh, Durham, and Chapel Hill, North Carolina. Sisters would wander by to spend a few minutes window-shopping, only to find themselves in the store hours later, captivated by all of that good-ole-black-girl stuff they hoped their designer and seriously ghetto-fabulous-faux-designer pocketbooks could handle.

The store's cash register rested on an antique glass display case, which held an assortment of crosses with exquisite jeweled settings, complemented by an array of matching cross earrings and bracelets. A corner table was dedicated to Bibles: classy leather-bound ones in black, pewter, and ruby along with chic Bible covers in rich suede, metallic leathers, velvet, and raw silk. Another lace-covered table held blessed and sanctified bottles of anointing oil—large, medium, small, and purse size. Right next to it, nestled in a nook, was a glass-doored corner hutch full of fine paper goods—sermons by the area's best preachers, Prayer and Praise Report Journals, pastel note cards, and legal pads with Bible verses printed on them, which were such a big hit with the local university students that Theresa couldn't keep them in stock.

The purses and hats were also a big draw. Miss Thang's purses were black-church-lady pocketbooks, pure and simple. Once, when asked by a friend, "Girl, what they look like?" a loyal customer held up her new black satin bag, with her church's name embroidered in sequins, and replied, "Now, do you want one of these, or should Miss Thang order you and your sorority sisters some royal blue silk clutch bags with 'Zeta Phi Beta' printed on the front with pearly white bugle beads?"

Cutting their lunch date short, that friend went straight to Miss Thang's to order twenty-five Zeta clutches for the Sorors and also treated herself to a ruby silk church bag with *Jesus* embroidered on it with silver silk thread.

And the hats—they were a visual feast, in every color and fabric. But everybody's favorite section of the store was devoted to what Theresa jokingly called her "Saved Hoochie Mama" merchandise. Tucked away in an antique mahogany armoire were pajamas and lingerie in silk, satin, and sheer chiffon, embroidered with expressions like "Saved," "Church Gurl," "Miss First Lady," and even "Bishop's Boo."

More than once, Theresa had been scolded and prayed over, with laying on of hands and anointing oil, when a conservative, super-saved customer went into the armoire looking for roomy, waist-high cotton drawers, support hose, and big longline bras, only to find filmy slips and camisoles, lace teddies, thongs, push-up demi-brassieres, and satin tap pants to match. In an effort to keep the "saved patrol" off her, Theresa tried to appease them by ordering their kind of underwear with "churchly" inscriptions. Now the big seller among the "saved patrol," which had first been special-ordered by a Holiness Church evangelist, Mother Clydetta Overton, was big panties with embroidery across the front reading "Nobody But Jesus Can See."

But the truth was that after a sister got lost in the sheer pleasure of looking at and touching the lingerie, she often came to her senses feeling embarrassed, especially when her eyes fell on the "Holy Ghost Corner" sign beside the armoire. Plenty of women got saved after rummaging through all that fancy, sexy, delicate bedroom wear and found themselves shamefaced, purchasing a new Bible, study guide, sermon, or Prayer and Praise Journal to strengthen their walk with the Lord.

The alarm system beep-beep-beeped, followed by a three-second blast of shouting music as the door swung open. Theresa's younger brother, Calvin, or "Bug," as he was called, insisted that the Holy Ghost had led him to wire that sound into the security system. Bug believed that if somebody came into the store who wasn't right, the shouting music would drive him *or* her out.

Theresa's assistant, Miss Queen Esther Green, was pushing through the door with her elbows, arms full of uniforms for area churches' Sunday morning service nurses in new colors—pale blue, pale purple, and off-white.

She had a box of gloves gripped under one arm and in her free hand, a carton of Krispy Kreme doughnuts that smelled so good it would have made Peter forget his fear when he hopped out of that boat to walk on the water with Jesus.

"Uhhh, baby? You gone keep standing in the middle of the floor, or you think you'll come and help an old lady out before Jesus cracks across the sky?"

Theresa rushed over to take the doughnuts out of Miss Queen Esther's hand.

"Baby, the doughnuts ain't heavy but these uniforms are."

Sniffing at the doughnut box, Theresa gathered the uniforms from Queen Esther's arms.

"These hats just came in—met the UPS man just as I was pulling up." Miss Queen Esther started dragging in two boxes from outside the door. "You know something, baby, that UPS man kind of cute. What church he attend?"

"He doesn't like organized religion. Said that on Sunday mornings, he grabs a cup of coffee and sits quietly, and then thinks about nature and science and agriculture and stuff like that."

Queen Esther frowned. "Well, then, we can forget about trying to get the two of you fixed up."

"Miss Queen Esther, the UPS guy isn't my type."

"You right about that. A man who get up on Sunday morning dranking coffee and thinking about tomatoes, instead of studying his mind on the Lord, show ain't your type. Baby, I should have known that something was up with him as soon as I saw them long dreadses hanging way back off of that big, half-bald head.

"Baby, the Lord has often led me to discover that when people hiding stuff about themselves, they give off telltale signs with their clothes, their hair, the way they keep their house and such. So, that hair is a blessing in disguise. 'Cause it's like the Lord saying, 'He may be cute and available, but look at his head—just look at the brother's head.'"

Theresa helped herself to a doughnut and bit into it with a laugh. "Miss Queen Esther, you know yourself is crazy."

"I ain't all that crazy, baby. I just depend on Jesus to help me see it and say it like it is."

Theresa shook her head, relieved that she'd escaped a lecture on being too persnickety about men. Single, forty-seven, and with no serious boyfriend, she felt awkward when Queen Esther kept pushing her toward the available men she came across. Though Theresa wanted badly to get married, she still hoped to find the right man: God-fearing, loving, as intelligent and hardworking as she was, and ideally, at least fairly attractive. But so far he hadn't come along.

Suddenly it struck her why she'd been so blue all day. The holiday season was rolling up on Theresa and she wasn't ready to face it this year.

She had a hard time with the holidays, and dreaded the thought of coming to dinner or a party alone and watching couples grinning and skinning all over each other and having fun. Sometimes her family, as loving as they were, didn't seem to understand how that made her feel left out. Worse yet, they even acted like it was normal for Theresa to be on her own, with no man, when that was the absolute last thing she wanted in her life.

Her eyes teared up as Queen Esther started to reconsider her opinion of Yoda the UPS man.

"Of course, baby, you just might be the Lord's way of reaching out to that Yoda. Technically, he really is a decent-looking man. All he need to do to look good is shave his head bald . . ."

Luckily, Queen Esther didn't notice her tears, distracted by the box she was cutting open. Pulling aside the gold tissue paper, she gently lifted out the hat inside and set it on the counter, next to the register. It was a fluffy confection made of the palest creamy yellow netting, twinkling with rhinestones. "Baby, you ought to keep this one for yourself. It is simply breathtaking."

She handed the hat over to Theresa so she could try it on.

Theresa settled the hat on her head and walked over to the full-length mirror near the Mary Kay cosmetics. The hat was so dreamy and romantic that she fell in love with it on sight.

"Baby, that hat is you," Queen Esther said. "Who made it?"

"Miss Bettie Lee Walker, the new designer with Essie Lee Industries in St. Louis."

"She young or old?" Queen Esther asked.

"Miss Walker is seventy-two."

"Young woman, huh?" Queen Esther said. She was seventy-six herself.

Theresa gave her a crooked grin in the mirror.

But Queen Esther missed it. She was shuffling through the rack of dresses and suits. "Here," she said. "This will knock that hat right out."

She was lifting the plastic off a pale, creamy yellow silk chiffon chemise and matching sheer tulle coat with ruffled sleeves designed to drape gracefully over the wrists. It was the kind of ensemble that delicately hugged the body and swayed with the wearer's every move—an outfit that would make a church man say, "Lawd, ha' mercy and thank you, Jesus."

"Oh yes, you gone need this." Queen Esther lifted the hat off Theresa's head and then proceeded to take it, along with the ensemble, to Theresa's office in the back.

"Miss Queen Esther . . ." Theresa began when she returned.

"Maybe it can be your Thanksgiving outfit."

"I think it's more for the springtime."

"Well then, Easter. That woman in the Bible days poured out some high-priced perfume and washed Jesus' feet with her hair and tears. So, I really don't think it's asking too much for you to look your best on Easter Sunday. And besides, you need a good man-catching suit, one to show off those long legs."

"We've got a customer," Theresa said to change the subject.

A Pepto-Bismol-pink Cadillac Escalade had whipped into the parking space in front of the store. The driver, who stepped down carefully, was dressed in pink from head to toe, wearing a pale pink silk pantsuit with a mint green silk tulip on the right lapel, a mint green and pink silk scarf draped over her shoulders, and pink alligator pumps with a matching shoulder bag. That outfit made Glodean Benson-Washington's exquisite chocolate skin look like the finest velvet. Though she was sixty-nine years old, not one wrinkle marred her beautiful complexion, enhanced only with a soft stroke of rose blush and shimmering rose lip gloss.

Glodean was notorious both in her own right and because she was married to Sonny Washington, one of the Gospel United Church of America's most controversial bishops. Back in the 1970s, after creating yet another major scandal at a church convention, Bishop Washington was exiled to a modest congregation in Fuquay-Varina, North Carolina. During his first year as pastor, Glodean urged her husband to persuade the members, who needed money for major repairs on the church building, to sell him and the first lady the twenty acres of land it stood on. After graciously deeding a few acres back to the church, Glodean proceeded to develop the rest into a strip mall with stores catering to the black community.

The thriving mall had made Mother Washington a millionaire several times over. And according to Gospel United Church gossip, that was how Glodean managed to get her husband, Sonny—an old-school, mean-as-a-snake street fighter if there ever was one—to stop beating her tail. Mother had pimp-slapped the bishop with so much money that if it even crossed his mind to look at her wrong, he had to stop and remember which side of the bread the butter was spread on—Glodean's side.

Emerging from the passenger door of the SUV was Charmayne Robinson, a real estate attorney, who did consulting work for high-roller developers and black business owners throughout the state. Theresa had known Charmayne since childhood, when they both lived in the Cashmere Estates, a now abandoned and blighted low-rise housing project in Durham. But while Charmayne could hardly bear to acknowledge the connection, her ruthlessness in business led many to observe that, beneath all that platinum-and-diamond jewelry and fancy clothes, she was still a "'hood rat," who had yet to shake the "ghetto dust" off her $400 stiletto-heel pumps.

The two women paused before the store's black-edged-with-pewter welcome mat, and Theresa could see Glodean taking in the facade. She was proud of the sign, with calligraphy script spelling out "Miss Thang's Holy Ghost Corner and Church Woman's Boutique" in velvety orchid neon light. She was glad that she'd decorated the windows for the holidays with silver and lavender silk ivy, glinting with tiny Christmas bulbs in starry white. And she felt a guilty satisfaction when Glodean demanded of Charmayne, in a shrill voice that carried from outside, "Why haven't you recommended some of these 'boutique touches' for my stores?"

Charmayne bit her lip to stifle a snippety retort. What kind of "boutique touches" could you add to a 7-Eleven? But Charmayne wasn't about to alienate a major client. Instead, she waved Mother Washington ahead while pushing the door open. Glodean put a foot in the store but jumped back when the shouting music came on.

"What a racket!" she said. "You ought to cut that out!"

Charmayne wrinkled up her nose as soon as she laid eyes on Miss Queen Esther Green. "What you doing here, *Queen Esther*?" she said. "Cleaning the toilets? Emptying trash cans?"

Queen Esther cut her eyes at Charmayne, but with a "Sorry, Father" opted to let the scripture be her answer. *"Do not speak to a fool,"* she said, *"for he will scorn the wisdom of your words.* Proverbs 23:9."

With that, Miss Queen Esther picked up a folder of invoices and bills to be paid, and headed back to Theresa's office.

"Mother Washington," Theresa began, fighting to keep laughter out of her voice. "I'm glad you're here. Your new hat has just arrived."

Whatever she thought of Glodean, any customer who ordered three hats worth $1,500 apiece—all designed to her exacting specifications—had to be coddled. "Let me open the box and you can try it on."

Theresa pulled at the second, sealed-up box on the floor, which seemed awfully heavy. Using her pearl-handled box cutter, she slit it open and peeled back the tissue paper. All three women peered down at the hat inside, which was covered in outrageous flamingo-pink feathers. It had a crown that would have swallowed an average woman's head and a hard, upturned brim sure to stand out a good eighteen inches from the wearer's face.

With a mighty heave, Theresa managed to get the big box onto the counter, then slit the sides so she could slide the hat out.

"Oh my, my, my!" Glodean exclaimed, reaching out for her new hat.

"I need to help you put it on," Theresa said evenly, estimating that the hat had to weigh at least twelve pounds.

It took some doing to maneuver the hat, which was like a three-foot sail, onto Mother Washington's head. Two months before, when Glodean had special-ordered the hat, describing it down to the last detail, Theresa was still hard-pressed to visualize it. The hat was so extreme—so bizarre and extravagant, and so pink—that she simply could not fathom how it would look on somebody's head. And now Theresa found it downright unsettling to see how very well Mother Washington wore it.

"I love it!" Glodean said, spinning around to see the

back of the hat so quickly that she lost her balance, as Theresa reached out to steady her.

"Oh yes, that's some hat," Charmayne offered.

"Umph," Glodean continued, with a smug, tight smile on her face. "No other woman will have a hat like this—or even anywhere close to it—at our district's next Annual Conference."

"I believe that," Theresa said.

Glodean started out taking small, careful steps, trying to figure out how to walk in the huge hat. Growing bolder, she eased into her signature stride—a slow, barely perceptible booty-swinging sway that never failed to turn some preacher's head and make the man resort to mopping his face with a handkerchief. She was in such a deep zone studying the hat that when the door beeped and the shouting music came on, she jerked and toppled onto a rack in the Holy Ghost Corner, sending an entire display of stockings inscribed with "Jesus," "Saved," and "Praise the Lord" tumbling all over the floor.

With arms stretched out wide to hold on to her hat, Glodean managed to right herself and back up onto a precarious perch at the edge of a table full of lap cloths. The cloths were wildly popular among the ultra-modest ladies at the Holiness Church, who liked to keep their knees covered during services.

"Here, Mother, let me help you," Theresa said, rushing to straighten out the hat on Glodean's head. Hearing all the commotion, Miss Queen Esther came running out of the back of the store, tightly clutching one of her bottles of anointing oil. She glared at Charmayne, who made no move to help her pick up the fallen rack or the packets of hose.

Struggling to keep her dignity, Glodean gave

Charmayne an imperious wave to signal that it was time
to leave. Charmayne carried both their purses to the cash
register, where Glodean handed her the mammoth hatbox
as if she were her personal maid. Then a hush of anticipation fell over the store as Theresa, Queen Esther, and the
new customers all waited to see just how Glodean was
going to navigate out the door.

"I hope you can drive with whatever it is you got on
your head," said the man who had just arrived, tilting the
crooked dark shades on his face toward the hat. Tapping
his white, red-tipped cane on the floor, he sniffed the air,
adding, "Lawd ha mercy, you a fine thang, ain't you, girl.
And you don't even look as old as you is, do you, baby?"

Glodean sucked in air through clenched teeth and bore
her eyes right through his shades. "I," she said, "I am
Mother Glodean Benson-Washington, wife of the Right
Rev. Sonny Washington. And you, and this, this . . ."

Glodean couldn't even find words to describe the man's
companion. The woman's hair, despite her obvious ma-
turity, was combed in three thick, coarse, steel-colored
braids; and she was passing off a blue-flowered house-
coat as a dress, accessorized with navy blue knee socks
and yellow jelly sandals. Strangest of all was her mouth,
which was filled with the most peculiar and conspicuous
false teeth Glodean had ever seen.

"Looka here, Miss High-Siddity-Preacher-Wife-Woman,"
the woman slurped out through those teeth. "You just
needs to get and gone on 'way from here, 'fore I have to
forget I'm a lady and whip yo' butt. 'Cause don't nobody
talk to my man, Lacy here, like that."

"Let it go, Baby Doll," the man said soothingly. "We

here to get you a treat. I ain't in no mood to peel you off nobody today."

Baby Doll calmed down and slurped out, "Yes, Big Daddy."

Charmayne couldn't believe that woman had called Mr. Lacy, who was a little, skinny red man with a face full of freckles, "Big Daddy."

"Charmayne," Mr. Lacy called out with authority. "Take this woman on away from here. She has almost ruined what started out as a beautiful day."

Charmayne had kept silent ever since Mr. Lacy and his girlfriend had entered the store. She knew he was blind, and he hadn't heard her, so how in the world . . .

"Baby girl, when you gone figure out that I have other ways of knowing who is around. Remember, I been knowing you since your mama, Ida Belle, went into labor at the Soul Family Picnic, and had you 'fore any of us could get her in the car to go to the hospital."

Charmayne wanted to snatch that cane from Mr. Lacy and beat him with it. Why did he have to tell that old tired story in front of the Bishop's wife? She had spent the last twenty years of her life trying to rid herself of those project roots and, even worse, project people. And here he was dredging up that mess.

"Charmayne, let's go," Glodean snapped. "You drive us back to Fuquay-Varina."

Under her breath she muttered, "Talking about ghetto . . ."

"Yes, Lawd. We's talkin' 'bout ghetto," Mr. Lacy's girlfriend said, as he tugged at her arm to forestall any trouble.

"Come on, Baby Doll," he urged.

Only by tipping her head to one side could Glodean fit her hat through the door. Queen Esther and Theresa watched from the window, amazed as she managed to twist herself gracefully into the car. Despite her initial difficulty at maneuvering in the hat, Glodean managed to climb up in her car like that overblown pink thing was a natural part of her head.

"Get out of that window looking country like that," Mr. Lacy admonished them.

"Lacy, we looking country, 'cause we country. Plus, she started it," Queen Esther said. "Didn't nam-nobody tell that heifer to come up in here, dragging that jacked-up Charmayne Robinson with her, like she did. Why, that—"

"Theresa," Mr. Lacy interrupted, "I want you to meet someone special. This here is my boo, Baby Doll Henderson. Baby Doll, this is the baby girl I've been telling you all about—the one with the store."

Baby Doll grinned, dabbing at some loose saliva, and said, "Girl, it show is good to meet yo'self. You know Big Da . . . I mean Lacy, here, got nothing but love for you. And that's sayin' somethin'. 'Cause I know you know, Lacy here don't take to everybody easy-like. Whole lotta people in Durham he'd just as soon cut with a straight razor if they so much as blink at him."

"Nice to meet you, Miss Baby Doll," Theresa said politely. She had seen a few of Mr. Lacy's women over the years, and every one was memorable, to say the least. But this one, without a doubt, took first prize.

"That your real name, honey?" Queen Esther asked, about to bust with that and the second question running through everybody's mind.

"Yes, it's the name on my birth certificate, signed at the old Lincoln Hospital right here in Durham. My mama named me that 'cause when she first saw me, she thought I was a big, pretty, brown baby doll."

"I see," Queen Esther said carefully, searching Baby Doll's face for evidence to support her name and coming up empty. "So," she continued. "Tell us how you met up with Lacy."

"Oh, that's a good story," Baby Doll answered beaming. She sucked back saliva to clear her mouth a bit. "See, I was waiting on the bus in a rainstorm, trying to get back to the homeless shelter before nightfall. And Lacy here, with his sweet self, pulled up and said he would drive me home."

"Excuse me," Theresa said incredulously. "Did you just say that Mr. Lacy offered to drive you home? In a car?"

Mr. Lacy, who had been "watching" them, tapped his cane on the floor and said, "I offered her a ride. That's all you bad-tailed busybodies need to know. Now get out of my business."

"Then, when we get to the shelter," Baby Doll went on, "Big Daddy said he didn't think somebody as sweet as me should be there, so he took me to his home and I've been there every since. Got me a job cleaning offices, and I am just so happy. I got a job, a home, and a man. "

"And now that Baby Doll has got me," Mr. Lacy said with such love and tenderness that it clutched at Theresa's heart, "I'm gone get my baby something pretty to put her teeth in. See, they ain't normal false teeth and sometimes they hurt her mouf, and she need to take 'em out. But she need somethin' to put 'em in—especially when we out in public."

"Yeah, Lacy right," Baby Doll added. "See, my nephew's girlfriend's baby daddy work at that hippity-hoppin' store for the young'uns, where they makes all the gold teefs and stuff, and them fronts or teeth grilles these chirrens stickin' up in they moufs. And when they makes the fronts, they makes molds of the teefs with this real light yellow, clay-lookin' stuff. The molds, they look like false teefs, but not all the way like false teefs."

Baby Doll gave them a big grin to fully display her "false" teeth, which were a putty yellow, or the exact color used to make the molds of teeth. "That boy who make 'em, did 'em for me for free."

Queen Esther tried not to say, "I see what you mean." But it came out before she could stop it.

Mr. Lacy cut his eyes at her because he knew Queen Esther knew better.

"I have the perfect box for Miss Baby Doll's teeth, Mr. Lacy," Theresa said softly. She reached under the table and found the cutest plastic box—perfectly sized. It was bright red with tiny metallic flowers stamped on it in blue, yellow, and green.

"Here, Miss Baby Doll," Theresa said, as she put the box in her hand. "This is a gift from me."

"Thank you, baby," Baby Doll slurped with a big grin on her face. Then she slipped her teeth into the box, snapping it open and shut a few times, and shaking it to be sure that they were secure. "Perfect," she mumbled through her gums, before putting the teeth back into her mouth. "I can get the teefs in and out of the box right quick. That'll do me some good when I have to take a meal."

Watching Baby Doll perform her ritual with the teeth, Theresa could practically hear Queen Esther trying to form her mouth to ask about the connection between the speed of getting teeth into and out of a box and eating food.

Feeling their eyes on her, Baby Doll got uncomfortable for the first time since she'd entered the store. "I can't eat good with my teefs in my mouf," she started to explain. "They real stiff and just for decoration, so my mouf won't look all sunk down in and bad."

Then she stopped, remembering that while these folks were nice, they might be a little bit uppity—and that not a one of them, including her Lacy, had ever gone hungry or not had a decent place to sleep in their entire lives. She was being stared at by some folk whose needs were so well supplied that they couldn't even imagine not being able to get some real false teeth.

"You folks is blessed and you don't even know how much you is blessed," she told them. "I know I am—I even used to be crazy until this evangelist lady over at the shelter prayed with me until I got healed of being out of my mind."

"Hmmm . . ." said Queen Esther. "So why haven't you come to church, Baby Doll? To be healed of that kind of craziness is a miracle, and you need to finish what was started and get saved. You and Lacy here need to come on back to church. You need to let the Lord know how much you appreciate your new life."

"Queen Esther," Mr. Lacy snapped. "Does everything with you always have to start and stop with Jesus?"

Queen Esther looked Mr. Lacy dead in the eye and knew that he could "see" her. "Yes, Lacy. Everything in this world starts and stops with Jesus."

Mr. Lacy squirmed just a bit under her glare, then

sighed and reached out for his girlfriend. He knew Queen Esther was right but he wasn't ready to give up making home-brewed spirits for his brother's illegal liquor house. And he was making a killing selling Virginia's state lotto tickets out of there, too. All that would have to stop when he took that long walk down to the church altar.

"You ready?" Mr. Lacy asked Baby Doll.

Baby Doll took his arm and made to leave, but then stopped mid-stride and turned to face Theresa. "I'm a good cleaning lady. You think I could work for you and keep your store all nice?"

Theresa was still processing what Baby Doll had been telling them about being blessed and prayed out of being crazy. Her first inclination was to say no, but something in Baby Doll's eyes made her think of the verse in Matthew about the sheep and the goats, when Jesus said that doing for the least of them was doing for the Lord.

"Look, I ain't no criminal and I show ain't no thief," Baby Doll was saying.

"You come to church on Sunday and to Bible study on Wednesdays, Miss Baby Doll, and I'll hire you to clean up on the weekends. That sound fair to you?" Theresa asked.

Baby Doll was hesitant at first, then stuck out her hand and said, "Deal."

"Come on, baby," Mr. Lacy said. "I think we need to hop on the bus and get on over to Kmart. You gone need some church clothes and a few extra things for work. You have to look nice when you working at a fine establishment like Miss Thang's."

"Ooooo, Lacy," Baby Doll slurped out, cooing. "You show is a good man. Handsome, too."

"Heh, heh, heh," was all Mr. Lacy said, as he hurried the two of them out the door, excited about having some extra money to take his woman on a shopping spree at her favorite store.

Watching them head out together in the dusk, Theresa was hit by a wave of loneliness. It was disheartening to watch Mr. Lacy carry on over Baby Doll like she was Gladys Knight, when the woman wore her hair in three braids, had on some yellow jelly sandals over dark socks, and didn't even have real false teeth. Yet Theresa—a prosperous businesswoman, with a retailing degree from Eva T. Marshall University, whom everybody agreed was nice-looking and goodhearted, if a little prickly sometimes—couldn't find a man who truly wanted her, never mind treat her like she was God's best creation since sweet potato pie.

For all her success at work, Theresa felt like a failure at life. Before she could help it, a tear slipped down one cheek.

This time, Queen Esther caught it. "Who are you to question God's ways in your life, Theresa?" she admonished. "Baby Doll has the same God-given right that you do to be loved and treated with kindness and respect by a man. And you are wrong—just plain wrong—to measure yourself against her like that."

"I know," Theresa began. "It's just that—"

"It's just nothing," Queen Esther interrupted. "Why—"

Before Queen Esther could launch into a full-blown lecture, the phone rang, four, five, then six times. When the machine picked up, the caller audibly clicked off, and then a minute later, the phone started ringing again.

"Who's that calling over and over?" Queen Esther demanded, punching the speakerphone button.

"Theresa, where are you?" asked an angry male voice.

Queen Esther definitely recognized that voice. Cutting her eyes at Theresa, she snatched up the receiver and thrust it at her.

"Hello," Theresa said, avoiding Queen Esther's glare.

"Why are you still holed up in that store?"

"Uhhh . . . did I forget something?" Theresa murmured.

"You certainly did," said Parvell Sykes, the owner of the voice. "You know that I'm waiting for you."

"Oh . . . where am I supposed to be?" Theresa asked gingerly, a little shocked that she'd forgotten her dinner date. She'd been seeing Parvell on and off for a couple of months but had found herself making excuses when he pressured her to see him. He was what most people would consider a "catch"—a wealthy and successful real estate agent, fifty-two years old, single, and an assistant pastor at Fayetteville Street Gospel United Church. But Theresa found that she just didn't like the man.

"You were to meet me at the Washington Duke Inn," Parvell was saying. "We set this up ten days ago because this was the first night you weren't 'busy' with some stupid little goings-on."

"I'm sorry," Theresa said. "Where are you right now?"

"AT THE WASHINGTON DUKE INN, YOU IDIOT!" Parvell yelled. "Get out of that flea market you call a store and get over here—*immediately*."

"But, but—"

The phone went dead in Theresa's hand. Parvell had hung up.

"I don't know what you're playing at, missy," Queen

Esther said, "going out with that low-down hound, Parvell Sykes."

"Well, he is a man of God," Theresa protested weakly.

"Humph. The only God that jackleg preacher worships is green, crisp, and folding. Don't you know he's mixed up in the plans to tear down the Cashmere and put up some of that rich folks' luxury housing?"

"Well, why not?" Theresa said. "Something has to be done with it. It's an eyesore and it's dangerous, with all those men breaking in there, drinking and setting fires. No one even likes to walk past it. It's too scary."

"That's our old home you talking about."

"Not for a long time now—not for me or you, either. Miss Queen Esther, I didn't know that you felt like that about the Cashmere."

"There's plenty you don't know that God will reveal in His own good time. And besides, that no-good Parvell Sykes is a dog. He wouldn't even be in the church if Bishop Eddie Tate didn't want to keep him close. "

"Look," Theresa said, defensively, "it's been almost two years since I've dated a man. I know Parvell's not ideal, but I'm trying to give it a chance. There aren't a lot of eligible brothers in my age group, you know. There *is* a serious shortage of available black men."

"Pooh-pooh," was all Queen Esther said, sighing in disgust.

"Pooh-pooh?"

"You heard me. *Pooh,* because I think you lying to yourself about wanting to give Parvell a chance. You know the cloth he's cut from. And *pooh!* because I am sick and tired of hearing about that black-man-shortage mess. The truth, as the Lord put it in my heart, is this:

Fear the Lord, you his saints, for those who fear him lack nothing. The lions may grow weak and hungry, but those who seek the Lord lack no good thing. That is Psalm Thirty-four, verses nine and ten.

"Theresa, if you heed those words in the scripture, you'll discover that what the world calls a shortage, the Lord considers a prime chance to show up and show out. In the world there's always a visible-to-the-eye shortage of something, but there is not a shortage of anything in the Lord. So you need to start getting down on your knees more than you been doing, and let the Holy Ghost get into your heart and guide your life."

Theresa didn't answer but her heart was sorely convicted. "I'm pretty late," she told Queen Esther.

Queen Esther lay a gentle hand on Theresa's arm. "Remember this: God can't put brand-new spiritual furniture in a cluttered-up house. You all distraught over the Lord sending you a husband, yet rather than clean your house, you messin' it up. You have to make room for your blessings."

As much as she knew Miss Queen Esther was right, Theresa also knew she had better hurry over to the Washington Duke Inn before Parvell busted a gasket.

"I've got to get going," she told Queen Esther.

"All right. But if you've heard anything I've said to you tonight, you'll go on over there and get that blessing blocker out of your life."

Chapter Two

THERESA ROLLED OVER A SPEED BUMP WAY TOO FAST, causing her brand-new, baby blue Lexus 470 to rise up high and hit the ground so hard she felt herself pop up a few inches. The thud of her dream car smacking the pavement knocked a little sense into her head. She needed to get a grip and calm down.

Here she was, rushing and panting to get to a dinner with a man Theresa wasn't so sure she needed to be bothered with. If God was truly her source for love and happiness, it shouldn't matter what the so-called Rev. Parvell Sykes did or thought.

When Parvell had completed his training in the Gospel United Church of America and went on to receive his preacher's license, many pastors in the denomination's North Carolina district, including their own, were up in arms about it. It was no secret that Parvell was a friend of Bishop Sonny Washington and had received full ordination from the bishop shortly after donating a tidy sum of $30,000 to one of Bishop Washington's church-based programs in Fuquay-Varina. Maybe the donation wasn't a bribe but it aroused suspicion, especially since, as Miss Queen Esther said, "About the only 'call' a reprobate like

Parvell would get would be somebody trying to get ahold of him on his cell phone."

Still, he was attractive to lots of women in the congregation. Parvell had no children, which meant no baby mamas to contend with. He was high yellow, with "good hair" and possessed a degree from Duke, even if his expensive hand-tailored suits made him look like he was headed to the local "playas'" ball instead of to an office. He was known to be a real mover and shaker in the Raleigh–Durham–Chapel Hill area, someone with a finger on every pulse—and in every pie.

Theresa had been alone so long that she couldn't help but be flattered by Parvell's attention, even if he never seemed all that happy to be with her, despite his insistence that they have dinner together. He was so stiff and boring on so many of their dates, Theresa often wondered if he needed some kind of "personality enema." Sometimes he acted like she got on his nerves when she talked about what was going on in the store, laughed too much or too loud, or acted in any way like the down-home girl from the 'hood that she really was. And he was always so busy talking on his cell phone at dinner, as well as making Theresa feel, in so many ways, that for all of her accomplishments, she was his inferior.

Parvell could act so ugly when he was annoyed—mouth turned down, breathing heavily through his nose, eyes hard and grating, and speaking with that nasty tone in his voice. Theresa knew he wasn't happy about waiting on her and didn't want to deal with him and his mess this evening. She quickly parked her car and dashed, breathless, into the dining room of the Washington Duke Inn, hoping that Parvell wasn't seated yet—a clear sign that he'd been waiting far too long for his taste. But there he was, sitting at his favorite table by the window overlooking the golf course, sipping iced tea with a sour expression on his face.

"I ordered my food," was all he said, not even rising to take Theresa's coat or help her into her chair. She sat down in silence as the waiter hurried over to ask what he could bring her.

"Just some hot ginger-peach tea for now," Theresa said. She was starving on the drive over, but Parvell's coldness had drained away her appetite.

Parvell was an expert at keeping women off balance. He knew that ginger-peach tea was Theresa's drink when she was upset and needed something to soothe her nerves. So he let the silence build a few more bars before reaching out, with a smile, to grab her hand. His uncle, Big Gold Sykes, who had been a pimp in Durham back in the day, when they all lived in the Cashmere, had taught Parvell how to work a woman's nerves, telling him, "Boy, you got to keep control of the situation. If you think a woman might go off on you or even leave, you got to turn the tables until you tired of her and ready to do the leaving. That's what Sykes men do. We keep women in their place."

"Take off your coat, girl," Parvell said smoothly, "so I can see how fine you looking this evening."

Caught off guard by his change in mood, Theresa mellowed a bit. It was nice to have a man admire the way she looked. She relaxed her hand and put her purse on the table, allowing herself to forget that Parvell looked a whole lot like a younger, taller, and thinner Ron Isley when he was portrayed as the Mr. Big character in some of the R. Kelly music videos.

*   *   *

Across the room, Lamont Green had made sure that his date, Chablis Jackson, was seated and comfortable before going to find his younger brother, James, who moonlighted as a waiter at the Washington Duke Inn. At thirty-six, Chablis was a little too young and self-absorbed for him, a mature man of forty-nine. But whenever he thought about cutting her loose after six months of dating, the girl would give him one of those late night phone calls that would leave his head spinning. He didn't know where that little young thang had learned all of that, but it sure was fun to try to figure it out.

He felt a tap on his shoulder.

"I see you are still kicking it with Table Wine," James said.

"Why do you always have to call her that? The girl's name is Chablis."

"Isn't that a table wine?" James asked.

"You know you wrong, li'l brother."

"Maybe. But what would I—a man happily married to a woman my age—know about being out there in the world tapping tail like it's going out of style?"

Lamont felt a brief sting in his conscience and tried to soothe it with what their mother and Auntee Queen Esther would call "*bull* ointment."

"Well, James, that's awfully easy for you to say. What do you think a single brother like me is supposed to do with all of my energy?"

"Get married?" James told him.

Lamont rolled his eyes and sighed. He said, "Negro, pleaz. Don't forget that I've been there, done that, and ain't gone do it no more."

"*You* the one complaining about what to do with your 'energy.' Last time I checked, marriage offered a pretty good solution to *that* problem."

"Look, James, I don't need advice. What I need is to find out if you've talked to Rev. Quincey about supporting my plans for the Cashmere. It would help a lot when Green Pastures goes before the Durham Urban Development Committee to have the backing of the church."

"You know Rev. got your back on this project, Big Bro," James said. "But I must tell you that he wanted to know why you, who got saved and married at the church, won't come to him yourself, let alone take some time out to come to service on Sunday mornings."

Lamont opened his mouth, wondering why a plausible and ready response wasn't resting on his lips. He lifted his hands slightly, acquiescing to his younger brother's well-founded rebuke.

"Thought so," James stated. "You and Gwen divorced nine years ago, and you haven't come to church with any decent regularity for six. Nobody works that hard—not even you, Lamont."

"Why do you have to make this so tough?" Lamont asked his brother.

"That's not what I want to do," James told him. "But you need to know that you're not the only one who wants to bend Rev. Quincey's ear his way. Our newest assistant pastor has his own development plans. He's determined to beat you at your own game. And he is sitting up in church next to the pastor each and every Sunday morning, while you, Big Brother, are recovering from a Saturday hangover from too much Table Wine."

"Who?" Lamont tracked James's gaze across the room to Parvell Sykes. "Him?"

"Yeah. Rev. Quincey told me that Parvell is working with Jethro Winters, and so is Charmayne Robinson."

"I get it," Lamont said. "Big, rich, white development tycoon hires himself two black flunkies to try to win the support of our community—or make it look like he has it."

"That's right. And since—unlike you—Parvell Sykes sits up in our church every Sunday, right up in the pulpit, he believes he has, or can get, the inside track."

"And if he can't get backing from Rev. Quincey, at least he can divide the community. Divide and conquer—that's the Jethro Winters way. I wonder if Parvell knows that I'm in the game. Maybe I better drop over and say hey to the good Rev. Sykes."

Chablis, who sat waiting at the table, couldn't hear what the brothers were saying, and she sure didn't appreciate being left high and dry by her date. Worse yet, Lamont wasn't heading back, full of apologies for abandoning her for so long. Instead, he was making his way across the room.

She almost started cussing when a waiter got in the way and blocked her view of Lamont approaching her girl Charmayne's man, sitting at a table with another woman. Chablis's jaw almost dropped right off the bottom half of her face when the woman turned her head slightly, allowing her to catch a glimpse of her profile.

Whipping out her cell phone, Chablis shot Charmayne a text message.

"Girl," she punched in, while trying to keep her eyes

fixed on that table, "your man is all up in Theresa Hopson's face, here at the Washington Duke Inn for all of Durham, North Carolina, to see."

Seconds later, her phone rang. "Girl," Charmayne barked, "are you sure that it's *my man* there with *Theresa Hopson*?"

"Sure as can be. And to make it worse, my man is in her face grinning and cheesing so hard, Parvell over there looking like he ready to start cussing. But he can't 'cause he *'sposed* to be a preacher-man."

"Hang up," Charmayne commanded, "so I can call Parvell's lying, cheating tail."

Lamont was shocked to find that the woman sitting with Parvell was Theresa Hopson. He was struck by how lovely she was and wondered why he'd never noticed those beautiful sepia-colored eyes and that gorgeous hair lying softly on her shoulders.

"Lamont Green!" Theresa exclaimed. "Why of all people! I see James and Rhonda at church all the time. But it's been ages since I've laid eyes on you."

"My Auntee Queen Esther tells me she's been working in your store and that you've made quite a name for yourself throughout the Triangle."

Parvell started clearing his throat loudly, then declared, "You are intruding on a private conversation."

Towering over Parvell, Lamont took his time looking him over. "That outfit must have cost twenty grand," he thought, as he took in Parvell's gold and black silk pinstripe suit, gold silk shirt, tie, and pocket handkerchief, the black mink draped over his shoulders, the mink fedora on his head, the diamonds on each pinkie, and the custom-made cane propped against the table.

"And it's an especially unwelcome intrusion, Green, since I've heard that you're bidding for the contract to develop the old Cashmere Estates."

"So, he does know," Lamont thought. But all he said was, "I don't get your point, Sykes."

"I'll take that as confirmation," Parvell said evenly, sniffed and tilted his head from side to side like a boxer warming up in the ring. "Do you really believe Green Pastures can beat out the Winters Development Corporation for that contract?"

"And why not, Parvell? What does Jethro have, other than an overdressed Negro like yourself, sitting here sweatin' in a mink coat in a hot restaurant? Seems to me that I really ain't got a thing to worry about."

"What you got is chump change," Parvell said, grabbing the shaft of his cane and smacking the head into his free palm, like he was resisting the urge to use it on Lamont. "You ain't got Jethro's deep pockets. The Cashmere is a wreck sitting on prime land that can be developed to bring in real money—folding money, *my brotha*. Not those nickels and dimes you like to jingle around in your pocket like some old church deacon looking for somethin' to drop in the missionary basket."

Lamont stuck his hands in both pockets, his right hand wrapping around an inch-wide wad of hundred-dollar bills held together by a platinum money clip.

"You keep smacking that cane, and I'm gone snatch it right out of your hand and slap it down on you and those dead minks riding on your back," Lamont said.

Parvell poked at him with the cane, and Lamont

reached out to grab it. But just then a few bars of Jay-Z's song "Big Pimpin'" blared out, and Parvell saw Charmayne's number pop up on the caller ID. He answered the phone, oblivious to both Lamont's and Theresa's surprised expressions over the song, and said in a cold, very businesslike voice, "I am unable to talk right now. But I will definitely call you in the morning," then hung up.

But almost immediately, the phone beeped to signal a text message waiting. With the phone on his knees, out of sight, Parvell read, "I know you are with Theresa Hopson. And you better cut this dinner short, or the dessert you are planning on getting will be gone."

Parvell had to work hard not to frown. Spotting Chablis, he realized that there was no point in denial.

"Excuse me," he said haughtily to Theresa, completely ignoring Lamont, "I need to make an important call."

Parvell hurried off to the restaurant lobby to dial Charmayne, who didn't answer. Finally, she picked up on his fourth try.

"Baby," he whispered, "I do want to see you tonight, and I'll get to you as soon as possible."

"You better," Charmayne said. "Because I don't know what you're doing out in public with that woman . . ."

"You know you're my boo, baby," Parvell said and clicked off. Hurrying back to the table, he found Lamont all up in Theresa's face. This was not turning out to be a good evening.

"I hope to see you at church soon," Theresa was saying.

"Yeah, I was just talking to James about getting more involved, you know, easing back in . . ."

Lamont looked up into Parvell's hard, angry eyes as he

approached the table. Lightly brushing Theresa's shoulder, he said, "Well, it sure was good to see you again." Then Lamont walked off without a parting word to Parvell.

Theresa turned to watch him head back to his table, still feeling the tingle of his fingers on her shoulder. Then, with stabbing disappointment, she locked into Chablis's dagger stare. Why did she think Lamont Green was about anything other than young, flashy women who could "drop-it-like-it's-hot" in a heartbeat? As kind and polite as Lamont had been, Theresa would bet her store that he was about as interested in a woman like herself as he was in getting an e-mail chain letter.

"That's about all the men my age want—an easy, drama-deficient booty call," she thought. "Trophy dates that make them look like they have absolutely no need for the 1-800-number for Cialis. With all of this kind of mess going on, who can blame me for going out with Parvell?"

Theresa turned back around, determined to finish this dinner on a good note, and smiled at Parvell. The look on his face was so punishing, she quickly turned down the corners of her mouth into a more somber position.

"I need to leave for a meeting," he announced, snapping his fingers to get the check. "First, you were late, and then you wasted more of my time flirting with that ghetto housing specialist, Lamont Green. Now my time with you this evening has run out."

"But, Parvell, I've known Lamont for years," Theresa protested. "You know we grew up together in the Cashmere."

"My Uncle Big Gold once told me that the hardest thing to get out of a project Negro was the need to connect with another project Negro who should have been long banished from their memory bank. I didn't bring you here to bask in the past. I brought you here to tell you something important."

"But I thought you had a meeting," she said evenly.

"I do. But the reason I wanted to see you, and then was so disappointed when you were late, was that I wanted to give you this."

Parvell reached into his pocket and pulled out what was obviously an expensively wrapped ring box.

"Parvell . . ." Theresa gasped.

Parvell had originally intended the gift for Charmayne, to cement their partnership. But now he could see that Theresa, who didn't yet know much about his ambitions—and who was a respected member in the church—might easily be swayed to support Lamont Green.

"Desperate times call for drastic measures," he told himself as he placed the ring box in her hand. He could see that Theresa was shocked—that she never dreamed that Parvell might like her that much. He worked hard to suppress a satisfied smirk, as he thought, "Who runnin' this thang now, Lamont Green? Who da man—who da man?"

Theresa unwrapped the box as Parvell paid the bill, but then he stopped her and pulled her up, helping her into the butter-soft, lavender leather swing coat that matched her leather pants. His eyes ran over her fast and efficiently, not missing the contrast of that black silk turtleneck next to her beautiful cocoa skin.

"Sweetheart, wait to open the box. I have to go and don't want you to see my gift without me."

"Okay," was all Theresa said. She sat back down as he walked away, now totally confused.

*   *   *

Lamont saw Parvell leave and immediately shifted his focus to Theresa. He became so absorbed with that lavender leather outfit and those black leather, spike-heeled boots that he was not even aware that Chablis was talking to him.

Chablis was fed up. Slipping her black suede poncho over her head, she rose from the table.

"Where you going, baby?"

"Does it matter?"

"We were supposed to have dinner and then—"

"And then what . . . ?" Chablis snapped.

"Uhh," Lamont said, knowing they couldn't go back to her place, because her mama, Miss Shirley, was always there cleaning and bumping around in the yellow rubber gloves she loved to wear.

Chablis snatched her purse off the table and started storming out, making sure that Lamont got an eyeful of her big, high behind held captive in those tight designer jeans.

"But, baby," Lamont began, trailing after her. Watching Chablis walking all mad in those jeans kind of gave him a need to put a hit on that thang.

"Negro, don't you baby me," Chablis said, whirling to face him. "There are men in Durham lined up to date me. And your old butt all up in 'Hallelujah Street' girl's face."

"Holy Ghost Corner," Lamont said. "That is the name of Theresa's store. But why are you worried about her?"

"Worried?" Chablis exclaimed and waved the palm of her hand up in his face. She turned to leave and Lamont followed, grabbing her arm.

Lamont could read Chablis like he did his twenty-three-year-old son, Montavous, when the boy thought he had one up on the old man. He really was too old for this girl, and he was going to have to straighten her out just like he did Monty.

"Let me tell you a li'l somethin' somethin', Chablis. Don't you ever get so caught up in how you look, what you do, and who you know, you begin to believe your funk don't stank. You got some good stuff, baby. But there ain't no coochie good enough for me to take some trifling street mess like this off of you."

Lamont could tell a cussing was bubbling up on Chablis's lips. He stopped her dead in her tracks so that he wouldn't have to get real down and dirty with her.

"Go home. Find your Bible and open it. Go to the Book of Esther. There's a whole segment on what happened to Queen Vashti, who was a 'Hoochie Royale' if there ever was one."

"Quoting scriptures now, Lamont?" she scoffed. "'Cause 'bout the only time I've ever heard you mention the Lord's name is during one of those moments you are definitely going to miss out on tonight."

"Well, at least I have called on Him a few times," Lamont said in a hard and cold voice. "What's your excuse?"

Chablis didn't say a word. She just stalked off, mad at herself for wanting to cry.

Theresa watched them, feeling sad that a man like Lamont Green was running after Chablis. She had never been one to appreciate getting what Miss Queen Esther always called "a man's bread-crumbs"—or, whatever time and affection he had left over after doing whatever or being with whomever he believed deserved the bulk of his time and attention. Tonight, both Parvell and Lamont had made her feel like they had tossed her scraps from stale pieces of bread.

"Though, to his credit and my surprise, Parvell did give me a ring," she marveled. Picking up her purse, she got up to leave herself.

James, too, had been watching while taking orders from a table of four. As soon as he entered their orders into the kitchen computer, he came up to the front of the restaurant where Lamont was standing, his eyes still glued to Chablis's departing form.

"So you gave Table Wine her pink slip?" James asked.

"Did you hear all that?"

"I got the gist of the conversation."

"Maybe it's for the best," Lamont said. "But there's a lot I'm going to miss."

James shook his head, then said, "Well, I be doggone. It looks like half the place is clearing out."

Lamont turned just in time to be face-to-face with Theresa.

"Dinner over so soon?" he asked.

"Yeah, I need to get home. Been a long day," was all Theresa said. She was feeling very confused. Just when she was sure the Lord had provided her with all the information she needed to stop seeing Parvell, he'd put a jewelry box in her hand. Now, here was Lamont in her face acting very concerned.

"You okay?" James said. "From where I stood, it looked like a whole lot was up back in that restaurant."

"Well, I guess . . ." Theresa really didn't want to say

too much around Lamont, since that Chablis girl was his "boo."

"Where's your date?" Lamont asked.

"He had an important meeting."

Lamont wanted to shake that girl. What in the world was wrong with her, going out with a chump like Parvell? He didn't understand it.

James could practically read his brother's mind. And if he were able to speak openly, he'd tell him why a woman like Theresa was dating a knucklehead like Parvell Sykes, who didn't even have the home training to make sure the girl got to her car safely.

"I'll walk you to your car," Lamont offered, not really interested in hearing anything about Parvell.

"That's all right, Lamont. You don't have to trouble yourself like that."

Lamont didn't respond to that nonsense. He took hold of Theresa's hand and began to pull her out the door and in the direction of the parking lot.

James looked around to make sure there weren't any white folks hanging around, put his hands up to his mouth, and gave a loud "Q-Dawg" bark. Heading back to check on his customers' orders, he passed the window table where Theresa had been sitting. And there he spotted it—a silver ring box.

That would explain Theresa's weird mood—being angry at a man and then not knowing what to do about it because he put an unexpected gift in her hand.

"A chip off the ole block," James whispered, thinking how much Parvell was like his uncle, Big Gold Sykes. Big Gold could write a dissertation on how to manipulate a woman. It was a miracle that he'd only been cut once, in the parking lot of Evangeline T. Marshall University (or Eva T.), when a woman discovered him cheating on her. "I will not be number two," she told him; and he replied, "What makes you think you that high on the list?" Livid, that old girl pulled out a straight razor and sliced his suit to rags, lopping off a good hunk of his freshly Jheri-curled hair in the process.

James flipped the box open and whistled when the light bounced off the huge diamond. He held the ring up to the light to get a better view. "Some people have too much money on their hands," he thought. "Because this is one *ugly* ring."

Lamont helped Theresa into her car, holding her hand a bit longer than necessary. At first Theresa felt comforted, but then she remembered his touch on her shoulders and how he chased after Chablis. No doubt about it, he was a playa, an expert at getting next to women, as nice as he seemed. And it was Parvell, not Lamont, who had given her a ring.

"Thank you for walking me out to the car, Lamont," she said.

"Drive home safely."

She nodded, and before she could stop herself said, "Maybe I'll see you around."

"No maybe," Lamont said, "because you'll definitely see me at your store sometime. I want to check out this famous Holy Ghost Corner."

"I'm sure Miss Queen Esther would like that," Theresa managed to stammer. Then, with a wave, she put the car in gear and pulled out of the parking lot, just as James came rushing out with the ring.

"What are you doing?" Lamont said. "You gone get fired from this job."

"It's all good, my co-workers got me covered," James said and handed the box to Lamont. "Look at this."

"You didn't waste any hard-earned tip money on this thing, did you?"

"It's not mine. It's a ring that Parvell gave Theresa tonight."

Lamont examined the ring carefully.

"Yes, it's definitely something Parvell Sykes bought—big, hideous, country, and shamelessly expensive."

"We better call her and tell her we have it," James said.

"Nahh, not yet."

James raised an eyebrow. "Don't you think Theresa would miss this? The ring couldn't have cost any less than fourteen or fifteen thousand dollars."

"Fo' real," Lamont said solemnly. "So you'd best put it away."

"Put it away?"

Lamont stroked his chin, grinning. Getting hold of one or *two* of Parvell's possessions felt good.

"Yeah, li'l bro, put it away for Theresa's sake. Let's say we keep it a day or two, or three for that matter. She doesn't need this ugly mess confusing her about something she needs to be clear on—like kicking Parvell to the curb."

"But what about our sakes when she discovers the ring missing, calls ole boy, and he runs to report the loss to the insurance company?"

Lamont looked at the ring again. "Why not have me take the ring to her store?"

"No, better yet," James said, "have her come by your office. That way the ball will be in your own court."

"I like your thinkin', playa," Lamont said as he held out his fist for some "dap" from his brother.

"But you do know that if you really want to get next to Miss Theresa Hopson that would mean no sleeping around. You'd have to get rid of all the honeys and definitely stay away from Table Wine."

Lamont shrugged with some reluctance.

"I can understand keeping clear of Chablis—she's high-profile and high-maintenance and hard to resist when you want some loving. But I'm a man. And a seasoned man at that."

"Look, if you want a woman from the world, go call Table Wine. She's beautiful, witty, and sexy," James said.

Just then, a sister in a short, black leather skirt, black lace stockings, black pumps, white T-shirt, and short black leather jacket bounced by. She smelled delicious in Coco by Chanel. Her short natural hair had a reddish tint, which was gorgeous with her beautiful butterscotch-colored skin. She pushed out her chest to reveal some natural D cups and smiled at Lamont.

"Evening, gentlemen," she purred.

"And a good evening to you, baby," Lamont said, sucking on one tooth.

She looked him up and back down from the ground to the top of his head, taking note of the size of his feet and hands, along with the rest of him. Then she opened her purse, pulled out a business card, and put it in Lamont's hand.

"I'm Prudence," she said. "I work in the admissions office at Eva T. Marshall University. Call me and I'll get you some season passes for the basketball team. My baby is a sophomore guard and starting this year."

Lamont read the card and said, "I just might do that."

"Good night, gentlemen," Prudence said and walked away slow to make sure Lamont got an eyeful of what he'd be missing if he didn't call.

"*That's* somebody mama, Dawg," Lamont said to James.

"Prudence," was all James could say. "She wouldn't know caution and discretion if her life depended on it."

"Who is concerned about caution and discretion if you've got a handful of that?" Lamont said, grinning. "Did you see the way she was workin' that thang?"

"That just what I mean, bro. If you're thinking about seeing Theresa Hopson, you can't even get a taste of that. Not even a whiff."

Lamont bit his knuckles as if that would help him. "*Umph!* Help me, Jesus."

"Tell me, Lamont. You've been down this road for a while. Hasn't it ever occurred to you that the lovin' you get from a good and saved woman, from an anointed wife, is beyond anything you might find out here?"

"No, I've never given it a single thought."

"Well, maybe you should."

"Maybe so, li'l bro—when I get ready."

"Okay." James threw up his hands. "But let me call Theresa about this ring business, since I was the one to find it in the first place."

"Okay," Lamont said. "And Rev. Quincey—what should I do about him?"

"We'll go see him. You know, Rev. Quincey has four

other black churches working with him, and two white churches have come on board."

"Oh really? I would think they'd throw their lot in with Winters."

"Nahh, Big Bro. Neither of the pastors at Canaan Christian Church and Mount Sinai Baptist Church like Jethro Winters or his wife, Bailey, and her family, for that matter. They have had several members complaining about the poor quality of the homes he's built and not being able to get any justice because Bailey Winters's father and brothers represent Jethro's corporation. And they are some ruthless attorneys. Rev. Quincey told me that Pastor Roy Lakefield at Canaan said that only Jesus is keeping him from punching Jethro Winters in the mouth."

Lamont started laughing. Jethro Winters was a big man who had played defense for Duke back in the early 1970s. Roy Lakefield was small and slender.

"Don't laugh. Rev. Quincey said that Lakefield and Winters have come close to blows on several occasions, and his money was on Pastor Roy. Plus, there's one other thing about Lakefield. The chair of the DUDC, Craig Utley, is a member of Canaan and one of Pastor Roy's staunchest supporters and closest friends."

Lamont smiled. "That's about the best news I've received all day."

"Yes, it is," James said. "But you don't have a lock on the situation. You need to start coming back to church. The Lord has brought you this far and He will give you victory all the way to your groundbreaking at the new Cashmere Estates. All you have to do is put Him first."

Lamont sighed. Sunday morning was about the only day he had to rest.

James started to press some more and then switched gears, as the Lord laid a simpler and more appealing plan on his heart.

"We could use some help with our annual Christmas Festival. It's on December 18 and it will be a lot of fun."

"Now, what would I do at a Christmas Festival?"

"Be Santa?" James asked tentatively.

Lamont laughed out loud and said, "Me, Santa? Negro, please."

"Negro, please, nothing. It would spoil it for the little kids if Santa was someone they recognized. You could pass for Santa, and you'd get the inside track with Rev. Quincey. And besides, you'd have fun dressing up and sitting a bunch of smart, fast-talking, hip-hop-dancing, *grown-acting* little black 'chiddrens' on your lap. It would be good for you."

"Santa, huh?" Lamont said, grinning and patting his flat, muscular stomach. "I think I could do a pretty good job at that. How about this? 'Come here, baby, and sit your fine self down on Santa's lap.'"

"You wrong," James scolded. "But . . . uhh, come to think about it, Theresa has agreed to play Mrs. Claus this year. And she loves working with the Christmas program."

"But won't they recognize her?"

"Mrs. Claus is different. She's not the one kids are coming to see."

"Hmm," Lamont said, stroking his chin. "I just might be the right man for the job after all."

"Be at church this Sunday for our first meeting. We meet right after service."

"Well, li'l bro, maybe I'll take you up on that offer. How's this? 'Ho-ho-ho, sweet thang,'" Lamont said in a silky smooth Santa voice.

James laughed. "You're exactly what our church needs, Playa-Playa Santa."

Chapter Three

THERESA PULLED INTO HER GARAGE. HOT TEARS HIT her cheeks just as the garage door pounded down with a heavy thud on the concrete. It had been the most trying evening. Parvell had heaped a helping of reproofs on her head when she first arrived, then practically dismissed her during dinner, only to twist all of that around into more confusion with the presentation of a ring box. And if that were not enough, Lamont Green had to invite himself to her table, get all engaging and cozy with her, only to flip over when that Chablis threw a hissy fit at her expense.

Theresa hopped out of the car, fuming with frustration. "What is it with these men?" she asked out loud. Did—could—Parvell really want to get serious or to marry her? If so, why didn't he ask straight out and why did he treat her coldly? If not, why the jewelry—from the looks of the box, a ring? And did she, Theresa, really want to be with him? If she did, why did she feel such a hopeless attraction to Lamont Green? Did she really care for Parvell or was she just desperate to have a man—any man—who might be a husband? Could Parvell be a real contender, when the truth was that she felt uneasy even thinking of inviting him to come anywhere with her during the holidays.

Wracked with conflict, she stomped up to her door, throwing it open and slamming it shut as hard as she could. She marched into the kitchen, threw her coat across a chair, dropped her purse on the floor, and reached down to take off her shoes. Then her house started beeping, annoying her because it would not stop.

All of sudden, Theresa realized that her alarm was about to go off in a matter of seconds. She ran to the control panel, suddenly forgetting the code. The alarm went off full blast with lights flashing all around the house, drawing her neighbors out of their homes with their hands covering their ears.

The phone started ringing, and in all the uproar, she could barely grasp that it was the alarm people. When she answered, she couldn't remember her own password, never mind the code to turn off the alarm. By the time she figured out the code, a police car had pulled up, and two officers hopped out with guns in hand.

Theresa finally cut off the alarm and ran to answer the door before the police opted to knock it down. It was only when she heard the security system lady calling out to her that she realized that she still had the telephone in her hand.

The police were now in the house running around the downstairs with guns drawn and aimed to shoot. The first cop stopped in his tracks when he noticed Theresa. "Are you okay?" he asked.

"Yes, Officer," she answered meekly.

"Is that your security service on the phone?"

"Yes, Officer."

"May I speak to them?"

"Yes, Officer," Theresa answered, conscious that she was repeating herself. She handed him the phone.

"This is Officer Yarborough Flowers . . ."

Theresa struggled to regain her composure while he talked to the dispatcher, then placed the phone back in her hand.

"Do you remember your password? Do you need to set a new security code?" the dispatcher asked.

"My password is 'The Lord is my Shepherd, I shall not want.' And no, I don't need a new code."

"You sure? 'Cause we can reset it for you."

"Yeah, I'm sure. Thank you," Theresa said and clicked off the phone.

Officer Flowers eyed her curiously. "Would you like to explain what just happened?" he asked in a firm voice.

Theresa, who was normally very poised and together, leaned against the wall and broke down into a rush of tears. She knew that she was acting like she had lost her last piece of gray matter, and she felt even worse as her neighbors began to gather to see what all the fuss was about. She waved them away for now.

"We'll call you to check on you later, girl," her neighbors, the Websters, said together.

"Okay," Theresa answered, hoping they would hurry up and leave. They were the kind of neighbors you needed, even if you didn't always want them around. The Websters kept tabs on everybody and everything happening on the street—earning them the distinct honor of being dubbed the official neighborhood "crime dogs" of the Durham police department.

They left eyeing each other and whispering, "What's up with Miss *Thang?*"

The officer's demeanor softened as he took Theresa's hand and said, "Are you sure you are all right?"

She nodded.

"Really? Because you look terrible, and you like to woke up the dead with all of this drama and excitement."

Theresa sniffled and smiled.

"Miss Lady, the Lord has just laid it on my heart that this is not quite how you handle things. Am I right?"

Theresa nodded, surprised and relieved. She had been bracing herself to be admonished some more, right before he wrote her a ticket.

"You think because I'm a cop, I don't listen to the Lord when I'm on duty?"

Theresa opened her mouth to answer him but he spoke before she had a chance to say anything.

"Baby girl, let me lay something on you. There ain't no way that I am strapping on a gun, then get big and bad enough to hop into a squad car without first praying and giving honor to God and asking Him to be by my side as I make my nightly rounds."

Theresa remained quiet. He had a point.

"Look, whatever is bothering you is so great it caused you to disrupt the flow of your whole street. Now, that ain't a good thing. You strike me as a church woman. But I believe you've taken matters into your own hands, and you are not trusting the Lord to handle whatever it is that He is trying to do for you. I don't know what it is, but I do know that you need to put God first in this matter. 'Cause if you don't, you will mess up worse than you did tonight.

"And let me tell you something, if I come up in your house like this again, I'll whip out a ticket on you so fat, you'll need Jenny Craig to help you take care of it. You hear me, Miss Lady?"

Theresa nodded, shamefaced and embarrassed. "Okay," she said, trying to give a cheerful, I'm-in-control-of-this-thing smile. "And thank you. Really. I'm grateful."

After seeing Officer Flowers to the door, Theresa took her favorite mug out of the dishwasher. It was sturdy, big, and pretty—pale gray with purple and silver butterflies on it. She filled the mug with hot water, dropped in a Constant Comment tea bag, stuck it in the microwave for one minute, plopped two heaping spoonfuls of honey in the tea, then took the mug, along with her coat and purse, upstairs. Setting the mug on the wide edge of her lavender Jacuzzi tub, she started running the bathwater. Then she caught sight of herself in the mirror.

No wonder Officer Flowers had tried to console her—she was a mess. Her hair was sticking straight up all over her head, mascara and tears streaked her face, snot was running out of her nose and over her lip, and her lipstick was so smeared that she looked as scary as Bette Davis in *What Ever Happened to Baby Jane?* Her sweater was damp with tears and streaked with her foundation. And the worst part was her boots. Theresa had been in the process of taking off her boots when the alarm sounded. Evidently from the one boot-clad foot, she hadn't even thought to remove the other one.

"Dang, so this is why I was walking so funny," she thought, bending down to remove the boot.

Theresa stripped off her clothes and eased into the comfort of the warm bathwater. Sipping her tea, she clicked the remote to turn on her favorite gospel station,

The Lite. One of her favorite songs, "I'll Live," by Jason Nelson, was playing. She was humming the melody of the vamp—"I'll live, I'll live"—when it suddenly hit her: *Where is the box from Parvell?*

Theresa put down her tea and, grabbing a bath towel, jumped out of the tub. Her coat and purse lay right where she'd dropped them, on the bathroom floor. She stuck her hands in both pockets of her coat and came up empty. Then, dripping wet and shivering, she dumped out her purse on the floor. No box.

A horrible sense of dread gripped Theresa. She'd never lost so much as a cheap earring, yet now it seemed possible—no, likely—that she had lost a very expensive piece of jewelry from Parvell. Putting on her favorite soft yellow pajamas and matching satin slippers, she raced out—making sure to shut off the alarm—to her car. A frenzied search in, under, and around the seats turned up nothing.

Theresa put her hands on her face and sighed heavily.

"I have messed up big-time. Lost Parvell's gift and don't even know what the heck it is. And if I don't find it before he hears that I've lost it, no reason to wonder if I should be with him because this thing will be over before it ever got started."

It was too late to call the Washington Duke Inn to ask if anyone had found a box. For all Theresa knew, it might have been picked up by someone dishonest. Feeling overwhelmed by defeat, she went back into the house and climbed into bed, clutching a pillow tightly to her chest as a new set of tears fell. Remembering Officer Flowers's words, she whispered, "Father, thank You for always being here when I need You. Show me what to do and help me find Parvell's gift."

She released the pillow and felt peace creep over her. Just before she drifted off into anointed slumber, a soft voice came to her, saying, "Put Me first in your life, let go of that which is not of Me, and I will give you rest and bless you with the desires of your heart."

Chapter Four

LIKE THERESA, PARVELL WOUND UP HIS EVENING IN A warm bath. He reached for his favorite inflatable pillow and meticulously pressed each suction cup against the wet porcelain. The music coming from the mounted wall speakers of Charmayne's state-of-the-art Bose sound system was "hot," "kickin'," "tight," and "all pumped up." Unbeknownst to just about everyone but Charmayne, Parvell was a closet rap and hip-hop aficionado, and he had an impressive collection of CDs by Ludacris, Snoop, Petey Pablo, Three 6 Mafia, T.I., Lil Jon, Trick Daddy, Mike Jones, the Ying Yang Twins, and Project Pat—just to name a few.

Tonight the radio station was pumping out a drop-it-like-it's-hot sweep of classic songs by Juvenile and the Cash Money Millionaires. Parvell reached for his glass of Crown, turned the Jacuzzi down to low, and sipped in complete satisfaction, as Charmayne massaged shampoo into his scalp.

It had taken some doing to get her to let him in, let alone run his bathwater, fix him a drink, *and* wash his hair. When he first knocked on the door, Charmayne opened it and let that evil toy poodle, Lulu, that she loved so much run out and chase him back to the car. Sometimes Parvell wondered if Lulu was Charmayne's alter ego. Charmayne was cool, smooth, and methodical, but the dog was wild, crazy, and almost uncontrollable—as if she was acting out the emotions behind Charmayne's very calculated and almost unreadable moves.

Finally, after Lulu got tired of acting crazy, Parvell made it onto the porch, where Charmayne kept him standing for a good ten minutes, while he issued no fewer than four *good* "Baby pleaz—pleaz baby—I need you, baby—ooo baby—baby, baby" begs. The crack in the door widened on number three, and number four was so good, it got him past the front door and into the foyer.

Uncle Big Gold had always told him that "Baby pleaz" worked like a charm, adding, "And boy, if you throw in some 'I'm such a fool,' 'I can't make it without you,' 'I'm hurtin', baby,' and 'You the only one who can take away this pain,' you in like Flynn."

He lifted his hand, and in a matter of seconds, his glass was refilled. Parvell, who loved luxury, ran his fingertips over the delicate engravings on the heavy crystal glass, enjoying watching it twinkle and glisten in the soft light of Charmayne's lush, sky blue bathroom with the pewter-colored metal fixtures. It was as big as a master bedroom and had everything you needed in it, including a wet bar, television, small microwave oven, and miniature refrigerator.

He sipped and closed his eyes, before opening his mouth to allow that sensual "ahhhhh" that always made Charmayne quiver and murmur "Oooooo, Daddy" to escape.

"Daddy?" she whispered, as her expert fingers slipped down to the back of his head, taking great care not to mess up her new manicure. Her nails were too expensive and took too long to put on to mess them up washing a man's hair. Her nail artist, LaShawn, had encouraged her to go with a more subdued, classier look. But Charmayne had just rolled her eyes at LaShawn, saying firmly, "I told you to hook me up, not have me looking like some church mother. You save that old tired mess for somebody like Queen Esther Green, and do these nails right."

LaShawn rolled her eyes toward the ceiling and pulled out what she secretly thought were the most "ghetto fabulous" nail tips she had in the salon. Charmayne was thrilled with them and rewarded LaShawn with a hefty tip. They were fluorescent red, with gold dust sprinkled on them ever so lightly, so as not to detract from the diamond chips embedded in each nail.

"Something wrong, baby?" Parvell asked, wondering why she had stopped rubbing the back of his head.

"Uhhh, no, Daddy," she answered. Glad as she was that Chablis had tipped her off tonight, she worried that her girl might not have sense enough to keep her involvement with Parvell a secret. The last thing she needed right now, when they were trying to clinch the Jethro Winters deal, was to have folks know that she was up to more than business with Parvell. Once the deal went through, she could start to push Parvell into claiming her publicly as his "boo."

Charmayne, who was nine years younger than Parvell, thought he was everything she wanted in a man and future husband. He was wealthy, educated, and an entrepreneur. But even more than that, the brother was from her neck of the woods, the 'hood. She loved the way he walked, dressed, talked, hustled, and put it on her. Only a brother from the 'hood could really speak her language.

Unfortunately, most of the *brothas* who qualified for her attention were happily married like James Green and his frat brother, Bug Hopson; didn't make enough money if they met her other standards; made enough money but the hustle was just a wee bit too shady for comfort; too young, too old, too fat, too country, too drunk, too ugly, or had a tad too few teeth for her taste; expected her to take care of them; or were far too self-righteous to be bothered with, like Lamont Green. Parvell Sykes was the only man she knew who fit the bill. And whether he knew it or not, she had appointed him as her desired man-to-be.

"Then, if nothing's wrong, you need to quit staring off in space and tend to your man like he means something to you."

Charmayne started to cup Parvell's head in her hand, but then she got mad. Here she was, sitting on the hard edge of *her* tub because Parvell didn't like sharing a bath with anybody, washing and massaging his head, handing him glasses of Crown like she was a bartender at Durham's favorite over-thirty-something black nightclub, The Place to Be, and he had the nerve to say some mess like that to her.

Worse yet, he was saying it after his tired behind had been caught with another woman. Parvell hadn't apologized enough to suit Charmayne, and he didn't even have the decency to mention the box Chablis had seen him give Theresa. Charmayne knew Theresa Hopson's support could help sway Rev. Quincey to back the Winters bid. And Charmayne knew that if, given the chance, Parvell would try to get more than "backing and support" from Theresa. Tall, shapely, and chocolate, with naturally long hair and the kind of long legs brothers loved to fantasize about, Theresa Hopson was a beautiful woman. The box—a ring box, according to Chablis—made her wonder just how far Parvell would go to gain such a chance.

She stared at her reflection in the mirror, admiring her pale, redbone complexion, greenish brown eyes, rich, cinnamon lips, and naturally dark golden hair with red and blond highlights. Charmayne knew she was sexy, with her large round behind, anchored with wide hips, and her neat bustline that was neither too small nor too big. There was only one thing wrong with her image in the mirror. Her bare ring finger.

Parvell held out his glass for another refill, sighing impatiently when she didn't respond on cue.

"My drink," he insisted, getting annoyed.

Charmayne rose, but instead of getting the Crown bottle, she grabbed the large pitcher she used to rinse Parvell's hair. Dipping it into the bathwater, she dumped what had to be two quarts right over his head.

"What the . . ." Parvell sputtered. "Girl, you aiming for a little tap on that behind, pouring all of that hot water all over me like that."

He stood up, eyes clenched tight to keep out the soapy water, hand reaching for a towel.

"Sorry, baby," Charmayne cooed, like she didn't have the faintest idea of what she had done. She left the towel on the rack, content to watch him squirm. Only when her satisfaction at watching him spit and sputter and swear over the soap in his mouth and eyes was complete did she put a tiny facecloth in his hand—a "towel" that belonged to one of her niece's dolls.

"What do you think I can do with this mess?" Parvell

snapped, one foot out of the tub, trying to dry off his face
with that little scrap of wet material.

"Poor baby," Charmayne said, without an audible trace
of sarcasm. She handed him a large towel but didn't bother
to help him get out of the tub.

Parvell dried off, mouth all tight, eyes stinging. When
he finally rinsed the soap out of his eyes, Charmayne was
smiling and dropping her light blue silk robe to reveal
her gold bra, with tassels on the tips of the cups, which
so beautifully offset her glistening gold-dusted, diamond-
chip nails. She shook a bit to make those tassels twirl,
snapped at the almost invisible golden strings on her
matching thong, and turned around to give a little shake
to the tassel hanging down the back.

"I bet Theresa Hopson don't know how to do this," she
said in a sultry voice.

Parvell wanted to get mad. But when Charmayne got
to twirling those tassels, shaking and twisting like she
was auditioning as a dancer on a rap video, he lost all
memory of what he wanted to scold her for. Seeing that he
was easing into a better mood, Charmayne decided to go
in for the kill. She spun the tassels some more, and when
Parvell broke into a grin, she dropped down into a squat
like she was doing a table dance, then worked her way
back up, still twirling those tassels.

Right on cue, Nelly came on. And as soon as she heard
"Drop down and get yo' eagle on, gurl," Charmayne
dropped it like it was so hot she'd spontaneously combust
if she kept still, popping and bouncing her big wide butt
with such smooth and rapid precision that she could have
put any of those young rap video dancers to shame.

Parvell twisted the bath towel and swatted at the

tassel hanging over her butt. Then he wrapped the towel around his waist and joined her dance, shuffling his feet and twitching his hips and butt from side to side in a stiff swing several beats off the rhythm of the song. Hard as she tried to sync up with him, Parvell's rhythm was so erratic that Charmayne almost fell when she hot-dropped it a second time.

"He really cannot dance," she thought, as she watched Parvell switch his hips to the left, then back to the right, as if there was a string running through his wide, square-shaped behind.

She wondered, as she watched his laborious move-ments, why brothers with butts shaped like that always had thick waistlines, pouchy stomachs, and little rusty-looking sticks masquerading as legs.

By now, Parvell was trying to do a dance called the Crypt Walk. He threw his arms up in the air, snapped his fingers, and started skidding/skipping a ways into the bedroom, trying hard to execute his own unique imita-tion of the dance, which most young people did so ef-fortlessly that it looked like they were floating across the dance floor.

Parvell looked back half-amused at the unspoken rep-rimand in Charmayne's eyes. The girl had some nerve acting like she was superior to him, when her mother, Ida Belle Robinson, as fine as the woman was, used to run so many scams on the welfare office that she had a part-time "business" selling food stamps, WIC vouchers, and government cheese from out her back door. And Ida Belle also made sure that any man in her life paid her bills and bought school clothes for her two bad-tailed children, Charmayne and her little brother, Charles, who now was clocking some serious dollars from Rumpshaker, his exotic hip-hop-dancer gentlemen's club.

Charmayne Chontelle Robinson was definitely a card-carrying member of her birth family, Parvell thought. Back in the day, she walked onto the campus of the University of North Carolina at Chapel Hill with ten packs of food stamps (a graduation gift from Ida's friends) and left with business and law degrees, earned with highest honors. And with those fancy degrees in hand, the girl had schemed, lied, cheated, and probably slept herself all the way up to where she was—a fancy six-figure-earning business that afforded her all the luxuries of a very comfortable upper-middle-class lifestyle.

Prior to starting her own business, she had worked for and been fired from the Housing Authority. If truth be told, even Parvell, who was ruthless, thought Charmayne's policies at the Housing Authority to be over the top. She seemed to hold the people she served in contempt, people living in the same kind of housing that had sheltered her until she went off to college to start a new life and establish an even newer identity. She had been described by one public housing resident, during television coverage of one of Charmayne's famous public evictions, as "an evil-tailed, ghetto-rat heifer, who was just mad 'cause she was born with a stolen plastic spoon hanging out of her lying mouth."

And still Charmayne had the nerve to look at Parvell like he was some sorry, played-out player, who needed to be rubbed down with some old-folks' nostril-clearing liniment. It would have made him angry if he didn't know that he was a prize catch—and if he didn't sense the truth of her love for him.

The music stopped and so did Parvell. Charmayne had slowed her roll two songs ago, when Parvell was doing his Geritol version of the Crypt Walk. Frisky, and with a buzz from the Crown Royal, he started grinning and licking his lips. Charmayne, who didn't have a taste for hard liquor tonight, took a swig of her bottle of sparkling water. She saw Parvell's eyes narrow into smoking slits and fought an urge to mouth what she knew were his very next words, when he dropped the towel and swaggered toward her.

"Girl," he said, "you think you grown enough to handle all of this?"

Charmayne wondered if Parvell knew he really wasn't as "all-that-and-a-bag-of-chips" as he tried to make her think he was. Chablis's words rang in her ears, as Charmayne remembered her friend's anti-Parvell admonitions when she first found out about this affair. Chablis wrinkled up her nose and said, "You sure you grown enough to take on a Negro who so ole-skool, he wears those black, elastic garter things on all his socks? You think Denzel wearing that kind of mess? Not a chance. And Denzel definitely ole-skool fine, with plenty of money."

She knew Parvell was waiting on her to give him some kind of "you-know-you-my-daddy, baby" confirmation. But that wasn't going to be the case tonight. She didn't feel like massaging his ego just yet. Just as she reached way back into her lyin'-to-a-wannabe-playa arsenal of snappy responses, Parvell's cell phone rang out the gospel song, "Don't Let the Devil Ride."

"Would you get that for me?" he said, grabbing the white terry cloth robe with a big, light blue Carolina Tarheel emblem embroidered on the back.

Charmayne couldn't believe that as big a devil as Parvell could be, he'd be bold enough to put that ring tone on his phone. She was just a teeny-weeny bit concerned about touching that phone while the song was still playing. She waited until the song had ended, then picked up the cell like it was a pair of Parvell's funky and sweaty draws. She checked the caller ID, but there was no name, just a phone number that caused her to sigh in relief and then grit her teeth with irritation. It was nearly midnight, and Charmayne was happy that it wasn't another woman or, worst of all, Theresa Hopson. But she didn't appreciate having her precious time with Parvell interrupted by a long and drawn-out conversation with Jethro Winters.

Over the past two weeks, Jethro had been running around Durham acting like he had some kind of Manifest Destiny rights to the Cashmere Estates land. Even worse, that clown had the nerve to "skool" the two of them about how he was getting what was rightfully his, and how they had better get on the stick and "recognize" if they wanted to continue doing his level of serious business in the Triangle.

It had taken every strand of Charmayne's "ghetto-fabulous" DNA not to go totally black on him and beat a few naps onto that mousse-stiff Just for Men dyed head of his. She handed Parvell the phone and turned her back, pretending that she wasn't listening.

"Well, I saw him tonight," Parvell was saying. "It sounds like Lamont is in the game."

Charmayne pricked up her ears and turned around, trying to fill in the blanks of their conversation.

"No, we 'brothers' don't all move in the same circles," Parvell said, rolling his eyes at Charmayne. "Green and

I don't like each other, Jethro, and his interests are different. He goes to every football and basketball game in the CIAA and SNAC leagues, while I, on the other hand, stay busy playing golf, swimming, and running with potential clients."

After a pause, Parvell explained that SNAC stood for the Southeastern Negro Athletic Conference, adding, "It's the conference that Evangeline T. Marshall University belongs to."

Jethro clearly said something dismissive because Parvell replied coolly, "And can I presume that the ACC is the only athletic conference among *historically white colleges* and universities in America?"

Charmayne felt like screaming, *Fast-forward to the good part!* This "who-da-man?" ritual was wearing her out.

Her wish was answered when Jethro bellowed so loudly into the phone that she could hear him: "I want to know, who's going to try to put Green's foot through the door for the contract?"

She could tell that Parvell was seething, though he was silent. She could almost picture Jethro now, questioning his words, wishing that he had a five-second delay to keep him from sounding like a bully. Parvell Sykes was obviously not the kind of man to yell at, because nothing could erase the ghetto edge that he cloaked with money, expensive clothes, a fancy education, and the right address in Southwest Durham. As more than a minute ticked by, Charmayne imagined Jethro scrambling for words to undo the insult, feeling pounded straight into the ground with regret for overplaying his hand.

Jethro finally came up with something, and Parvell answered icily, "Well, anyone with a semblance of sense should be worried about Lamont. He's small-time, but if he's in it, he could become the popular favorite. After all, he grew up in the Cashmere."

Charmayne knew that Parvell was angling for a payoff when he added, "Though, of course, so did I."

She was right.

"Twenty-five," Parvell was saying, calmly. "It'll take a lot of palm grease to get you what you want."

Jethro must have counteroffered, for Parvell answered, "Eighteen."

Another long silence ensued, making Charmayne wonder whether Jethro was bargaining Parvell down. Finally Parvell smiled. "Deal," was all he said and then hung up without so much as a thought to say goodbye.

"So . . . what was all of that money talk about?" Charmayne asked calmly, hoping nothing about her demeanor betrayed the anxiety she felt.

"Not much," Parvell began, mind racing to stack up several lies side by side. "Jethro is on to Lamont Green, and he's getting desperate to know something, anything, on what he is planning to present to the DUDC. He asked how much money I thought he'd need to pass around to get that info."

"And you told him what?" Charmayne said, knowing that Parvell had negotiated something at her expense.

"We agreed on twelve. Five that I could use and the rest he'd have to do on his own."

"What about me?" Charmayne said.

"Twenty-five hundred of the five is supposed to go to you. That's more than twenty percent." Parvell lied so smoothly and effortlessly that he wanted to give his own self some dap on that one.

"I see," Charmayne replied flatly, knowing full well that Parvell was cutting her out.

Sensing her mood, Parvell offered, "How about if I throw in an extra thousand. Can you work with that, Charmayne?"

"But that would only leave you with fifteen hundred to work with," she said, feigning ignorance.

"That's about all I need. I'm figuring you have a better chance of finding someone to give up the goods."

"Yes, that's true," Charmayne lied. She'd be able to grow two extra cheeks on her butt by the time she could get somebody affiliated with Lamont Green to double-cross him and give her, of all people, that information. No one that close to Lamont liked her any more than they did Parvell. Except for one person, and that was a longshot.

"Well, it's done," Parvell said smoothly, glad to have put Charmayne on the case. He knew she'd bring back something useful when there was money to be made.

"Thank you, baby," Charmayne said sweetly. More and more she was just playing along to stay in good with Jethro Winters. She figured that, whatever happened, he would still need her to negotiate his deals with the black community. The phone conversation was just one more piece of evidence that she and Parvell were perfectly matched—each working for a leg up, for some edge or a little advantage. She thought that maybe Chablis wasn't so right about Parvell after all. Ole-skool players, even the ones who wore garters, still had a lot of game left in them.

Parvell walked into the bedroom and tuned into the

Quiet Storm on the radio. Frankie Beverly was singing about the day's end, voice smooth and soothing. He turned down the pale blue silk spread and piled the soft smoky gray pillows behind his back. Charmayne's bedroom was very elegant. But the best part about this room was that it felt so comfortable and tasteful to men.

"Now, if she could just get those fingernails to match this room, I might be inclined to put the girl on my arm in public," Parvell mused softly, climbing into bed and leaning back into all of those pillows.

"I'm getting sleepy, Charmayne," he said. "Come in right now and tend to you man."

"My man," she said softly, and slipped out a slightly harsh laugh before calling out sweetly, "Just hold your horses, Daddy." She grabbed a sheer, gold silk chiffon scarf and did a slow sexy stroll into the bedroom, making sure that Parvell got an eyeful of a round thigh each time she moved.

Chapter Five

BABY, QUIT EATING SO FAST. YOU GONE GIVE YOURSELF a horrible case of indigestion, wolfing your food down like that."

Lamont tried to slow down. He knew Aunt Queen Esther was right. No good would come of eating his breakfast so fast that he practically missed the taste of it. But he was not only very hungry, he was itching to get to his office, to strategize with his staff on how to win over Craig Utley. Listening to Parvell Sykes boast about his connection to Jethro Winters at the Washington Duke Inn, had worked up Lamont's appetite for food and a good old knockdown, drag-down, roll-all-in-the-dirt fight. When James mentioned that Craig Utley belonged to Canaan Christian Church, he had immediately hit on the plan of calling Utley, the most open-minded member of the DUDC, at home. Lamont was going to take Craig on a tour of the Cashmere and hope that the man had enough imagination to see what *he* saw whenever *he* walked the expanse of the now abandoned development.

All Lamont had ever wanted to do, since he first opened his business back in 1992, was to rehab and build homes that folks like his parents, his aunt and uncle, his brother, and the like could afford. Durham was a vibrant and fast-growing community, with plenty of beautiful new neighborhoods to live in. Yet, unfortunately, nearly all of these neighborhoods, a great number built by Winters Development Corporation, were out of reach for the average family, never mind those in the lower income brackets. Recovery of the Cashmere for the people it was designed to serve—the struggling lower middle class and the poor—was turning out to be a calling for Lamont.

"Baby, you are being entirely too fretful over this project," Queen Esther told him. "The Bible says in Philippians, chapter four, that you are *not to be anxious for anything, but in everything by prayer and petition, with thanksgiving, present your requests to God.*"

Lamont patted his aunt's hand.

Queen Esther, who was married to his father's older brother, Joseph, was a Holy Roller to the nth degree. There were times when her own husband said, "Anna the Prophetess in Luke don't have nothing on my Queen."

"Auntee," Lamont said, "you think that everything can be solved with something as simple as a prayer and some anointing oil. But some things need just a bit more than falling on your knees and worrying God."

"Lamont Kenneth Green, I ought to wash your mouth out with soap for spewing that filth out in my house. I rebuke you in the name of sweet Jesus of Nazareth and pray that God will forgive your ignorance about the power of prayer. You know, for all of your learning and smooth ways, you don't have a clue about how things really work."

Lamont almost smiled, but caught himself. For Queen Esther, rebuking in the name of Jesus was like taking a spiritual belt to someone's behind. When he was younger, her rebukes often felt worse than a physical whupping. Once, when he was a teenager, she'd caught him and his best friend, Curtis Parker, on the back porch smoking a joint and drinking Boone's Farm apple wine straight from the bottle like a couple of winos. That day she'd beat them so badly that they started calling for Jesus long before she did.

But by far the worst part of that punishment was when Auntee and her girl and prayer partner, Doreatha, Curtis's grandmother, made the two of them dip their "weed-debased" lips into a bowl of anointing oil in front of their whole prayer team. That had to be one of the most humiliating chastisements Lamont had ever received—and it worked. To this day, Lamont got sick to his stomach if he even saw someone rolling loose tobacco in those cigarette papers.

"Finish your food," Queen Esther commanded.

"I'm not hungry anymore," Lamont said carefully and made a move to push his plate away, all the while watching his aunt out of the corner of his eye, to gauge her reaction. Though he was a grown man, with a grown son of his own, he still cringed at the thought of messing with Queen Esther Green.

His aunt headed into the dining room as he admired the fact that, from the back, she looked like a woman almost half her age—standing five feet five, with a very trim and voluptuous figure. Even from the front she was still beautiful at seventy-six in that Lena Horne, Diahann Carroll, Gladys Knight, Anita Baker kind of way. She was the color of butterscotch, with wavy gray hair cut in the cutest pixie style, full lips, and beautiful golden brown eyes that twinkled like topaz stones when she read her Bible, prayed, or smiled at her husband, Joseph.

Queen Esther returned carrying a large, ornate crystal decanter made to hold fine wine. But when Queen Esther received it as a gift from Doreatha Parker, she immediately proclaimed it to be too exquisite for wine and perfect for anointing oil. It was from this decanter she had poured the oil to "cleanse" Lamont and Curtis's "weed-debased lips." He stifled an urge to say, "Help me, Jesus."

Queen Esther set down the decanter and took off her pale green linen apron, with embroidered apples in silken thread, to reveal a very flattering yellow knit tunic top and matching skirt, with ivory trim around the collar, sleeves, and hem. She wore stockings under her matching yellow-and-white Allen Iverson athletic socks and some white K-Swiss sneakers with yellow stripes on them.

"Why Allen Iverson, Auntee?" Lamont asked playfully, hoping to divert her attention away from whatever it was she was planning to do with that bottle—no, "decanter"—of anointing oil.

"Boy, you know how much I like that Allen Iverson—him and that fine Alonzo Mourning. He's not a Boy Scout but he just needs Jesus and somebody like myself out there praying for him during a game."

Lamont flashed on an image of his Aunt Queen Esther in an NBA locker room, praying over Allen Iverson and his team members during a game, and anointing them with oil. It was a rather forbidding image.

"You know what's distracting those boys?" his aunt was saying. "The devil, that's what. If they took the time to focus on Jesus first, He'd help them see what they needed to do to win an NBA title."

She caught Lamont's half-smile and shook her head, wondering why everything always had to be so black and white to her nephew. She'd heard him bragging on a number of occasions that he was the "quintessential left-brain man," and declaring, "I am a brother with intention. I *be* the *linear brotha* who is focused on progressing from one point to the next without any deviations from the start to finish."

But all of that mannish thinking was just arrogant foolishness. Things didn't always go straight from point A to point B. Sometimes it required that nonlogical, nonlinear, topsy-turvy path, invisible to the left-brain-trained eye, to get to the truth. Sometimes the truth could only be seen with spiritual eyes—with that wondrous gift that only came from the Lord. That's why she always remembered to thank the good Lord for making her left-handed and in her "right mind."

Lamont had drained his glass of orange juice and was smacking his lips. His aunt's orange juice had to be the best in Durham County. She made it fresh several times a week from the sweetest and juiciest oranges she could find, using a selection process she'd explained over and over to Lamont. But try as he might, Lamont couldn't seem to pick oranges as good as his Auntee's.

"Of course you can't," she'd thought when he had shared that with her, "not with that left-brain thinking clouding your vision."

She watched her nephew push his chair back from the kitchen table and get ready to leave.

"Mister Man," she said, "before you hightail it out of here, we got some business to take care of. We need to pray."

Lamont started to protest but her stern expression stopped him dead in his tracks.

"Okay," he said, desperately hoping it wouldn't take too long.

Queen Esther gestured toward the place where she wanted Lamont to kneel. She opened the decanter and, while still holding the stopper, stretched her arm up in the air. She lowered that arm and stretched out the other one.

"Lamont," she said, *"commit your way to the Lord; trust in Him and He will make your righteousness shine like the dawn, the justice of your cause like the noonday sun. Be still before the Lord and wait patiently for Him . . ."*

Lamont unwillingly bowed his head as she continued to speak the words from Psalm 37, while bending and stretching out her torso.

"Why," he thought, "does Auntee have to do warm-up exercises like she is getting ready to go on a run before praying?"

Queen Esther knew that most people, her nephew being one, viewed prayer as a passive activity. But to her, praying was linking up with the Lord, coming to Him for help in every area of life; giving praise for His blessings; thanking Him for His salvation, praising Him for being God and God alone; for defeating life's problems; for offering healing, overcoming trials and tribulations, going through the storm and coming out of it as pure as the purest gold. Praying was anything but passive—it was doing battle and waging spiritual warfare. As far as Queen Esther Green was concerned, praying had to be one of the most aggressive acts any Christian worth her "salt-and-flavoring" could do.

Queen Esther finished her stretches and then started jumping up and down like a fighter waiting on the first-round bell to ring. She cracked the kinks out of her neck and poured some oil onto her hands, placing them on her nephew's head as she began to pray in tongues. Lamont started to squirm a bit, like he used to do when he was a little boy, and Queen Esther felt a need to hold on to him in prayer.

She took his hands in hers and prayed, "Lord, this baby need Your help and guidance, and he needs to feel You moving in his heart and soul. 'Cause he runnin' round here thinking that hard work and thinkin' and plannin' and frettin' and controlling how he and all the rest of his team at Green Pastures work and handle this thing, gone be what truly makes the difference in what he trying to do. But while hard work and thinkin' and frettin' and bullying folks and plannin' will . . ."

Queen Esther paused a moment as she thought about the words she'd just spoken. Rev. Quincey was always cautioning them to put a stop guard on their tongues as written about in the Book of James. Words were some mighty powerful things when a body considered the words in the first chapter of the book of John, *"In the beginning was the Word, and the Word was with God."*

"Well, not bullying, Lord. Nobody ever got anywhere in a decent way by bullying and threatening and subjugating and mistreating folks, even if they were right on their concerns about the issue that prompted this behavior in the first place. So, Lord, in continuance of what I was saying, let the baby know that while the other means will help, only Your will truly makes the difference. And as for the frettin' . . . well, that's better left to those folks who've just made Jesus' acquaintance, and don't know enough about him to know better than to sin by scurrying up a fret."

She studied her nephew a moment, amused at his pitiful efforts to act like he wanted to be kneeling here listening to her pray. Lamont was a very good man. He had given his life over to the Lord when he was twenty years old and, for the most part, had endeavored to live right. But living for Jesus required a steady prayer life, going to church, reading the Bible, and growing stronger each day in your walk with the Lord—which was a whole lot more than he had been doing over the past few years. Yes, he was saved—technically, that is. But he had to get right and let Jesus rule over his life for a change—and to be in the pastor's office talking about Jesus and not just strategies to rebuild the Cashmere.

"Can I get up now, Auntee?" Lamont asked, trying hard to keep the impatience out of his voice. He knew that the absolute worst thing he could do was to rush his aunt during one of her infamous prayer sessions.

"No," she answered, clinging tightly to his hands as he began to pull away.

"Lord, in the name of Your precious Son, Jesus," she prayed, "I ask that You lead Lamont in the way that You would have him to walk. Lord, Lamont needs You to bless him with that contract to rebuild our old neighborhood. And Father, I ask that You do it in such a way that this hardheaded, think-the-business-strategies-of-the-world-is-the-way-to-go, left-brain-dominated, linear-thinkin' boy can't help but bow down in praise and worship before Your throne, simply awed by Your miracle-working power. Let him know, Father, that when his back is to the wall, all he has to do is call You up and tell You what he wants in accordance with Your perfect and holy will.

"And Lord, it's getting to be past high time for this boy to get married again. Ain't right for a man as fine and sweet as my baby boy to be running around alone and loose, with his male nature working on him and making him prone to lying up with those loose-legged women like that Table Wine girl, and the one with that big ole panther tattoo on her booty that he think I don't know about."

"Auntee!"

Queen Esther put Lamont in his place with barely a flicker of a narrowing of her beautiful topaz eyes. Lamont grew quiet, annoyed his aunt would try to dip into his personal business like that. He was a grown-tailed man, and big and bad enough to run his own life. But he knew better than to say so.

Finally, Queen Esther took a very deep breath, and then let it go, releasing all that she had just prayed on into the very expert and capable hands of God.

She loosened her grip on Lamont's hands, opened her eyes, and gave him the sweetest smile. Lamont always thought his aunt was most beautiful when she finished praying. More beautiful still was the thought that now he'd be dismissed at last, for Queen Esther was saying, "Come here, baby," as she drew him to his feet. "You better head on over to your office and study on this prayer, so you can hear the Lord speaking to you and telling you what you need to do to be blessed with the contract."

Lamont kissed his aunt, thanked her for breakfast and the prayers, and got ready to leave.

"Oh, don't forget to call the pastor before the day is out."

"Why?"

"Because James told me that you are volunteering to play Santa this year. You want to tell him that and also let him know that you will be at the meeting for the Christmas Festival next Sunday, right after service."

"I'll do that if I run into Rev. Quincey before the meeting. I wasn't planning on attending the morning service," Lamont said.

Queen Esther frowned. She never did like it when folks came to church asking for help but didn't think enough of it to participate in the morning worship service. Politicians, especially white politicians, were notorious for skipping out right in the middle of the service after coming to ask black church folk for some much needed help and votes.

"You'll be asking the church to raise a lot of money," she scolded Lamont. "Enough to make a dent in your closing-cost program. You are also depending on Rev. Quincey to back you, using his savvy and good standing here in Durham, to persuade some more preachers to join him. Now, I don't know about you, Lamont. But if it were me, I'd be ashamed to ask for all of that from some people I didn't think enough of to sit through church with. You either want the church's help or you don't. Don't be trifling about something this important."

She opened the door.

"All right. I'll come to service and then attend the meeting."

"And the dinner? Don't you want to come to that as well?"

"I would think that sitting through the entire service would suffice," Lamont answered in the same voice she'd heard him using when giving orders to people working for him.

But since she didn't work for him, and certainly wasn't inclined to take orders from him either, she said, "Well, I guess it would *suffice*, if all you wanted was a few sufficient words about yourself from Rev. Quincey during Sunday morning service. But if you are aiming for some real support, and some help from above, it *suffices* me to say, that taking some extra time out of your day to spend with your pastor, at his church, would *suffice*."

"Just make sure you get me my plate, so that I don't have to stand in that long line, trying to convince one of your girls on the food service committee to part with an extra leg of chicken."

Queen Esther stuck out her hand and said, "Deal," suppressing a small smile of victory. She'd done her part by getting Lamont back to church. Now God would do the rest.

Charmayne had been driving around the neighborhood where the old Hillside High School used to be for close to an hour, taking mental notes. She wondered if Jethro Winters should back off of trying to get the property in this area. The historically black North Carolina Central University was so busy expanding and building that she seriously doubted that he would be able to bulldoze the powers that be at the school. She pulled over and picked up her cell to dial Jethro, wishing she'd put his number in her voice recognition system.

After several rings the voice mail came on. And just as Charmayne was about to give a quick report, she saw Lamont Green coming out of his aunt's house. She clicked the phone off and then back on, this time speaking, "Chablis," into the receiver.

"This is the Jackson residence," Chablis's mother, Miss Shirley, answered, in that stiff and proper voice, with over-pronounced words, that she used when answering the phone. Charmayne always wondered why Miss Shirley didn't use her regular voice because she still sounded ghetto and country, especially when she put "ers" on the end of everything when attempting to talk *proper*.

"Hey, Miss Shirley. Has Chablis left yet?"

"Naw, baby," Miss Shirley answered in her regular voice, which was flat, slow, and always sounded like she was chewing on a wad of gum when she spoke. "Blee still hangin' 'round the house."

"May I speak to her?"

"Sure, baby," Miss Shirley said and then yelled, "BLEE, Charmayne Robinson on the phone."

"Okay, I got it, Mama," Chablis yelled into the receiver.

As soon as Miss Shirley hung up, Charmayne said, "Do y'all always have to holler and scream in the phone like that?"

"What's going on, Charmayne?" Chablis said, ignoring her comment.

"You hungry?"

"Yeah, why?"

"Let's go over to Mama Dips for breakfast."

"Why don't she come over here and eat?" Miss Shirley boomed.

A silent moment passed.

"Mama," Chablis finally asked, "when did you get back on the phone?"

"When I felt like it," Miss Shirley answered and hung up.

"I'm in your driveway," Charmayne said. She turned off the car and walked up on the Jackson porch. But she felt compelled to linger there to let her gaze sweep the block, with its small, well-tended lawns and homes with warm personal touches—a red door here, white window boxes filled with colorful flowers there, and across the street, a small neighborhood park with swings, a seesaw, and a modest picnic shelter.

"What are you staring at?" Chablis asked, wondering what was so intriguing about this street, with its old-school ranch houses, to Charmayne. She had visited their home many times.

"Never realized how nice this street was," Charmayne said, feeling a slight ache in her chest. What a shame that it was on Jethro's "must-hit" list.

"Well, get off the porch," Miss Shirley admonished, pulling on a pair of yellow rubber cleaning gloves and heading back to the kitchen, mumbling, "Don't know why you two heifers think Mama Dips's food better than mine."

"Why," Charmayne wanted to know so badly, "does Chablis's mama always wear those things?" She knew Miss Shirley's elevator bypassed a few floors on the way to the top, but did she always have to let everybody know how many stops it missed by wearing those big, hot, yellow rubber gloves?

"Okay, Mama," Chablis said tightly, trying so hard not to snap at her mother. "We'll eat breakfast here."

Charmayne followed Chablis into the small but immaculate kitchen, the floor shining and smelling so fresh that she really could have eaten off of it. As soon as they sat down at the gleaming pinewood table, she pulled out the Cashmere business plan that she'd been working on all morning.

"Look at these numbers, Chablis," Charmayne said and pushed the paper over to her friend.

Chablis's eyes scanned the spreadsheet quickly before coming back to rest on Charmayne.

"Impressive. But what does this have to do with me? Maybe you're making money from this, but I'm not."

Charmayne rolled her eyes and blew air out of her mouth. What was she thinking? Chablis was very self-centered and a little obtuse at times. Of course she wouldn't give a hoot about these numbers or anything else until she saw how it affected her directly. Charmayne flipped through the papers in front of her and pulled out the building plans.

"Look at this section of the new neighborhood."

Chablis took the sheet and studied it. She was about to hand it back to Charmayne when her eyes fell on the building designated for a blend of living and business spaces. The stores proposed for the larger slots were all very high-end and chic, but interspersed with them was an assortment of small, more affordable retail spaces.

Although Chablis had built a thriving event- and concert-planning business out of her home, she believed that it would soar if she could find the right location. Right now, she got customers through word of mouth and advertising in the Black Pages, or the black-owned-business phone book, the radio, and targeting the black Greek associations, along with a growing number of churches who wanted to celebrate anniversaries and annual choir concerts in a big way. But to go further and expand her clientele across both color and economic lines, she needed a location-*location*-location.

And then, maybe she could even afford—at last—to indulge in a home of her own, where she could kick up a little dust whenever she wanted.

"Perfect for your business, isn't it, Soror?" Charmayne cooed, forming her fingers into a dainty triangle. She knew she was fighting dirty by playing the Delta Sigma Theta card on Chablis. But what else could she do? She was desperate and needed help to get the skinny on Lamont Green. Chablis was the only one associated with Charmayne who could possibly get next to him and be willing to share what she knew with her.

"What do you want?" Chablis knew there was a price.

"Lamont's strategies. I need to know what my boss is up against—"

"Mama, you all right?" Chablis called out, as flames shot from the stove and her mother doused what was supposed to be their bacon with baking soda.

Miss Shirley whirled around to glare at Charmayne, who stared back as hard as she dared without risking a reproach. "There's some trickery going on," Miss Shirley proclaimed, seemingly out of the blue.

Chablis handed the plans back to Charmayne, torn between wanting to guarantee her space at the fancy new building and those big yellow warning signs on her mama's hands. There were times when her mother simply wasn't as crazy as she wanted folks to believe.

"So, what do you think?" Charmayne asked, determined not to wilt under Miss Shirley's withering gaze.

"I'll see what I can do," was all that Chablis dared to

respond. She wanted store space so badly that she could practically taste sawdust. But she was also on the outs with Lamont and unsure of how to get back into his good graces.

"Let's go to Mama Dips," Miss Shirley said, brandishing the hot, baking-soda-smothered bacon skillet like a weapon.

"Good idea," Charmayne replied. But having made her point, she knew she'd never win by confronting Miss Shirley head-on. She checked her watch and hurriedly collected her papers. "On second thought, I'd better head on over to Jethro Winters's office."

"You sure you don't want to tag along, baby?" Miss Shirley asked sweetly, as she took off her gloves and stashed them in her voluminous fake burgundy patent leather purse.

"No, ma'am," Charmayne mumbled as politely as she could and left, feeling that she'd at least planted a seed.

Chapter Six

CRAIG UTLEY STOMPED DRY, RED DIRT OFF HIS SHOES as he walked around the brick ruin of one of the remaining buildings of the original Cashmere Estates.

"Why," he wondered, "would anyone want to preserve the Cashmere?"

It was an abandoned low-rise housing project with crumbling garden apartments, centered on a garbage-strewn lot that used to be the main square. And it was only the powerful plea of Lamont Green, who had done good work around the state, that had made Craig come out to see the place for himself—rather than rely, like the rest of his DUDC colleagues, on reports from the county's urban planners. If the most recent report he'd read was any indication of their feelings about this property, the last thing the city of Durham needed was to resurrect the kind of community that was buried beneath the rubble that he and Lamont were forced to make their way through this morning.

He walked around the building again, this time paying more attention to its design rather than being distracted by its decay. This two-story brick house had to have been a beauty back in its heyday. Even in this dilapidated state, it still retained some of its former glory from the period when this community was flourishing. Or, at least that's what Lamont had told him. Back then, Craig lived in one of the "whites only" sections of town and never found occasion to visit the "most thriving Negro neighborhood in Durham," as his black colleagues labeled it.

Craig came and stood over Lamont, who was sitting on the stoop of the building staring out over the blighted landscape.

"You have a point. It is a shame to have let all of this deteriorate," Craig stated, not feeling as convinced as he hoped he sounded, as he glanced at the stone plaque set in the brick wall. "So, this was the Meeting House I have heard so much about, huh?"

"Yes, the Meeting House in two senses of the word," Lamont said, wondering why white Durhamites had so much trouble understanding why this particular building meant so much to black Durham. If this had been a decaying house owned by a Duke or any other white town father or town mother, they wouldn't even be having this conversation.

"Daniel Meeting," Lamont continued, "was an early-twentieth-century black architect who trained a whole generation of designers and builders here at Evangeline T. Marshall University, or what was then the Eva T. Marshall Normal School for Colored People. He was a fierce advocate of Social Gospel thinking, which motivated him to instill in his students, that the poor, like everyone else, deserved—and also needed—to have beauty in their everyday surroundings. The Meeting House is one of the finest examples of his work, and even in the midst of this decay, it remains one of the most architecturally significant buildings in the state. And, you know something?"—Craig could hear the pride swelling in Lamont's voice—"I even got to meet the noble professor when I was a teenager."

"What was he like?" Craig asked, feeling sorry that the designer of the place some in Durham still called the Mecca of black urban family life might have come to a tragic end. "Was he broke? Miserable? An alcoholic? Demented? Depressed and sad?"

"Pleaz," Lamont answered, laughing. "Daniel Meeting lived to be 103, was healthy until the last two years of his life, and remained rich, happy, and still trying to flirt."

"Flirt?"

"Yeah, flirt. This brother took on the state of North Carolina during the Jim Crow era, lived to brag about it, and kept his position as a professor at a state-funded school. He outlived three wives and then spent his last years just enjoying his freedom. You don't really think that a man with that much gumption would pass up hitting on a good-looking woman, do you?"

Craig smiled, relieved that such a great black man came to the end of his life with the same joy and passion that he lived it. He said, "I see what you mean."

Then he stammered, "Uhhh, uhhh—I had no idea there was such a rich history attached to a building in the . . ." He stopped, not wanting to insult Lamont by calling his birthplace "the ghetto."

Lamont smiled at Craig, whose face was now a bright red. Utley was good people, even if he didn't know as much as he needed to know about black folk.

"I don't understand," Craig went on, "why the state didn't grant this building landmark status."

"I do," Lamont replied evenly. "Daniel Meeting was a

strong proponent of civil rights. He sued the state for the right of a private black developer—not unlike myself—to buy this land and build on it when the Cashmere was first proposed after World War II. Although he lost that battle, and the county was allowed to own the land, he did win the right to design and select who would work on the actual construction of this building."

Lamont kicked at a rock. "No, Craig, I don't think there were any state legislators clamoring to honor this site when the community began to spiral downward in the eighties."

Craig scanned the Meeting House's facade. He was tempted to walk up onto its broad veranda and push open what was left of the large, fire-scorched mahogany door to peek inside. Now he wished he'd taken Lamont's advice and gone online to look up Daniel Meeting and see the pictures of the old Cashmere before coming over here. "You'd think that the black movers and shakers in the city would be all over themselves to preserve this place," he said.

"You'd think," Lamont answered. "But unfortunately, there are too many black folk in Durham who remember the Cashmere only as liquor and numbers houses, as those makeshift confectionaries on back porches selling cornflakes and powdered milk, Stanback and BC headache powders, hairnets and hair grease, and cheap toilet paper stolen off delivery trucks. Of course, in the late eighties and early nineties, it wasn't just sundries folks were selling but marijuana, heroin, cocaine, and finally crack."

Lamont rested his cheeks on his hands, with his head down, as all those wonderful memories about the

Cashmere he loved came rushing in. He stood up and put his foot on the loose, rotten steps leading up to the veranda of the house. He thought about the drug dealers who had taken an entire community hostage, reducing the Cashmere to this sorry wreck of a place. His aunt was right when she said, "The vermin who destroyed this community probably drafted the blueprints of hell."

As if reading his thoughts, Craig said, "It's a doggone shame that some devils got up in here and drove all the good folks off."

"But here's the question," Lamont replied. "Why is it that we allow the devils to get a stronghold in neighborhoods where poor folk live? If somebody started selling crack over there on Dover Road in Hope Valley, right across the street from the country club, what do you think would happen?"

"I know what would happen," Craig said with a dry, harsh laugh. "I live on Dover Road. If somebody like that crackhead character on the old Dave Chappelle show turned up, a SWAT team would descend on him before he even lost his high."

"Hey, what you know about the Dave Chappelle show?" Lamont asked, smiling. Craig Utley was full of surprises. He looked as straitlaced as could be, standing there in the classic white-boy uniform—expensive khaki slacks, finely tailored navy blue jacket, light blue oxford shirt, and red/yellow/blue striped silk tie, accessorized by brown loafers.

"More than you think, and even more than you know," Craig said, and then burst out laughing.

"What is so funny?"

"You, standing there with your mouth open because I watch Dave Chappelle. He's a nut and he makes me laugh."

"Yeah, that Negro is definitely a straight-up fool."

"That he is," Craig said. "But you'd better not tell anybody I said that. Last thing I need is an irate black man or woman all up in my . . ." He snapped his fingers, face wrinkling in a frown, as he tried to remember the phrase.

"You mean, all 'up in your grille.'"

"Yeah, yeah, that's it . . . all up in my grille."

Craig stretched out his palm, and Lamont slapped it on "the black-hand side." The gesture was corny and dated, but it brought to mind that special era when the Cashmere Estates was making its mark as the premier neighborhood for working-class black families.

"My house used to be right over there," Lamont said, as he pointed to a pile of bricks on what looked to be a fifth of an acre of land behind the Meeting House. "Used to sit on my front porch and watch all of those famous folks staying at this place."

"Famous people?" Craig asked. "Here?"

"Don't look so surprised," Lamont told him. "There were only a few places famous black folks could stay when they visited Durham—the Meeting House, the Elegante Hotel, the homes of prominent black Durhamites, and what used to be Lester Lee's Boarding House over near Eva T. Marshall University."

"But who stayed *here*?" Craig asked again, pointing to the house.

"Elroy Thorn and the Gospel Thornbirds, Big Johnnie Mae and the Revue; several major bishops in black denominations, like Bishop Percy Jennings, Bishop

Murcheson James; other artists like Carlton Quickly—
you know, he wrote those gritty novels about urban black
life during the forties and fifties."

"Carlton Quickly?" Craig said, now excited. "I've
read everything he's ever written. What did you think
of him?"

"He was brilliant but humble and real and down-home.
He wrote about my world—my life—and he gripped my
heart and inspired me. Why, we even had our own *Blind
Man with a Gun* here in the Cashmere, shooting at the
pushers who finally forced him from his home."

"Really!"

"Oh, yeah."

"You're so lucky!" Craig said.

"Lucky? I guess. But really I was in the right place at
the right time, to gain an understanding of the world I
lived in—and of myself!"

"Your Cashmere was a pretty great place to grow up
in, huh?"

"Yeah," was all Lamont could say. He couldn't explain
to Craig why his Cashmere was so wonderful—that it was
a place full of laughter; of arguments over checkers and
bid whist games on front porches; of double-Dutch jump
ropes hitting the pavement; of the clapping hands and
singsong rhythms of hand games; of metal roller skates
in the street, and of car horns honking at the skaters; of
Aretha Franklin, Archie Bell and the Drells, Freda Payne,
Gladys Knight and the Pips, Sly and the Family Stone,
James Brown, the Dells, the Delfonics, Al Green, and
Johnnie Taylor blaring from the radios in the windows; of
mothers calling their children in to eat juicy homemade
burgers or famous North Carolina chopped barbecue

sandwiches, fried chicken, macaroni and cheese, collard greens, red velvet cakes, and sweet potato pies; of soft whispers of mothers and fathers who'd put their children to bed early so that they could become lovers, completely unaware that their laughter and shared kisses wafted out of windows left open to catch the soft breeze of a Carolina pine-scented night.

"Tell me about it?" Craig's voice broke through his reverie.

"The Cashmere was sweet, warm, safe, and homey—a black Norman Rockwell painting just waiting for the first stroke on a canvas. There were hardly any robberies—certainly no shoot-outs—and about the only reason the police came cruising through, other than to keep a few known parolees on their toes, was to smell where the best rib and chicken dinners were being cooked. It was a community that loved celebrating with block parties and rent parties. There were rallies and concerts, with even outdoor trunk shows offering cheap and stylish clothes, hats, shoes, purses, local artists' paintings, eight-track tapes, books by black authors, and some furniture from New York.

"There were so many families living in Cashmere Estates who had very little money, but Lord knows those folks were rich in spirit, and faith in God. Everyone, even the marginal folks, had clean homes, enough food to eat, decent-looking clothes, medical care when they needed it, a safe haven from the harsh realities of inner city life—and they had love. There was enough love floating around Cashmere Estates to cure the national deficit, then and now."

"Sounds lovely," Craig said.

"More than lovely, it was home—a place where being neighbors really meant something, and family life was just the way it was. The Cashmere was what inspired me to become a builder," Lamont finished with a sweeping flourish of his arms to take in the whole Cashmere.

"It showed me that it was possible for people to live in dignity, even if they were poor."

Lamont knew he could rebuild this place. But it was going to take a miracle of Old Testament proportions. Jehosophat—sometimes he felt just like his name was Jehosophat.

Craig was staring at him, listening intently.

"I'm sorry," Lamont told him. "I didn't mean to ambush you with a speech and all. But you can see that this is more than just a development to me. Where other folks see blight, I see heritage—heritage that we black folks owe it to ourselves and our children to preserve."

"I can see that," Craig said.

"And you know that if Jethro Winters starts building here," Lamont added, "he's not gonna stop. Once this prime central-city location is developed, all the surrounding neighborhoods . . ."

Lamont waved a hand to indicate the established black communities in view of the Cashmere.

". . . will be fair game—if you think the word *fair* is applicable to Winters. Because working folk—teachers, nurses, police officers, librarians, construction workers, and small-business owners—will be pushed out. And where will they be able to find homes and a neighborhood as nice as that, at the prices they paid, elsewhere in this city?"

Lamont sighed. He was preaching again. But he didn't

know what else to do or say to reach Craig Utley, the one reasonable and fair-minded individual on the DUDC.

"Lamont, I want you to win that contract," Craig announced.

"Huh?"

"I get it. I really get it. The Cashmere is history, culture, and heart. It has traditionally been a home for good, hardworking people. Jethro Winters has no sense of history, and especially not of black history. He is a boor, and a pack of rabid, hungry wolves has more heart than he does. He doesn't need to build here—not at the cost of destroying history, of destabilizing an entire segment of the population. That's what those professional reports don't figure in with any reliability. Remember all those 'urban renewal equals Negro removal' deals of the past? You're giving me the reasons to fight that."

"How so?" Lamont asked. "I feel like I'm up against a huge cash machine, the public, with an urban commission that was formed to 'eliminate blight' on the surface, and stick it to 'the folks,' when you get down to the nitty-gritty of it. And once 'blight removal' gets a toehold into this area, property taxes will increase as fast as the new and improved luxury houses go up. How can I compete with what will look like progress and more revenue to run this city?"

"For starters, you have to raise enough money to fund a closing-grant program to make sure that lower-income people can qualify to successfully complete a contract to buy. The DUDC will need to see that you can deliver a certain number of creditworthy buyers, or people who have someone to co-sign. That can be a hard mountain to climb when you're dealing in building affordable housing developments."

"I know," Lamont said with a heavy sigh. "There are plenty of folks in Durham who can afford to pay a monthly mortgage, but can't afford the closing costs. And there are lots who can't raise enough money to tighten up their debt ratios and credit reports."

"True," Craig stated. "Good folks who are good risks, despite some glitches in their credit history. I've battled underwriters for years about this at my bank. And right now, we are in a rough-enough economy, which calls for some compassion and faith when assessing lending. Of course, men like Jethro Winters can get their hands on hundreds of millions of dollars, with all kinds of breaks and allowances. But when somebody like your aunt, Miss Queen Esther, comes to get a loan, they act like she is trying to cheat them and get something for nothing."

"So what can I do?"

"Well," Craig said, "Winters's strength is that he has promised to give DUDC eleven million dollars if they give him the contract—three million up front when he breaks ground, one million when he starts construction, one million when he finishes, and the rest to come over a three-year period to begin once the units start selling."

Lamont scratched at the almost imperceptible whiskers on his chin. Eleven million dollars was a lot of money—a whole lot more than he had to offer through his company. Craig held up his hand and finished.

"That sounds awfully good, I know. But the only problem is that Winters is always late on paying his notes for new construction. And although the banks continue to give him money, they will take any extra funds that he has available if he's late. So, all of that money he promised will come in much tinier dribbles than you'd imagine. And of course, there are other incentives."

"Green 'Benadryl Cream' to soothe some very itchy palms?" Lamont said.

"Well, you know Durham politics. You're not naive," Craig replied.

"I'd bet Winters is paying a couple of the DUDC's members kickback money."

"How'd you know that?"

Lamont smiled and said, "I have connections in places you would never think to look. And my connections tell me that Terrell Richards and Dotey Matheson will hop in bed with anybody with a fat-enough bank account."

Craig raised his hands to stop the conversation.

"No more. I know too much already. Despite how I feel, I have to remain as impartial as possible. And I have to work with these people."

"Better you than me," Lamont said, "'cause CNN would make a beeline to get here and report on all the damage done, once I started pimp-slapping jokers left and right, up and down, and every which a way."

"You're not alone," Craig said with a chuckle. "And I would not reserve the 'pimp-slaps' for the men, either. Those two lone women on the committee—Clara Perkins and Patricia Harmon—are pieces of work. And one of them is sneaking around with Winters. I don't know which one, though."

"Must be Patricia," Lamont said matter-of-factly. "All of Winters's other women look like Patricia—tall, thin, and blond with those gigantic boobs that don't move when she does—and gray or light brown eyes."

Craig thought about Patricia Harmon's boobs for a moment and then laughed. "You are absolutely right on that one, Lamont. Patty Harmon's boobs never move. They look just like coconuts, and, like they'd hurt your hand if you tried to squeeze one of them."

"Does your wife know that you've given this much thought to Patty Harmon's coconuts?"

"No. Besides, there isn't anything a hard-edged and greedy woman like Patty can do for me but go somewhere and sit down."

"I hear you," Lamont said. "On that and on the other valuable advice you gave me. You know, there are black churches planning to work with their members on problems with closing costs and creditworthiness."

"Well, that's where you'll need to concentrate your efforts, at least as a start."

"I'm already on it," Lamont assured him.

"Good. And thanks, Lamont. You've taught me a good lesson today about the importance of a past that I didn't understand. We don't always consider the value of what we are losing when we try to map out the future. If you can make the finances work, I'll have your back."

"Naw, man. I'm the one who should be thanking you," Lamont told him.

They headed toward Craig's silver Range Rover and then clasped hands before Craig climbed into his car. As he drove off, Lamont spun around for another look at the Cashmere thinking about how much more he could have told Craig.

The Cashmere bred so many colorful characters—many with clever scams that managed to keep them one carefully placed footstep on the right side of the law. Parvell Sykes's uncle, Big Gold, was one of them, with his liquor houses, and most inventive of all, his "Telephone Friendship and Comfort Service." As much as Lamont hated to admit it, Big Gold was way ahead of his time—imagine finding eight women who were willing to install a second telephone line in their homes so that they could provide "friendship and comforting coversation" to men for a monthly fee.

But even though Big Gold was a petty felon himself, he deeply resented the new criminal element—ill-mannered, nondressing, noncommerce-minded, "treasonistic"-acting, "New Jack City" Negroes that practically chased him out of the Cashmere.

And, of course, Mr. Lacy was on his mind when he told Craig about the "blind man with a gun." Mr. Lacy had had tears in his eyes on the day that Lamont and James helped him move out.

"Son, I tried to hold on but I have to go," he told them. "Couldn't even entertain my lady friends with all of those trifling-tail Negroes hanging around outside every night. And that isn't good. You know a playa need his 'entertainment' or he'll get mean and ornery. Liked to make me shoot out the window on a Wednesday night, it was so bad."

"Why," Lamont mumbled, as he made his way to his car, "would Durham, for all of its talk of needing decent and affordable housing, let a vibrant community like the Cashmere crumble away into this mess?"

He sighed heavily, shaking his head in disgust, as he

got in the car and drove off. He didn't know how he was going to do it, but he had to win that contract. No other developer, no matter how much money and clout he had, could bring the same understanding, sense of history, and love to rebuilding the Cashmere. Green Pastures was the only firm that could do it right.

Chapter Seven

THERESA TUGGED AT HER SKIRT. EVERY TIME SHE moved, it rose up to the middle of her thigh, making her feel like one of those middle-aged hoochie-mamas who believed they could beat down old age with something as inept as a short, tight Ultrasuede skirt. She thought about changing for the second time this morning, but dismissed that notion as soon as her eyes landed on an e-mail from "silkygatorfeet."

"'Bout time," Theresa mumbled, as she tugged at her skirt for the third time, before opening Parvell's e-mail. She hoped that he had taken the time to check his schedule and shed some light on his plans for the Christmas holidays. She had three party invites lying on her desk and the RSVP dates were closing in.

Until this morning, she had not even heard from Parvell. And to make matters worse, they had not gone out together since that ill-fated dinner at the Washington Duke Inn, phone tag between them was no longer the exception but the definitive rule, and about the only contact she'd had with the man was when he shook her hand while he was standing next to Rev. Quincey in the receiving line at church.

And to add insult to injury, Parvell did not even take a

moment to chat with her that Sunday. He just gave her one of those blasé handshakes preachers gave to bothersome folk who hopped in the line simply to irk, dress down, or hit on a minister. She had noticed, though, that he took a whole minute to talk to Charmayne Robinson, apparently impervious to the audible sighs and coughs of the folks standing behind her. In fact, he never released Charmayne's one hand from the two of his, while she deliberately held up the line just to agitate any woman in church with her sights set on Rev. Sykes before sashaying out of the sanctuary.

Watching the two of them carry on like that made Theresa so mad she decided to hop back in that line, push that old high yellow Charmayne out of the way, and give Parvell a good piece of her mind. But just as she spun back around, Bug pulled her aside and tried to direct her attention to Parvell's stark white clerical robe with the fancy white brocade stole with "Communion Sunday" embroidered all over it in iridescent bugle beads. Theresa studied the robe a moment and then stared back at her little brother as if to say, *"And?"*

Bug put the bulletin in her hand and pointed to the date.

"SO?"

Theresa's brother closed his eyes and shook his head.

"What Sunday is it?" he asked her.

"Fourth, why?" Theresa answered with just a taste of exasperation. Here she was trying to get Parvell straight, and Bug was worrying the daylights out of her over the man's robe. *ROBE—Parvell's robe.* She read the date on the bulletin again. It was the fourth Sunday, and that fool

was all dressed in white like it was the *first* Sunday—
Communion Sunday.

When Parvell released Charmayne's hand, he glanced
at Rev. Quincey's unpretentious, but finely tailored, black
silk robe, smirked, and proceeded to caress the bugle-
beaded words on the stole with his fingertips.

At that point Rev. Quincey stole a look at that first Sunday Communion stole and proceeded to do what he did
best to a wolf whose sheep's covering was slipping off his
shoulders—engage the fellow in a friendly round of what
his wife, Lena, called "Negro Checkmate."

"Man, you must have paid a fortune for that robe,"
Quincey said to Parvell, never missing a beat with shaking hands with his parishioners.

"Why would you ask me something like that, Obadiah?" Parvell replied. "It's no secret that I invest quite a
bit in my wardrobe. Everything I put on my back costs a
pretty penny."

"Oh," Rev. Quincey said mildly, pausing in the conversation to kiss each cheek of the group of little girls waiting patiently to give the pastor the biggest and brightest
smiles they could muster on their pretty brown faces. He
smiled at them, thinking that they resembled a garden—a
garden filled to the brim with the loveliest array of flowers
in every hue of brown imaginable.

He turned back to Parvell and said, "I hear you, Dawg.
There is no doubt that you drop some serious cash on your
clothes. But something tells me that you outdid yourself
on this particular garment."

"Why is that," Parvell said, trying to talk and keep
the flow of parishioners steady like he'd seen Rev.
Quincey doing.

"It's fourth Sunday, Reverend," Rev. Quincey said smoothly. "And since you are standing there all decked out in a first Sunday Communion outfit, the only thing I could conclude was that it was too expensive to go to waste on one Sunday out of the month."

Theresa and Bug barely made it out of earshot of the two preachers before they collapsed into a fit of hysterical laughter. Aside from the pastor's smooth *"punking"* of Parvell, the expression on his face after being *"punked"* was almost as priceless as his Communion robe appeared to be.

Parvell snatched his hand away from the stole and cleared his throat, searching hard for a plausible lie as to why he was standing up here making a fool out of his own self.

He said, "I've been inundated with ministerial requests lately, and with this one exception, the rest of my robes are dirty and being cleaned. And I just hated going up into the pulpit in a mere dress suit—just didn't seem suitable, if you'll pardon the pun."

Rev. Quincey rolled his eyes upward, as if making a silent "Jesus, give me strength" plea and shook hands with the last of the folk standing in the line.

"So, do you still think *Pimpalicious* is the man for you, Big Sis?" Bug asked Theresa, hoping that this display on Parvell's part would be the straw that broke the camel's back in their alleged courtship. Because from what he could see, Parvell looked more to be Charmayne Robinson's man than he ever did his sister's.

"Hey there, Brown Sugar," the e-mail began. Theresa smiled, then frowned. The sweetness of this salutation was so out of character for Parvell, she read the line twice to make sure that her eyes were not playing tricks on her. But there it was, in bold brown print—*Brown Sugar*. Parvell had never, ever called her anything sweet. In fact, she didn't ever remember him calling her anything that came close to a weak sugar substitute.

Theresa's eyes scanned down the e-mail, landing on the link to an e-card.

"Nice touch, Parvell," she said, then wondered if he were okay. She dismissed that notion, clicked on the link, and waited for the card to open. Anita Baker's song "Serious" started playing, and Theresa sat back in her chair, anticipating something sexy and endearing in the note section of the e-card. It didn't take long for Theresa to discover that not only was Parvell okay, but that he was in rare form when she read:

"Anita sings the word 'serious' so eloquently until I was compelled to attach the song to this note to further clarify what I want to say to you. Theresa, my darling, we are through—Seriously speaking, *thu-roo!* I am serious, so serious, Parvell Sykes."

Theresa's mouth hung wide open so long she barely caught the drool that was about to spill out of her mouth and onto her skirt. The song was coming to an end and before she could close this e-mail, a P.S. popped up.

"the ring . . . I want the ring back."

"What ring?" Theresa asked herself. Then she panicked when she remembered the ring box she'd lost.

"That was a ring worth returning? I figured it cost a lot, but not that much."

Theresa closed her eyes and shook her head in disgust. She should have been hurt—her so-called man was breaking up with her. But about the only thing she felt was

relief, and then anger. How dare Parvell end their relationship with an e-mail playing one of her favorite songs?
That was so mean and *so* Parvell. And then, for him to
have the nerve of Job's wife to ask for that ring back, put
the icing on the cake.

And what made this situation go from bad to past abys-
mal was the fact that Theresa had to come up with a ring
she'd never seen, and was clueless about where it could
possibly be. It was a shame she had to give up the ring
if she ever found it—it would have been nice to sport a
flashy ring at holiday time, pretending that she had a special man in her life. It had been years since Theresa had a
man in her life, a piece of significant jewelry to show for
it, and especially at this time of the year.

She closed her eyes. What *would* it feel like to have
Parvell by her side on Christmas morning? In her mind's
eye, she saw herself getting up and running down to a
gigantic Christmas tree, warm and cozy in a beautiful
red velour robe, trimmed in white satin, with a perky
red velour Santa hat on her head. Theresa practically slid
under the tree and pulled at the biggest box she could
find. She had been eyeballing that box all day, Christmas Eve day, when she first spied Parvell placing it underneath their tree.

Theresa stopped tearing at the wrapping paper on the
box for a moment to admire their Christmas tree. It was
eleven feet tall, thick, lush, and smelled so good. The silver and lavender ornaments, orchid velvet bows, violet silk
ribbons, and silver and lavender brocade skirt wrapped
around the base of the tree was so pretty one of the
neighbors called the Durham newspaper and asked them
to feature it in the Christmas Eve edition. The headline

read— "Durham's Premier Boutique Owner and Hubby
Do a Christmas Room to Put Santa's Elves to Shame."

Theresa pulled the box out from under the tree and
finished ripping the bright red foil paper off, frowning
for a moment—that red definitely clashed with all of
that beautiful lavender and silver. After plowing through
yards of plain white tissue paper, she found a small box
and grinned from ear to ear.

"Diamond earrings! Six carats—three for each ear,"
Theresa exclaimed with glee, and opened the smaller box,
face dropping so fast the rapid change in emotional alti-
tude made her dizzy. Nestled in black tissue paper was her
gift along with a note that read:

"You have not done a thing to please me this past year.
If your name was Virginia, and I told you, 'Yes, there is
a Santa Claus,' I would be compelled to present you with
these two pieces of coal . . . Respectfully yours, Parvell."

The imaginary Theresa started to cry, and then proceeded to break down into hysterical sobbing. This made
the real Theresa so mad, she reached out to slap the imaginary self upside the head for crying over that trifling and
no-good man, and succeeded in slapping the mess out of
herself. Theresa's head was ringing so hard, she didn't
even hear the telephone until a second before the last ring.
She glanced at the caller ID and frowned—the call was
from Lamont Green's company, Green Pastures.

"Why him now," Theresa said. Last thing she wanted
to do was talk to Lamont Green. Bad enough she had to
read Parvell's e-mail and then get her feelings hurt in her
own fantasy about him. She pushed the button and waited
for somebody to answer.

"Green Pastures. This is James Green speaking."

"Whew," Theresa said. She was so glad Lamont had not answered that phone.

"Huh?"

"Uh . . . James . . . uh, hey . . . how's . . ."

"Theresa?"

"Yeah," she answered, trying to sound chipper and nonchalant. "Uh . . . I noticed that your number was on my caller ID."

"You mean my brother's number, right?" James asked, grinning. He could not believe that the oh-so-together Theresa Hopson was all discombobulated over this call to Lamont's office. Maybe the Big Dawg had made some headway with Miss Thang after all.

"Well, yes, kind of . . . I . . . uh . . . thought that I should call back. You know, to find out."

James was enjoying this. But being the good Christian brother that he was, decided to put an end to the sistah's misery.

He said, "I called you, Theresa, because I have something that belongs to you and thought that you might be looking for it. I could . . ."

James glanced at his watch. Lamont was on his way to the office. If he could get Theresa over here soon, she'd run right into his brother.

"You know something," he said smoothly, "why don't you come by Lamont's office?"

"There . . . as in Green Pastures?" Theresa asked, hoping that she didn't sound as goofy as she was feeling.

"Yeah, here—Green Pastures," James responded, trying not to laugh at her. He'd forgotten that Theresa was not the coolest woman when it came to men.

"Can't you just drop it off by the store?"

"I could," James began, "but I won't be able to get to you until tomorrow. My plate is pretty full today. If the expensive jewelry box I am holding is any indication of the contents, Theresa, I am thinking you'll want to get this as soon as possible."

All of a sudden, Theresa sighed with relief. Here she was having an anxiety attack over the lost ring and one of the most trustworthy people she knew had been keeping it safe all of this time. She could have saved herself a whole lot of grief if she'd only done as Miss Queen Esther had instructed her to do, and follow the advice of 1 Peter 5:7 . . . casting all of her anxiety on the Lord because He truly cared for her.

"I could meet you at Green Pastures if you can get over there in about thirty minutes," James said.

"I thought you were already there," Theresa said.

"Company phone."

"Okay. Well then, I'm on my way," she agreed, hoping to get over there and out without running into Lamont.

Theresa turned off the computer and went to run the comb through her hair and dab some gloss on her lips. She did a quick check of her outfit, now wishing that she had chosen something else to wear this morning. Even though it was one of her favorite outfits, she didn't relish rolling up in Lamont's place of business dressed like she wanted to be seen by a man. Because this was definitely a man's "eye-candy" outfit—snug and short peach, Ultra-suede skirt, a creamy white silk mock turtleneck, peach fishnet stockings, and peach, cream, and dove gray suede high-heeled boots with a matching applejack-styled hat.

She grabbed her dove gray suede jacket and headed out the door. The last time she wore this outfit, Parvell had practically busted a gasket. They were attending a reception at Eva T. Marshall University, and just about every other brother they ran into—young and old—commented on her ensemble, especially those sexy high-heeled boots. About the only brother who didn't compliment her was Parvell.

Theresa backed up from the front door and hurried to check herself out in the foyer mirror. Good—that's how she looked—awfully doggone good. What in the world was wrong with a man who couldn't recognize the striking sister staring back at her? Maybe her people were right—Parvell leaving her would be the best thing that ever happened to her.

As Theresa pulled into a parking spot right in front of the building, it occurred to her that she had never been in Lamont's office suite on Consultant Place. His building was in a great location—up on a hill that offered a pleasant view of Martin Luther King Parkway below, along with the clusters of pine trees that contributed to Durham's lush and woodsy landscape. Plus, it was in walking distance of the grocery store, movie theater, Fuddruckers, Starbucks, Bruegger's Bagels, CVS pharmacy, and several other businesses, in an area frequented by just about every manner of folk in the city.

It occurred to her that she had walked right past Lamont's building plenty of times when visiting Bug and Vanessa's office suite for their accounting firm. Theresa had driven by a few of Green Pastures houses and developments, and read newspaper articles on the company. But she'd never given much thought to what the company was all about, or taken the time to stick her head through the office doors to say hello.

Theresa was impressed as soon as her feet crossed the threshold into Green Pastures' chic lobby. Large picture windows afforded a great view of the busy parkway below. The café-au-lait walls showcased original African American paintings set in burnished copper-colored frames. A chocolate leather sofa and matching oversized chairs, along with an elegant, chrome-trimmed glass coffee table accentuated with a large crystal vase filled with purple, yellow, peach, and cream-colored flowers rested comfortably on a plush carpet that matched the walls.

Theresa knew without asking that her friend Yvonne Fountain had decorated this office suite. Because Yvonne, who had apprenticed under Rosie Vicks-Hall in St. Louis, was about the only decorator, other than Rosie herself, who could so perfectly match up an interior with its owner. This suite may have had Yvonne's expert touch but everything about and in it was Lamont Kenneth Green.

It was hard to believe that no one had heard her come in. She knew that somebody had to be somewhere in the vicinity. This was a black business with a lot of fancy and expensive stuff in it. Black folk, especially ones who had been raised in the 'hood, did not leave their offices open and unattended.

Theresa sat down on the sofa and started flipping through a local black business magazine. In it was an article featuring North Carolina's freshest crop of black millionaires across the state. Number six on the list was none other than Lamont Green, whose company was estimated to be worth $13 million, with profits totaling $2 million in the last year.

She ran her finger up to the top of the list, and then down to number ten, looking for Parvell's name. Her finger slipped to the end of the page, where she spotted his name, situated in a three-way tie at the bottom of the "Almost There, Honorable Mentions" list, with profits skimming the half-million-dollar mark.

"Who woulda thought it," Theresa murmured to herself and put the magazine back on the table. She nestled down into the comfortable chair, eyes scanning the very tasteful room, trying to still her impatience. She'd hoped that she could meet up with James, get the ring, and leave without running into his brother.

Theresa glanced at her watch and realized that she'd been here all of six minutes, even though it felt more like fifteen. She picked up the magazine again and hurriedly flipped to the article on Lamont, peeking over her shoulder to make sure that no one was around to see her reading it.

Spread across an entire page in living color was Lamont Kenneth Green, grinning and skinning, legs akimbo, hands on his waist, with the jacket of his navy suit pulled back far enough to reveal a mint green shirt. Theresa felt her face flush, staring at that man like that. Lamont was way too sexy for his own good. And even worse, he knew it.

"That is one of my best pictures."

Theresa jumped, more unnerved by the feel of his lips near her ear than by not knowing he was there. Just how long had that mannish rascal been standing there watching her?

"Hi Lamont," she barely whispered, wondering why she was so shy and uncomfortable around this man. Here she was, a well-educated, respected businesswoman, and the only response she had for Lamont Green was the same old tired one she always had, from back in the day when they were teenagers at Hillside High School.

Back then, he and his boy, Curtis Parker, were star members of the basketball team, and she was a member of the Pep Squad. Theresa being the grade-conscious, hard worker that she was, always made sure that the team had the utmost support. And Lamont, who thrived on his reputation as a smooth player, both on and off of the court, drove her crazy with all of his empty flirting, and eyes that gave the impression they could penetrate the thickest Hillside Hornet Pep Squad sweatshirt. He made her uncomfortable and got on her nerves then, and he was still doing it now, more than thirty years later.

Lamont took great delight in his effect on Theresa, especially when he noticed the ruby tint spreading across her cheeks. In fact, he was especially delighted with this unexpected opportunity to "fellowship" with the good Sister Hopson this morning. And he found himself a bit mesmerized by the way Theresa's naturally long, heavy, dark brown hair—the kind of hair sisters spent a heaping of good weave-money on—fell around her pretty face, accenting those large, dark brown eyes. Lamont had been privileged to observe many a well-dressed black woman in Durham. But he'd rarely seen one who always managed to choose an outfit that was so appropriate for the moment, classy yet sexy, and clearly demonstrated impeccable taste in clothes.

Theresa's purse shook and gave off a low rumbling moan. She politely moved her ear away from Lamont's warm lips, and dug around in the bottom of her purse for the cell phone.

"You still there?" James asked breathlessly, as he whipped his car into the parking space next to his brother's and hopped out.

"Yes," she answered. "Where are you?"

"I'm in the building," James said, as the door flew open and he was face-to-face with Theresa while still talking to her on the phone.

"Girl, I am so sorry. I got stuck behind a school bus *and* one of those slow mowers and couldn't get around either one to save my life," James said, still frustrated.

He reached inside of his breast pocket and put the ring box in Theresa's hand.

She closed her hands around the box just like she did the first time the ring was given to her, not even thinking about looking at it.

"Aren't you going to open the box, Theresa?" James asked, just itching to see the expression on her face when she laid eyes on it. He had examined the ring several times, marveling that something so ugly could cost so much money.

"Uhhh yeah," Theresa answered, hoping they would go about their business and not stand there watching her open the ring box. Last thing she needed was for either one of them to figure out that she didn't have a remote notion of what that ring looked like.

It was clear to both Lamont and James, however, that Theresa was clueless concerning the contents of that overpriced box. There wasn't a woman in Durham with active brain cells who would have been as composed as Theresa was right now, if she had an inkling of what was in that ring box.

"Why you taking so long to inspect your property, girl?" Lamont asked. "You standing there acting like you're about to open up something you're not going to like."

"Why wouldn't I like it," Theresa exclaimed a bit too sharply. "It's a big, expensive ring, right? I'm a woman. I'm supposed to like that kind of thing."

"How do you know it's a big expensive ring? It could be a piece of cheap costume jewelry in a big fancy box from Dollar General," Lamont stated, avoiding James's glare because he knew he was being so wrong.

Theresa cut her eyes at Lamont and bounced the box up and down in her hand like it was a big rock. She wanted to throw it upside his head so bad. But she triumphed over that urge, and snapped open the ring box, which contained a four-carat yellow diamond, set in the middle of eight stones—two sapphires, two rubies, one white diamond, and three emeralds. The ring was big, obviously expensive, and the ugliest piece of jewelry she had ever seen.

In fact, the ring was so ugly, it *out-uglied* the fake diamond and ruby ring owned by Dayeesha, the night clerk at the Kroger grocery store several doors away from Holy Ghost Corner. Whenever Dayeesha rang her up, she waved that ring, which she wore on her right forefinger, and started bragging like there was no tomorrow, exclaiming: "You know, Miss Theresa, my second and fourth babies' daddy, Metro, put this heah rang on my fanger, just to let his third, fifth, and eighth babies' mama, Trygliserod, know that I'm number three, and not number five like she is. 'Cause that heifer know she trifling and ghetto with that medicinal turninology name."

"Why don't you try it on," Lamont said, mischief lighting up his eyes.

Theresa took the ring out of the box and held out her ring finger, looking like she was going to puke the closer the ring got to slipping down her finger.

"What's wrong?"

"Nothing, Lamont. Nothing at all," Theresa managed to say through clenched teeth. She felt like putting the ring on and then using it on him like it was a pair of brass knuckles. And she would have hurt him, too, as heavy as that thing was.

"Then, if nothing, 'nothing at all' is wrong, you shouldn't have any problems putting that thin . . . ring on your finger."

"Well, I think I'll wait and do it in private," Theresa said, wishing he would just shut up and leave her alone before she forgot she was saved and got to talking all ugly up in his business *es-stablishment.*

"Hmmm, that's odd," Lamont replied.

"Odd?" Theresa managed to say.

"Yeah, odd. Most women receiving a ring that large can't wait to put it on. But, Theresa, not only can you wait until you can do it in private, you lost the ring. And just a few moments ago, Miss Lady, you were clueless about what it even looked like."

Theresa opened her mouth.

". . . and," he continued, dismissing her attempt to fabricate some nonsense just to save face, "I betcha that if I looked in the player's manual about you and this ring, I'd stumble right on the term *odd,* missy."

"Ms."

"Huh?"

"Ms., Lamont. As in Ms. Hopson. 'Cause I'm grown."

Lamont was not going to allow Theresa to get away with that. He got all up on her and whispered, "How grown are you, baby?"

James closed his eyes and shook his head ever so slightly. His brother was so wrong. And poor Theresa was, as always, outdone when she came up against his big brother.

Theresa, who was clearly out of her league, was searching hard for a *comeback* with enough *umph* in it to put Lamont in his place, when their uncle, Joseph Green, who was Lamont's office manager, came strolling in. His eyebrows lifted ever so slightly when he spied Theresa Hopson standing with her left hand outstretched and scowling at his oldest nephew.

Joseph took that same hand to extend a greeting, but as soon as he laid eyes on that ring, all he could say was, "Peter, James, and John, and Paul and Jesus' baby cousin, too. *Man!* Baby girl, your ring is so ugly, it makes Mr. Lacy's new girlfriend's fake false teeth look real."

James could not believe his uncle went there like that. Uncle Joseph was so wrong, even if he were so completely on point about that ring.

"Theresa," Uncle Joseph went on, "you need to go and call the police and have them put out a warrant on the man who gave you that mess. Better yet, take it over to that hippity-hoppin' store, Yeah-Yeah, ask for Trucie Smith's grandbaby, Jaequon, and let him take that ring off of your hands. He's a jeweler, and will make one of these rappers who come to the store when they in North Carolina, one of them there pairs of fancy teeth grille things with the stones. Give you a good price for it, too."

"Don't you think I should just give the ring back to its original owner?" Theresa replied, thinking that "gettin' on yo' nerves" had to be a genetic trait in the Green men.

"Depends. Who gave it to you?" Uncle Joseph asked.

"Parvell Sykes."

Joseph refused to even position his mouth to respond to her question. He simply held out his hand and said, "Give me that thang and I'll take it over to Jaequon myself. Is there anybody you think could use a few grand?"

"Mr. Lacy and his new girlfriend," Theresa told him.

"Good thinkin'. Those two definitely need some extra cash. 'Cause that Baby Doll needs to get her self some different shoes before the first snowfall. I don't think she will like walking around in ice and snow wearing those yellow jelly sandals she always has on."

Theresa bit back a smile. She was glad that she wasn't the only one who had noticed Miss Baby Doll's shoes. She'd recently seen Miss Baby Doll and Mr. Lacy at Kroger, and Baby Doll was still wearing those yellow jelly shoes. Only this time her socks were a bright red, a noticeable contrast to the orange shirt and hot pink skirt she was wearing that day. And even more noticeable was the way Mr. Lacy was looking at her—like she had a freshly fried pork chop hanging around her neck.

All Theresa could think at that moment was, "Lord, what am I doing wrong here?"

"Theresa," James said, "I'm expecting to see you at the first Christmas Festival meeting at church next Sunday."

"Sunday?" she asked, trying to shake her mind clear of Miss Baby Doll and Mr. Lacy. Sometimes, she had to pray so hard about being jealous of Miss Baby Doll. Theresa knew she was wrong but she couldn't help how she felt—no matter how crazy or ridiculous those feel-ings were. She owned a fancy boutique, made plenty of money, was attractive, and about as man-less as a nun. And Miss Baby Doll, with those yellow jelly shoes and men's socks, could go on and on ad nauseam about how Mr. Lacy couldn't keep his hands off her.

"No, next Sunday, as in the Sunday after next. You will be there, right? And you and Yvonne are still doing the decorations?"

"I'll be there. And it's more like Yvonne is doing the decorations. I just take orders and put things where she tells me."

James smiled. Theresa was right. No one at their church could decorate like Yvonne Fountain. And ever since she moved back to Durham after her divorce from that stuck-up husband of hers, she had been very busy with projects at the local churches and Eva T. Marshall. He liked Yvonne, and was always tempted to introduce her to his frat brother, Coach Parker.

"Are you still gonna be Mrs. Claus?" he asked more for Lamont's sake than anything else. Theresa was not one to promise to do something and then renege and not do it. Lamont, on the other hand, had been gung ho about playing Santa at first, then got cold feet when he saw the costume, tummy pillow and all.

He had said, "Do you honestly expect me to put this on and then proceed to go out in public? How can I be big-pimpin' with the honeys bringing their babies to see ole Santa in this thing? I'll be looking like a fat old man."

"Uhh, Big Brother? If my memory serves me right, Santa *is* a fat old man. And on most occasions he tends to be of the Eu-ro-pe-an persuasion," James had told him.

"And therefore, a black Santa with some serious 'dap,' talking junk to the honeys while he is placating their little darlings won't have much trouble at this festival, big round tummy and all."

"So, you think that li'l Junior, Man-Man, T-Joint, and Tarsha/Tasha/Teisha's mama might wanna spread some good tidings by hopping up in ole Santa's lap and dancing him up some holiday cheer?"

At that point, James had moved away from his brother.

"I do something wrong?"

"I'm not partial to the way lightning feels when it strikes. Lap dances for Santa at church. Talkin' 'bout your naughty and nice scenario," James had told him.

"So, who is Santa this year?" Theresa asked.

"Who you want it to be?" Lamont said, suddenly re-thinking his decision to back out of the Santa gig. Miss, no *Ms.* Theresa would make one fine Mrs. Claus. And she'd certainly fit all nice and snug on Santa's lap.

"It's more like who I don't want it to be."

"As in . . . ?" Lamont questioned.

"As in Brother Jesse Mumford," she said matter-of-factly.

"Ewww," Nina Rhodes said as she walked into the lobby, arms full of drawings and plans for Cashmere Estates. As the head architect at Rhodes, Rhodes, and Rhodes, the firm she co-owned with her two sisters, Nina was in charge of figuring out what kind of units Lamont needed to build to blend in with the historical buildings they planned to keep and renovate on the grounds of the property.

"That is so nasty. Jesse Mumford. Ewww. He has so

many teeth in his mouth, he looks like a shark. And he is always trying to hit on somebody at a church event, when he thinks his wife isn't looking. I can't stand him."

Nina handed James some of her papers.

"And one of these days Shark Tales is gonna roll up on the wrong saint, and get his feelings hurt bad."

"Does Mr. Mumford still wear a Jheri curl?" Theresa asked, curious.

"What else would you call 'good hair' that converted to finger-ripping naps at the edges and the roots?" Nina put in.

"I didn't even know that they still did curls," James said.

"You can get a Jheri curl over at Yeah-Yeah," Uncle Joseph said.

"Is there anything that you can't get over at Yeah-Yeah?" James inquired.

Uncle Joseph started to expound on the things that were not available at Yeah-Yeah, and then thought better of it. Last time he was at Yeah-Yeah, he bought some chitlins off the food truck they kept in the back parking lot. Yeah-Yeah had the best chitlins in town—had so little fat on them, a ten-pound box didn't whittle down to six when you cooked them. In fact, they barely went below eight.

"You can get just about anything you want and need at Yeah-Yeah."

Theresa glanced down at her watch and realized that she had a little more than twenty minutes to get over to her own store. She picked up her purse, and started moving in the direction of the door. Lamont grabbed her by the wrist.

"Slow your roll, Miss Thang. We need to get something straightened out before you run out of my place of business."

"And that is?"

Lamont tilted his head back and scratched his chin.

"Well, I just want to make sure that my Mrs. Claus is a fine woman, and someone I believe I can work with, like yourself, before I totally commit to working for the festival."

Theresa started to blow him off. She hadn't forgotten how she felt while watching him with that Table Wine girl at the Washington Duke Inn. But the irresistible smile radiating from Lamont's face stopped her from saying something ugly.

"Santa, Santa, Santa," Theresa began lightheartedly. "For you to even contemplate whether or not you and Mrs. Claus can work together is a travesty. In my humble opinion, Mrs. Claus has to be the quintessence of the concept of 'helpmeet.'"

Lamont opened his mouth to retort but nothing could come out that was on par with what had just been said. Theresa grinned and then signified by lightly flicking some imaginary dust off her right shoulder.

Uncle Joseph took a big gulp of his orange juice and said, "Girl, if you gonna be a pimp, just gone and dust you shoulder off," to the surprise of everybody in the room.

Nina, who was twenty-nine, said, "Gone, Uncle Joseph, with your bad self. Didn't know you liked Jay-Z."

"Me neither," James mouthed to Lamont, wondering if there might be some extra-frisky stuff blended in with that fresh-squeezed orange juice their uncle was so busy slurping out of a mayonnaise jar.

Theresa clasped her hand on Lamont's shoulder and said, "So, you game for working with me, Santa?"

"Ready and willing to handle anything you want to throw my way, *Miss Thang*," Lamont answered with so much heat in his voice, Theresa felt warmth starting to spread across her cheeks. But the progress of that warm flush was quickly chilled with disappointment when the lobby door opened and Lamont's ex-wife, Gwen, along with Nina's oldest sister, Lauren Rhodes-Ramirez, walked in.

Lamont gave Lauren a big smile and then turned toward Gwen, who came and stood next to Theresa and gazed into his eyes like they were about to go out on a date. Theresa moved back a few steps, not quite sure what to do, and Gwen quickly absorbed her spot, commandeering all of Lamont's attention.

"Hey you," she said, not making any attempt to speak to anybody else.

"Hey yourself," Lamont answered.

Theresa walked over to the table and retrieved her purse. It was time to go. There was no way she was going to stand here and watch Lamont let his ex-wife monopolize his attention at her expense.

And to add insult to injury, the girl had come up in here to have a detailed and serious discussion about her trip to the Super WalMart store in Raleigh. From the way she was going on, it would make you think Wal-Mart was some exclusive department store and Raleigh the only location ritzy and exotic enough to host such an establishment.

Theresa made her way toward the door.

"You leaving?" James asked her.

"I have to get to the store. But I just wanted to thank

you for keeping the ring safe." Up until this moment, she'd forgotten that she was supposed to be returning it to Parvell. "Too bad," Theresa thought. She really didn't want to talk to Parvell again, and giving the ring away would be the perfect excuse for not calling him.

"Well okay," James said and kissed Theresa on the cheek right before she walked out of the door. He glanced over at his brother and frowned. Lamont hadn't had any romantic feelings for Gwen since they parted ways ten years ago. But he had never learned how to draw the proper boundary lines with the girl. And that had cost him dearly by running away good women who refused to be second-placed by Gwen. Women like Theresa Hopson.

As soon as the door closed behind Theresa, Lauren went over to Uncle Joseph and whispered, "I'm going to have to use that mack approach with my husband."

"Girl, what you talking 'bout? Who up in here mackin'?" Uncle Joseph asked, all loud and unconcerned about who heard him.

"Shhh," Lauren said and nodded at Gwen and Lamont.

Uncle Joseph drained the mayonnaise jar and said in a slightly lower voice, "I don't know why that boy won't put that girl in her proper place."

"Who?" Nina asked, coming from the kitchen nursing a cup of hot tea.

"Them," Uncle Joseph stated, with a finger pointed boldly at Lamont and Gwen. His nephew may feel it necessary to handle Gwen with kid gloves but he didn't.

"He won't do it, Uncle Joseph, 'cause he allows Gwen to make him feel guilty about filing separation papers and carrying out that divorce when he came home that time and found the locks changed and his good suits strewn across a wet lawn," James said.

"Yeah, I think you right on that one, son," Uncle Joseph said. "But Lamont needs to give that up, and Gwen, too, for that matter. It's over with and that boy ain't coming back to her no matter how much she calls him, and finds ways to talk on and on about nothing when she 'round him. And when he finally decides to remarry, Gwen is gonna get her feelings hurt, and so will Lamont. 'Cause no wife worth her salt is going to stand by and let that girl be all up in her husband's face without kicking up some dust."

Uncle Joseph leveled a firm eye on both Nina and Lauren.

"You two heed what I'm saying. Don't you ever let your girlfriends talk you into being cold and mean to your man when you are going through a few bumps and bruises with him. If you love the man, and you know he is a good man, you better sit down and work it out with him. But if you listen to your friends, you'll end up losing your man. And when he is gone, you'll have to watch him be happy and in love with somebody else. And mark my words, that new woman will not be interested in catering to you and your feelings simply because you let a good man walk out of your life."

"Y'all better listen to Uncle Joseph," James said, "because he's right. I've seen it happen too many times. And good brothers do not come back when you lead them to think you don't want them anymore."

"So, you think Bossman is interested in Theresa Hopson?" Nina quizzed, more eager for info on her boss's future than a lingering past that should have been laid to rest a long time ago.

"You a nosy little something, Nina," Lauren scolded.

"Forget you, Lauren," Nina countered. "You not the boss of me."

"Stop it," Uncle Joseph commanded. Those Rhodes sisters ran the best architectural and contracting firm in the state. And their work was exceptional. But sometimes they made him want to go outside and get a fresh switch and use it to whip their behinds.

"Well, she started it," Lauren said and made a face at her sister, who said, "You 'sposed to be somebody's mama, and here you are acting like you are the child."

Lauren backed down. She took great pride in being what she thought was a mature mother of her three boys.

Finally, after the uncalled-for drama subsided, Uncle Joseph answered Nina's question.

"Lamont likes Theresa—and a lot more than he is willing to own up to. But he has been so contented with bachelorhood for so long that he, despite a rich arsenal of playa skills, has forgotten how to woo a woman like Theresa Hopson."

"What you mean, Uncle Joseph," Nina said, in what everybody who knew her always called her "old woman" voice, "is that Boss-man can put a smooth move on a temporary 'shorty.' But he is out of his league when he runs into that brick wall we call commitment."

"I hear you, li'l sister," Lauren said. "That's why Gwen gets away with so much. She runs off all his 'temps.'"

"Yeah," Uncle Joseph said. "But that ain't a good thing by any means. Lamont has just let Gwen help him run off Theresa. And that fool boy, as smooth and cool a player as he thinks he is, doesn't even know it."

Lamont gave Gwen a kind pat on the shoulder and

stared at his watch, hoping that she took the hint and left. He didn't remember a word she'd said to him and was piqued with himself for allowing his ex-wife to run off a woman he was interested in. Sometimes he could kick himself for letting Gwen do that to him.

"Is Theresa gone?" he asked, realizing that the members of the huddle before him were all up in his business.

"Yeah," James stated. "Left as soon as you let Gwen monopolize your time with tales of her travels to the land of Kmart."

Lamont frowned and said, "Target, James."

"No, I think it was Super Wal-Mart, boss," Lauren said.

"Well whatever it was," James replied, "Theresa left because you let another woman push her off to the side over some nonsense. Gwen isn't your wife and not eligible for any special privileges where you are concerned."

"Gwen is Monty's mother," Lamont said with a hard edge in his voice. "Furthermore, she is a good person, a great mother, and deserves to be treated with respect."

"You are absolutely right, big bro. Gwen is a wonderful person, and she definitely deserves your respect. But what she doesn't deserve is the right to think that she can be treated special like the two of you are still a couple."

At that point, both Lauren and Nina thought it best to go to the conference room and prepare for their meeting, as much as they would have loved to stay and watch *the colored brothers' showdown*. Uncle Joseph, on the other hand, sat down on the couch and waited for the show to begin.

"You didn't have to go there, James, and you know it."

"Yes, I did. I hate to see you guilty over hurting Gwen

when you realized that you couldn't go back into that marriage after she put you out, told you that she wanted a divorce, then changed her mind after you believed her and left. Your divorce is a decade old and you need to let that go. When you do that, you'll find that Gwen will act better and not expect you to shout her up and down simply because she dropped Monty in the doctor's hands."

"But I'm not angry at Gwen, don't have any issues with her," Lamont said defensively, deliberately skirting the issue of guilt.

"No one said that. And no one in their right mind believes that foolishness you just threw at me, either. All I am asking you to do is to let go of guilt over a decision you believed you needed to make. Because if you really believed that you were wrong to divorce her, you'd been back with her years ago. But you are not with her and that speaks volumes in my book."

"And," Uncle Joseph added from his chair, "the first thing you need to do to help put this matter to rest is rededicate your life to Christ. When you do that and get the Holy Ghost, you'll find your relationship changing for the better with Gwen. Because then you will have forgiven yourself because you'll know that God has already forgiven you. And you will feel comfortable about insisting that Gwen respect the boundaries you need to establish between you and her, and not care whether she likes it or not."

Uncle Joseph got up and started walking back to the conference room. He and Queen both knew that when Lamont put the Lord first in his life, God would see him through this and his struggle to get that contract for the Cashmere.

Lamont sighed heavily. Sometimes he got tired of hearing about him and Gwen and wished folks would just leave this matter alone.

"You think Theresa will still play Mrs. Claus?" he asked his brother, hoping to change the subject.

"I know she will. And if you want to have a great time with her doing this, I suggest that you get over to her store as soon as you can and try to make amends."

Lamont nodded. James was right. He had to remember that women didn't take too kindly to a man teasing and flirting with them, only to cut the interaction short to talk to another woman.

"I'll drop by before our meeting at church."

"Sounds good," was all James said, as they both went down to the conference room to try and figure out what to do to build their case for that contract.

Chapter Eight

JETHRO HADN'T EVEN REALIZED THAT HIS TELEPHONE was still off the hook until that annoying sound kept buzzing in his ears, reminding him to put it back on the receiver. Lately, most of his conversations with Parvell Sykes ended on a very expensive and sour note. As he sat there fuming, he realized that tonight was no better—no worse—than the last time he did a round with that black, jackleg preacher.

"Twenty-one freakin' thousand dollars," Jethro exclaimed. "And this is on top of the first eighteen grand I've thrown that nnn . . . man's way."

"What twenty-one, eighteen thousand dollars," his latest mistress, Patricia Harmon, asked. She had never been one to miss out on any mention of money—intentional or otherwise.

"Patricia, why are you so concerned about *my* money?" he snapped.

"Yeah, it might be *your* money," she thought, "but it came from that same petty cash flow you use for *me*." Twenty-one thousand dollars would have paid her mortgage for seven months.

Patricia held her left hand under the light on Jethro's desk to admire the monstrously expensive ring he told her was for his wife. It had to be worth at least $15,000. She wanted that ring for herself, to prove to her close girl-friends that she was the one other woman capable of luring Jethro out of his marriage to Bailey Catherine.

Jethro held out his hand for the ring. Patricia slipped it off her finger and tossed it in his hand, with what she hoped was a lot of attitude. Sometimes she envied black women's ability to convey a thought without so much as moving a tongue muscle. Those *sistahs* could say a "mouthful" with something as simple as the snap of their necks, or a flick of the wrist.

"You're going to have to spend a little more time over on Fayetteville Street, to perfect that kind of body language," Jethro said, and then gave a harsh laugh when Patricia sent him a frosty glare.

"Naa . . . scratch that thought," he said. "I'd hate to see one more misguided and totally unnecessary news report on our historically black Hillside High School because one of those teeny-bopping 'sista-girls-in-training' put you in your place with a dress-down you'd never forget."

Patricia was seething, her faux, coconut bosom heaving fiercely with each breath, face so red, it looked like Jethro had slapped her. She snatched up her purse and car keys, signaling that their evening, which had only begun thirty-five minutes ago, had come to an abrupt end.

Jethro really didn't care what she did. Patricia thought she was far more important to him than she was and needed to be put back in her place. He picked up the telephone and dialed the number for his building's security office, and said, "Send Anthony up here to escort Mrs. Harmon to her car," and hung up.

"May I ask just one question?" Patricia spat out.

Jethro nodded calmly, hoping that this wasn't going to be one of those diatribes women went into when they were insulted by a man, and were too concerned about losing him to really get him straight.

"When did you ever care anything about the blacks in this city?"

"I beg your pardon," he said icily.

"I find your concern for poor, little black Hillside High School interesting," she went on. "Because if you have your way, not one of the parents of those little mouthy 'sistah-girls-in-training' will be able to afford to live in what used to be their own neighborhood."

Jethro walked over to Patricia, who was now standing at the open door. He lifted her chin with his fingers and held her eyes to his. When she tried to pull away, he tightened his grip on her.

"I'm rich, I'm greedy, and I don't put much stock in ethics and morality. And even though I love to twist the truth to suit my needs, I do know the truth when I see it. And these things are true. Hillside is not the jungle some people in Durham try to make it out to be. Parvell Sykes successfully defrauded me of thirty-nine thousand dollars. Charmayne Robinson is smart, I need her to get what I want from the blacks, and I intend to ahh, *hit that*, as the *'brothahs'* would say, first chance I get.

"And you know what else, Patricia? The truth is that you are going to help me win over the DUDC because you want to keep me in your bed, along with all the money that goes into your account throughout the duration of this affair."

Patricia bristled.

"You know something," he said cheerfully, while

clenching her jaw so tightly it felt like it might crack in his hands. "If I didn't want to go home and make passionate love to my wife, I'd sit back in my chair and treat you to a mouthful."

Patricia managed to wrench her chin away and raised her hand. But Jethro reached up and grabbed her wrist with the speed and dexterity of the conference title quarterback that he used to be. When she tried to lower her arm, he relaxed his grip and said, "Go home, take a long, hot soak, and ask yourself if you can handle this affair, Patricia. It can last as long as you want it to last. But know that this is all there is and all there will ever be."

Tears welled up in Patricia's eyes and Jethro handed her a monogrammed handkerchief, just a teensy bit remorseful that he made her cry. It was never a wise thing to get your mistress so upset she felt a need to seek revenge on you. And Patricia Ann Harmon was just the type of woman who would get you in the messiest and the most inconvenient ways.

Her last lover almost lost everything—his wife, family, million-dollar home, and a chunk of his income to the astronomical spousal support payment his wife's lawyer was asking for if she divorced him. Desperate and fearing bankruptcy, the fool managed to patch things up with his wife, and remained in what Jethro always secretly believed was a horrid marriage to an ugly, boring, no-leg-shaving, Birkenstock-wearing woman.

To make a wretched situation worse, the clown still lost money when his lawyer recommended an out-of-court settlement, when Patricia threatened to put all of his business in the street with a vicious and very public civil suit. No, it was not wise to let this woman leave this room mad, hurt, disappointed, crying, and feeling rejected. Jethro took the handkerchief out of Patricia's hand and gently wiped a tear off her face, leaving a pale streak where her "natural tan" makeup used to be.

"Babe," he said softly, and kissed the spot where the tear had been, wishing he didn't want to rush home to Bailey, who had called right before Patricia walked into his office, whispering a naughty tale about what she was and wasn't wearing. "I'm sorry. Can I make it up to you this weekend?"

Patricia nodded through a loud sniffle, hoping that he wasn't planning on sneaking off from the golf course to spend a quick hour with her. She needed more time with Jethro after tonight, and was about to tell him so, when his soft nibbles on her earlobes sent hot promises of what was in store for her if she just said yes.

"Good," Jethro said with a wink and a sultry smile, all the while opening the door and pushing her right out when he heard the security guard's heavy footsteps in the hall. He closed the door and started cleaning off his desk, giving himself fifteen minutes before heading down to his car. Last thing he needed was to run into Patricia. He didn't want her tonight. He wanted and needed his wife.

The vibration of his cell phone tickled his waist. He looked at the caller ID and smiled. It was Anthony, the security guard, one of the few black men that he liked. There were several he respected—Lamont Green, his most fierce adversary, being one. But there were very few that he liked.

"Coast is clear," was all Anthony said and hung up.

Jethro smiled again, grabbed his briefcase, and hurried out. It was good to be white, fifty-three, male, rich, Southern, feared, envied, and handsome. And Jethro knew he reminded folks of a tall, husky version of the actor Ray Liotta. Women loved his rich coloring, thick silver and black hair, and dark gray eyes with thick black lashes. He was also a well-dressed man, looking awfully striking this evening in a dark gray pinstriped suit, dove gray shirt, lavender silk tie, dark gray silk socks with tiny lavender "Js" embroidered in them, a pale gray undershirt in the softest silk/cotton/lycra blend, gray silk boxers, and a pair of sleek, black lace-up Cole Haan shoes.

He hurried down the corridor to the elevator, and then paused just one moment to admire himself in a large mirror hanging on the wall.

"I love being a *'white boy,'*" Jethro thought smugly and grabbed at the "package" that made so many of his mistresses say *"oh my."*

He pushed the down button and tapped on the wall impatiently when it seemed like the elevator was stuck at the lobby level. It finally moved to his floor, and he had to wait several more minutes for the maintenance crew to push that cumbersome cleaning cart off. Then they took up even more of his time, when the man just stood at the back of the elevator, not making any effort to come off until the woman said, "Get off now."

Jethro had seen some interesting folks working in the building's maintenance department. But he didn't think any could top these two. He made a point of treating the cleaning people as if they were invisible. But he found it difficult to ignore this couple. The man was wearing eyeglasses with lenses that were so thick they looked like the bottoms of two vintage Coca-Cola bottles fused together. And it was all he could do not to stare at the woman's teeth. They looked like they were made of that yellowish putty dentists used to make molds of your teeth. He got on the elevator thinking, "I hope they don't clean my office."

As soon as the elevator was down on the lobby level, Baby Doll looked up and down the hall to make sure that nosy security guard, Anthony, wasn't around and then whispered, "No one's around," to Mr. Lacy, who took off the glasses and slipped them into his coat pocket. He massaged the tender imprints on the bridge of his nose and put on his shades.

"Girl, them thangs must weigh a ton."

"But they worked, Daddy," Baby Doll answered. "Those things were so thick, nobody could see your eyes good enough to be able to figure out that you blind."

Baby Doll placed her forearm up under his hand and guided him, along with the steel cleaning cart, down the hall and straight to Jethro's office suite.

She rolled the cart into the middle of the floor, took out some Pledge and a dust rag, and laid it on Jethro's desk. Mr. Lacy felt around the cart and located some trash bags, which he placed on top, to make it look like he was emptying all the trash cans.

"Girl, you gone be able to find them papers?"

"I think so," Baby Doll whispered as she reached for the trash can Jethro kept under his desk and put it on his black leather chair, with a built-in massage system she sneaked and used from time to time. She put on a pair of rubber gloves and then rambled through the crumpled-up papers in the can.

"Here it is," she said softly and triumphantly, holding

the paper up for Lacy to "see," wondering why people like Mr. Jethro Winters were so full of themselves they played themselves at their own game. It was never a wise thing to act as if the person cleaning your office when you weren't around was less than you.

"Read what's on it to me," he said.

She slipped her mold teeth out of her mouth and scanned the paper before reading the contents out loud.

"Can I just give you the gist of what's on it? This stuff is real boring, Daddy."

"That's fine," he answered impatiently, thinking that there were times when being blind was such an inconvenience. "Just tell me what's on the daggone papers."

"After Mr. Winters gets the contract to rebuild the Cashmere, he plans to get Ida Belle Robinson's baby girl to help him buy up all the land around it."

"But there are houses, very nice houses I might add, around the Cashmere. What they plan on doing, just asking all of them peoples to move?"

"Something like that," was all Baby Doll said, then asked, "You think this is something Lamont Green would want to know?"

Mr. Lacy started grinning.

"Come on over here and give me some sugar, baby. Not only would Lamont want to know this, it's just what he needs to stop Jethro dead in his tracks."

Baby Doll was about to empty the remaining contents of the can into a large trash bag when something pressed on her heart to look at the rest. She pulled out two small folders that had once held room keys for the Siena Hotel in Chapel Hill with Jethro Winters's name scribbled across one and Patricia Harmon's name written neatly on the other.

"Looka here, looka here."

"You find something else useful in that trash, Baby Doll?"

"There are some hotel room key holder things with Mr. Winters's and his girlfriend's names on them."

Mr. Lacy snorted in disgust. Men could be so stupid when they ran around on their wives. Some of them actually behaved as if they wanted to get caught.

"Keep that, too. Might come in handy if those other papers don't get Lamont the edge he'll need going up against someone like this sly Jethro boy."

Baby Doll put the papers and the key holders in her purse at the bottom of the cart.

"Daddy, we better hurry up and finish this office. That no-good Anthony'll be strolling by here shortly to check on Mr. Winters's office. That lazy, no-count Negro walks around here actin' like he Mr. Winters's personal assistant."

Mr. Lacy felt for the carpet sweeper and began working on the large area rug, while Baby Doll finished emptying all of the trash cans before she started dusting. She was so excited about what they'd found and tried not to rush through her work. Many years ago before she got too crazy-acting, she'd been a part of Durham's black community. She had a good memory of most of the people she was now becoming reacquainted with, even if none of them remembered her.

Baby Doll had come a long way from where she used to be. A lot of the folks she used to hang around were dead, so crazy they didn't know their butt from their toes, so sick they couldn't do anything for themselves, or just hanging around on the fringes of life in the community trying to pretend like they were in the mix, making fools of themselves because it was clear to everyone that they were not.

But the Lord had blessed her by taking her from the fringes and given her a toehold back into the mainstream of her community's daily life. She hoped that by helping Lamont Green beat out that no-good Mr. Winters, she'd be able to get her whole foot through the door.

Jethro's large, plush, and sparkling chocolate Mercedes sedan made a smooth left turn into his neighborhood. When Bailey had first decided that they were moving into the Surrey Green development, right off Hope Valley Road in Southwest Durham, he balked—it wasn't flashy enough for his taste. But after driving through the quiet neighborhood, and basking over the price she'd negotiated for a very plush house, he capitulated and wrote the check.

That was just one of the things he appreciated about his wife—her exquisite taste and eye for a delicious bargain. Their house, in one of the newer and more opulent Triangle communities, would have cost them tens of thousands of dollars more—not to mention demanding a much higher tax rate. And like Bailey had once told him, just because they were rich didn't mean they shouldn't look for a good bargain.

Bailey Catherine Fairfax-Winters, unlike his women, was the real deal—a classy Southern belle. She was tall, gorgeous, with thick, shiny chocolate-colored hair Jethro loved so much he special-ordered his six-figure-tagged car in the exact same color.

Bailey was Jethro's ideal woman. His numerous mistresses were generally thin, slender-hipped, and blond with big, silicone implanted breasts. But his wife was lush and voluptuous with real D cups. And those things were so soft and warm Jethro could get all hot and bothered just thinking about them.

But it was Bailey's laugh that made her absolutely irresistible. His wife had the most engaging, heartwarming, and rib-tickling laugh he'd ever heard. It was that laugh that caught his attention the first time he saw her surrounded by a bunch of basketball players when they were undergraduates at Duke.

Jethro slowed the car down, so he could enjoy what he cherished most about the close of his obscenely busy days—a languorous drive around his neighborhood before pulling up into his paved-stone circular drive.

Jethro adjusted the earpiece to his cell phone, called out a name, and waited for the number to dial itself.

"Hello," a woman's sultry voice traveled through the sound waves to his eager ears.

"What are you wearing?" he asked with so much heat in his voice it made his windows fog up.

Charmayne blinked at her caller ID to make sure the number was right. She almost said, "Negro, you got some nerve," but stopped when she remembered that Jethro was very white. Instead, her mind flipped through her mental file of ghetto comebacks and she said, "A gun."

Jethro started laughing. Charmayne was the only woman, other than Bailey, who could make him laugh out loud with her sassy, in-your-face one-liners. And just like Bailey, the girl was definitely a piece of work, which made her all the more intriguing and desirable.

The phone line was deathly silent. Jethro knew that he had committed a serious breach of etiquette by crossing that particular color line with Charmayne. She was part of that generation of black women who did not take too kindly to a white man hitting on them just because his sweet tooth was craving some brown sugar.

"Come on, baby," he whispered in his deep "good ole boy" drawl. "You too full of sweet brown sugar to be wearing anything as cold and menacing as a gun."

"You need to get your color scheme straight 'cause I'm a redbone."

"Huh?" Jethro said, trying to pull up a mental list of black vernacular so that he could figure out what the heck Charmayne was talking about.

"I'm not brown sugar. I'm high yella, light-skinned, a redbone sister," she retorted nastily.

"Is that how you talked to folks back when you were a bona fide 'hood rat?" Jethro asked, delighted that he'd struck a nerve, when he heard a sound that made him wonder if Charmayne was sucking on her teeth.

She said, "You better be glad that there is a telephone line protecting you from being slapped back into the twentieth century."

"Do me a big favor and make it the nineteenth. That way I'd have legal right to order myself up a lap dance or anything else I wanted from you, Charmayne."

"Why are you calling me and getting on my last nerve, Jethro?" Charmayne demanded. She was tired and sleepy with tons of works to do, and in no mood for foolishness.

He opened his sunroof and sighed with relief when

the chilly pre-winter wind whipped through his hair and cooled him down enough to remember why he had called Charmayne in the first place.

"I called to tell you that my investors came through with the seed money I promised the county when the DUDC gives me the contract."

Charmayne smiled. That *was* good news—good enough to make it worth putting up with Jethro's craziness.

"Is there anything you want me to do?" she asked.

"Focus on the neighborhoods surrounding Cashmere Estates. Find out how much was paid for each house, how much they're worth now, and start drawing up contracts to offer the owner fifteen hundred dollars more than the home's estimated worth."

"That's not giving them a lot to work with, Jethro," Charmayne said. She doubted if the owners would be able to take that money and find a comparable home outside that community.

"Charmayne, we are out to make as much money as we can. So, offering a better deal to those people is out of the question."

She didn't say anything. She was one of "those people" Jethro was referring to.

"Don't go and get a conscience on me now," Jethro said sharply. "I told you what was going to happen when I first mapped out my plans with you. Those folks are getting way more from you than they ever would from anybody else, black or white, including your precious Rev. Sykes.

"Charmayne, you are ambitious, aggressive, driven, hot, and sexy. But you are not greedy. That is why I hired you for this job. I need someone who will be thorough and honest when it comes time to do the figures on what those properties are worth. That will be very important when the community is up in arms and accusing me of taking property for less than it's worth."

"You also hired me because I don't have any problem with telling you no," she said matter-of-factly.

Jethro laughed softly.

"Baby, I'm just a country boy with a bit more testosterone than I probably need."

"No, you're a crazy white boy who wants to be the HWMIC in Durham County. You have too much money and way too many old-school debs trying to break up your marriage and steal you away from your wife."

"HWMIC?"

"Head White Man in Charge," Charmayne answered.

Jethro hollered with laughter and said, "You are dead on all of my money with that one, baby. But tell you what—just make sure you are in my office on Monday at seven-thirty A.M. sharp."

"Parvell told me that the three of us are meeting at nine."

"We are. But you and I need to plan how to buy out that extra property without Parvell. He's not in on this part of the deal."

Charmayne smiled and licked her lips.

"I see," she said, very pleased with the way things were going, especially after Parvell had lied about the money he squeezed out of Jethro. She heard a loud rumbling of metal.

"What's that?"

"My garage. I need to go—have some housekeeping of sorts to tend to," Jethro said, grinning at Bailey standing in the garage wearing nothing but a full-length chocolate-colored mink coat, chocolate thigh-high fishnet stockings, and brown patent leather pumps with clear heels.

"I just bet you do," Charmayne said in a very naughty voice and hung up.

Chapter Nine

THERESA TOOK A BIG GULP OF COFFEE, BIT INTO A breakfast bar, and flipped the newspaper open to reveal a grinning Lamont Green plastered across the front page under the big bold print that read, "Will Green Pastures Successfully Till the Field of Affordable Housing, or Be Mowed Over by a Bigger Plow?"

"My baby boy show does wear a hard hat well, don't he," Queen Esther said, as she read the article over Theresa's shoulder.

Theresa nodded, not wanting to let on that she thought Lamont was looking very sexy in that hard hat, blue jeans, Timberland boots, baby blue cable-knit sweater, and buckskin-colored suede jacket. She'd never paid attention to how broad his shoulders were, and could barely pull her eyes away from them.

"Now those arms on that boy show designed for holding a woman tight," Queen Esther said proudly, hoping that Theresa agreed with her.

"I guess so," Theresa mumbled. The last thing she needed to be doing was becoming too interested in how well Lamont Green's arms could hold somebody. She'd bet some money that his arms were prone to holding a lot of women real tight, and figured the smart thing to do would be to keep her distance. There was nothing worse than loving the feel of a man's arms, only to discover that you weren't the only woman with a penchant for the comfort of those arms.

"You guess so?" Queen Esther questioned, wondering what was wrong with that girl.

"Yes, I guess so," Theresa snapped, wishing Miss Queen Esther would leave her alone about Lamont Green. She was not in the mood to discuss the merits of an unavailable man.

"You kind of touchy this morning, ain't you, missy?"

Theresa wished she had it in her to be contrite and apologetic but she didn't.

"I'm not touchy," she answered evenly, trying to keep the snap out of her voice.

"Well, you show is something," was all Queen Esther said, as she headed toward the front of the store.

Theresa didn't know why she felt like slamming things around on her desk. But every time she looked at Lamont Green grinning from ear to ear, a shovel in his hand, hard hat cocked on the side of his head like he was at the club, she wanted to take something and throw it at somebody, anybody.

She made sure that Miss Queen Esther wasn't in earshot, and was about to slam her hand down on the desk and stomp her foot when the shouting music came on, denying her a great opportunity to take out her frustrations on the poor desk and floor. Theresa took a deep breath and hurried up front, trying to remember if she'd scheduled any appointments before regular store hours.

Mr. Lacy was "looking" around, touching everything he passed in the store, while Miss Baby Doll was in deep conversation with Miss Queen Esther about one of her cleaning gigs.

Theresa surmised that the conversation between the two women was getting awfully good when Miss Baby Doll took the mold teeth out of her mouth and placed a hand firmly on one hip. She almost looked regular to Theresa, standing there talking like she and Miss Queen Esther had been friends for ages.

"You lying, Baby Doll," Queen Esther exclaimed in a tone of voice that let Baby Doll know that she actually believed every single word coming out of her mouth.

"If I'm lyin', I came outta my mama's womb with these here teefs I'm holding in my hand, in my mouf," was all Baby Doll said.

Mr. Lacy stopped "looking" around the store and made his way over to the two women, saying, "My baby ain't tellin' a lie, Queen. Now, I know she kinda special . . ."

"Ooo, Lacy, you is so sweet, Daddy," Baby Doll slurped out, blushing and hunching up her shoulders like she was in middle school.

"But she ain't never been no liar. She wasn't a liar back in the seventies when she got all tangled up with Big Gold Sykes, thinking she was in love with that Negro, and upped and lost her husband, got to drankin' hard and taking them pills, went crazy, and then lost her chirrens to the Social Services peoples."

"How you know all that 'bout me, Daddy?" Baby Doll questioned, shocked that somebody knew who she was.

"Didn't you live next door to me and my third wife, when you left your mama's house to marry that Henderson boy?"

Baby Doll just nodded, feeling kind of tearful every

time she thought about her first and only love until she met Lacy, Davy Crockett Henderson. He had been a bit on the ugly side—light brown, big wide mouth with widely spaced teeth, big ears that seemed to move of their own volition, and skinny with the biggest feet she'd ever laid eyes on. But he had to be the sweetest, kindest, hardest-working boy in the Cashmere. And back in the day, when she was walking around thinking she was too fine for words, Davy Crockett loved himself some Doll.

Queen Esther gave Baby Doll a thorough once-over and then shook her head in disbelief.

"Doll Henderson? Your daddy name is Skillet, right? *That's* who you are, girl?"

Baby Doll nodded her head and said, "Yeah, I'm Skillet's oldest baby girl—the one he got on the sly right after he married Miss Ella."

"Yeah," Queen Esther said. "I remember that. Was a big mess. Your mama's name was Zenobia, and she used to press heads at the old beauty parlor that used to be off Fayetteville Street, over near where the old St. Joseph's AME church used to be."

Queen Esther stared at Baby Doll's new hairstyle for a moment, wondering why her deceased mama's skills at giving a good press and curl had not passed down to her child. The woman's coarse, steel gray hair was parted in a bunch of triangles all over her head, with stiff braids that were held in place with multicolored rubber bands. She looked like she had just been told "thanks but no thanks" at an audition to play Topsy in the remix of *Uncle Tom's Cabin*.

"You know I really don't want to speak ill of your mother, God rest her dear departed soul," Queen Esther began. "But girl, that was a hot affair that she carried on with your daddy. She absolutely couldn't stay away from Skillet. Would drive by his wife, Miss Ella's, house, and blow for Skillet to come out and leave with her. Your mama messed up a good marriage to Mr. W.L. Just like you upped and messed up your own marriage to Davy Crockett."

Mr. Lacy leveled his eyes on Queen Esther. Ever since he'd known her from back in the day at Hillside High School, Queen would blurt out what most folk thought was best left unsaid.

"Yeah, from what little I've been told about that, seems like me and Mama were cut from the same cloth on messin' up. Sometimes I wonder what happened to Davy Crockett and my children after Social Services took 'em from me."

This time Queen Esther smiled.

"Davy Crockett came and got your four children, married a lady from Memphis, and moved back there with her. From the little bit I've heard, they all turned out fine."

Baby Doll sighed with relief and felt a deep prayer of thanksgiving. She'd always felt in her heart that the children had fared well without her. But it felt so good to have that feeling confirmed.

Mr. Lacy reached out for her hand and patted it gently when he felt the tears welling up in her over those babies. He knew that she cried over them at night and always asked God to take care of them for her.

Theresa, who'd been busy fussing over the latest shipment of nightwear for the Holy Ghost Corner, trying to act like she wasn't in "grown folks' business," couldn't resist moving a little closer to the three of them to hear more. She didn't know why she'd been so surprised to learn that they knew Miss Baby Doll in her former life. Mr. Lacy and Miss Queen Esther were old-school black Durhamites—they knew a little bit of something on just about everyone who had ever claimed to be black in Durham County.

Baby Doll turned to Theresa.

"You been satisfied with my cleaning? You ain't had all of that dust and the store smells better since I've been taking care of it."

"Yes, ma'am," Theresa answered honestly. "My store has never been as clean and fresh as it has been under your care."

"You think you want to handle me as permanent part-time? 'Cause I just got on part-time to clean the church and part-time is all the time I have left. Had to look for another job quick after Lacy and I went through Jethro Winters's things."

Baby Doll reached inside of her big yellow patent leather pocket-book with a tarnished gold chain strap and pulled out some crumpled-up and motley papers.

"Here, Miss Queen Esther. Give this to your nephew. Like I told you on the phone, the papers got everything he'll need to build the Cashmere back up."

Queen Esther took the papers and then gave Baby Doll a big hug.

"Girl, we owe you. Now, when you coming to church and letting the Lord know you thankful for all of the blessings He's been dropping down out the windows of heaven into your lap?"

Baby Doll took her mold teeth out of her mouth for a second time and went to the back to rinse them with some cold water. She wished those heavenly windows would open wide enough to pour down enough money to get some real false teeth, instead of these painful things that hurt her gums when she wore them too long.

She swished the cold water around in her mouth, and then rubbed some of that stuff you put on babies' gums when they were teething on her own tender gums.

Within a few minutes she came back, still at a loss as to how she should answer Miss Queen Esther. On the one hand, Miss Queen Esther was absolutely right—Baby Doll really did need to go back to church. Yet on the other hand, she was having a hard time with her excruciatingly slow walk to putting her life back together.

Baby Doll wished she were more patient because she certainly didn't end up where she was overnight. And even though she was thankful to the Lord for how far she'd come, there were times when she wished the changes she prayed for happened sooner than later.

She dabbed the wet mold teeth dry with a paper towel and put them in the container Theresa had given her. She took a deep breath and then took a stab at sharing what was on her heart.

"See . . . I want to come back to church but . . . I didn't want to come back like I am. If I'm trusting the Lord to put me back together, don't it stand to reason that I'd want to come back with a testimony?"

Queen Esther, Theresa, and Mr. Lacy were staring at Baby Doll like she had some real false teeth in her mouth.

"That has to be the craziest thing that I've ever heard come out of your mouth yet, Baby Doll," Mr. Lacy said, adjusting his shades as if he were trying to get a better look at her. He turned toward Queen Esther.

"Don't you have a scripture to rebuke off that foolishness coming from my woman?"

Queen Esther sighed, mind racing to find the right scripture.

"Here, Miss Queen Esther," Theresa said, as she grabbed an Amplified Bible off of a table and flipped through the Book of Psalms. "You think this one will work?" she asked, pointing to the beginning of Psalm 71.

Queen Esther read it over silently and then turned to Baby Doll.

"It says right here . . . *In You, O Lord, do I put my trust and confidently take refuge; let me never be put to shame or confusion."*

"So, what's your point?" was all Baby Doll said, wondering how that scripture applied to her.

"Do you trust in the Lord or not, Baby Doll?" Queen Esther asked her.

"I'm beginning to more and more," was all that she said.

"Well then if you are learning to trust the Lord and depend on Him, and you take this scripture to heart, why would you think that He would not take care of whatever you're concerned about if you went back to church, say . . . this Sunday?"

"Good point, Miss Baby Doll," Theresa chimed in. "You know, you and I did have an agreement about church. I've let you come and work for me and you owe us some church time."

Baby Doll turned to Queen Esther.

"So, what you're saying is that if I take this scripture to heart, it means that the Lord will make it comfortable for me when I come to your church on Sunday? And maybe even give me a way to give my testimony, huh?"

"Umm, hmm," was all Queen Esther had a chance to say when the shouting music came on, pulling everybody's attention to the door.

"What brings you into this neck of the woods?" Queen Esther asked, surprised and curious about why Lamont had deigned to set foot in Miss Thang's this morning.

Mr. Lacy took a deep breath and thought that whatever reason Queen's nephew gave her, it certainly would not be the full story, judging from the scent of the cologne he was wearing this morning. Because if Mr. Lacy didn't know anything else, he knew for certain that Lamont was smelling like a man intent on capturing some woman's attention.

"I was in the neighborhood, had some papers for Rev. Quincey to sign, knew you were here, was wondering if you were planning on going by the church today, and if so, hoping you would drop them off for me."

Queen took the envelope and nodded.

"Tell him to look over everything. And if he doesn't have any problems with what's being proposed, to sign the forms indicating that he is raising money to fund the closing cost program. I'm going to need that to have some leverage when Green Pastures makes the presentation to the DUDC."

"Hey, girl," Lamont called out to Theresa, who all of a sudden had found a dire need to rearrange the shelf she'd just got through stocking minutes ago.

"Hey," she said quietly, wanting to join them but not

sure if that was the right thing to do. Last time she became too chummy with Lamont, he cut the conversation short to run off and talk to Gwen about some insipid reason or another. That hadn't felt good and she wasn't in a hurry to relive that experience.

Lamont wasn't sure if he should go over to where Theresa was working, or just finish up his business with Aunt Queen Esther and leave. He had seen her entire face light up when he walked into the store. Now, she was over in that corner being unnecessarily industrious and very careful with him. Pity. Theresa was looking absolutely delicious this morning in a pair of booty-hugging jeans, a mint-colored, snug-fitting long-sleeved cotton T-shirt, mint crochet poncho, and some of the sexiest navy leather ankle boots he'd seen in a long time.

He absolutely adored the way her thick hair hung around her face, lightly touching her shoulders. And that mouth, with those full, wide lips stained with a deep blackberry-colored gloss, was practically begging to be kissed.

"Umph, umph, umph," he thought as he tried to take in all of the dimensions of that high round booty, giving off the slightest bounce when she moved. "What my hands could do with all of that."

"Lamont," Queen Esther practically yelled in his ear.

"Yes, ma'am," he said, jumping to attention, hoping she hadn't seen him staring at Theresa's behind.

"If he read the Bible as hard as he staring at that girl's butt, he might learn something he needs to know from the Lord," Queen Esther thought before she said, "Lamont, have you forgotten your home training? You busted up in this store without a word to Mr. Lacy and his lady friend standing here."

"Sorry," Lamont murmured, as he stuck out his hand toward Mr. Lacy, who grabbed it with such speed and dexterity he could have sworn that old man could see where he was standing.

"Son, this sweet lady standing next to you is my boo, Baby Doll Henderson."

Baby Doll grinned and then remembered that she didn't have her teeth in her mouth. She reached down in her purse for the red teeth box but was stopped by the gentle pressure of Mr. Lacy's hand on her arm.

"Baby, you don't need to do all that. Lamont is family. And when he sees what you have for him, he won't care if you ever put your teeth in your mouth whenever he's around you."

Theresa bit her lip to keep from laughing. Sometimes folks treated Miss Baby Doll's fake false teeth like they were a member of the family.

Lamont stuck his hand toward Miss Baby Doll, who grabbed it in a grip as firm as any man's. He thought her to be the most paradoxical woman he'd ever seen. On the one hand, Miss Baby Doll, with her deep copper-toned and very smooth and beautiful complexion, dark brown eyes, slender yet well-built frame, and thick silver hair that was begging for a perm, had the potential to be a striking woman, despite those missing teeth. Yet her natural attractiveness couldn't make up for her appearance. That "Topsy" hairstyle; the blue denim, calf-length, A-line skirt, purple plaid, flannel peasant-styled shirt; the purple silk men's hosiery; and those yellow jelly shoes, made it seem as if she was funny-looking, when in actuality she was far from it.

"It's a pleasure to finally be able to meet you, Mr. Lamont Green. I always read about you but I'm glad to have a chance to see you face-to-face."

"Thank you, ma'am," Lamont said, humbled that this woman took the time to read about him.

"Here, Lamont," Queen Esther said and handed him some crumpled sheets of yellow legal paper and the card holders for two hotel room keys.

As soon as Lamont saw that there were names on the key holders, he thought, "How dumb can you get?"

"Where did you get this?"

"From Baby Doll," Queen Esther told him. "She used to clean Jethro Winters's office and got this out of his trash can."

"This is some pretty condemning evidence. Miss Baby Doll, have you ever seen Patty Harmon and Jethro Winters together?"

"I done seen them together a lot—more than I done seen Mr. Winters with his own wife. Sometimes they'd be all over each other like they on one of them reality TV shows. Use to make me wish I was blind as my Big Daddy, so I didn't have to be exposed to all of that."

"Who?" Lamont queried, hardly believing that she had called little red Mr. Lacy *"Big Daddy."*

"Lacy here, Mr. Lamont Green. He my man and I loves to call him Big Daddy."

Mr. Lacy puffed out his chest, winked at Baby Doll through his shades and laughed, "Heh, heh, heh," causing her to grin and blush like he was her very first boyfriend.

Theresa dropped one of the boxes of note cards she'd

just started putting out on the floor. All of that "heh-heh-hehing" and blushing, skinning, and grinning was a bit unnerving. She couldn't imagine Mr. Lacy and Miss Baby Doll exchanging a simple chaste peck on the lips, with or without her mold teeth. But the thought of them doing anything worth "heh-heh-hehing" about was a bit too much to digest.

There were times when she truly wondered if she was missing the mark in her prayers for a husband. Theresa just couldn't believe that she was so undesirable that about the only romance she could experience was watching a feisty exchange between a little-red-rooster-looking blind man and his girlfriend who sported *fake* false teeth, and then wore dark men's socks and yellow plastic shoes as if she was making a fashion statement.

"Baby Doll," Queen Esther said sternly. "You and Lacy need to get saved and get right with the Lord, and get married. Y'all don't want to be running around Durham doing all of this 'heh-heh-hehing' and be unable to even get your feet off the ground when the Rapture comes."

"Auntee, does it always have to be that way with you?" Lamont asked, wanting know more about the information this Miss Baby Doll had obviously collected and not about her hot and torrid romance with Mr. Lacy of all people.

"Hand me that Bible again, baby," she commanded Theresa, mumbling, "Lord, do I have to do all of the work around here, to help these people get saved and steadfast on Thee?"

She looked up, muttered, "Help me, Jesus," and flipped open the Bible, thumbing through page after page until she found the right scripture.

"Hmmm, here's something that should get some folks straight around here," she said, cutting her eyes at Lamont.

"In the Book of Joshua, chapter twenty-four, verse seventeen, Joshua tells Israel that . . . *it is the Lord our God Who brought us and our fathers up out of the land of Egypt, from the house of bondage, Who did those great signs in our sight and preserved us in all the way that we went and among all the peoples through whom we passed.*

"Baby Doll, if my memory serves me right, you once said that you used to be so crazy, you wore a winter coat in July in North Carolina. I believe your exact words were *monkey-fool crazy.* Girl, that is crazy. Now here you are standing before me as in your right mind as everybody else in here is. Because the good Lord saw fit to deliver you from bondage some poor souls find themselves caught up in until the day they die. You blessed and you need to recognize."

"But . . ." Baby Doll began. She knew she was blessed but she didn't want to lose the one person she knew loved her.

"Don't get it twisted and let this little red Negro put you on the bullet train to hell," Queen Esther admonished. "If Lacy truly loves you and wants your good lovin' as much as you obviously want his, he'll do right by you."

Baby Doll ran her tongue over her gums and sighed. She really wanted to do right but it was a hard thing Miss Queen Esther was asking of her. She often wondered why such requests came from people who were happily married and getting all the love and care they could possibly want or ever need. Didn't seem fair to her.

"Give it a rest, Queen," Mr. Lacy said as soon as he felt the pain shooting through Baby Doll over the mere thought of losing him.

"I know you mean well but you coming at it all wrong," Mr. Lacy said to Queen. "Unlike you, Baby Doll has not had the pleasure of being wrapped up in the arms of a good-loving man when she falls asleep at night. And until very recently, she was not a part of our community—just standing outside the lines looking in at everybody else on the inside. So, back off and show some understanding that lets me know that you are the good Christian woman I have always believed you to be."

"I'm sorry, Baby Doll," Queen Esther said with a convicted heart. Standing on the Word and being bold for Jesus wasn't always as easy for Queen Esther as most people thought it was. She completely understood Baby Doll's reluctance to lose what she believed was the best love she'd ever had. But when Baby Doll put the Lord first in her life, He'd supply her every need—and that included true love between a man and woman. Plus, that kind of true love could not fully develop and flourish without Jesus smack dab in the middle of it all anyway.

Queen Esther took Baby Doll's hands in her own and said, "I know it appears as if I am asking you to give up what you've been wanting and needing for so long. I wish that I could say this a better way. But I can't do that because I can not and I will not disobey the Lord by sugarcoating what He has placed in my heart to share with you and Lacy. And truth is—you and Lacy need to get saved and married."

Baby Doll held her head back to keep the tears from falling down her cheeks. She knew that Miss Queen

Esther was right. God had to come first—there simply was no other way to get around it. She just wished that she didn't have to give up all the love and the warmth that she got from her Big Daddy.

Mr. Lacy reached out and took her hand and said gently, "Come on, baby, let's go down on Main Street and get a marriage license. I couldn't stand to lose all of that good loving because you want to do right. If marrying you is what you need, then marrying you is what you got. 'Cause I ain't never loved no woman like I have come to love you, Baby Doll."

He took off his shades and quickly closed his eyes. He got down on one knee and raised his head toward hers.

"Will you do me the honor of becoming my wife today?"

Baby Doll had been praying for this day every since Lacy had picked her up in that rainstorm. Tears fell down her cheeks as she reached into her purse for her mold teeth. Didn't seem proper to experience this moment without any teeth in her mouth.

She popped them over her gums and said, "Yes, Lacy. I will become your lawfully wedded wife."

"Then help me up, girl, 'cause these old stiff knees 'bout through, and we have to make it downtown in a hurry. 'Cause, girl, there so much sweetness and love in you, it's got my blood boiling. And I don't know how much longer I can keep my hands off of you."

Baby Doll reached out and helped her man/husband-to-be up and said, "You so mannish and crazy, Big Daddy."

"Heh, heh, heh."

Mr. Lacy put his shades back on, grabbed Baby Doll's hand, and made his way toward the door.

"Make sure you give Mr. Lamont the rest of the infor-

mation, Miss Queen Esther," Baby Doll called over her
shoulder as Mr. Lacy hurried her out of the store, pausing
just long enough to cut a shouting step when the store's
music came on.

Theresa made a quick exit to the back of the store before her own tears of hurt and disappointment streamed
down her cheeks. She knew that not only should she
be happy for Miss Baby Doll, but she was supposed to
have joy in her heart for being blessed to witness God's
miracle-working power in someone's life. It was a powerful testimony that God answered a woman's prayers about
love and marriage. But all Theresa could do was feel sad
that she didn't have what Miss Baby Doll had. Imagine
a man loving you so much, he married you just so his desire to hold you in his arms wouldn't interfere with your
desire to get right with God.

Lamont started to follow Theresa. He could tell that
she was very upset, but couldn't for the life of him figure
out what had triggered this response. One minute she was
fine, stocking merchandise and trying to look inconspicu-
ous while trying to listen in on the incredible exchange
that just took place in her store. And then in the blink of
an eye, Theresa was on the verge of tears.

"Give her a moment," Queen Esther said, thinking,
"Your butt is partially to blame for all of this wallowing
in faithless self-pity. 'Cause if you had sense enough to
take that girl in *your* arms, she wouldn't have a need to
run off like some silly woman in one of those daytime
soap operas."

She placed the sheets of crumpled papers in both of
his hands.

"I told you the Lord would make a way for you,

Lamont. Read what's on those papers in Jethro Winters's own handwriting."

As he scanned the contents of the papers, he shook his head in disbelief. For the second time since he'd come in the store, he couldn't believe that Jethro had been too dumb to destroy this incriminating information. And to have possession of these two key holders *with names on them* was like holding manna from heaven right in the palm of his hands.

"Auntee, please tell Mr. Lacy and his bride-to-be that I am so grateful for their help."

"No, you tell them yourself. Go over to their house and tell them. I'm sure they don't have a lot of company. And your presence will be just what the doctor ordered."

"You know where Mr. Lacy's house is?"

"Over on Dupree Street, not far from North Carolina Central University. But call before you come. They just ran off to get married and you might get your feelings hurt busting up on them unannounced."

Lamont blushed. He could not even begin to imagine something as incredible as that. In fact, he counted it a blessing that he didn't have the ability to imagine *that*.

He hugged his aunt and started to rush off.

"Where you headed to now?"

"I wanted to go over to the Cashmere and take a look around. Sometimes, I just need to walk around and remember and then think about what it can be again."

"Why don't you take Theresa with you? Might do you good to help somebody else see what you dreaming up."

"You think she'd be interested in seeing the site?"

"Yep," was all Queen Esther said as she hurried over to greet the first customer of the day. It was that worrisome Mother Clydetta Overton, who was always going on and on about her concerns over distracting her pastor during a sermon with glimpses of her legs. Queen Esther's best friend, Doreatha Parker, had been in the store once when Clydetta was carrying on about the pastor and her legs. Doreatha gave the woman a quick once-over and then whispered, "Girl, have you seen her pastor?"

Queen Esther nodded. Clydetta's pastor was a big fine-looking high school football coach who had every churchgoing hoochie in Durham County panting after his behind.

"Then, you'll know," Doreatha continued, "that this heifer buying all of those lap cloths 'cause she just stuck on stupid."

"Mornin', Queen," Mother Clydetta said as she pulled a church fan with her pastor's picture on it out of her purse and started waving it around. "Umm, y'all got some air up in here, 'cause I feel like I'm having some hot flashes."

Queen Esther wanted to snatch that fan out of Clydetta's hand and beat her across the head with it.

She thought, "Hot flash, my butt. That ain't nothing but lust flashing all that heat on your crazy, lying self."

If Mother Clydetta came up in this store one more time claiming to live like Anna the Prophetess after her husband died forty-six years ago, Queen Esther was going to forget she was saved and beat that heifer down. She knew that Clydetta had run around on her deceased husband when he was alive, and then sneaked and slept with half of the old black men in Durham County after he died. The only reason that dried-up hoochie was "chaste" now was because she was too old, too stiff, and way too slow to be slipping in and out of hotels and other folks' houses without being noticed.

Mother Clydetta looked at the picture on the fan, waved it across her face a few more times, and put it back in her purse.

"Queen, Theresa called and told me that my order had come in."

"Yeah," was all Queen Esther said, as she went behind the register, sat a box on top of the display case, and opened it for inspection.

Mother Clydetta pulled out a yellow flannel nightgown, trimmed in white satin, with "Saved" embroidered all over it in white silk thread. She stuck her hand back in the box and held up several pairs of big pastel-colored cotton panties with "For Jesus Only" printed on them. She laid the panties on the counter and removed a white satin turban with tiny Santas embroidered all over it. The turban stood almost a foot high on her head when she tried it on. And if that weren't enough, Mother dug back in that box and pulled out a matching handbag, along with a pair of white satin gloves with little Christmas trees on them.

Queen Esther took one look at that merchandise and thought, "I'm gonna have to have a little talk with Theresa about this new made-to-order policy of hers."

When Mother Clydetta pulled out lap cloths shaped like Christmas trees, Queen Esther thought, "I am really going to have to sit down and talk to Theresa about this."

Chapter Ten

THERESA COULDN'T BELIEVE THAT SHE HAD GOTTEN so torn up over Baby Doll becoming a bride-to-be right in her store. Folks in the community always joked that you could get blessed simply by setting foot in Miss Thang's Holy Ghost Corner and Church Woman's Boutique. But until today, she never imagined just how much a blessing being in her store could be. If only she could step up in here and get a blessing like that, all would be just fine.

"You okay, girl?"

Theresa closed her eyes a moment and thought, "Great. I'm back here buggin' out over Baby Doll and now Lamont is all up in my grille."

She swirled her prized lavender leather chair around to face him with what she hoped wasn't too tight a smile plastered on her face.

"Sure. I'm fine."

"Well, to be honest," he said, "you don't look so sure, even though you sure are fine."

Theresa relaxed instantly and said, "Boy, pleaz," and hit his arm playfully, laughing.

"Can you get away from the store for a while?"

"Yeah. Thanks to Miss Baby Doll, I don't have to do

any cleaning or straightening up. She is very efficient. Everything in the store that is not ready to be shelved is now back here, categorized and arranged by what section of the store it is to be placed in."

"Kind of makes you wonder why all of that efficiency does not extend to her wardrobe, doesn't it," Lamont said.

"Stop it. You know good and well that Miss Baby Doll is kind of special."

"Yeah, she is definitely that, judging from those 'sexy mama' socks she was sportin'," he said with a laugh.

"Mr. Lacy don't seem to have a problem with those socks. Remember, he just ran off to get married so his love supply won't be cut off when Miss Baby Doll gets saved."

"Mr. Lacy is also quite blind," was all Lamont could say. It was pretty hard for him to imagine running off to marry somebody to stop the booty from being shut down 'cause your woman suddenly caught a case of "some of that old-time religion."

"Yeah, he blind," Theresa said. "But I've never known him to be crippled or crazy. So, she must be working something in those socks and yellow jelly shoes."

Lamont was cracking up with laughter.

"Theresa, can you imagine Miss Baby Doll doing a 'sexy mama' dance in those socks and shoes?"

"No . . . but I have one even better than that," she said, thoroughly tickled at that thought herself. "Can you imagine Mr. Lacy *watching* her do that dance in those socks and shoes?"

"You know you are so wrong, Theresa Hopson," Lamont told her, dabbing at his eyes. He pulled on Theresa's arm to get her out of that chair. "Come on. Get up. There's something I want to show you—won't take too long."

Theresa grabbed her purse and followed Lamont out the back door.

"I need to tell your aunt that I'm leaving."

"Call her on your cell. You don't want to go up front because her favorite customer, Mother Clydetta, is out there giving Auntee a fit."

"I hear you," was all Theresa said, as she flipped open her cell phone and dialed the store's number.

As soon as Theresa heard, "Miss Thang's Holy Ghost Corner, your one-stop shop for the best in church lady merchandise," she said, "Miss Queen Esther, I'm gonna take . . . wait . . ."

Lamont tapped Theresa's arm until he knew he had her attention long enough to mouth, "I'm going to get the car."

She nodded and went on, "I'm going with Lamont to take a look at something. Won't be gone long."

"Okay, take your time," Queen Esther said, wishing they would take Clydetta Overton with them.

Theresa walked outside looking for Lamont and realized that she didn't know what kind of car he drove, when he pulled up in a sweet, silver blue Chrysler 300 sedan with what one of Bug's sons told her were eighteen-inch customized rims. A close inspection revealed that the eight-pronged chrome rims had "Green" emblazoned in the center with burnished chrome letters.

Lamont pulled right up to the curb where Theresa was standing and was about to get out when she slipped into the passenger seat with such grace and panache, he was tempted to ask her to do it again.

The platinum-colored leather seat was so comfortable it felt like it had wrapped itself around her as soon as she sat down. She rubbed her hand across the luxurious leather and inhaled the spicy and rugged smell of the car. This was definitely an "ole-skool" brother's car.

"How long have you had this car?"

"Not long. And man, do I love this car. It drives like it's a smooth and sexy sister," he answered, giving her a sultry wink right before he slipped a CD into the stereo system.

"You like Kem?"

"I love that brother's work. Have you seen him in concert? That little slender chocolate boy can work it."

"I concur," Lamont said as he turned on the music. "You heard this CD, yet? It's his latest."

"Just bits and pieces. You know he performed some of these songs the last time he gave a concert at the Carolina Theatre."

"I was at that concert. Kem threw down."

"I concur," Theresa answered, making him smile at her use of his term. "So, where are you taking me?"

"It's a surprise. Thought it might lift your spirits a bit. You were looking like you had the wind knocked out of you back at the store."

Theresa bit her lip, embarrassed that he'd seen how upset she was. Lamont placed his hand over hers and held it firmly when she tried to pull away. When her hand relaxed, he slipped his fingers through hers and caressed the palm of her hand with his thumb.

Theresa sighed softly. That man's hand felt wonderful. She could just imagine what those same hands would feel like on her arms, holding her waist, and caressing her cheeks. When Theresa started thinking about his fingertips on her lips, she pulled her hand free. She adjusted the passenger seat so that she was now sitting up straight with both hands folded primly in her lap.

Lamont thought Theresa looked like she was sitting in a lobby waiting to be interviewed for a job.

"Baby, relax. It was only your hand."

His voice was so sexy, with a low, gravelly sound to it, Theresa started to squirm. She was feeling heat in places that heat did not need to be.

"Are you all right?" he asked in that same sexy voice, knowing full well that he had "hit the spot," just like he intended on doing.

"Yes," she answered, while crossing her legs back and forth one time too many.

"You sure you all right, baby?" he asked again, making sure that "baby" had plenty of that dirty-South, black-boy drawl in it.

"I'm sure."

"I hear you, sure," he replied with a low chuckle that made her uncross and cross her legs just one more time for good measure.

Lamont turned into the entrance of what had once been Cashmere Estates. "I bet you haven't been back here in years, have you, Theresa?"

"No."

"Ever miss it?"

"Sometimes—especially if it's near a holiday. This Thanksgiving, I had an urge to drive over here on the way to Bug's house."

"Why didn't you do it?"

"Don't know. Thought that I was being kind of stupid."

"Nahh. Nostalgic maybe. But stupid? Never—not you, girl."

He parked the car right in front of an old fire hydrant.

"You remember this spot, Theresa?"

She shook her head.

"It's where you had your first business—right here on this corner during one of our many neighborhood festivals."

Theresa smiled at him. Lamont actually remembered her very first business—a small stand decorated in red, black, and green, with all kinds of accessories and novelty items for the home.

"Doesn't seem like it was thirty years ago, does it?" he asked.

"Nope. Time passes so fast."

"Too fast sometimes," Lamont said, thinking about how little time it took for his son to go from being a baby boy to a man. "But you have to admit. This was a great place to grow up in."

"It was a wonderful place to grow up," Theresa said. "Best-kept secret in Durham. Folks thought we lived in the projects. But where we lived was in a community full of hardworking people, and brimming over with support and love."

"I like the way you over there talking, girl. Too many folks like Charmayne Robinson and . . ."

He hesitated at Parvell Sykes's name because the last thing he wanted to do was remind this girl of the man she'd just recently stopped dating. As hard as it was for the player in him to admit it, Lamont was falling for Theresa and he had trouble with the thought of her being in another man's arms.

". . . and Parvell," Theresa said for him. "Too many folks like Charmayne and Parvell want to forget about this place. That's why they are so bound and determined to help Jethro Winters turn this place into something it was never meant to be—a bunch of overpriced condos and town homes for upper-class folks (mostly white) who have a penchant for so-called sophisticated urban living."

"Yeah," Lamont added with a heavy sigh. "I've always wondered why it's the inner city when *we* live here and something like 'sophisticated urban living' when white folks start moving back in."

He drove around the corner and stopped in front of one of the few houses left in the community. He turned the car off and got out.

"I remember this house," Theresa said, as she hopped out of the car and clapped her hands in pure delight. "It's the Meeting House, where all of the fancy folks used to stay when they came to NCCU or Eva T. Marshall. I used to love to sit on the steps of this house, just to see who would come out of it."

"Me, too," Lamont told her. It felt so good to have someone, other than his design team or family, share his appreciation for the Cashmere. No other woman understood what he was talking about. The one time he tried to show this very house to Chablis, she'd turned up her nose and started dialing clients on her cell until he finished inspecting it.

"This house is going to be renovated and will be the focal point of the new Cashmere Estates. I'm working with Rhodes, Rhodes, and Rhodes architectural firm and—"

"Those old bad-tailed Rhodes sisters make up your design team?" Theresa asked with a hearty laugh. "They put my store together and did some work on my house. But I have to tell you, those three are something else—always arguing and just being plain bad."

"I know," Lamont said. "They have to be one of the best firms in the state. But Lawd knows those are some headstrong, need-they-butts-beat women. Smart, witty, funny, and just as crazy and different from one another as night and day. That little Nina is a genius of a designer but she can work a nerve down to the last strand of DNA."

"And Nicole," Theresa added. "She comes across as all quiet but don't mess with her on legal matters."

"Who you tellin'," he said. "I've seen her make puree out of folks without so much as working up a sweat. And then that Lauren. You put that little roughneck on the job and your buildings go up and they definitely won't come down."

"Lamont, you have to win that contract, you just have to."

"I sure do, don't I," he said, smiling into her eyes.

Theresa stared down at the ground and swirled her shoe around in the dirt until she felt her chin being lifted gently by strong fingertips. She started to look down again, when she heard a soft "uh, uh," and felt his lips pressed against her own.

"That was nice," he whispered and kissed her again, only this time with more boldness as he pulled one of her lips between both of his.

"Ummm, that was even better, baby," Lamont murmured right before placing his hands on either side of Theresa's face and kissing her deeply.

She felt his hands slide down her back, only to rest firmly on her waist in very much the same way that she'd imagined it while still in the car. She wrapped her own arms around Lamont and held him tight.

"Ohhh," he sighed. "It's been so long since a woman has wrapped me up like that. I believe I could stand here like this practically all day."

"Me, too," Theresa whispered back.

He stepped back a few inches and unclipped his vibrating cell phone from his waist and glanced at the caller ID.

"Excuse me, Theresa, but I have to take this," Lamont said solemnly, giving the impression that it was an important business call, and then walked away several feet, so he wouldn't be in earshot of Theresa. But that only made her ease over closer, so she could hear better.

"I'm kinda of busy right now," Lamont said. "Can this wait until I get back to the office?"

"No," Theresa overheard Gwen Green say so loudly until it made her wonder if Lamont's ears were ringing.

"But why?" he asked. "I've already talked to my brother and he said that Monty's application had been approved and he could pledge Omega this spring."

For several minutes, Lamont remained quiet, as if what was being said was the absolutely most important thing that could be said this morning.

"No, Gwen," he said with a sigh. "Monty cannot go on line before that because there will not be a new line of pledges for Durham's graduate chapter until the spring."

"But what about Greensboro?" Gwen's voice rang out.

"Why would the boy pledge in Greensboro when he clearly lives in Durham County? That—"

Lamont sighed heavily and then said, "Look, I'll have to call you back."

He flipped his cell closed and shook his head, completely unaware of how closely Theresa was watching him. Why did Gwendolyn always have to have long and detailed conversations about matters that did not warrant immediate attention? Theresa knew from conversations with Miss Queen Esther that Monty was very independent and did not want his parents in his personal affairs.

Lamont put one hand on his hip, looked up, and sighed heavily. He turned back around to continue the "conversation" he'd been working up on with Theresa, only to discover that she was sitting in the car with her seat belt on. He sighed heavily again.

"Women," he muttered, before slipping into the driver's seat and turning on the gospel radio station. He needed something to soothe his ruffled feathers and put him in a better mood—especially after the chilly reception he had just received from his passenger.

"Are you all right?" he asked her, hoping to get some feedback on this sudden change of heart. Minutes ago, he could have sworn that the girl had gotten heated up enough to practically melt in his arms. And now, he could just about see her breath puffing up like smoke in the frosty confines of the car.

"Yes."

"You sure?"

"Do I look like there is something wrong with me?" Theresa snapped, wishing she could act like there was nothing wrong. She didn't know why those impromptu, ill-timed, unexpected, and lengthy calls over what sounded like inconsequential concerns bothered her so much. And they hurt, too, because those phone calls always seemed to spring right up whenever Theresa felt a warm connection building between her and Lamont.

Lamont's first inclination was to leave this matter the heck alone. Nothing worse than exploring what appeared to be a trivial issue with a woman who had just said some asinine foolishness like, "Do I look like something is wrong with me?" Of course she looked like something was wrong. And he knew that if Theresa said that junk, whatever was wrong, was much deeper than she was willing to reveal.

He was about to put the car in drive, when he glanced at Theresa out of the corner of his eye. She was sitting straight and stiff like she was too much of a sophisticated, twenty-first-century black woman to get so mad that she lost it and put on what his brother called "the colored woman's show"—neck snapping, finger waving, hand-on-hip, tooth sucking, and "let-me-tell-you-one-thang" perched on the tip of her tongue.

"Whew," he exhaled softly, knowing without even asking further that Theresa's anger had been ignited by that long and very unnecessary telephone call. Maybe Auntee was on the money when she kept getting on him to put Gwen in check.

Lamont took one of Theresa's hands out of her lap and raised it to his lips, kissing it softly, gently, and with so much love, it almost made him gasp as loudly as Theresa in complete astonishment. All of these years he'd been running from falling in love, and he hadn't even realized it until now.

"I'm sorry," he said softly.

Theresa relaxed some, took a deep breath as if she were about to say something.

He let go of her hand, turned the radio down, and sat back, obviously anticipating one of those long, drawn-out discussions women were so famous for when they finally decided to give you the *411*.

"Lamont, how long have you and Gwen been divorced?"

"Over ten years."

"And you have no intention of ever getting back together?"

"Nope," he answered firmly and without any emotion, good or bad.

Theresa took a real deep breath. She wasn't too sure about how he would take what she had to say next. But it needed to be said. As far as she could tell, Lamont wouldn't have full peace and healing from his past until he realized that it was just that—the past, nothing more, nothing less.

"You and Gwen can be inconsiderate of other people's feelings."

Theresa could feel Lamont bristling from her words. She wasn't trying to be unkind to him, or to Gwen for that matter. But the truth was the truth. She waited a few seconds to see if he was going to try and dispute what she was saying, but all he did was say, "Go on."

"Lamont, there have been moments, like today, when you and I have made a very wonderful connection. And then that phone rings, it's Gwen, and you cut off whatever was going on between us, to run off and talk to her about absolutely nothing."

"I don't think of my business as 'absolutely nothing,'" he said testily.

Theresa was about to back down, give up, and just wait for him to take her back to the store, when she remembered something her first lady, Lena Quincey, once shared with her. Lena said that whenever somebody had a hard time hearing the truth from you, "speak the Word of God because that Word never failed to stop them right in their tracks."

She averted her eyes from the hard glare in Lamont's and pressed on.

"In Ephesians chapter five, husbands are called to love their wives like Christ loved the church. They are also directed to love their wives as their own bodies. No man in his right mind would treat himself as shabbily as you have treated me when you talk to Gwen on that phone of yours, even though I am not even your girlfriend.

"But if you were to be so unwise and unthinking as to let that kind of thing happen to whoever becomes your wife, you would not be in line with the Lord's will for you as her husband. Because as your wife, she would deserve your utmost allegiance, respect, and consideration even if it meant stepping on somebody else's toes when they themselves stepped outside of what is the proper way to act towards a married man."

"I see," was all Lamont said because he was too full of what his aunt always referred to as "Holy Ghost conviction." Everybody had been getting on him about Gwen and those calls. But this was the first time anyone had ever put it to him in a way that made sense and went straight to his heart. Theresa was right. He couldn't let his past barge into his present, his future, and hurt the woman he allowed to cup his heart in the palm of her hands.

Lamont blinked back his tears. Last thing he wanted was to appear weak and like a wuss to Theresa. He reached over and grabbed her hands, which looked to him like they had been especially designed for holding his heart.

"Thank you," he whispered and kissed her hand one more time.

His cell phone began to vibrate and before Theresa could get half an eyebrow raised, Lamont glanced at the caller ID, smiled and said, "Miss Nina Rhodes, with her busy, little redbone self."

Theresa smiled, once again happy that the tension had been broken between them. It was hard to open up to a man, and then call him out after you had opened yourself up to him.

"Hello, Nina."

"Bossman," she said loud enough for Theresa to hear. "Bossman, get on over here. I have the first phase of the design ready."

"First phase? What about the whole phase, girl? We have less than two weeks to get this thing ready for the DUDC and you talking about phase one?"

"Take your panties out of a bunch," Nina replied with so much little-bad-tailed sassiness, Theresa started laughing, and then tried to stop when Lamont frowned at her.

"We are not taking the entire presentation into the meeting. Just the first part, which looks like the whole thing but it's not. We got to fool them, so we'll see what they have to put on the table before we pull out the big guns."

"And why is that?" Lamont inquired, not so sure he wanted to buy into this.

"Because I ran into Craig Utley's secretary's baby daddy, and he told me that his baby's mama wanted somebody on our team to know that we are not to bring in our final product. Said that is how Jethro Winters beats out the competition every time—by letting them think that what he presents is all that he has to offer, when it isn't. He uses that strategy to get the scoop on the competition, then he finagles another meeting, submits a better proposal, and wins the contract. And since Patricia Harmon is letting him tap that tail, I know he'll be able to get a second meeting at your expense, Bossman."

"I see," was all that Lamont could say. Nina Rhodes was a mess. And a nosy little redbone who knew everything. If he ever looked up "the 411," Nina's picture would be right next to the definition.

Theresa was cracking up with laughter over Nina's very accurate, albeit "ghetto-fabulous" low-down on the situation. Nina heard a woman laughing and asked, "Bossman, who the heck is that you got with you laughing like that? It show don't sound like that 'Lee-press-on-weave' hoochie, Table Wine, either."

This time Lamont started laughing. That girl was a nut. He said, "No, missy, Chablis, or Table Wine, as you so affectionately call her, is not with me. It's Theresa Hopson."

"Oh . . . snap, Bossman," was all Nina said, and hung up.

"You think it's time for us to get back to work?" Lamont asked Theresa.

"Yes, Bossman," Theresa replied in such a perfect imitation of Nina Rhodes that Lamont laughed and said, "You 'bout as crazy as that little redbone back at my office."

He put the car in gear and pulled off, taking a quick moment to look at Cashmere Estates in the rearview mirror. For the first time in weeks, he was filled with an inexplicable feeling of a pending victory.

Chapter Eleven

LAMONT CLICKED THE ALARM BUTTON ON HIS KEYS, just as James slid his gold Expedition in the space right next to him. His sister-in-law, Rhonda, hopped out wearing a striking rust-colored hat she could have only found at Miss Thang's. From the very beginning, Theresa had kept her store stocked with a most unique and eye-catching array of church lady hats. It was refreshing to see that she had not lost her touch in that area of retail.

Folks—men and women alike—always said that a trip to Miss Thang's was a treat. And several of these people had also testified to receiving some very sweet and timely blessings when they visited the store and fellowshipped with Theresa and his aunt. They were right on the money, too. Lamont had certainly not expected to receive that blessing the Lord sent through Miss Baby Doll the day he was at Theresa's store.

And even better, Lamont had been blessed a second time, when he found himself holding Theresa Hopson in his arms—something he'd been aching to do since their chance meeting at the Washington Duke Inn. Now that was a heaping helping of good woman—the kind of "sweet thang" a brother could snuggle up to, and be guaranteed that he would remain warm throughout a chilly Tarheel night.

Lamont walked up to his sister-in-law grinning.

"You awfully clean there this morning, girl. You've been taking all of your hard-earned dollars over to Miss Thang's?"

"Yes," she said, smiling and patting her rust-colored silk hat, with its pleated crown, a short brim, and the gold, rust, charcoal, and silver paisley-printed ribbon around the crown. "And . . . uhh . . . I heard that you made a trip to Miss Thang's your own self."

"Well, you know how it is," Lamont responded, scratching at his chin like one of the brothers on the corner. "A brother needs to know what's all in that store you good saved sisters always raving about. And from what I've seen, there is a whole lot of good stuff up in that store."

"Show is," Rhonda said and did a quick twirl, so that he could see the rest of her outfit—a snug-fitting rust suede suit with a silk shell that matched the ribbon on the crown of the hat, rust and charcoal suede purse, with matching rust and charcoal suede pumps with chrome-colored spike heels.

"And," she added, "the best thing in that store is Miss Thang herself."

"You crazy," was all Lamont said with a deep chuckle.

"Yep, my baby is just as crazy as can be," James said, as he helped their two boys and one baby girl out of the car. He was pretty sharp himself in a deep rust–colored suit, dove gray shirt with tiny rust and charcoal pin-stripes, along with a rust silk tie with tiny charcoal and silver Js on it.

"I won't cut my fingers this morning, if I touch you,

Dawg," Lamont said as he walked over to his little brother, grabbed his hand, and leaned toward him in that masculine greeting of a combination hug/handshake.

"You're not doing too poorly yourself, Big Bro," James said, admiring Lamont's chocolate suit with deep cream chalk stripes, ivory jacquard print cotton shirt, and chocolate tie with the tiniest cream, silver, and pale blue stripes in it.

"You dressin' to impress this morning?" Rhonda asked, hoping that Theresa Hopson was at church for the eleven o'clock service. Her brother-in-law was already a fine-looking man. But if somebody looked up the words "pimpin'" this morning, all they would find were pictures of Lamont in that suit.

Lamont sniffed at the air and sucked on a tooth, before he said, "Well, you know how it is."

"Naw, I don't know, *Dawg*," Rhonda said, egging him on. "But you sure can try and tell me about it."

"Well it's like this, li'l Sis," he said. "See, I had to make sure that I was in my best at-tire when I came up in my Father's house. 'Cause me and the Lord workin' on me learning to make better use of His mainline. That way, when I call Him up, I'll know just what to say when it's time to tell Him what I want."

"And what do you want, Big Bro?" James queried.

"That contract for one," he answered him.

"And for two?"

Lamont stroked his chin and casually looked across the parking lot, where Theresa Hopson, her brother, Bug, his wife and kids, along with their mother, were making their way up to the church door.

He said, "Well, you know, some things really need to

be left in the good Lord's hands. Don't need to go broad-casting *everything* I plan on asking for."

"I hear you loud and clear, Big Bro," James said, as his eyes followed Lamont's gaze. As soon as he knew that Theresa's brother, Bug, had seen them, too, James gave his fraternity brother the Omegas' "throwin' up the funk" sign—that unmistakable raising of both arms with the hands held up, open-palmed and in the shape of the Omega symbol. In reply, Bug put his hand up to his mouth and gave out a deep, loud Omega Psi Phi "dawg" bark.

Theresa didn't know why Bug had to bark like that all the time and at church of all places. Here she was trying to get her mind set on Jesus, and her brother was out in the church parking lot acting like he was getting ready to throw down in a fraternity step show. And to make matters worse, James gave his own exceptionally loud bark, only to be followed by another bark and "funk-throw" by Bug. She glanced over at her sister-in-law to gauge her reaction. No help from that love-struck girl. The child was worse than her husband, grinning and cheesing like *she* was a Q-Dawg.

Theresa shook her head and started walking away, in-tent on getting in and finding good seats for the whole family.

"Morning, Miss Lady," Lamont called out, as he hur-ried up to where the Hopson clan was. Theresa thought the greeting was meant for her. But in case it wasn't, she didn't say anything. She did, however, slow her pace considerably.

"You not speaking to folks this morning, Miss The-resa?" Lamont asked, as he tipped his chocolate derby at her and scanned her person from head to toe.

What Theresa had on was a better advertisement for her store than any of her commercials airing on the black radio stations could ever be. Lamont didn't know a whole lot about women's hats. But he did know that Theresa's black hat, which was covered in black silk, beaded tulle, had to be one of the best-looking ones he had ever seen.

And that outfit? The cashmere and silk blend of the black suit was of the same quality as the material used for the finest menswear. But instead of being severe and too masculine, the suit was quite elegant, and awfully sexy, too, with a snug jacket grazing the hip of the straight and short skirt that rose a good three inches above the knee. Theresa's long, sinuous legs were showcased in silky black hosiery with a tiny star pattern and a pair of three-inch-high, black suede ankle-strapped shoes.

"Theresa," Bug's wife said, "aren't you going to speak to James's brother?"

"Uhh sure," Theresa answered. She raised her hand in one of those stiff and proper Miss America waves, and extended him an even more stiff and proper smile.

"Praise the Lord, Lamont," she said, causing her own family members to turn and stare her down. Her mother cleared her throat until she had Theresa's eye, and then looked at her as if to say, "Did you fall out of bed and right on your head this morning?"

Theresa tried to play dumb and said, "What?"

"You know what, *Prophetess*," Bernice Hopson answered loudly.

Both Bug and Vanessa started cracking up. Bernice always called somebody Prophet or Prophetess when they were not acting right in church—especially when the person was hiding behind "Saved" lingo to put someone else off from them. And if she called you "Apostle," you were really cutting the fool.

Lamont was having a good time watching the cool, saved, always-did-and-said-the-right-thing Theresa Hopson fidget under his scrutiny, as well as that of her mother. He experienced a hot thrill knowing he'd gotten so far up under her skin, and then be able to act like he hadn't purposely pushed all of Theresa's buttons like that.

"Why so formal, baby?" he asked in a sultry voice. "I thought that we had a real nice connection thing going on between us."

Theresa blushed and then caught herself when she realized that her mother was staring at the two of them so intently one would have thought she was watching one of her favorite television shows.

Lamont peered into Theresa's dark, almond-shaped eyes.

"Well? We do have a connection, don't we?" he stated.

"Do you or don't you have a connection with this man, Theresa Elaine," her mother asked with some mischief in her voice, and her poker face in place, so as not to give away her burning curiosity about what *was* going on between those two. Last time she heard anything about her daughter's love life, the girl was calling herself dating that punk-tailed Parvell Sykes.

"And now, looka heah, looka heah," Bernice thought, "the oldest Green boy is eyeing the girl like she's a piece of piping-hot, fried-to-golden-brown-perfection chicken."

Bernice and Bill Hopson had known the Green boys since they were in elementary school. They had always secretly thought that Lamont was just what the doctor ordered for their duty-bound baby girl. As far back as grade school, Theresa worked hard to outdo the kids in her class and didn't have a clue about the joys of just being regular like everybody else. It was a contrived perfection that both parents believed had been very costly to her. Because for all of Theresa's perfections, she never figured out how to disable her ability to let two wonderful "wannabe" husbands slip right through her fingers because they had some flaw that she did not possess.

Bill always said, "Bernice, that girl is going to have a time finding a husband. I mean, who can bear to sleep next to pristine perfection each and every night. 'Cause let's be real, baby. There are times when a man wants his woman to leap at the chance to get to the point where she sweats back the roots in her perm for her man."

Bill was right, too. Because that is exactly what your man wanted and needed. And watching Lamont pick at Theresa made Bernice think that he was probably the one man capable of making her want to mess up that immaculate coiffure of hers.

"I need to quit giving you a hard time, Miss Thang," Lamont said sweetly but without as much heat in his voice. He had not missed Bernice Hopson's rapt attention to his and Theresa's conversation.

"Yes you do," Theresa said smiling, working hard to hide just how much that man had gotten next to her, and pulled at the church door.

"Girl, let me do that for you and your mother," Lamont said, as he held the door all the way open for them.

"Thank you," Theresa said with a gorgeous smile lighting up her face.

"Yes, thank you," Gwendolyn Green chimed in as she hurried through the door after Bernice, stopping right in front of Lamont, pulling on his arm, and gazing up in his eyes as she struck up a conversation with him.

Theresa's sunny smile disappeared behind the cloudy expression that was settling on her face. She gave Gwen a polite greeting and walked off without a backward glance at Lamont. Why she believed that anything she said last week would get through his obviously thick skull was foolish thinking at its best.

Gwen was talking and smiling and looking up at Lamont, who didn't hear a word she said. He sighed and closed his eyes, wishing that he would have had sense enough to excuse himself from Gwen and go and stop Theresa from rushing off like she did. Why couldn't he get it through to the girl that he only wanted to be considerate of Gwen's feelings—nothing more, nothing less?

"I'm going to sit down," Gwen said and then repeated, "Lamont, I am going to sit down, okay?"

"Yeah, okay," he mumbled and waved her off, stretching his neck and trying to get one last glimpse of Theresa before she slipped through the sanctuary doors.

Bernice followed her daughter, thinking, "And Miss Theresa walking around Durham thinking the only man willing to date her is Parvell Sykes."

While the other ministers were deep in their preservice prayer, Parvell, who had decided to forgo wearing his clerical robe this morning, was already in the sanctuary profiling his new holiday attire—a Christmas green velvet suit, white silk shirt and matching tie, green, slip-on gaiters with red leather piping, and a snow-white, floor-length mink coat, which was draped around his shoulders.

Chablis Jackson and her mother hurried and slid into

their seats because Miss Shirley did not like standing out in the vestibule socializing on the Sundays they made it to eleven o'clock service. As soon as they were situated, Chablis gave her mother the eye, hoping she'd take the cue to remove the yellow rubber cleaning gloves from her hands.

"Don't be eyeballing me," was all Miss Shirley said as she stubbornly refused to remove her gloves, wishing that Chablis had not challenged her, so that she could have gotten those sweltering hot things off her hands as soon as they sat down.

"You act as if I am the only person who is touched in the head in this sanctuary," she continued, and then started pointing a yellow rubber finger at Parvell. "Look over there. Ain't that Charmayne's boyfriend, Mr. Big from the Isley Brothers?"

"No, Mama," Chablis snapped, wishing her mama wouldn't always have to point and talk so loud.

Miss Shirley loved the singer Ron Isley's character "Mr. Big." Every time a "Mr. Big" music video came on BET, Miss Shirley stopped cleaning, took off her gloves, and said, "Umph, umph, umph. Just looking at that fine Mr. Big can rock my world."

It vexed Chablis to no end that her mother loved coming to Fayetteville Street Church just to see "Mr. Big's" taller and thinner and younger look-alike, Rev. Parvell Sykes.

Parvell's mink was beginning to feel hot and getting heavier by the minute. He knew that Rev. Quincey would flat out refuse a request to carry the coat on his arm during the processional. He scanned the sanctuary in search of a trustworthy person to watch his mink. He thought about asking Chablis and her mother. They were definitely trustworthy enough—but not the best choice since Chablis was tight with Charmayne and Miss Shirley was always trying to flirt with him.

He kept right on looking until he spied the president of the Daughters of Naomi Missionary Society, Roxanne Daye, who always managed to be in his immediate vicinity whenever they were at church. Maybe it was time the two of them had more contact with each other.

Parvell walked over to Roxanne's pew and said, "Praise the Lord. Sister Daye, I must say that you are quite lovely this morning in all of that green."

Roxanne gave a coy giggle and smoothed an imaginary wrinkle on her forest green silk suit that was the exact same shade as the one Parvell was wearing.

"Thank you, Rev. You know I think we're looking like twins today."

Parvell squeezed out a smile, as he thought, "Why do black folk *love* being twins with somebody," and then answered Roxanne with a polite, "I guess you could say that. But what I'm wearing," he continued, moving deftly into a playa lie, "can't hold a candle to you, my dear."

Roxanne tapped him lightly on the arm and said, "Rev., you so crazy."

Queen Esther, who was sitting several rows behind Roxanne Daye, thought she'd puke listening to the two of them. She leaned over and whispered to her husband, Joseph.

"Baby, that mess they handing out to each other so full of syrupy poop, I feel like I'm about to catch a case of the sugar diabetes."

Joseph nodded. As far as he was concerned, Rev.

Sykes, who was prancing around the sanctuary dressed in a mink like he was The Mack or Superfly, wasn't worth a pinch of dissolved table salt. And Roxanne, who was waving to fifty from the forty-something shore, was determined to marry a professional man with high visibility in the Gospel United Church.

Roxanne, who had been skinnin' and grinnin' all up Parvell's face just moments ago, frowned. He gave his mouth a blast of Binaca, sneaked and sucked in a few puffs of air to make sure Roxanne's frown wasn't caused by his breath, and then followed her troubled gaze around the church to where Theresa had just sat down.

Parvell had forgotten that Roxanne Daye hated the ground Theresa Hopson walked on—which made this thin woman, with few womanly indentations on her figure, all that more attractive to him. Parvell decided right then that it was high time he gave Ms. Hopson payback for not calling him after he broke up with her, and for failing to return his ring.

When Parvell saw Theresa looking in his direction, he took his mink and draped it around Roxanne's shoulder with a great show of "chivalry."

"I thought you might like this to keep you warm and remind you of me," he said in what he had been told by Charmayne was his sexiest voice.

"Thank you, Rev.," Roxanne gushed as she inhaled his cologne and rubbed her hand over the luxurious fur, making Parvell worry that the oil from her hand would get his coat dirty.

He took both of Roxanne's hands in his to get them off his coat. When she frowned a second time, he turned around and spotted Charmayne and her mother,

Ida Belle, taking their seats in front of Chablis and Miss Shirley.

"Is everything all right, my dear?" he asked.

"Yes," she lied, hoping that he had not seen Charmayne. Rumor had it that Parvell's car pulled up into Charmayne's driveway during those late night times known as the "booty call" hours. As much as Roxanne hated to admit it, she knew that Charmayne Robinson, with that naturally blond hair, and bouncing boobs and "rumpshaker" butt, was some stiff competition.

Plus, to make matters worse, Charmayne was always putting it out there that she had some serious "skills." Roxanne, on the other hand, was president of the biggest missionary group in the church, and not at liberty to release the same information. And even though there were some men at the church who knew that she "served it up" behind closed doors, it took some maneuvering for her to get a man behind them without drawing unwanted attention to herself.

Charmayne had not missed Roxanne's fierce scrutiny. She waited until she knew both Roxanne and Parvell were looking her way, and then licked her lips like the warmth of her tongue on them was just about the best thing she'd ever felt.

Roxanne stiffened. Parvell tried not to think about Charmayne's mouth. He tore his eyes away from her and refocused his attention on Roxanne. The pastor and the choir were filing into the sanctuary. Parvell squeezed Roxanne's hands and hurried to the back of the church.

"I'm going to have to have a little talk with Charmayne," Parvell thought, all the time wondering how he was going to do so without making her so angry she shut down his booty calls.

"Don't you think it's time to find a new and improved strategy for handling Gwen?" Lamont's sister-in-law, Rhonda, said as she came up on him from the direction of the ladies' bathroom. It was taking all her strength not to haul off and slap the black off him, for letting that little transaction happen between the two of them.

"I'm just being considerate and polite, Rhonda," Lamont said. "When did that become a crime?"

"Here's a news flash for you, Big Brother," Rhonda said solemnly. "If you were truly being considerate and polite, you wouldn't have been rude and thoughtless to Theresa."

"I didn't realize that I had been rude to anyone," Lamont responded defensively.

"Big Brother," Rhonda pushed, determined not to back down on this one, even if they had to have a good old-fashioned sibling spat right in the church lobby. "You can't sacrifice Theresa for Gwen, just to make sure that you are being . . ."

She raised her hands and made the quotation sign with her fingers, ". . . *considerate and polite.*"

"Don't you know that if you are falling in love with Theresa, her feelings have to come first? And don't you know that when you marry again, that your wife's feelings cannot be put in second place on those occasions when it isn't comfortable for you to put them first and you believe it's time to be *nice*?"

"You need to go in that sanctuary and stay out of grown folks' business," Lamont told her. He was having a hard enough time admitting that he was falling for Theresa. Last thing he needed was a baby sister chewing him out over how he was treating someone he didn't want to admit he was falling for.

Rhonda rolled her eyes, sucked on her teeth, and then went and found her husband and children, mumbling, *Negroes,* under her breath.

Lamont checked his watch. He would need to get into the sanctuary and take a seat in a few minutes. He inhaled the masculine smell coming from the fine leather, cognac-colored bench he was sitting on. Then he inhaled a second time, taking special note of the smell of what he always called "church air."

It had been six months since he had attended a Sunday morning service, and he had almost forgotten how good church felt and how comforting the smell of "church air" was to him. Lamont couldn't say just exactly what "church air" smelled like. But anybody who grew up in church knew it when they smelled it. It was a combination of things—breathing in the wood on the pews and the furniture polish used to keep it clean, the scent of heavy choir robes, meals that were being prepared by the kitchen ministry, new hats, perfumes and colognes, Communion wine and crackers. It was like you could smell the very beginning of each service—a smell that touched and warmed your heart the moment you stepped up in church.

The smell of Fayetteville Street Gospel United Church of America made Lamont feel good. It made him feel safe. It made him feel like all the burdens of these past months were being taken off his shoulders and handled. It made him wish he'd come back home to church months ago. It made him feel good, at home, comforted, and convicted all at the same time.

His church was beautiful. As a man who built houses for a living, he had a special appreciation for the architecture, the landscaping, and the design of the interior of Fayetteville Street Church. The church had been built with custom bricks that were a pale terra-cotta with flecks of a muted apricot color in them. It was a one-story building that spread across several blocks, and was nestled comfortably in the midst of a small hill of velvety grass, lush shrubbery, an award-winning rose garden, and bright wildflowers in yellow, orange, red, and hot pink.

The simple yet sophisticated interior was stunning with its color scheme of cognac and Caribbean blue. The walls were cognac, the cool ceramic tiles were blue and golden brown, and the furnishings were either golden brown wood tables, or cognac leather benches. Plants and flowers gave the interior of the building a warm and almost tropical feel. There was a detailed and very colorful map of the Holy Land that covered one wall, while another wall showcased photographs of the members engaged in various church activities, along with a large oil painting of the pastor, first lady, and their five children hanging on the wall opposite the one displaying the photos.

Lamont thought this year's Christmas decorations were especially nice. The church's unofficial decorator, Yvonne Fountain, had used the church's color scheme to decorate the nine-foot tree in the lobby, fashioned the bronze-toned silk ribbons for the wreaths at every door, and outlined the windows in the lobby with blue and white Christmas lights.

"You better get in church before you have to wait for

the ushers to let you in, Bossman," Nina Rhodes's voice
rang out, cutting into his quietude. She was standing over
him, holding one of her bad little nephews' hands, clutching a Bible under her other arm, and dressed to the nines
in a hot, electric blue silk suit and matching hat, black
lace stockings, and electric blue patent leather pumps with
black heels. Her man, the pastor's son, Lamar Quincey,
came in behind her. Lamont didn't miss Lamar's quick
perusal of Miss Nina's generous backside and those cute
little legs of hers, before he remembered he was in church
and started behaving.

"Yeah, you're right," Lamont answered and hurried toward the sanctuary doors before the processional began.
His eye caught a flash of some very royal purple on one
of the minister's robes. Lamont smiled to himself when it
dawned on him that the owner of the robe was their presiding bishop, the Right Rev. Eddie Tate.

Chapter Twelve

LAMONT HURRIED AND TOOK HIS SEAT WITH THE REST of the Green clan. For more than forty years, the Green and Hopson families sat in the exact same location on Sunday mornings. The church itself had changed a lot in the past four decades, even if the habits of the parishioners remained pretty much the same. The hard, dark wooden pews and olive green carpet of yesteryear had been replaced with the same color scheme that graced the lobby and vestibule.

The choir loft could seat over one hundred people comfortably, with a separate section for a handcrafted pipe organ, grand piano, drums, conga drum, keyboard, and other members of the instrumental ministry in the church. The pulpit area and altar were bathed in the golden light of sunshine that regularly shone through the stained glass windows of Jesus blessing the fish and loaves for the multitudes. And the ceiling had been transformed from an ornate plaster job to all-mahogany wood beams that made Lamont think of the inside of Noah's Ark.

The actual pulpit contained several large and very comfortable chairs. Members with complaints of stiff and painful joints sang the praises of the Rhodes,

Rhodes, and Rhodes design team for constructing an altar that rose a foot off the floor, allowing easy access to the soft pew cushions that were the same color as the carpet during Holy Communion and altar prayer.

Countless bake sales, church dinners, plays, fashion shows, and raffles had provided the initial seed money to remodel the 138-year-old church, which began as a summer prayer meeting in a pastoral plot of land that was now the rose garden. Once Fayetteville Street Church had raised enough money to dare to dream of a new and improved interior, the previous pastor preached a sermon on tithing that convicted every heart, young and old, igniting a fire to give back to the Lord unprecedented amounts of money. And now, over twenty years later, Fayetteville Street Gospel United Church of America had the blessed distinction of earning most of its impressive income from tithing.

As Lamont surveyed the sanctuary, it occurred to him that he wasn't the only truant member who had decided to come to church this morning. There was nothing like a visit from one's presiding bishop to draw everybody and their grandmamma to Sunday morning service. He saw that Charmayne Robinson and her mother, Ida Belle, were present. And, as was her custom, Ida Belle was dressed more for that Durham "grown folks only" hotspot, The Place to Be, than church. It was hard to miss her gold-sequined, cropped pantsuit with the baseball-styled jacket, black silk tank top, gold lamé boots and matching purse, and gold-sequined baseball cap on top of her blond natural.

He felt a poke in the side and then quickly read the note James had just passed to him from Rhonda.

"Table Wine and her mama, Miss Shirley, are sitting right behind the Robinsons."

Lamont tilted his head, and sure enough, there was Chablis and that crazy Miss Shirley sitting right behind Charmayne and Miss Ida Belle. Chablis was looking so tasty this morning in that low-cut black sweater she was wearing it made him sigh with just a twinge of regret. He knew that outfit well—the snug black cashmere sweater and matching skirt, over sheer black hosiery and ruby patent leather pumps with clear heels. The last time she wore it for him, the girl almost made him forget he was jumping up in fifty's face with a fully grown son.

There was another poke in the side, along with a new note, only this time it was from his mother. Her note read, "Do you think Table Wine's mama brought her yellow rubber gloves to church this morning?"

Lamont was about to give his mother the "you know you are so wrong" look when, out of curiosity, he glanced over at Miss Shirley just as she raised a hand and removed a thick, yellow rubber cleaning glove from one of her hands.

James bent his head over and coughed to try and drown out his laughter.

Lamont bit his lip and closed his eyes to try and stop himself from staring at Miss Shirley and those cleaning gloves. He whispered to James, "Do you think she wears those gloves all the time?"

"No," his mother answered before James could stop laughing long enough to speak. "I know for a fact that she takes them off whenever she is with one of her men."

"Men?" Rhonda, James, Lamont, and Lamont's father all whispered in unison.

The organist started playing and anyone who hadn't taken a seat moved quickly to find one, or claim the spot being saved for them by a family member. Lamont's father's second cousin on his mama's side, Cousin Buddy, stopped pouring water into the assortment of white altar flowers from a small pink plastic cup—even though no one had asked him to do it—and hurried to sit with Queen Esther and Joseph. He sipped the little bit of water left in the cup and then adjusted the strap of the Carolina Blue football helmet he was wearing on his head, to make sure that it wouldn't slip off during the service.

James wiped at his eyes, shaking his head, and whispered to Lamont, "Do you think white people have this much going on in their churches, just sitting in the pews waiting for service to start?"

"No, this is definitely a black peepes thang, and they wouldn't understand."

"I hear you, Big Bro," James replied and held out a fist for Lamont to hit it with "some dap."

Lamont turned his head slightly, so that he could study Theresa discreetly, only to find that she was watching him intently. He gave her a fresh wink, and then grinned, as she struggled to act like nothing had happened between them in those few seconds before the congregation rose for the processional. Theresa was so funny, with her "good-church-girl" acting self.

He'd always liked her and didn't know why he never made a play for her after Gwen divorced him. Theresa, along with the rest of the Hopsons, was solid, hard-working, kind, generous, salt-of-the-earth black church folk. But then again, he did know why he never thought about pursuing her—that is until now. When his divorce became final, the last thing he'd wanted, or felt he needed, was a beautiful and good-old saved "church girl," compelling him to walk back down that aisle into matrimony.

Lamont liked being a bachelor. As he always told his family, he was happily single and content to stay that way. What reason on earth did he have to get married when every one of his needs was being met to his ultimate satisfaction? In fact, if he were to take a poll among some of his married friends, he'd bet the contract to develop the Cashmere that he was getting a whole lot more "action" than they were. Because while the word "no" graced the lips of too many wives far too often, girlfriends, on the other hand, treated "no" like it was the plague.

The choir members of the youth choir moved into place in the sanctuary's center aisle. Rev. Obadiah Quincey walked in behind them, with Bishop Tate at his side, his two assistant pastors close at his heels, and the third, Rev. Parvell Sykes, trailing behind those two. Lamont liked and respected two of the three assistant pastors. But he didn't know for the life of him why Rev. Quincey continued to put up with Sykes.

The Rev. Dr. Sharon Simmons-Harris, daughter of Bishop Theophilus Simmons and Mother Essie Simmons, was a beautiful and brilliant woman—tall, graceful, with a captivating smile radiating out of a face that made her look like a female version of her dad. She was also one of the best youth ministers in the state, building a reputation for breaking down the gospel with hip-hop style and winning countless teens to Christ.

The second assistant pastor, Rev. Alvin "Al" Albertson, was a powerful attorney in Durham, and just about the coolest saved brother Lamont ever had the pleasure to meet. Rev. Al, as he was affectionately called by everyone at church, once preached a sermon titled "The Perils of Mack Daddy" that was one of the most memorable he'd heard at his church.

During that sermon, Rev. Al came out of the pulpit to demonstrate on his wife what he had called "the Mack Daddy's art of mackin'," causing the entire congregation to slap palms, give "dap," and howl with laughter. At the end of that sermon, five young men, two from North Carolina Central University, and three from Eva T. Marshall University, located right where Durham County ran into Chatham County off Highway 751, joined the church and gave their lives over to Christ.

But that last joker, Rev. Sykes, had no business in the pulpit as far as Lamont was concerned. He'd met people at The Place to Be nightclub who had more business in the pulpit than Parvell—a sad commentary at best. And how that Negro had finagled his way to an ordination was a subject worthy of a book on church folk.

Rev. Quincey adjusted his gold and rust brocade stole and made sure that it, along with the diamond-studded cross he was wearing, were lying straight on his black silk robe. He gave his wife, Lena, a slick "playa" wink when he thought no one was paying attention, and then signaled to the musicians to prepare for the opening of the service.

Cousin Buddy knocked his fist against the football helmet and whispered, "Rev. Quincey was making boyfriend eyes at our first lady," to Uncle Joseph.

"The Lord is in His Holy temple. Let all the earth

keep silence before Him," Rev. Quincey called out in that smooth, low, flat, and very sexy voice that sent far too many shivers up the spines of some of the women with all the wrong motives in their congregation.

It was fourth Sunday and the youth choir, under the direction of Chablis's seventeen-year-old nephew, Jarnquez Jackson, was very excited about singing this morning for the guest minister, Bishop Eddie Tate and his wife, Evangelist Johnnie Mae Tate. Bishop Tate, a contemporary and close friend of the renowned Bishop Theophilus Simmons, had built one of the most effective ministries for black teens in the country. Over the course of the past thirty years, countless young people could bear testimony to how Tate's "Ladies and Gentlemen of Distinction in Training" program had contributed to their growth, development, and triumph over worldly adversities.

Eddie Tate loved being around young people. Despite being in his early seventies, with teenaged grandchildren, he was loved and admired by most young people in the Gospel United Church of America. And unknown to many of the grown-ups in the denomination, it was rumored among the teens that the Bishop had a slammin' collection of hip-hop music.

Jarnquez walked the thirty-five members of the youth choir down to the altar, turned to face the congregation, and as one of the teens would later say to a group of friends the next day at Hillside High School, "church was on."

For months, the musicians and lyricists in the choir had labored to turn out an acceptable gospel version of the rap song, "From the Window to the Wall," by Atlanta

rap artists, The Ying Yang Twins. The song had a seriously "crunked," dirty-South beat and had been quite
popular when it was released several years ago. The
choir had been waiting for it to become "old enough" to
be eased by the old-schoolers in the church. But more so,
the youth choir had to wait until the right Sunday morning to perform it. When Bishop Tate walked into the
choir room for prayer, those children almost lost their
minds, and Jarnquez ran and got the sheet music for the
song and passed it out to the instrumentalists.

Plus, they had a brand-new processional song that
Jarnquez had written a couple of weeks ago. So, this
promised to be what they would consider as a "madd
cool" Sunday. They had some hot new songs, Bishop
Tate was visiting, and the members of the church's
kitchen ministry were putting the finishing touches on
what smelled like a fabulous dinner after the service.

Jarnquez called out, "One, two, one-two-three, hit
it," and pointed to the bass player, who immediately
plucked out some funky, booming chords. The drummer
followed suit, and was soon joined by the lead guitarist
and organist. They played several riffs of the song long
enough for the choir members to get the sway in motion,
before they started singing "Get-get-get Ya Praiz On."

The members of the choir bobbed their heads, moved
from side to side, lifted their hands in the air, and proceeded with a hip-hop version of the traditional march
to the choir loft. Rev. Quincey, who loved jazz, laughed,
raised his hands in the air, and got in sync with that
rocking hip-hop beat. Revs. Simmons and Albertson
were grinning and having a good time marching in with
a few smooth movements of their own.

Bishop Tate raised his hands in the air like the kids and moved down the aisle as smooth as any young person.

Parvell, who couldn't stand the bishop, didn't want any Holy Ghost "crunk in his system" this morning. He walked down the aisle without giving any mind to the tempo guiding the processional.

"Get . . . get . . . get-get-getcha praiz on . . . get-get-getcha praiz on. God is good . . . all the time . . . all the time God is good . . . and since He's always blessing you . . . you need to get-get-getcha praiz on."

"Sang li'l *chil*-drens," Bishop Tate called out, causing some of the teens' parents sitting in the congregation to laugh out loud, as everyone started clapping and swaying with the choir while the processional members progressed to the choir loft and pulpit.

But not everyone was delighted with this processional and the music. Several of the "old heads," especially the ones with deep pockets, found "this display" off-putting. This was particularly true for Dr. N. P. Nance, who had recently donated $8,000 to buy new choir robes for every choir in the church *except* the youth choir.

He huffed and puffed and then said, "Lawd, soothe my ears and give me strength to stomach this discordant excuse for sacred melody," loud enough to be heard by the people sitting nearby.

Eddie Tate, who had never been a conventional preacher, even back in the early 1960s when he was a young man, locked eyes with N. P. Nance. This wasn't the first time the two of them were at odds and it certainly wouldn't be the last. But as the presiding bishop and the "Head Negro in Charge," he was not about to let

this man ruin this delightful and sincere expression from
the congregation's youth. Adults constantly complained
about the problems associated with black children. And
when a visible number of them were at church, acting
right, and singing their hearts out for Jesus, some of
those very grown-ups displayed disdain for their youth-
ful style of worship.

"Some of these old buzzards need *to get some crunk
in their system*, and get as excited about serving the
Lord as these youngsters," Eddie thought and shifted his
focus from N. P. Nance back to the youth choir.

N. P. Nance didn't miss the bishop's casual dismissal.
But then why should he have been surprised that Eddie
Tate liked all this nonsense—from the music, to that
dancing down the aisle, to their "uniforms" of fash-
ionable, loose-fitting blue jeans, crisp, white oversized
oxford shirts, white athletic shoes, and navy fitted caps
with the church's initials embroidered on the brim in silver, worn tilted to the side like the rapper T.I.

Nance had never liked or approved of Eddie Tate,
from the first time he laid eyes on him and his then future wife back in the 1960s at that infamous Triennial
Conference in Richmond, Virginia. As a staunch sup-
porter of both Bishop Giles and Rev. Ernest Brown out of
Michigan, the thought that Tate and his cronies usurped
Rev. Ernest Brown's run for an Episcopal seat was still a
bone of contention more than forty years later.

And when Bishop Tate ran for an Episcopal seat,
Nance fought him tooth and nail. It didn't matter that
the bishop was a dedicated, saved, and anointed pastor
with impressive credentials—an earned Ph.D. in sociol-
ogy from the University of Chicago, consultant for the

chaplain program at Cook County Hospital, two books published on ministering to black teens, and a thriving church with five thousand members. N. P. Nance did not believe that Eddie Tate, with his cool, streetwise ways, and reformed hoochie-mama for a wife, was worthy of being a preacher, let alone being elected to serve as a bishop.

Parvell Sykes narrowed his eyes as his gaze sliced into the bishop's back. He and Dr. Nance made a quick exchange that rolled right by everyone but Queen Esther and one other person—Baby Doll Henderson-Lacy—who had managed to slip into the back of the sanctuary with her new husband, unnoticed despite her eye-catching attire.

Queen Esther could not stomach either Rev. Sykes or that hissing, spitting venom, snake-in-the-grass, Nathaniel P. Nance, whom she always referred to as *"Negro Please* Nance." If there was some mess going on in their church, she could bet one of Joseph's Viagra-strength glasses of fresh orange juice that *"Negro Please"* was bound to be somewhere in the midst of it.

"You got your lips so tight, baby, I'm beginning to worry that you can't get any air in your mouth," Joseph leaned over and whispered to Queen Esther, wondering what had caused that fierce, fire-spitting expression on her face. It was fourth Sunday, her favorite worship Sunday because the kids sang today. And Bishop Tate and Mother Johnnie—two of Queen's favorite people—were at church this morning.

"Sorry, sweetie," she sighed. "It's just that the devil is so busy this morning and service ain't even really started." She dug around in her purse and pulled out her bottle of anointing oil.

"Now what in heaven's name do you think you are going to do with that?" he asked.

"Anoint the bishop?" she said sheepishly, all the while pouring a drop of the fragrant oil in the palm of her hand.

"Anoint the bishop when? While he is conducting service from the pulpit?" Joseph pressed.

"Uhh, well . . . yeah," she answered with a whole lot more conviction than she felt. *Somebody* needed some oil on them this morning. In addition to the mayhem stewing in Nance and Sykes, Charmayne Robinson, along with Lamont's ex-girlfriend and their mothers were at church and sitting together.

As soon as every choir member was in place, Rev. Quincey said, "The hymn of praise, 'God Will Take Care of You,' can be found on page two of your bulletin and page 220 in your hymnal."

Queen Esther had been so busy with all that was going on in church, she hadn't been paying attention to the progression of the actual service. She grabbed a hymnal, stood, and waited as the pastor commenced with the lining of the hymn.

"Be not dismayed whate'er betide, God will take care of you. Beneath His wings of love abide, God will take care of you. God will take care of you, Thru' every day, O'er all the way; He will take care of you, God will take care of you."

"Without further lining of the hymn," Rev. Quincey said, "let us sing this wonderful testimony of God's ever-present help and love in our lives."

The congregation rose and prepared to sing, pausing for a few seconds, when it dawned on them that the rhythm had been kicked up a few notches. Jarnquez rolled right over that traditional hymn style and pushed everyone to keep up with his updated version of the song. The members of the choir started grinning and singing the song with an enthusiasm they had never previously displayed when they sang what they referred to as "one of those old-fogey church songs."

Queen Esther, who loved this choir and all of her babies in it, raised her hand in the hip-hop style Jarnquez had shown her and called out, "Sang babies. Let Jesus know you love Him, even if ya' gotta put a li'l dap in your praise."

The youth choir sang even louder and with more fervor. A few of the teens raised their hands and two shouted out, "Praise the Lord somebody! Praise the Lord!"

"Girl," Charmayne whispered back to Chablis. "Your little nephew is serving it up this morning."

"I know," Chablis answered.

"Baby," Miss Shirley said, "you got some hand lotion?"

Chablis dug around in her purse and handed her mother a tube of Sensi perfumed lotion.

"Baby, I can't use this fancy stuff on these hands," her mother said and raised up a brown hand, which looked like it had powder on it as a result of wearing her yellow rubber cleaning gloves. "I need some grease."

Charmayne, who wanted to hear more of the song than Miss Shirley's discussion of hand grease, passed her purse over her shoulder to Chablis.

"There should be a tube of that creamy Vaseline in my purse."

As Chablis dug around for the Vaseline, she found samples of blond hair tracks stapled to a card with instructions for weave selection from Charmayne to her hairstylist, LaShawn. She quickly put the hair back and pulled out the tube of Vaseline. A note fell out with instructions for buying out homeowners in the neighborhood where her brother and his family lived for prices that went way below market value.

Chablis could hardly believe that Charmayne was working with Jethro Winters to sell out hundreds of hardworking black people like Jarnquez's father. She gave her mother the Vaseline and slipped the note into her own purse before giving Charmayne hers. Even though she was barely on speaking terms with Lamont, she was giving him this note. Because there was no way she was going to sit back and let anyone, including her girl, Charmayne, swindle her brother and nieces and nephews out of their home.

Chablis loved making money, and as much of it as she possibly could. But it was a shame for Jethro Winters to have such disrespect for working-class black folk that he was willing to systematically destroy a pretty, safe, loving, and affordable neighborhood. She fought back her tears and then smiled when she saw her nephew, who was a child who truly loved the Lord, getting so caught up in the music that he had started dancing his way out of the choir loft, and commenced to doing some mighty fancy footwork once he was on the floor.

By now the entire congregation had gotten caught up

in the music and was clapping and swaying as Jarnquez shouted and danced.

"Lawd, that boy out there working like he trying out for the gospel *Soul Train* hour," Joseph whispered to his wife.

All Queen Esther could do was nod, wishing she could get out there and dance like that with Jarnquez. He looked like he was having the time of his life—dancing with all his heart, and all his strength, and all his might for the Lord. Now that was some dancing.

Lamont was so tickled. He had been away from church far too long. Nobody could have church like black folk. He turned around to see how Theresa was taking this all in. She always seemed so reserved to him that he wondered about her reaction to things that were clearly filled with unadulterated emotion and joy. Much to his delight, Theresa was clapping and smiling and having the time of her life.

Parvell Sykes was sitting back in his seat hoping that this display of "Negromania" would end soon. The song wasn't *that* good. He wished he could reach over and slap Bishop Tate, who was now up on his feet waving his arms in the air in that hip-hop "raise ya' hands in the air, and wave 'em like ya' just don't care" style. But Parvell certainly thought twice about that. Bishop Tate was six feet six and just two M&M's short of 275. Plus, that Negro was one of those old-school, brawling bishops—the kind who packed heat and would punch you down almost as fast as he would pray for you.

The song ended and two ushers brought in a big red basket and sat it at the foot of the altar.

Bishop Tate walked up to the pulpit and said, "Christmas is fast approaching and there are people who need a helping hand. Fayetteville Street, I'm asking you to open your hearts and your pocketbooks, so that we can send a bounteous gift to the folks who are still struggling from Katrina. If you have a decent home to go to after service, you should run down to give something to somebody in need. Ushers, I want you to start with the back rows, so that we can do this quickly and in an orderly manner."

Charmayne pulled out a five and stood and grinned at the usher when he reached her row like he was her new man. She gave him her hand when she stepped into the aisle, let her eyes drop down to his waist, and whispered, "God is good and His *provisions* are great."

The usher grinned from ear to ear and pimped to the next aisle.

Roxanne sat there hot and sweating from the heavy mink on her shoulder, gritting her teeth with every step that Charmayne took down toward her hoped-for man. She thought, "Why does that conniving skank always have to look so good?"

As soon as it was time for Roxanne's row to get up, she hopped in front of some people, anxious to find out Parvell's reaction to Charmayne in that ruby St. John's suit, with rhinestone buttons down the front of the jacket, black clear-heeled pumps, and a ruby silk shoulder bag with "Charmayne" embroidered on it with sequins. And to make matters worse, the girl had a full-length, silver fox coat draped around her shoulders.

About the only other woman in church who could top that outfit was the bishop's wife, Mother Johnnie, who was dripping St. John's herself. Known for her sexy outfits, Mother Johnnie, who was now well into her sixties, caused several men to whisper, "Lawd, ha' mercy," when she walked into church this morning wearing a snug navy blue dress, with sterling silver buttons all the way down the front and on the sleeves. Her navy patent leather pumps with the silver trim around the edges of the shoe were complemented by the navy patent leather clutch she was carrying. But it was the navy, full-length mink with "Johnnie" embroidered in navy silk thread all over the silver lining that set Mother apart from the other women in church.

Johnnie wasn't wearing a hat—instead, opting for a sleek, shoulder-length style, a wisp of shiny silver hair, falling over her eye whenever she moved her head. Mother was so fine and sexy, she gave being in your sixties a whole new meaning. She had scored several points with the teens this morning in that outfit, especially when she smiled, revealing what they considered to be an enviable white gold tooth with her infamous sapphire in the middle of it. They couldn't believe that their bishop's wife, one old enough to be their grandmother, was sporting gold and sapphire in her mouth.

Jarnquez had whispered, "Mother Tate looks like she used to dance in music videos back in the day," when he saw her tooth.

"They didn't have music videos for her to dance to back in the day, fool," the bass player had hissed to him. "They probably didn't even have TVs when she was young."

"Yeah . . ." Jarnquez mused. "Ya' probably right. No TV, no music videos, no hip-hop. Lawd, they musta been bored stupid."

"They were," one of the girls hissed. "Why ya' think she went and got that tooth? She was bored stupid."

Charmayne flipped out a hand-painted, ruby-lacquered fan and waved it furiously in her face.

"Hussy-heifer," Roxanne mumbled, as she pulled Parvell's sweltering mink closer to her body.

As soon as the last person took a seat, Parvell stood at the pulpit podium and raised his hands for this special offering to be blessed. When the ushers took it away, he stayed at the podium and started flipping through the Bible, obviously intent on giving the scripture reading.

Eddie Tate, who was now seated in what was traditionally the pastor's chair, noticed the frown on Rev. Quincey's face and knew that this fool had overstepped protocol and appointed himself to do that reading. He picked up his program, grabbed the pen resting next to his glass of water, and wrote, "Why is that joker up in your pulpit without permission, Obadiah? And where is his clerical robe? He looks like an oversized gangsta elf in that outfit."

Rev. Quincey smiled. His bishop was so crazy. He wrote, "Man, I have had about enough of that Negro. But the presiding elder ignored your last e-mail to let him go because he wants Sykes to help the district buy some land in Johnston County."

"Bump the presiding elder," Eddie Tate wrote. "I'm the bishop and I say get rid of him. We have enough riff-raff in the denomination and don't need to add any more to our ministerial ranks."

"Done," Rev. Quincey wrote.

"Good," the bishop wrote back. "Does he look like Ron Isley to you?"

Rev. Quincey nodded and covered his mouth with a handkerchief, hoping no one figured out that he was laughing.

"Whew," Eddie scribbled, "I thought it was just me."

Parvell didn't miss the note passing and took the liberty of reading from several more scriptures. Both Rev. Quincey and the bishop had to hurry and flip through their Bibles to keep up with him. He was now reading from Psalm 71. Eddie frowned as he listened to Parvell jump around the text in search of words to use against him and the pastor, which was a serious breach of ministerial etiquette.

". . . *for my enemies speak against me,*" Parvell read from the first part of verse ten, before jumping down to verse thirteen. *"May my accusers be put to shame; may those who want to harm me be covered with scorn and disgrace . . ."*

Parvell paused a moment to turn and glare at his pastor and the bishop, before facing the congregation again, only to give Lamont the same menacing stare. After he had handled his own business, he then moved to the parts of the scripture Eddie had selected for the text of his sermon this morning.

Parvell read, *"Since my youth, O God, you have taught me, and to this day I declare your marvelous deeds. Even when I am old and gray, do not forsake me, O God, till I declare your power to the next generation, your might to all who come."*

The bishop frowned. Parvell, who had read the first part slowly, was now rushing through the text, after he had given clear directions in Rev. Quincey's office for this part of the scripture to be read slowly, so that all the young people had a chance to absorb verses seventeen and eighteen from Psalm 71. Eddie knew that Parvell had read the scriptures any kind of way, to be spiteful.

But Eddie Tate had not been in the ministry all of these years for nothing. He was an old dog, whose bite was a whole lot worse than his menacing bark. He had stood by his best friend, Bishop Theophilus Simmons, through one of the stormiest moments in their denomination's history, and they were all still standing. He was a man of God and an esteemed member of the episcopacy but he was also a street Negro and didn't take this kind of mess off of anybody.

"Rev. Sykes, read from verses seventeen and eighteen again," the bishop called out, like he was talking to an impertinent child.

"Excuse me," Parvell said, not fully believing what he was hearing.

"You heard me, Rev. Read it again. I don't think anybody got anything out of it the first time, with the way you were rushing through the text."

Parvell coughed, stalling for enough time to think of something to say that would put the bishop in his place. He was not about to let Bishop Tate clown him like that in front of the congregation, even when he knew good and well that it would be a serious breach of church protocol and ministerial manners to say or do anything disrespectful to your senior pastor and any bishop.

He squared off his shoulders and said, "It appears as if our representative from the denomination's esteemed episcopacy has mistaken the members of this great congregation for someone from his own previous church."

Parvell turned around to make sure his point had been

driven home. Satisfied with the "Negro, is you crazy?" expression on Rev. Quincey's face, he continued.

"Our congregation, unlike far too many churches in the denomination, has been blessed with a disproportionate number of highly educated people, who don't require that the gospel be spoon-fed to them."

At this point, Eddie Tate had enough. He stood up and gripped Parvell's shoulder in what felt like an iron vise.

"Son, the Lord appreciates when a man or a woman wants to become a better citizen by completing his educational training. But even more than that, God delights in a man or woman whose heart and mind and soul are turned to heaven with a desire to serve Him to the fullest. And if every single man, woman, and child in my old church was so dumb they didn't know how to pour a glass of water, I would rejoice and consider myself a blessed man if they all found Christ and were saved, sanctified, and full of the Holy Ghost.

"Now you read that scripture right and give *my* Father the honor and glory He is entitled to. Because I've had enough of watching you stand here sinning, 'cause you so intent on serving *yours*."

"Ooooo," Jarnquez said under his breath to the pianist. "Bishop done told Rev. Sykes that his daddy is the devil."

Queen Esther, who was of the same mind as Eddie Tate, stood up and called out, "Thank you, Jesus. You ain't never been scared to throw a money changer out his stall, when they come a callin' in the house of our precious Lord."

"Amen and Praise the Lord," James shouted out, clapping his hands with such fervency that Lamont found he couldn't stop himself from standing up and joining his brother in praise.

Several other folks, who wholeheartedly agreed with the bishop's bold move, stood up and clapped and called out a few "shout outs" to the Lord. At that point, the organist, who felt the shift in the mood of the church, hopped up and started playing what Bug always said was "that old Negro spiritual, 'The Shouting Song,'" to fan the sparks of the Holy Ghost into full-blown flames.

Theresa, who had been content to stay seated and just watch the drama being played out in church like it was a TV show, suddenly felt the anointing of the Holy Ghost pouring over her so strong, it made her rise out of her seat, lift her hands up, and call out, "Thank you, Jesus, Thank you for coming up in this house and cleaning it out."

Charmayne stood up and waved her hands around like she was feeling the spirit because she wanted to make sure that Parvell knew she was in the congregation and having some fun at his expense. She twirled around to see what the rest of the folks were doing and caught Lamont Green watching Theresa Hopson like she was something good to eat.

"Umph, *Miss Thang* got a li'l thangy-thangy going on up in here and she too saved to pause a moment and see it," Charmayne thought to herself.

Lamont was enjoying watching Theresa praise God so much, he could feel that joy spreading all through his chest like a warm and soothing liquid. She was absolutely breathtaking standing there in such deep praise. He'd always wondered why Uncle Joseph looked at

Auntee like she was some red-eye gravy when she got the Holy Ghost and shouted. Now he knew—the anointing of the Holy Spirit made a woman a man loved even more beautiful than she already was.

Charmayne liked the way Lamont Green's biceps bulged every time he clapped his hands.

"Umph, I sure wish that brother was clapping on me," she thought and then hollered out, "Lawd, ha' mercy," when just the thought of that particular thought got too much for her.

By this time, Roxanne was fit to be tied. She had not missed Parvell watching that heifer, Charmayne, so hard she thought his eyes were going to pop out his head. She decided it was time to get to shouting and bring some attention from her hoped-for-man-to-be onto herself.

Roxanne ran down the center aisle, right in front of the altar, and very carefully "fell out" on the floor like she had been slain in the spirit. But Charmayne could see right through Roxanne Daye and decided to put that lollipop-head hussy back in her place. She got up to the altar and fell out, too, right on top of Roxanne, who lay there trying to figure out a way to get this heavy heifer off her without letting on that she was faking it.

Parvell, who had been working on a strategy to add Roxanne to his "in-the-dark-only" booty call list, knew he needed to get down there and attend to the girl. But to do that would only raise Charmayne's ire and cause him to forfeit his booty call privileges with her. And he could tell just by looking at Roxanne that she did not have the same gold-medal "skills" as Charmayne.

Uncle Big Gold had taught him the proper pecking order for his women. Said, "Boy, don't ever place your

'I-need-to-call-somebody' woman higher than your 'gold-medal-girl.' Because about all the 'call somebody' woman can do for you is take the sharp edge off of your hunger. But that 'gold-medalist' is capable of serving it up and then some."

Charmayne, who was lying across Roxanne with the end of her weave brushing the girl's face, was determined to stay on her as long as she thought she could get away with it. Plus, she wanted to find out what Parvell would do when his undercover woman and wannabe undercover girl were simultaneously in need of his assistance.

Roxanne was getting tired of this heavy heifer lying on her. She couldn't get up because she was supposed to be "out with Jesus." So, she took her fist and poked Charmayne in the back as hard as she dared without bringing attention to her movement.

Charmayne wanted to jump. That bony fist hurt. Instead, she pressed heavier on Roxanne, then quickly jumped back up when she felt a track of her weave being snatched out of her head.

Roxanne acted like she was coming to, called out "Jesus" so sweetly and softly Parvell couldn't help but choose to come to her aid, and collapsed again when she felt his arms on her, tracks of dark blond weave clutched tightly in her hand.

"Here," Parvell whispered, "let's get you out in the lobby for some air," as he helped the "weak and helpless" Roxanne to her feet. "You need anything?"

"No, Rev. Sykes," she answered in the most pitiful voice she could muster. "All I need is some fresh air and Jesus."

"Amen," Parvell said in a rare bout of sincerity, and

led her out of the sanctuary as gently and carefully as he could.

Roxanne surrendered completely to Parvell's leading. She may have a big lollipop head and no shape to speak of but she knew how to work a man over. Being overcome with "savedness" and weakness were a winning combination for some men. And she figured correctly that Rev. Sykes was more the rule than the exception to this very basic fact.

"Lawd, help that boy," Uncle Big Gold whispered from his seat in the back of the church. He couldn't believe that his nephew had succumbed to the okey-doke like that. At least he could have picked a woman as fine as Ida Belle's baby girl. At first he was glad he had come to church this morning—so much drama this morning, it was better than watching a DVD. But to have to witness the demise of a playa was just too much for his reprobate heart to handle. Made him wish he hadn't decided on church when he was roaming to and fro in the neighborhood searching for some entertainment.

Charmayne was so upset over what had just happened, she didn't even notice the usher at the front of the sanctuary vacuuming up her hair tracks with the small DustBuster in his white-gloved hand.

She smoothed her hair over the blank patch on her head and whispered to herself, "That hard-knot, conniving hussy just stole my man *and* my hair in church of all places."

"That's the best place to steal a man," Miss Shirley murmured, more to herself than to Charmayne.

"Huh?"

"I said," Miss Shirley stated firmly while snapping

on the fingers of her yellow rubber gloves, "Church is the best place to do your man stealing. Best man heists I've ever seen have been right up in church, just like this morning."

"You ain't never lied," Ida Belle said, thinking about the men she'd stolen while in church and all the fun she had doing it.

"And if I were you," Miss Shirley continued, deliberately ignoring Chablis nudging her to be quiet, "I'd go find that Roxanne and make her pay for my weave tracks. 'Cause I know they was expensive from the looks of it. And I bet you wearing some real hair from South America that's been dyed good."

Charmayne turned all the way around in her seat and asked, "Miss Shirley, how you know so much about weave hair?"

Miss Shirley snapped two fingers on the gloves and chuckled.

"Baby, I takes medication for my cleaning problem and don't get out too much. So, Chablis always has me doing research on the Internet for her. And when I get bored, I just look up stuff on whatever interests me, like what kinda hair you got sewed up on your head."

She snapped some more of the fingers on the glove and blushed.

"Got me a real nice man on that there Sista/Brutha Hookem Up Internet dating program, too."

This time Ida Belle turned all the way around in her seat.

"Shirley, I didn't know you had a man?"

"Show do. Name is Clyde."

"That's his Internet name?" Ida Belle asked. "I've

never known anybody to call themselves by a regular name on the Internet."

At this point, Charmayne turned back around and stared at her mother. She knew the girl always kept a man in her back pocket. But Mama on the Internet? Just the thought was enough to make her want to get saved.

"What would he call himself, if not by a regular name, Ida Belle?" Shirley inquired in complete innocence. She figured from the shock on their faces over her having a man, it would probably be best not to tell them that Clyde was white.

"Mama, maybe you don't have enough to do," was all Chablis could say.

"Yes, I do, baby," Miss Shirley answered sweetly. "I just know how to get a whole lot done real fast, so that I can clean, and then have time to sit down and talk to Clyde in the evenings."

They had been so deep into Miss Shirley's business that they hadn't paid a bit of attention to the progress of the actual service. And it came as a bit of a surprise when Charmayne's usher walked up to their pew to direct them up and out of their row for the regular morning offering.

Charmayne didn't want to get up and gave her money to her mother, who was happy to get down to that altar so that she could get in closer proximity to Bishop Tate. Now that was a man. Not some cyber-person like *Clyde*. Ida Belle felt a quiver at just the thought of that big ole Big Daddy preacher, wavy-gray hair still full and thick, and just as sexy and "gangsta" as they came.

She took her time dropping her envelope in the basket and gave Eddie Tate a wink before heading back to her seat. Eddie, who had sworn off hot, bold church women when he met his wife, didn't move a muscle. It had been a long time since a woman had gotten bold enough to hit on him right in front of his wife. He hoped that Johnnie wasn't watching.

That girl had earned a degree in banking and finance from Chicago State University. Yet, despite graduating with the highest honors and being appointed by the bishop presiding over their district to serve as the financial and investment consultant for the Chicago churches, she was still a 'hood rat who would take you out in a moment's notice. And this was especially true if it involved what she would describe as a "wanton skank trying to roll up on her man."

Johnnie, who was sitting on the first pew, had not missed Ida Belle's solicitation of her husband's attention. She ran her fingers through her silky silver hair, making sure that her wedding ring, an opulent five-carat, emerald-cut diamond set in platinum, was in plain sight to Ida Belle.

Coming on to a man in front of his woman had always been a powerful aphrodisiac to Ida Belle Robinson. When the bishop's wife flashed that incredible ring, it fueled her desire to get her hands on him even more. She cut her eyes at Johnnie, licked her lips when she caught Bishop Tate's attention, and then returned to her seat satisfied.

Mother Johnnie Tate was not the kind of bishop's wife that you played games like that with. She capitalized on her status in the church this morning and signaled for an usher to come to her side. When the man reached her pew, she had a note ready for Ida Belle which read:

"Skank-Hussy-Heifer, I will bust a cap in your rusty behind if you try that with me again."

The usher took the folded note and did his best to sneak and read it before he reached Ida Belle's seat. Ida read the note quickly and sent one of her own back to the bishop's wife:

"Bring it on, *Mother.*"

Johnnie read the note and chuckled. She'd dealt with plenty of rough-talking, butt-kicking women on Chicago's South side. She sucked on her tooth a moment and handed the usher her purse.

"Baby, I want you to take this to that woman, open it up, show her the contents, and then bring it back to me."

The usher took the purse, which he thought was awfully heavy. When he reached Ida Belle, he did exactly as Mother Tate had instructed. Both his and Ida's eyes got big, when he opened the purse to reveal Johnnie's prized .357 Magnum.

Ida stared down at Mother Tate, who was sitting in her seat as cool as a cucumber, smiling sweetly at her husband. She leaned over and whispered, "I have to go," to Charmayne, who suddenly became curious herself concerning the contents of that pocketbook.

Miss Shirley, who had not missed a thing, thought, "Serves Ida Belle right. Always trying to mess around with somebody else's man."

Cousin Buddy hit on both sides of his helmet with both hands. He grabbed his pink plastic cup off the pew and raised it to his lips for a sip of water. He frowned—the cup was dryer than his throat. Folks always whispered that he was different, which was probably true. It wasn't too hard for him to figure out that he was the only person in church wearing a helmet.

"But if I'm different," he said softly to himself, "what in the world is that lady in the gold? Just 'cause a person don't wear a helmet on they head to church don't mean they is right."

Uncle Joseph saw Cousin Buddy's mouth moving but could tell that his conversation wasn't directed at anyone. He leaned over and poked him in the arm gently.

"You all right? Need any more water?"

"Nahh. I'm just fine. Just thinking to my ownself," he answered.

Chapter Thirteen

BISHOP TATE SHOOK HIS HEAD AT HIS WIFE, AS IF TO say, "Girl, you know you know better." He looked at what was left of that woman in the gold nightclub suit's departure, and thought, "Serves you right—thinking you could roll up on a preacher's wife like that."

Eddie sighed heavily. What had started out as a wonderful and anointed service was rapidly disintegrating into what his boy, Theophilus Simmons, once coined as *"Histrionic Religioses,"* in a sermon to fellow ministers at the last Triennial Conference.

Theophilus told them: "Church, when you see this form of neurotic narcissism masquerading itself as pious buoyancy for Jesus, stop, drop, and roll on down to the ground, and get prostrate before the Lord. 'Cause when all of that is happening within the humble four walls of your sanctuary, you best believe you got to bind up and pray out some devils intent on blocking somebody's salvation by diverting their attention away from Jesus."

And that is just what was happening in church this morning. There was somebody in this sanctuary on assignment—the wrong assignment. That somebody didn't want anyone who had gone astray to find their way to the

Lord and get saved. And what better way to accomplish this than to sit up in here full of "hell," hoping with a heart that was anything but clean and clear, that something in the service would make someone with a heart turning toward salvation think twice about taking that step.

Both Eddie and Theophilus had discovered that oftentimes, the people creating the most distractions—like the two "Jezebels" and that one spiritually lukewarm "congregation worker bee"—were not necessarily the ones who were the most invested in preventing the church from doing what it was supposed to do on a Sunday morning. They were just what Theophilus's daughter, Sharon, had once described as "being so wrongly in the right place at the right time, that they inadvertently stir up what the rest of us needed to be praying completely out of the service."

Eddie heeded the advice of his friend and goddaughter and brother and sister in Christ. He put his hand to his heart and whispered, "Father, there is someone in this sanctuary who came to get saved this morning. Reveal that person or those persons to me. And Lord, direct my eyes to the one who would be delighted if no one found his or her way to You this morning."

The youth choir had just begun a slow and very soulful ballad. In that moment Eddie closed his eyes and felt so much love from the Savior, his eyes welled up with tears. He loved being a minister, he got a great deal of pleasure in being a prominent bishop, and he had great fun when he pastored his church in Chicago. But what gave him the most satisfaction was letting the Lord use him to find someone who desperately wanted to turn their life over to Christ and didn't have a clue as to the first step to take.

He opened his eyes and the first person he saw was a woman dressed in an outfit that his wife wouldn't be caught dead in. In fact, if Johnnie were dead, and he got crazy enough to dress the girl in that hot pink plaid polyester skirt, gold peasant blouse, and gold silk men's socks worn in those yellow jelly shoes, she'd come back to life, pistol-whip him, change her clothes, and then go on back home to glory. Yet, as fascinating as this woman's attire was, Eddie knew that he wasn't supposed to scrutinize her through his own myopic human vision.

Eddie was being led by the Lord to view her through the kind of anointed lens that gave sight to those blinded by human shortcomings and frailties. What he saw, when he looked at her right, was "the woman at the well," "the woman the Pharisees wanted to stone to death," "the woman who washed Jesus' feet with costly perfume and tears of sorrow-filled repentance." And what all of these women had in common (including the woman in this church) was a desire to be saved.

When the choir had finished singing, the bishop walked up to the pulpit podium and reached underneath for the Amplified Bible.

"The Lord has just laid it upon my heart to change the order of service a bit. And the first thing that He wants me to do is to offer the following scripture reading:"

And behold, a woman of the town who was an especially wicked sinner, when she learned that He was reclining at table in the Pharisee's house, brought an alabaster flask of ointment (perfume).

And standing behind Him at His feet weeping, she began to wet His feet with [her] tears; and she wiped them with the hair of her head and kissed His feet [affectionately] and anointed them with the ointment (perfume).

Now when the Pharisee who had invited Him saw it, he said to himself, If this Man were a prophet, He would surely know who and what sort of woman this is who is touching Him—for she is a notorious sinner (a social outcast, devoted to sin).

Eddie stopped reading from verses 37 to 39 in the seventh chapter of the Book of Luke and stared right at Baby Doll, hoping that she knew that these passages were meant for her. When she lowered her head a bit, and held tight to the hand of the little red man in the shades sitting next to her, he skipped over to verses 46 to 50 and resumed his reading:

You did not anoint My head with [cheap, ordinary] oil, but she has anointed My feet with [costly, rare] perfume.

Therefore I tell you, her sins, many [as they are], are forgiven her—because she has loved much. But he who is forgiven little loves little.

And He said to her, Your sins are forgiven!

Then those who were at table with Him began to say among themselves, Who is this Who even forgives sins?

But Jesus said to the woman, Your faith has saved you; go (enter) into peace [in freedom from all the distresses that are experienced as the result of sin].

The Bishop closed the Bible, wiped his face with a pale purple cotton handkerchief, and turned around to face Rev. Quincey.

"Pastor, I apologize for moving this service in a different direction. But when my God calls, the only thing that I can say is: *Lord, here I am, send me.*"

"Praise God," was all Rev. Quincey said.

Revs. Albertson and Simmons simply smiled and nodded in agreement with their senior pastor. They had perfect peace about this change and were eager to find out who had come to church this morning specifically to get saved. As Albertson would later say to Sharon Simmons, "This is really what our job is all about—sending as many folks to heaven as we possibly can. Anything else is a moot issue when you consider that."

"Now," Bishop Tate began again, "there is somebody out there who would give anything to have the Lord say to her what He told the woman with the perfume and tears. I am standing here before you, as one who has been forgiven much and been blessed to love much. And all I can say is, if you come down to this altar and bathe it with tears from a repentant heart, and confess Jesus Christ as your Lord and Savior, you will be saved."

He raised his hands, signaling to the congregation to stand.

"We haven't had a sermon this morning. And to be completely honest, except for this good singing, we really haven't had much church in the good ole tradition of our beloved Gospel United Church of America. But church, as much as I love this denomination, I love the Lord even more. So, with the permission of Rev. Quincey, I am opening the doors of the church."

Rev. Quincey came down and stood beside his bishop, eager to see who this new child of the King was. Since he first joined the ranks of the ministry, there were two things that got him excited. The first was discovering that two people loved each other so much they wanted to immerse themselves into that incredible mystery called Holy Matrimony. And the second and most important was when somebody got saved. That had to be the most incredible rush he'd ever felt—to watch somebody accept Christ as their Lord and Savior.

The fire in Baby Doll's chest area alerted her to the possibility that this bishop man might be talking to her. She rose up out of her seat slightly and then sat right back down, dismissing the fire as heartburn—she had been suffering from acute attacks of acid reflux disease for about six years. She popped an antacid tablet into her mouth but to no avail. The burning started again but unlike heartburn, it didn't hurt. In fact, it felt good, like holding cold hands over a warm fire, or coming into a warm dry spot after being forced to stand in the icy rain for hours on end.

Baby Doll rose up out of her seat again, only this time to stand all the way up. She made a move to the center aisle and then stood there frozen, not sure what to do next. Her new husband stood all the way up, took her hand and, using his senses, walked her to the altar and placed Baby Doll's thin, work-roughened hand into the bishop's large one.

Eddie felt the sorrow and the hurt, the loneliness, the despair, the aching for help and not knowing where to turn in the woman's tiny hand. He gazed into her eyes and saw a testimony that was guaranteed to bring somebody else to this altar.

Queen Esther began to cry so hard, Joseph had to encircle her in the protection of his arms. Cousin Buddy hit his helmet a few times, then reached into the inside pocket of his baseball jacket and pulled out a starched white handkerchief that he had been saving to give to a lady in distress. He'd once seen a movie where a man handed a crying lady a clean hankie, and thought that had to be about the sweetest and kindest thing a man could do. He had been waiting for many years for an opportunity to do the same, and was glad that it was for his favorite lady on earth, Queen.

"Don't cry," Cousin Buddy said sweetly as he gave his prized possession to her.

Both Lamont and James were upset to see their favorite aunt cry like that, until it occurred to them that perhaps her tears were filled with joy. She had, after all, been after both Miss Baby Doll and Mr. Lacy to turn their lives over to Christ.

"You have an incredible testimony, don't you?" Eddie asked, anxious to discover how the Lord had moved in this woman's life.

"Yes," Baby Doll whispered, surprised at the calm she felt.

She had always thought that getting saved would hurt—that it would be a violent wrenching from the world as she knew it, to become a child of God. Queen Esther was so right when she always said, "You know the devil is a straight-up liar." Because the lie she had believed all of these years was that her sins were so great, her life so poorly lived, her mistakes so expansive, it would take a

whole lot of pain to get saved. She thought that she would
hurt real bad, like the time she was beaten mercilessly
by a petty drug dealer when she was a dime short the
first and last time she took a mind to work in that area of
"commerce."

"Mister," she slurped out, drawing Eddie's attention to
her mouth and what looked like the putty cast a dentist
took of your teeth. He thought that her maneuvering of
those things like they were real dentures had to be one of
life's great mysteries.

Ironically, to those who knew Baby Doll, she was actually looking pretty good this morning. She wasn't wearing dark-colored socks in those yellow jelly shoes, her
face was softer and rounder, she had gained some weight,
and her clothes were not hanging off her body. Her hair
was different, too. Gone were the funny-looking braids,
colored rubber bands and barrettes. Instead, her coarse,
natural gray hair was clean and shimmering in a becoming arrangement of sophisticated twists.

"Mister," she slurped again, "I have lived down in
the hellhole of sin. I've seen thangs, and heard thangs,
and done thangs, and thought about doing thangs that
would give most of these finely dressed folks up in here
nightmares on end. I've been insane, locked up in the
crazy house, homeless, drunk, high, you name it. But
I am still here and I am blessed. And my friend sitting
over there . . ."

Baby Doll pointed to Queen Esther.

". . . she told me all about Jesus and made me know just
how much I've been blessed. And I want to tell the Lord
that I am sorry for all of my sins. And I want the Lord to
forgive me. And I want to be saved and receive the Holy

Ghost and to give my life entirely over to Jesus. Can you help me do that, Mister?"

Eddie and Rev. Quincey started laughing, as two of the three assistant pastors came and joined them at the altar. This was something they all wanted to be a part of.

"Mother," Eddie said to Johnnie, "did you bring your anointing oil with you?"

Johnnie nodded as she dug in her purse around that big gun and found the oil. The same usher who had been doing her bidding all morning hurried to her side to get the bottle. He placed it in the bishop's hand and sighed with relief when Mother Tate smiled at him.

Eddie poured oil onto the palms of his hands and then passed the bottle around to every minister except Parvell. When everybody was "oiled up" to their own satisfaction, they surrounded Baby Doll and laid hands on her.

"Give the church your name."

"My name is Baby Doll Henderson-Lacy because I just married my man, Lacy, here last week, y'all," she chirped and slurped, every bit the blushing bride.

Mr. Lacy puffed up at that announcement and laughed his trademark "heh, heh, heh."

Rev. Quincey had heard the term "love is blind" practically all his life. Never had it been as applicable as it was right now. He'd never met a couple who so perfectly balanced each other out. He sneaked a glance over at his wife, Lena, who was so tickled, she could hardly sit up straight and keep her mind "stayed on Jesus."

Obadiah narrowed his eyes to make Lena behave, working hard to keep those "church chuckles" welling up in him from spilling out. There was nothing worse than something happening right in the midst of the most serious part of a church service and it was so funny it made your sides hurt from keeping the laughter in check.

Bishop Tate put his right hand on Baby Doll's forehead and said, "Do you confess that Jesus is Lord? Will you make Him Lord of your life? Do you believe that Jesus was raised from the dead? And do you humbly confess and repent of your sins?"

"Yes," she stated loudly. "Jesus is Lord. He is Lord of my life. The Bible says that He was raised from the dead and I believe the word of God and I believe He was raised from the dead. I humbly confess and repent of all of my sins."

Eddie smiled broadly.

"You are saved, Mrs. Lacy, in Jesus' name."

Rev. Quincey smiled at her and said, "Let the congregation say amen."

"Amen."

"Louder. Y'all, somebody just got saved. That's something to shout about!"

"AMEN!" The congregation said loudly and with great enthusiasm.

"That's it, Mr. Pastor?" Baby Doll asked sweetly.

"Not quite," Rev. Quincey said. "Don't you think you'll need a church home to grow in your newfound salvation?"

This time Baby Doll started to cry. It had been a long time since anybody had invited her to join anything.

"You mean I can join this church and be a member?"

"Yes, you can. Just turn around so that the congregation can extend you the right hand of fellowship."

Baby Doll turned around and smiled. Then she held up

her hand and said, "Mr. Pastor Man, may I please give a gift to my new church?"

"Yes," was all Rev. Quincey said.

She looked up at Jarnquez in the choir loft and said, "Baby, I can sang. Will you help the musicians to follow me as I sang this song for the Lord and my new church?"

At that point, everybody, including the ministers and the bishop, took a seat and got real quiet. Parvell, who had just been readmitted into the sanctuary by the ushers, sat down next to his Uncle Big Gold—whose presence at the service this morning was a shock even to him—and waited to hear this song.

Bug leaned over to Theresa and whispered, "I show hope your cleaning lady can *sang*."

Baby Doll reached into her skirt pocket and pulled out the red plastic teeth box. She slipped her mold teeth out of her mouth and then put them in the box and snapped it shut. She started humming the hymn "Come, Ye Disconsolate."

Jarnquez gave the pianist and organist her key and instructed them to play one verse of the song. Baby Doll smiled and held out her hand for the portable microphone Mother Johnnie's usher had just retrieved from the bishop and started into her song. It had been a long time since she had sung anything in front of anybody but Lacy. And nobody but the Lord had ever heard her sing a church song. She hoped that her memory didn't fail her with the words too badly when she opened her mouth to sing:

Come ye dis-con-ti-nent . . . where is de language . . .
Come to ha' mercy street . . . fervently kneel.

Com'ere brang yo' wounded hearts, Com'ere tell yo'
    quaintance;
Earth ain't got no sorrow heaben cain't heal.

The only thing that kept that church, especially the
youth choir, from howling with uncontrolled laughter was
how beautiful Baby Doll's voice was. She sounded like
Gladys Knight. So, when she started singing the verse
once more, folks forgot her words and only heard what
the Lord wanted them to hear, which was:

Come, ye disconsolate, where'er ye languish,
Come to the mercy seat, fervently kneel.
Here bring your wounded hearts, here tell your
    anguish;
Earth hath no sorrow that heav'n cannot heal.

At first, Lamont was just as tickled as the next person
at Miss Baby Doll's rendition of the hymn. But as he sat
there, hymnal in hand, reading the correct words while
listening to her beautiful and obviously anointed voice,
tears started streaming down his cheeks. Here he was,
with so much to be thankful for, and a woman who had
seen every negative aspect of life imaginable, was standing in the very spot where he needed to be.

Mr. Lacy had heard his beautiful wife sing to the
songs on the radio and sound better than some of the artists she was singing with. But he'd never heard her sing
for the Lord, and the difference between the two was
night and day. When they first walked into the church,
all he wanted was for his Baby Doll to find Jesus and get

herself right with the Lord, so that she would feel better about herself. He'd never had much use for church or church folk. And in fact, Lacy had found far too many of them either truly lacking in the faith they professed, or as big a hypocrite as there ever was—like the so-called Rev. Parvell Sykes, who he didn't think was any better than his Uncle Big Gold.

But this morning, Baby Doll's testimony got next to him. It made him remember what colors looked like before he lost his sight in the Vietnam War. It made him remember what a Carolina sky looked like when it was truly "Carolina blue." It made him remember just how good one of those big, sexy ghetto booties looked in a tight red skirt. Lacy remembered, if only for a fleeting moment, the beauty that filled a woman's eyes when she knew that you were truly making love to her with all your heart.

And when his wife started singing that incredibly beautiful song with all those crazy lyrics, he remembered the promise he made to the Lord if he sent a platoon to rescue him, when he'd been shot down by "Charlie," and was lying in a pool of his own blood, suddenly blind and hoping that he wouldn't die in a foreign and hostile land. At the moment, Lacy told the Lord that he would give Him his life if he lived to see another day in the good ole US of A. It wasn't until this day, that he was born all over again to see so many new days with eyes that were not born of the flesh but of the spirit of his sweet Lord.

Lacy fell prostrate at the foot of the altar, hoping that his tears didn't turn into heart-wrenching sobs. God had been so good to him all these years, and all he had given Him back in return for those blessings was a heart hardened by the pain and bitterness of knowing that he'd never be able to use his natural eyes to see again.

"Father, please forgive me all of my sins. Please redeem me, save me, and make me worthy of one day living in Your Kingdom so that I can see Your face and hear Your voice say, *Well done my good and faithful servant.* For I would rather be a doorkeeper in Your house, Lord, than to set foot in the finest palace filled with wickedness and people who don't know You."

Baby Doll ended her song and bent down to help her husband get up, so thankful that the Lord had answered her silent prayers for her dear, handsome Lacy.

Rev. Albertson and Rev. Simmons hurried to give their assistance, while Eddie said, "Church, the Lord has done some mighty work up in here this morning."

"Amen," sounded out all around the church.

"And, I believe He has one more mighty work to perform. You see, there is someone in here who was raised to know the Lord, was saved at a young age and then strayed away from what he knows to be right. You know who you are. God is waiting on you to come back home."

Once more the church was quiet and still. A whole lot of folk were practically praying for the strength to *stay still*, and not start looking around the sanctuary to find out who the "you know who you are" was.

Lamont felt a fire in his heart and then something he'd heard talked about but never felt himself. In fact, he hadn't been too sure that "fire shut up in your bones" was even a real phenomenon. But if he weren't sure then, he sure was certain now. That fire that started in his chest had now spread across his entire body and felt like it was shut right up in the marrow of his bones.

Lamont stood up and walked as coolly as he could down to that altar. As soon as he grabbed ahold of the bishop's hand, his mother stood up and started shouting, while his aunt ran right out into the aisle and did the holy dance without one note of music.

That did it. He couldn't stay cool one second longer. Lamont fell right down on his knees at that altar, and raised his hands up high, and called out, "I love you, Lord. Thank you, Jesus. I'm home, I'm home."

Jarnquez got up and said, "Start singing: *Just as I am without one plea, But that Thy blood was shed for me. And that Thou bidd'st me come to Thee, O Lamb of God, I come! I come!*"

Rev. Quincey reached out and helped Lamont to his feet. He had been praying for his friend for years. And there were times when he almost felt like giving up because it seemed as if Lamont was so hardheaded and prideful that the Lord wouldn't be able to make a dent in his rigidly set heart. But here was the answer to his prayers standing before him with a repentant spirit and a thirst for the Lord. The tears streamed down his own eyes as he beckoned to James to join his brother at the altar.

James had been praying on Lamont, too. And like the pastor, had agonized over his brother's determination to hold on to the world. As good a man as his brother was, he had that hard edge that comes from being in the world. Lamont believed his hardness accounted for his "confidence" and "business acumen." At least he believed that mess until he ran up on the brick wall called the Durham Urban Development Committee and realized that he needed a serious and very *un-worldly* friend—Jesus.

And James also secretly thought that same worldliness

is what made Lamont so reluctant to find a better way of relating to Gwen. In the world, folks come up with all kinds of inept ways to compensate for a wrong they've committed against someone. But in the body of Christ, that same person would go to the Lord, ask for His forgiveness, repent, and then seek out someone to pray for and with them on the matter. In Christ, Lamont would diligently seek the Lord's guidance concerning the matter.

James put his arms around his beloved big brother and said, "We've been waiting on you for a long time."

Bishop Tate knew that what he'd been sent to the church to do this morning was now complete. He hadn't even known that the Lord had a specific task for him until he located the two individuals on assignment to stymie the flow of the Holy Spirit during the service and interfere with the salvation process. The first was Parvell Sykes. And the second was the extremely well-dressed misanthropic older brother (who bore a striking resemblance to Sykes) sitting all the way in the back laughing at the service like he was watching a comedy show. But that changed in a heartbeat when Mrs. Lacy got saved and turned the church out with anointed singing that gave new meaning to the term "malapropism."

As soon as she belted out that first line of side-splitting misapplied lyrics, that man hopped up and left the church so fast the heavy swinging doors practically revolved in a 360-degree turn.

"If there's one thing the devil can't stand," Eddie thought, "it's the conversion from sinner to saint."

Chablis Jackson thought she'd seen everything when that lady joined the church and took her teeth out to sing a song, sounding like Gladys Knight and using all of the wrong words—a Kodak moment if there ever was one. Then, to put icing on the cake, that blind man fell out and got saved, even though he looked like he could sniff a fifth of Hennessy dry before he got around to taking the first sip from his shot glass. But what truly should have given sight to that little red blind man was her ex-man rededicating his life to Christ.

"Lamont Green is a man of God," she whispered incredulously, wishing that whatever was rolling up on folks in this church this morning would rub off on her mama long enough to make her remove those yellow rubber gloves and stop trying to sneak and wipe off the back of the pew with a tiny hand-wipe.

Shirley was wishing the same thing herself. She knew Baby Doll from back in the day. And if that girl could get saved and delivered, there had to be hope for her and her condition. Just the thought got Shirley all worked up and anxious to get down to that altar for prayer.

Gwen was absolutely flabbergasted. In all of the years that she'd known her ex-husband, she couldn't have ever imagined him getting to this point. At times she'd wondered what it would take to get him to give his life back to Christ. And all the time it was being faced with a problem that couldn't be solved with hard work, discipline, organization, multitasking, and confidence. He finally recognized that everything he had and was and could do, even his revered "confidence," was from God.

Bernice was so thankful for all of the people who had turned their lives over to Christ. And it was such a blessing for Baby Doll to come to church and get right when Big Gold—the man who had single-handedly helped her right out of her mind—was making a rare appearance in church. When God said that vengeance was His, He was not playing. She glanced over at her daughter, Theresa, and almost started laughing. That girl was ecstatic over Lamont rededicating his life to Christ and getting filled with the Holy Ghost.

Bernice knew from experience what it meant to have a saved husband. With a saved man, time and energy were not wasted on harsh words, too little compassion, limited understanding, and a hardness of heart that interfered with the man's ability to love his wife as his own flesh.

Men who had not given their lives over to Christ listened with what they believed were rational, linear, intelligent and "just the facts, ma'am" ears. Saved men asked the Lord to open their hearts and ears to what their beloved was saying, no matter how emotional and "nonlinear" the words might appear on the surface. If a saved man had trouble understanding his wife, he knew he could always go to a better source than her—the Lord—to make even the most convoluted conversation crystal clear.

Theresa held her head back so that the tears wouldn't roll down her cheeks. To see Baby Doll get saved and then bring Mr. Lacy to the Lord was something. But watching the big, bad Lamont Green humble himself before the Lord was a miracle.

"Lord," Theresa began praying silently, "touch Lamont's heart and let him know that I am the one you have picked out for him," before it occurred to her that this was the first time she'd had this kind of revelation concerning her feelings for him.

Charmayne reached into her purse to send a text message to Jethro Winters that he might be in for a serious fight with Lamont Green, then changed her mind. She didn't have a clue as to what she could say to help Jethro understand what he was up against, now that Lamont's confidence and skills would be girded up with weapons from the Lord. That would be just too "Negrolistic" and obscure for Jethro to wrap his very carnal intellect around.

Chapter Fourteen

Less than two weeks after that memorable service, Lamont attended his first meeting with the Trustee Board to plan for the church's Christmas Festival. Generally, this activity was planned and implemented by the missionary groups. Rev. Quincey, however, had requested the administrative change this year, to aid in the Fayetteville Street Church's efforts to raise money for Green Pastures' closing cost grant program. There were several families in the congregation who wanted to live in the new Cashmere Estates, and many of them would need assistance with securing financing and money to purchase a home.

Lamont had hesitated about joining the Trustee Board when the pastor first issued the invitation. But James and Bug, who were also members of the more powerful Steward Board, were overjoyed to be able to work with Lamont on behalf of their pastor and church. And they both believed that he would receive so many unexpected blessings from giving of himself and his time in this way.

If there was ever a time when Lamont could benefit from unexpected blessings, it was now. The pending battle between Green Pastures and Jethro Winters's company could get nasty. Plus, there were so many opposing con-

cerns embedded in this challenge—black/white, sacred/
secular, rich/poor, old-guard/new-school, old money/
need money. The morning paper had, in fact, displayed a
cartoon with a tiny Lamont Green looking up at a gigantic
Jethro Winters while holding a slingshot in his hand.

Lamont was the first one to enter the men's parlor. He
had forgotten how much he liked this room, with its inviting masculine decor—high-backed black leather chairs,
black lacquered conference table, platinum carpet, gray
silk draperies, and an enormous lead crystal vase stuffed
with fresh lilies.

He had stood in this very room waiting to get baptized
at twelve. He had knelt down on his knees in this room
when the church fathers had blessed him and prayed for
his business. He had stood in this room waiting to enter
the church for his first marriage over twenty years ago.
And he had slumped down in one of those black leather
chairs when the pastor told him that his wife wanted out
of the marriage.

Lamont sat down in what for him was the most comfortable seat in the room—at the head of the table.

"Good evening," came from a biting voice that sliced
right through Lamont's peace. His home training kicked
into gear, and forced him out of his chair and on up to
extend a hand, despite the fact that he felt like doing just
the opposite.

"Sykes."

Parvell grabbed Lamont's hand in what he thought
was one of those threatening, hand-crushing grips. He
frowned when Lamont stared him dead in the eye and
then gripped his hand in a painful iron vise, refusing to let
go until he saw color draining from Parvell's face.

"Still play-acting with God, Green," he said, in an effort to recover some of his dignity after that excruciating handshake.

Lamont sat back down, refusing to honor Parvell's petty retort with a response. If *anybody* knew about "play-acting with God," it had to be Sykes, with his closet full of costumes to go with his starring role.

Parvell took a seat directly across the table from Lamont, gingerly fingering the sterling silver lion head carving on one of his signature canes, as if he were waiting for the most important meeting in Durham County to start. Lamont couldn't help but wonder why he would wanted to be involved with something as unpretentious as the Christmas Festival the church sponsored every year.

Lamont thought about calling James on his cell and telling him "thanks but no thanks," when Theresa walked in with Bug and Vanessa, only to be followed by James with Rhonda in tow.

He couldn't take his eyes off Theresa, who was looking awfully fine in butternut-brown suede jeans, a cream silk turtleneck sweater, chocolate suede ankle boots, and a chocolate suede baseball cap on her head. He loved the way she wore her makeup—a whisper of pale brown shimmer on her eyes, sexy eyeliner that gave her eyes that smoky look, warm blush on her rich brown cheeks, and a sheer reddish brown tint of gloss on her full and pouty-shaped lips.

And that perfume—Euphoria—made Lamont want to pull the girl on his lap, give her round behind a good, open-palm slap, and whisper, "Who's yo' daddy, baby," in her ear.

About the only person in the room who missed

Lamont's reaction to Theresa's entrance was Theresa. James and Rhonda wanted to shout, along with their co-conspirators, Bug and Vanessa.

They had been praying on Lamont and Theresa so much and so hard until Rhonda now had a joke about it, where she said, "The phone rings in heaven. Gabriel answers it. The Lord says, 'Who is it?' And when Gabriel says, 'Guess?' God just sucks on His teeth, shakes His head, and says, 'I've got some uprisings, a war, and a host of other needs to attend to, and they 'bout to worry my last heavenly nerve on Lamont and that Theresa girl. Handle my business, Gabe, before I have to hurt somebody in Durham, North Carolina.'"

Parvell knew he should have taken Roxanne up on her offer and gone to her house for dinner. There was nothing worse than having to watch a woman who used to belong to you get all excited over the mere sight of another man. Because that is exactly what Theresa did when she laid eyes on Lamont Green.

But that was all right. After next week's meeting with the DUDC, he had something that would loosen Green's grip on things. Parvell was confident that this committee, made up of four-white-folks-strong with one-lone-black-voice-for-decoration, was not voting to rebuild "the projects." No, those folks wanted to build the committee's war chest, get a few developers with deep pockets in the palm of their hands, and get their scratchy palms soothed with green from time to time. Plus, they wanted to get more white folks in that expanse of well-placed land and real estate near Downtown, Highway 40, Bull Durham Ball Park, and Duke University—land now inhabited by folks who would not be able to afford houses with a minimal asking price of $350,000.

This project was only the beginning. Parvell was looking to expand his business from selling real estate to development. All of those underdeveloped and currently unvalued properties extending from Downtown Durham, down Mangum Avenue, and East Durham were ripe for the picking. He could make a killing if he played his cards right.

Parvell contemplated leaving for the second time in less than thirty minutes. Rev. Quincey was running late. There was one too many Greens in the room. The chance that Queen Esther Green would make an appearance was great. And it would be his misfortune that Baby Doll Henderson and her new husband would roll up in here quoting scripture in the exact same way that she belted out the words to that hymn the day they joined church.

If that woman came up in here grinning and slurping at everybody in the room but him, he would lose it and snatch those ridiculous denture casts right out of her mouth. Anybody who knew anything about Baby Doll also knew that there was no love lost between her and the Sykes family. This was especially true for his Uncle Big Gold, who had pretended to be her first husband's friend, just so he could get up in their house and have a clear path to the man's wife. Then he lied to Doll, who was young, pretty, frustrated taking care of those babies all day while her husband, Davy Crockett, slept, and lonely at night while he worked and the babies finally went to sleep.

Parvell was about to leave when he started vibrating. He glanced down at the cell attached to his belt and checked the number—Charmayne.

"I'm in a meeting," he said with obvious irritation in his voice.

"At church," she asked, as she pulled up next to his Mercedes in the church parking lot, her worry over him being with Roxanne Daye gone.

"Why?"

"I have the check from Jethro for the Christmas Festival," she told Parvell. "He thought that throwing a li'l somethin'-somethin' at the church would make it hard for Rev. Quincey to choose a side when the press contacted him. Because you know that the press is coming to him to get an opinion on all this. And there's nothing like money to help somebody forgo expressing one."

"Why didn't you tell me that when you first called?" Parvell demanded, and got up to meet her at the door when it was clear that everyone in the room, including the newcomers, Rev. Quincey and the first lady, along with that dag-blasted Queen Esther Green, and Cousin Buddy Green of all people, rolled up in the conference room. There were just too many Greens in this room.

Charmayne's cell went off and she thought Parvell had hung up on her. She was about to push redial and cuss him clean out, when she saw him standing at the door and holding it open for her.

"Thank you," she said and then stared him up and down, trying to figure out what was off about him. He wasn't wearing a suit. In fact, his gray cords, matching gray silk turtleneck, and navy suede field jacket were so sharp, the outfit *almost* made him look like one of the rest of the brothers.

"The check—how much?" Parvell queried, miffed that Jethro hadn't even told him he was donating some money, and then had given the money to Charmayne, providing her an edge over him in all of this. His cell vibrated again—Roxanne.

"Excuse me," he said smoothly and walked away from her to take the call.

At first Charmayne decided to be polite and wait as Parvell took his call. Then she heard his voice go down to the "girl let me hit that" decibel, when he said, "Hmmm, baby, you really wearing that? My, my, my."

Charmayne moved closer to where Parvell was standing. He moved and she moved again. He moved some more and she moved some more. He inched away another foot, she inched up on him a foot and a couple of inches. Finally, he stopped talking, gave her a nasty look, and then tried to shoo her away.

Charmayne sucked on her teeth and backed up off of him. Then, when he wasn't paying her any mind, she eased on into the men's parlor to handle her business.

"*Suck-ah,*" she whispered and laughed softly. If she had just a teaspoon and a half more tolerance for Roxanne, she would have called that heifer and encouraged her to give Parvell a hard time for not rushing over to see whatever the skinny skank was "wearing." But she couldn't stand her. Plus, the skank was on a mission to become Parvell's *"boo,"* and probably wouldn't be inclined to have some fun at his expense with one of his other women.

The first person who saw Charmayne was Theresa, who thought she was dressed more for an audition for a video by the rapper 50 Cent than church—even if it were a Tuesday night. Because that tight, sage green, jersey knit V-neck dress was so short, it showed off more of those Tina Turner–quality legs in sage fishnet stockings than was necessary.

The men couldn't resist taking a quick peek at her sparkling green patent leather, ankle-strap shoes with those four-inch clear heels. Rhonda and Vanessa wondered if Charmayne had a stripper's pole somewhere in her house.

"Are you sure you're in the right room? No," Bug continued, "let me be more frank. Are you sure you're even in the right building? This is 'chutch' and the Christmas Festival Committee meeting . . . and not . . . uh, The Place to Be."

Charmayne couldn't stand that Bug Hopson from way back in the day, when they were at W. G. Pearson Elementary School. She ran her tongue across her lips, and went and stood right up on Bug, but quickly retreated when she saw the "I will slap you" expression on Rhonda's face.

"Too bad that heifer is up in here tonight," Charmayne thought. "'Cause Bug Hopson is looking kinda appetizing with that Omega Psi Phi fishing hat dangling on his head."

Another glance at Bug, who bore too strong a resemblance to Theresa for her comfort, brought Charmayne back to her senses. No matter how tempting the "hors d'oeuvre," Bug was still a Hopson. And the Hopsons and the Robinsons never did have much love for one another.

She flung her new weave around and then reached down in her cleavage and pulled out a check. She curled up her lips and said, "I know exactly where I am, *Dawg*. And why don't you take this check from one of my more prestigious clients."

James took the warm, perfume-scented check and

opened it—$1,800.00. He smiled. Sometimes white folks like Jethro Winters truly believed that black folks, especially what he considered to be the "churchy" ones, could be bought for what amounted to a few fried fish and slaw dinners.

"Your *esteemed* client is kinda cheap, ain't he?"

"Cheap," Charmayne said, indignant. "You ought to be glad he gave you twenty-five cents, with the way your brother been dogging him out."

James fingered the check and then gave it to Rev. Quincey, who opened it and laughed. Quincey put the check in Lamont's hand and said, "We don't have to take this, you know."

"No, take the money," Lamont answered him, thinking that once more the Lord had been on his side. Because in an effort to encourage Rev. Quincey to keep his opinion about Jethro Winters's business dealings to himself, Winters had given the opposition a signed document—his own check—that proved his "support" of whatever the church's Christmas Festival money was used for—in this case, Green Pastures. And there was a whole lot more money pledged than this chump change. Lamont didn't have anywhere close to the resources of Winters's corporation, and he always kept ten grand in his petty cash flow. So, he knew this tidbit didn't amount to much more than booty call money for Jethro's "boo," Patty Harmon.

Bug removed his fishing hat and sat down. No need to argue with Big Bro on that one—especially when it occurred to him what Lamont was already thinking.

Rev. Quincey picked up on the train of thought, too, and grinned. He held his hand out for the check and said, "Ms. Robinson, I believe that our manners have been remiss. Please tell Mr. Winters that Fayetteville Street Church is grateful for his donation and will put this check to good use."

Charmayne, who'd been gearing up for a fight, suddenly felt all her steam evaporating into dry nothingness. Something didn't feel right. These Negroes were just too slap-happy over this little miserly check for her comfort. She studied Lamont Green for a moment.

"You need anything else?" the pastor was asking, hoping she'd take the hint and leave. Last thing he wanted was Jethro Winters's satellite sitting up under them, gathering information to send back to her command center.

"No," Charmayne said and walked to the door, bumping into Parvell.

"Have I missed anything?" he asked.

"No," Charmayne said again and left. She wasn't about to tell him a thing. Charmayne loved Parvell and she was going to get him good for not returning that love. She couldn't stand that the Negro acted like nothing was going on between them in public. And worse than that, he was now parading that old stuck-up, Roxanne Daye, around like she was the best thing since being able to buy tickets for the new North Carolina lottery.

"Well," Rev. Quincey said, "maybe we can get down to the business we're here for—the Christmas Festival. Miss Theresa, Bug told me that you are playing Mrs. Claus? And Lamont, you are Santa, right?"

Before Lamont could say yes, nod, shrug, or catch a twitch, Parvell hopped up. He just couldn't stand being in this room another minute and not address the real reason he was here.

"You know, I have some real problems with a meeting about something as asinine as who is going to play Jolly Old Saint Nick and his *'boo,'* when there are some more pressing issues that need to be on the table—like who should win the development contract from the DUDC."

"Uhh . . . this church isn't bidding for a contract, Rev. Sykes," Rev. Quincey said coolly.

"Oh, really?" Parvell spat out. He pulled last Sunday's bulletin out of his black alligator briefcase, turned to the page with a detailed history of the old Cashmere Estates, and tossed it on the conference table. "Because you certainly had me fooled."

"Well, you know what, Parvell," Rev. Quincey said like he was talking to a brother itching for an altercation on the street. "This church does support Lamont and everything that Green Pastures is trying to do to restore what used to be a wonderful and very affordable place to live."

Parvell scoffed. He was so sick of these Negroes. He said, "Everybody in this community isn't stuck on some misguided nostalgia for the seventies like you, the Greens, and members of the Hopson family," Parvell shot out.

"A few of us remember that we are in the twenty-first century and are anxious for some progress. Frankly, I am having a very difficult time figuring out what you have against building luxurious units right in the midst of black Durham."

"Because if *you* build it, many black Durhamites will not be able to afford to park in the parking lot and the area will suddenly become very white," Lamont countered evenly.

"What do you know about luxury housing?" Parvell challenged him. "You are, after all, the king of the 'new jack ghetto unit.'"

"And you really believe that 'Nino Brown' wannabe white boy you work for is coming up in this community to restore it in the right way—a way that benefits people who look just like you, Parvell?"

"Uhh . . . Dawg, there ain't too many brothers . . . err . . . people who look like him," Bug said, as he eyed Parvell's black snakeskin cowboy boots with spurs and toes so pointed he could have killed a posse of roaches in a corner.

Theresa, Rhonda, and Vanessa looked down at Parvell's feet and felt like they were going to holler with laughter. If his feet didn't look just as crazy, they didn't know whose did.

Rhonda caught her husband's eye and whispered, "I am definitely going to ask God *why* when I get to heaven."

"Let me put it to you this way, Sykes," Lamont said in a hard voice, "Jethro Winters has gone into two communities just like the one he and I am fighting over with his fancy plans, and made a big mess. The homes in Lavender Meadows in Greensboro started out selling just fine until the new residents discovered that all of those rowdy, spinning-rims, car-bass-booming Negroes in the neighborhood weren't going anywhere."

"Last time I checked, Lavender Meadows was thriving and new units were scheduled to go up in the spring," Parvell said.

"Lavender Meadows," Lamont said slowly and firmly, as if he were talking to a disobedient teen, "was bought out by a very savvy group of young black men who wanted in on a good real estate deal in the black community. They got the property for a song, lowered the prices of the townhouses to a reasonable price, sent the early buyers what amounted to real estate rebate checks, and then proceeded to sell more units to folks with strong ties to that community.

"And," Lamont went on before Parvell could open his mouth, "Winters's other fiasco, Greenleaf Park in Wilmington, went up in smoke. It seems like somebody in that neighborhood didn't appreciate those overpriced homes bringing the threat of high property taxes and possible displacement to make room for regentrification. Soon after the first five houses were built, they mysteriously burned down to the ground. His insurance company wouldn't pay unless he promised not to rebuild in that area. And he could have saved time and money, and made some money, if he would have listened to the people who practically begged him to build affordable housing in that community."

Lamont threw up his hands in exasperation. "I don't know why, for the life of me, that Durham is even entertaining becoming involved with anything that Jethro Winters is involved with. A mess waiting to happen, that's what that is."

"And Springland Hills in Charlotte is evidence of this pending disaster, right?" Parvell stated. "Because I believe that Winters tripled his investment on that development. So, what do you have to say for yourself on that one, Green?"

"He ain't got to say jack to you on nothing about nothing dealing with that no-good nothing you supporting,"

Queen Esther, who had been unusually quiet this evening, said and stood up holding a roll of quarters in each hand, looking like she was just itching for a fight.

"Buddy," she ordered, when he rose to stand at her side, "go on back over there and sit down."

"But I'm ready to go home and watch my show," he said, still standing with his helmet up under his arm like he'd seen the football players holding theirs at one of the Eva T. Marshall University home games.

"Buddy," Queen Esther stated firmly, "I told you before we left the group home, that Mr. Quentin would record the *Powerpuff Girls* for you and put the DVD in your room. Now, go back over there and *sit down*."

Cousin Buddy scurried over to his favorite seat and threw his helmet on the floor. He bent over and picked it back up when Queen Esther shot him a glance that clearly said, "I ain't playin' with you, Buddy."

Rev. Quincey removed his glasses and put two fingers on the bridge of his nose, not daring to look at his wife, Lena, and praying that he wouldn't break down in laughter. Buddy Green, despite his obvious special needs, was a character—all of those Greens were, including Lamont, who thought he put the K in Kool.

"Green, are we going to keep wasting time with Forrest Gump here, or attend to the matter at hand, before that unnecessary disruption," Parvell snapped.

"'Cccccuse me, Rev. Sykes," Buddy interjected politely, "but Forrest Gump ain't in this room. I hope you ain't been dranking nasty, drunk-man-on-the-corner wine to make you think that a made-up movie person is in this room. Even I know that, and I have to live in the special home Lamont built for me and my friends 'cause I cain't live by myself."

At that point, Rev. Quincey, along with everybody but Parvell, broke down into hysterical laughter, making Buddy wonder what was wrong with what he said.

Lena Quincey saw the concern cross Buddy's face and said, "It's okay. What you said was absolutely perfect, Buddy."

"Say Amen, lights," Rev. Quincey said and laughed some more.

"Not a thing will be this funny, when the DUDC announces that I have won . . ."

"I?" James quizzed him, wondering when this two-bit player in the housing game became the *"I"* in that white boy's company. Cousin Buddy was on to something. This Negro *had* to be drinking "nasty, drunk-man-on-the-corner wine" to say some foolishness like that.

"Yeah, Rev. Sykes," Queen Esther said, "you are a much bigger fool than I've ever thought you were, to think Jethro Winters is gonna give you more than an 'I-full' of some house Negro scraps from his table."

"Sister Green, Sister Green," Parvell said, the tone in his voice set to appease her, as if she were kind of crazy and he was trying to stop her from flipping out. "There is no need to dig specks out of my eye, when your vision is a bit askew due to the board in your own. We are in church . . ."

"If you don't shut up talking to me, with your old Mr. Big-dressing, pimp-daddy, Beelzebub self, I'm gone catch a case up in this here church so bad, somebody going over to Mr. Duke's hospital, and it ain't gone be me," Queen Esther said, as she gripped those rolls of quarters in her hand tight, and started making her way over to where Parvell was standing.

James, Lamont, Rev. Quincey, and Mr. Lacy, who had just come in looking for the pastor, hurried over to Queen Esther to stop her from doing some serious damage to Sykes with those quarters.

"Boy, what you do to make Queen act like this?" Mr. Lacy demanded, coming through the door, cane pointed in Parvell's direction. "Do you realize that *I* taught her how to use those quarters on a body when she was working at Duke and had a long walk to her car at night?"

Parvell was still, as he gave serious thought to Mr. Lacy's claim. He needed to leave this alone. Everybody from the old neighborhood knew that not only could Mr. Lacy fight, but he loved a good, down-and-dirty physical altercation. Nobody bothered Mr. Lacy back then and nobody bothered him now.

Uncle Big Gold, in his quest to rule over the old Cashmere Estates, had once taken it upon himself to challenge Mr. Lacy—he got a beat-down that folks in the Durham 'hood still talked about to this day. And to add insult to that injury, Mr. Lacy had chased and jumped his uncle, when Big Gold tried to run off, thinking that he couldn't catch him because he was blind—*wrong*. As soon as Uncle Big Gold started running, Mr. Lacy had shaken his head, sniffed at the air like a police dog, and then took off running right behind him, jumping over and dodging everything in his way. Then, he proceeded to beat him down with those two rolls of quarters he had balled up in his fists.

Theresa, Vanessa, Rhonda, and Lena had been huddled up on their end of the table passing notes back and forth about everything that had been going on at this so-called meeting. It seemed as if everything was being put on the table but what they were going to do for the Christmas Festival.

"I luv chutch meetins'," Rhonda wrote, then passed the note over to Lena, who sneaked a peek at her husband before adding her portion to the note:

"Don't you kinda wish they would have let go of Miss Queen Esther?"

She passed it to Vanessa, who nodded and slipped it down to Theresa, who wrote: "No! Cousin Buddy would have turned it out. He can fuss with Miss Queen Esther, but nobody else better be crazy enough to mess with her around him."

The note went back around and they all stole a quick glance at Cousin Buddy, who was sitting quietly in the corner, fidgeting with his helmet and watching Parvell like a hawk.

"Nahh," Rhonda whispered. "They betta keep a good hold on her, or else it will be on up in heah."

They all nodded in agreement. Sometimes folks forgot that at six feet four and weighing in at 257, Cousin Buddy was potentially a formidable opponent.

"Look," Rhonda, who never missed anything, whispered to Lena, and sneaked and pointed to the open doorway.

"You'd think," Lena started, on a fresh piece of paper, "that we hadn't had enough drama for one evening. And now, here comes Miss Baby Doll resplendent in one of her dramatic interpretations of clothing."

Rhonda took in Miss Baby Doll's outfit and prayed that Mr. Lacy wasn't "watching" them because Baby

Doll had outdone herself this evening. She was wearing purple velvet, 1970-style knickers with rhinestone buttons on the knees, a sheer, red chiffon blouse over a gold lamé tank top, and gold tights.

"Miss Baby Doll has on some new shoes," Vanessa wrote.

"Stop! Before Mr. Lacy 'sees' us," Theresa wrote back, simply amazed at Miss Baby Doll's rainbow-colored jelly shoes.

"Where did she get those shoes?" Rhonda wrote. "They kinda crunked."

"You are so wrong," Lena whispered, making sure that Obadiah didn't see her acting up. He'd loved himself some Miss Baby Doll and would, as he said, "cut a Negro" over her.

"HER TEETH!" Rhonda wrote. "MISS BABY DOLL HAS REAL FALSE TEETH!!!"

They turned to stare at Miss Baby Doll's mouth.

"Bishop Tate paid for them," Lena whispered.

"But how did she get them so fast?" Rhonda asked too loudly, drawing attention from Mr. Lacy.

"Never you mind how she did that, missy," he admonished, losing patience with those four and all of that note writing. "You just thank Jesus that she has them. Looks good, too. Don't she?"

Rhonda almost said, "How do you know how she looks?" But she bit back those words so fast she drew blood from her bottom lip.

Before Mr. Lacy could get on her, Theresa whispered, "I didn't know she was that cute."

"Me neither," Vanessa said carefully, hoping Mr. Lacy wasn't still all up in their business.

"I'm leaving," Parvell said.

"About time," James said, as he let go of his aunt, and took the rolls of quarters out of her hands.

"You don't think you can get rid of me this easy, do you, James?" Parvell scoffed. "I am, after all, your assistant pastor, Dawg."

"Not anymore," Rev. Quincey said calmly and emphatically. He should have done this the day after Parvell came to work at his church. It never ceased to amaze him how much chaos and mess was always brewing or occurring whenever Parvell was anywhere around—a clear sign that this man was not of God and he had no business occupying the pulpit at his church.

The Lord had been pressing on Rev. Quincey's heart to get rid of Parvell. And now, he couldn't avoid the inevitable any longer. He said, "You're fired. You have a right to remain here as a member but you can't work with me anymore. And I'm sure I speak for the congregation when I say that we have had enough of you and your mess."

"You just made the biggest mistake of your life, preacher," Parvell shot out.

"No, I've just undone two of the biggest mistakes of my life," Rev. Quincey countered. "The first was letting my presiding elder convince me that you were worth keeping an eye on. And the second was not getting rid of you the first time I knew you weren't worth the trouble."

"That's what I'm talking 'bout," Lamont said out loud, throwing off the silence that blanketed the room.

"God is good," James added.

"All the time," Rhonda called over to him.

"And all the time, God is good," Theresa said as she stared Parvell dead in the eye, and then flicked her tongue out at him.

Baby Doll, who had taken a seat quietly by the door, thought that the novel she'd recently read, *Church Folk*, hit the nail on the head when it came to talking about folks who went to church.

"And to think," she murmured to herself, amused at Big Gold's nephew trying to worm his way out of this confrontation and this room without looking like the pushover that he was, "that I once thought church business was dry and stale and boring. Humph, I'm beginning to wonder if everybody up in this room need some of those medications I used to have to take when I was crazy."

As soon as Parvell had stormed out of the men's parlor and slammed the door behind him, Rev. Quincey lifted his hands and said, "I ought to know better than to allow any meeting to commence without prayer. But if we didn't start right, we show can end right. Stand so we can get this meeting adjourned."

They all stood and formed a circle holding hands.

"Father," Rev. Quincey began, "we thank you for this meeting and the blessings that came in the disguise of an altercation. For, if this meeting had not gone the way it did, I wouldn't have had the courage and impetus to get rid of Parvell Sykes. Forgive me for not having that same bold assurance in You as the Apostles on the day of Pentecost. Forgive me for not following the example of Peter, who when led by the Holy Spirit, castigated the wickedness of Ananias and his wife, Sapphira. They dropped dead, Lord, when their hidden evil was stripped bare and exposed by the Light of Truth.

"Forgive me for not trusting you and saying no when the denomination first asked me to let such a reprobate serve as a minister in this church. For, we can get so concerned with what can happen to us if we don't come across as a team player until we fail to remember the words of Psalm 56:11 when it says, *In God I have put my trust; I will not be afraid. What can man do to me?"*

"Amen, Lord," Queen Esther whispered, as the last bit of stress generated by her encounter with Parvell faded away and was replaced by the kind of peace that only Christ can give.

Cousin Buddy held tight to both Queen's and Rhonda's hands, his helmet strap secured tightly under his chin. He knew he was different. But what he loved about church, and especially his church, was that it didn't matter. People loved and cherished him in spite of his disabilities. When Buddy was at church, he felt what he had learned when Queen taught him the Bible despite his problems with reading—that God was no respecter of persons.

Lamont laced his fingers through Theresa's and felt the warmth of her hand in his heart. He didn't ever remember feeling such love and peace and comfort from the touch of any woman's hand other than his mother or his aunt. He'd felt all kinds of good things from the touch of his women. But he'd never felt it like this in his heart.

As soon as Rev. Quincey finished praying, the members of the Christmas Festival committee gathered up their things. They had not spoken one fraction of a word about the Festival. But that was all right. They knew it would come off just fine. And even better, what they were really trying to do was already done. All they had to do was sit tight and watch the Lord fight this battle just like He did for King Jehosophat, when the enemies of Judah and Jerusalem cut the fool and took each other completely out.

Lamont waited as Theresa finished comparing notes about all that had occurred at tonight's meeting with her "girls," and then collected her coat and purse.

He tapped her on the arm and said, "Come on, baby. Let's get you to your car."

Theresa gave Lamont a shy smile and followed him out of the room, trying to ignore the series of whispers and giggles lingering behind the two of them.

He grabbed her hand and lifted it to his lips as they walked to her car together. A light blue 1975 Oldsmobile Cutlass Supreme, with a white vinyl roof pulled up beside them, and eased back down low on the ground with its custom hydraulic system. Lamont reached inside his coat, making Theresa not wonder *if* he was packing, but *what* caliber of hardware was up in that jacket.

The bass on the car was booming so loud, Theresa could feel the thumping jolting her chest. It was only when they made out the tune as a gospel song by Keith "Wonderboy" Johnson that Lamont relaxed his hand and removed it from the inside of his coat.

The window rolled down just enough for them to recognize Baby Doll's face from the passenger side.

"I just wanted to wish y'all a good evening."

"Thanks, Miss Baby Doll," Theresa said, wondering what was so different about the way she was talking until it dawned on her that the new teeth made it easier for her to enunciate her words.

Baby Doll rolled the window back up and the car drove off.

"All I want to know, is where in the world did they find a '75 Cutlass Supreme in such excellent condition? And, where in the world was Mr. Lacy if Miss Baby Doll was on the passenger side?" Lamont asked.

"The first is a good question, Lamont. But I'm not so sure I want to know the answer to the second one."

Lamont laughed.

"Yeah, you have a point there, baby."

Theresa was about to comment when his telephone rang as if on cue.

Lamont looked at the caller ID and frowned, mumbling, "What in the world does she want?" as he walked away to take the very unexpected call from Chablis.

"Yes," he said impatiently.

"Look, this will only take a minute," Chablis said, wishing that she had to call anybody but Lamont Green. But she was not going to sit by while Jethro Winters rolled over her brother's neighborhood without trying to do something about it.

"I have a paper that kind of . . . uhhh . . . fell out of Charmayne Robinson's purse on Winters's plans for the neighborhood surrounding the Cashmere, when what he is calling 'Phase I' is complete. Charmayne is my girl and all. But she is not gonna help that greedy white boy roll up on my brother and his folks in that neighborhood. I just wanted to make sure that it was all right with you, if I mailed it to you."

"Sure, sweetie," Lamont said, not even thinking about

how that endearing term sounded to Theresa, who was waiting on him and looking at him like he was crazy. All he knew, was the girl had something that would blow Jethro Winters out of the water when they made the first appeal to the DUDC.

"It'll be in the mail tomorrow. I'm sending it certified."

"That sounds like a good idea. I'll call you as soon as I have it in my hands. Thank you, baby," he said and hung up the telephone, walking back over to Theresa with the biggest grin on his face.

Theresa stormed off toward her car, hurt and wishing she didn't feel like crying. Lamont hurried to catch up with her.

"Baby . . . baby . . . wait."

That was it. Theresa had reached her limit. Upon hearing that second "baby," she snapped. Walking up to Lamont, Theresa snatched that cell phone right out of his hand and threw it on the ground.

"What the—"

The surprise on his face felt good for a mere second. But it wasn't enough to satisfy the frustration that had been building up in her for some time. When the phone started ringing a second time, she jumped up in the air and landed with both feet on top of the phone. And she jumped and jumped and stomped on that phone until there were nothing left but silver and black fragments on the pavement of the church parking lot.

Satisfied and tired, feet sore from stomping on that hard metal-like plastic, Theresa hopped in her car and drove off before Lamont could say another word.

Lamont was standing in the middle of the skid marks

from Theresa's car, staring at the silver and black fragments of material that used to be his cell phone. No woman had ever even thought to challenge him on who called that number. A cell phone was, after all, sacred territory. It was the one phone a brother could expect to receive calls on and not have to deign to answer the "who was that" look. And to have a woman snatch the cell out of his hand and then to jump on it and smash it to pieces was tantamount to her rummaging through his things, finding that "black book" (which in his case was chocolate brown leather), reading it, and ripping it to shreds right before his eyes.

James, who had witnessed the entire episode, turned into the smart-alecky little brother that he was and started singing his own version of Brian McKnight's "What We Do Here." He walked up to Lamont, clasped his hand on his shoulders, knowing he was being so wrong, held up his own cell phone like he was talking on it, and sang:

"Who I talk to right heah . . . is none yo' biznez . . . And I wanna make it clear . . . oh my Theresa . . . that even tho' you're a dear . . . I'm tellin' you . . . Don't ask me 'bout what comes from heah."

James started laughing and Lamont got angrier. He did not see any humor in that little ditty, or what just happened.

"What I want to know," Lamont snapped in a nasty voice, clipping James's laughter, and making Rhonda ease away to where Vanessa and Bug were standing talking to Lena Quincey, "is what made that woman think that she could clown me like that?"

"Nothing made her think she could clown you, Big Brother. She just did."

Lamont continued to frown. James was definitely not helping with this matter.

"I don't know why you standing there acting like Theresa committed a capital crime because she tore up your precious phone," James said as he started laughing again at just the thought of Theresa jumping up and down on Lamont's cell phone. "Oh sorry. Look, you asked for it, Lamont. Even though she shouldn't have messed up your phone like that, you still asked for it."

All Lamont did was continue to frown and look at James like he had a big booger hanging out of his nose.

"Why don't your trifling butt just fess up? You've talked to some women on that cell phone like they were the 'bestest' thang in the whole wide world right in front of Theresa. And nothing or no one could persuade you to do otherwise—that is until today. 'Cause I bet you'll give some real serious thought over what you say, how you say it, and who you say it to on that cell the next time some woman calls you whenever Miss Theresa is around."

Lamont raised his hands in surrender.

"Okay. I have not handled telephone calls right around Theresa. So, sue me."

"See," James sighed heavily, "that is the problem. Your main concern is that it bothers Theresa and hurts her feelings . . ."

"Isn't it enough," Lamont queried, "that I am concerned that my calls bother Theresa?"

"No," James answered him matter-of-factly. "The calls are just a symptom. The problem is that you don't think there is anything wrong with these calls because they don't mean anything to *you*. See, you love this woman. She has first place in your heart. But you have to make it clear to her and everybody else that she has first place in your life."

"Wait a minute. If I love her—and I do—then, if I marry her, doesn't that say it all?"

"No," James replied gently, wishing that another man had explained this very womanly issue to him when he first realized how much he loved Rhonda. Could have saved him a lot of grief and frustration, if he would have just understood what he hoped to convey to his brother.

"Lamont, when you fall so deeply in love with a woman that you are going to make her a permanent part of your life, you have a responsibility to protect her from the slights and transgressions of others who may have difficulty digesting a change in how you relate to them because this woman is now in your life. What seems normal and easy for you may be something akin to an anathema to them. And without even meaning to, they will take it out on Theresa—and it's not fair for you to allow that to happen to her. You following me on this?"

Lamont nodded and got into his car.

James knew he'd said enough.

"You're still playing Santa, right?"

Lamont smiled and tapped the middle of his chest with his fist to signal that he was, and drove off.

Rhonda, Vanessa, and Lena were standing together talking and absorbing as much of James and Lamont's conversation as they could without getting caught and called on the carpet for eavesdropping.

"You better call the girl and make sure she's all right, Vanessa," Rhonda directed. She'd never seen Theresa lose her cool like that.

Vanessa pulled out her cell phone, dialed it, and walked a few paces away from her girls. She'd tried to keep her nose out of Theresa's business. But that little peeling off and burning-tire-rubber episode demanded some attention from somebody. Before Theresa could finish getting hello out of her mouth, Vanessa leaped right into the conversation.

"Why did you run off like that?"

"I don't want to talk about this with you, Vanessa," Theresa answered in her businesswoman voice.

"Oh, it's like that, huh?" Vanessa countered. She couldn't stand it when Theresa got her butt up on her shoulders like that and then got to talking in that harsh voice. "Look, I didn't mess over tires expensive enough to pay all of my bills this month—screeching out of the parking lot like I didn't have any daggone sense."

Theresa didn't say anything. And she had the nerve to try and sneak out a sniffle after all of that big, bad, and nasty talking.

"Is your behind crying? Where are you?"

"In my garage."

"Girl, how fast were you driving?"

"I dunno."

Vanessa sighed out loud. Sometimes Theresa could make you want to throw her up in a tree. She said, "Look, the Lord laid this on my heart some time ago and I have just gotten to the point where I have peace about sharing this with you."

She felt Theresa tightening up all the way through the phone and wondered if she should continue, and decided that it was now or never.

"I don't understand how you can be so assured and

faithful in the business world and then fall flat on your face when it comes to believing the Lord for a husband. Nobody can get around you when it comes to that store. But you run your own self in circles when it comes to finding a man.

"I've sat back and watched you run off a few good brothers because of your ridiculous specifications. I've heard you ask some nice man who just wanted to take you out for a cup of coffee if he'd been tested for AIDS, and then wonder why he didn't call you back. Did you really think that the good Lord would send you somebody who was HIV positive, when He knows your every thought and concern?"

Vanessa took a real deep breath and went for what she knew Theresa would swear was her jugular vein.

"And Lord help the brother who starts to like you and reveals that he hasn't always had the best credit. What hardworking black man do you know who hasn't had to deal with less than perfect credit at least once in his life?"

Theresa started breathing hard into the telephone. Having good credit was something she was so proud of, and she had trouble understanding others who didn't.

"Umm . . . hmmm," Vanessa said, sucking on her teeth. "You need to work on that one, girl. 'Cause your own brother has had a few 'flags' on *his* credit report. And one more thing—I'm not so sure you know what to do with a brother, like Lamont, who walks and acts like his 'stuff' is the best there is in all of Durham County."

"VANESSA!" Theresa exclaimed. "We don't need to be all down in that boy's clothes."

"Well, if he were your husband that is exactly where

you'd need to be. Because he is the kind of man who wants one of those Betty Wright women."

"What is a Betty Wright woman?"

"Well, okay," Vanessa said. "He wants a Millie Jackson woman."

"Vanessa, if my ears serve me correctly, Millie Jackson's music is more risqué than what I've heard Betty Wright singing. So, what's your point?"

"Lamont wants what Betty Wright calls *'a lady in the streets, a mama to the kids, and you-know-what-in-the-sheets.'"*

"Of course Betty Wright would sing like that, she's the Clean-up Woman for goodness sake! And why would I want to be like that?"

"Because that's what yo' man gone want."

"What man?"

"Lamont," Vanessa answered, thinking that this conversation sounded a whole lot better when she rehearsed it with the Lord in prayer.

"So, how did Lamont Green suddenly become my man?"

"When the Lord decided that is who he would be," Vanessa said with such an anointed conviction, Theresa felt it and knew in that instant that she was right. Only the Lord could have revealed that to Vanessa in such a way that she could believe it without a shred of natural evidence.

"You know Lamont is your husband. That's why you get so mad when Gwen calls, and then cut the pure-tee fool when Chablis called him this evening."

"That was Chablis?"

"Yes. And from what I've been able to gather from

sneaking and reading the text message James sent to Bug, Chablis has some information that is gonna rock some of the members on the DUDC's world. That is why he was so sweet with her—she had something he wanted, and this time it had nothing to do with going over to her house for an impromptu 'wine tasting.'"

Theresa started laughing.

"Girl, you are so wrong and so crazy."

"I just call 'em like I see 'em," Vanessa said, glad that Theresa was finally calming down. "Anyway, you need to let the Lord fight this battle for you. Lamont is just a man—brown dust, like a blade of grass, and no match for God. He is your husband and you know it, too. Don't you?"

"Yeah," Theresa said, wondering how it came to be that the Lord decided that her husband would be a boy from her old neighborhood—a boy just like her. And all these years, she'd thought that her husband would be some kind of "big-time something or another" with one of those impressive black family pedigrees.

But then as Romans 8:28 clearly stated in her Amplified Bible, *All things work together and are [fitting into a plan] for good to and for those who love God and are called according to [His] design and purpose.*

A sweet calm came over Theresa. It was the peace that was so perfect it pushed her past the hurt and fear of being alone without an anointed and God-selected husband to share her life with. As the Lord told Jehosophat when faced with a treacherous and powerful army bent on turning his people every which way but loose, *the battle is not yours, but God's.*

Like so many women, she'd been fighting her own

battle of loneliness and fear of never being married, instead of trusting the Lord and knowing that no matter how long her time without a husband may have appeared to her, the God of Abraham, Isaac, and Jacob was not about to leave her hanging with a heavy heart silently pleading for deliverance from the place she was in.

Ruth was out in a field gathering food so that she and Naomi would not starve. She found food, love, a husband, and the distinct honor of being King David's "Nana" or "Big Mama." If the Lord hooked up this widowed and impoverished Moabite woman in a foreign land, Theresa knew He was doing the same for her in her own hometown, with the boy next door.

Chapter Fifteen

I T HAD BEEN A COUPLE OF YEARS SINCE CHARMAYNE had been in This Ain't Your Carolina Blue Sports Bar and Grill. As she sat quietly taking in the setting, she understood why. This place, though quite comfortable and pleasing to the eye, had a bit too much early-1960s, white Southern flavor for her taste.

Most of the walls consisted of polished walnut paneling. The two large picture windows, framed with navy and white plaid curtains, offered wonderful views of Duke's east campus several stories below. The smoking lounge epitomized shabby chic with the large and comfortable chairs—some in aged and cracked black leather, others in worn navy velvet with slick nap on the arms. And adding to that ambience was the superfluous supply of Duke athletic accessories hanging everywhere. It could make a Carolina grad like Charmayne feel very out of place, especially during a heated Duke vs. Carolina basketball game.

About the only things that spoke of twenty-first-century life were the two large, flat-screen televisions in the main area. Otherwise, the sturdy wooden tables surrounded by matching chairs that were almost too heavy to lift, rough wooden floors with antique and sometimes threadbare

Oriental area rugs, kept right in step with another time—one where black folks were invited in only to make sure that the surroundings were clean and comfortable enough for the next day's crowd.

For most white folks (along with a decent showing of black folks) who wanted to hang out after work or on the weekends, the This Ain't Your Carolina Blue Sports Bar and Grill was an ideal spot that was always crowded. But whenever Charmayne wanted to hang out like this, she preferred to be in the company of people at The Place to Be nightclub, located not too far from Eva T. Marshall University.

Now, The Place to Be definitely didn't represent old-money elite like this place. But it sure was a whole lot more fun. You could get all dressed up and go over there, eat some good food, drink some good liquor, hear some good music, and dance until you sweated past your weave tracts down to the roots of your real hair. Plus, some of the Triangle area's finest and sexiest brothers were always on-site at The Place to Be.

Charmayne rattled the ice around in her drink before she drained what remained, and then dipped her fingers in the glass to get a piece of ice to suck on. She loved the taste of residue liquor on ice almost as much as she liked the taste of the liquor itself. She didn't care for prissy drinks—the ones that were all pretty and pink and dressed up with some kind of sugary something or another. Charmayne preferred old-school, black-people liquor—Crown Royal, Rémy Martin, Hennessy, and of course, Grey Goose.

"You are working the heck out of that ice, baby. Think you could do some of that twirling around on me?"

Charmayne glanced up and then around to make sure nobody was close enough to hear Jethro. She was not into white boys and didn't want to risk having a brother watching and listening, and thus ruining her chances with him. Nothing worse than having one brother say to another, "Don't waste your time, Dawg. You know she loves her Vanilla," when it was chocolate you were craving all along.

"What's wrong, *baby-gurl*," Jethro teased, as he reached out to pinch her upper arm, knowing full well that he was not supposed to touch Charmayne with that level of familiarity. As much as he enjoyed being a *white boy*, Jethro hadn't played college football and a few years with the pros for naught. He'd learned a lot from the "bros" during that time. One lesson being that very complicated maze of unspoken rules and regulations on touching that black people adhered to like it was part of the U.S. Constitution.

According to the "Black Code Handbook," only your man, or a man you wanted to be your man, was supposed to touch that tender part of the arm in a public setting. Anybody else was subject to "getting told" or worse, "slapped." But Jethro had never seen a black woman implement what he considered to be a true slap.

A slap in *his book* was pulling your hand back slightly, and rapidly hitting the cheek with a flat open palm that was meant to stun and sting. When a black woman "slapped" you, however, she pulled her arm all the way behind her. Then, with the support of her body weight, swung her arm forward, and let any and every part of her hand connect with your head, thus knocking the living daylights out of you with one "slap." Whenever he had the distinct privilege of seeing a "slap" like that, he could swear he heard the word *"WHAM"* roar through the air.

"What?" he asked, holding up both hands out to the side. "You *skeared* one of yo' homies gone see this white boy trying to get himself a li'l taste of that brown sugar the bruthas been hoarding all these years?"

Charmayne hated it when Jethro tried to be cool and use black lingo to hit on her. She said, "When will you get it through your head that you ain't got it like that with me?"

"Oh," Jethro said and sat down. "So, you think that I haven't ever crossed over that particular color line before? You think you're the only black woman I've tried to sleep with, Charmayne?"

She didn't open her mouth.

Jethro started laughing and said, "Sugar-darling, I'm a multimillionaire. I'm handsome and I'm packing more than you think."

He reached under the table and grabbed himself to press his point.

"And, there are some 'sistahs' who really think that green is the color of choice."

"So, what do you want with me, if you have a stable of brown fillies at your disposal?"

Jethro leaned toward her and whispered in the most seductive voice he had in him, "I like a challenge, baby. I like a good fight. And I've always wanted a black woman who has never wanted to sleep with a white man. Just the thought makes me hot."

Charmayne blushed. Jethro's eyes had so much lust and heat in them she felt the need to reach for another piece of ice. She'd never heard a white man talk like that.

"You sound like you got a lot of freak in you. That's what I think," she finally managed to say with a great deal of attitude.

Jethro stroked the back of her hand with one finger. Charmayne moved her hand fast. She didn't want to be touched like that again. She could feel that light touch all over her body.

Jethro laughed. He was having a ball. He would not have thought that the big, bad, bold Charmayne Robinson would blush or get shy with a man. He liked that—modesty in a woman, even a woman who'd been around the block a few times. Maybe that is what was missing from Patty Harmon—shame and modesty. And right now, watching Charmayne practically choke on a piece of ice because she honestly didn't know what to do with him, only made his unadulterated lust for her get stronger.

Charmayne had to put this white boy in his place and fast. He was far too slick and seductive for his own good. She went straight for the kill, hoping and praying that it wouldn't hurt their business alliance.

"Jethro, I will give you credit where credit is due. There are women, and especially white women, in Durham who would mow your wife down with their cars if they thought they had a chance to get with you. I've heard a few whispering about you and your *package*. And I will give you some 'dap' that you have been rocking a few worlds in this little Southern city.

"But let the record show that I have seen you dance at one or two Christmas parties. And I have concluded that you can't do a doggone thang fo' me. See, it takes a whole lot of rhythm to rock my world, *DAWG*."

Jethro sat back and snapped his fingers.

A tiny redhead with the cutest bob hairstyle scurried over to him, pen and pad in hand.

"You need anything?" she asked, obviously impressed with this extremely well-dressed gentleman, whose face she remembered from a newspaper article that didn't seem all that interesting at first glance. She wished she had taken the time to read it—could have used the knowledge to increase her tip.

"I snapped my fingers didn't I, sugar?" Jethro asked, voice full of his good-ole-rich-boy drawl that had so many of Durham's aging debutantes practically throwing their underwear at him. He took in her short navy skirt, white oxford blouse with the white lace bra peeking out, navy lace stockings, and black low-heeled shoes.

"Yes, sir," she said with a blush, "you did."

"How long you've been working at this bar, sugar?"

"Six weeks."

"I see. Well, I come in here a lot and I want you to remember what I drink, and make sure that each time you see me come up in here, to fix it and bring it to my table as soon as you lay eyes on me. Comprende?"

"Yes, sir."

"Now go over to the bar and get me a glass of Southern Comfort with a twist of lemon, a squirt of lime, a dab of brown sugar, and no ice."

"The name of the drink, sir?"

"Jethro Winters."

"Excuse me, sir. I just need the name of the drink."

"Jethro Winters."

"But—"

"Look, baby girl," Charmayne interjected impatiently.

"The drink is called Jethro Winters, after him. Now go and get it 'cause you are getting on my last nerve."

A tight smile crossed the girl's lips. She took in the information but refused to acknowledge Charmayne.

"I'll get the drink ASAP, sir."

"Jethro Winters."

"Sir?"

"That's his name, heifer," Charmayne snapped. She had enough of watching this little skeezer dissin' her, while she tried to keep the charm turned on for Jethro.

"I'll get your drink, sir," the waitress said once more and walked off. She returned in a few minutes with Jethro's drink, laid a napkin on the table, and placed the drink on the napkin. She turned to walk off without Charmayne's empty glass but was stopped short.

"He's married and not a bit more interested in leaving his wife than he is in making me the CEO of his corporation."

"How would you know?" the waitress inquired icily.

"Because I work for him and he told me," Charmayne stated and put her empty glass in the girl's hand.

When the waitress turned toward Jethro as if he needed to do something, all he did was laugh, drain his whiskey, and put his glass on her tray.

"Bring us another round. Charmayne, you want some Jethro Winters?"

This time Charmayne couldn't get mad. She started laughing.

"Naw, I don't want none of that tired mess. If you are buying me a drink, get something I can relate to."

"A Jethro Winters and some Crown."

"Now you talking," Charmayne said.

"You know something, girl," he said with one of the nicest, cleanest, and most honest smiles Charmayne had ever seen on his face. "You're not bad company, for an old mean, won't-give-anybody-any, black girl. You're a basketball fan, right?"

"Boy, pleaz," she answered. "What good Nawth Carolinian worth his or her salt ain't a b-ball fan?"

"You want some tickets to the ACC—center court?"

"What do I have to do to get those tickets?"

"Nothing, Charmayne," he said sincerely. "Look, I'll be honest. If you ever give me an inkling that you're going to give me some of that good-looking stuff you're toting around, I'm jumping on that quick. But you have my word that I'll work real hard to behave myself. I like your style, baby. You've got class and some good 'balls' for a girl. I just thought that you'd be fun at an ACC game."

"I would be," Charmayne answered him, just as serious. "But while I can take you and your mess, I'd have to cut one of those other white boys trying to hit on me. So, tell you what. Why don't you give me a box at the CIAA? It's a whole lot of fun and some doggone good basketball, too."

"Can I come and hang out with you and your folks?"

"Yeah."

"Will there be any fine sisters there interested in giving a little taste to a white boy like me?"

Charmayne just shook her head. Jethro really was something else. And even though she'd rather have her freshly done weave snatched out track by track before she admitted this—he was a handsome man. A big, rich, and well-dressed handsome man.

"Yeah. There will be some serious gold diggers dipped in hot chocolate in that box, who'll pretend to be *I Dream of Jeannie* and hop out of a magic lantern if you ask them to. You do have some deep pockets, and you're quite capable of setting somebody like that up in style. Plus, you can be fun, too, when you're not concentrating on being ruthless over making more money than you need."

The little redheaded waitress sauntered up to their table. She put Charmayne's glass down any kind of way, heedless of the spill on the table. Then, she took great care with Jethro's drink, even placing a Duke blue linen napkin in his lap.

"Speaking of gold diggers," Charmayne mumbled.

The waitress swung around, face almost as red as her hair.

"I beg your pardon," she said in a very cold and nasty voice. She was sick of this black woman giving her a hard time.

"You heard the lady," Jethro said in a voice that was so hard, she could feel his words pressing up against her cheek like cold steel.

"Sir?"

"I said—you heard the lady. She called you a gold digger. And that is absolutely true. You *are* a gold digger and you are a slut, too. Because when you went back over to the bar and found out exactly who I was, you were all prepared to do whatever you needed to do for a big tip if an invitation came your way."

"Sir, I don't know you from Adam," she exclaimed, indignant and puffing up with crocodile tears.

"Oh, you definitely know me from Adam, missy," he argued. "Because Adam is over there . . ."

Jethro raised up his drink and waved it at Adam the bartender, who nodded back grinning.

The waitress turned around to glare at her co-worker. She couldn't believe that Adam played her for a fool like that.

"The tips that I send his way to keep greedy little redheads off me are worth much more than him being concerned about you and your phony tears. Here," he added as he drained a second drink and set it on her tray. "Go and get me another . . ."

She spun around to storm off, when his voice cut right through her.

". . . another waitress before I have you fired."

"Well, I guess you got her told, now didn't you?"

"Seems like I did," he said to Charmayne grinning. "You know, as much as I like a good rump in the sack with a good-looking woman, I've never cared much for a woman who thinks she can use that rump to control me. You either want me or you don't—it's just that simple."

"So, how do you explain Patty Harmon? Because she is a gold digger if I ever saw one."

"I want Patty's vote. And she does this littl—"

"TMI . . . " Charmayne said, putting her hands over her ears. "TMI!"

"What is TMI?"

"TOO MUCH INFORMATION," she answered in a loud whisper. "Honestly, Jethro, if you weren't always trying to hit on me, I'd wonder if you've mistaken me for one of the boys, with all of the 'guy stuff' you tell me."

He smiled. Not a grin, or a smirk, or even a suggestive thought tugging at the corner of his mouth before he opened it to speak—a smile. His dark eyes sparkled and his cheeks flushed a soft, warm pink.

"Hmmm," Charmayne thought, enjoying the genuine warmth of his smile. "So that's why you have so many women and Bailey hasn't cut you with one of those extra-sharp, overpriced gourmet knives that I just know she has lying around in the kitchen."

"Penny for your thoughts, Charmayne," he said softly, wondering why this black woman from the projects reminded him so much of his wife, an old-money, crème de la crème, white Durham debutante. She was about the only woman, other than Bailey, whom he respected, and whose company he enjoyed as much.

She held out her hand and started laughing when he dug around in his pockets and pulled out a fifty-dollar bill, a platinum money clip with diamond chips formed into a J, and his Harris Teeter grocery store card, then shrugged when he couldn't find that much desired penny.

"Well, I guess you won't be getting any thoughts from me today, huh?"

"That's okay. We'll have other times to talk."

She reached under the table and pulled her briefcase up on the table.

"I like that," he said, admiring the soft blue leather satchel with Cs embossed all over it in metallic navy, gray, and brown. "Where'd you get it and would you mind if I got one for Bailey?"

"My friend, Chablis Jackson, had it special-ordered from Miss Thang's Holy Ghost Corner and Church Woman's Boutique."

"That black lady churchy store all of the black women in Durham always running to?"

"One and the same."

"Hmmm, never knew it carried merchandise that classy."

"There's a lot you don't know about black people, Jethro," Charmayne stated calmly and honestly, without any intention to offend.

He frowned and she quickly moved away from that subject.

"If you'd like, I'd be happy to call Chablis and have her get you one. Any particular color?"

"Orchid is my wife's favorite color. Orchid with purple and gray Bs on it."

"Done," she said, then added. "You're crazy about Bailey, aren't you?"

"Umm, hmm. And so few women have figured that out."

"Then why not let them go before Bailey gets tired of your extensive whoremongering?"

"Let me see what you have for me," he stated, face hard and closed.

Charmayne regretted that "Jethro Winters" was back. The man who had been sitting across from her over the past hour was so much more likable than "Jethro." She pulled out the new workup on the neighborhood bordering the Cashmere. She'd lost her notes to the original proposal—which was very uncharacteristic of Charmayne—and had to go back and do some research all over again. Although this was a good report, it would have been so much better if she didn't have to spend so much time in research at the last minute.

"Figures look good, even if the text is dry," Jethro

mumbled. "Your proposals are usually quite interesting, if not entertaining reading at times."

He kept reading, reaching inside of his breast pocket for a pen to jot down some notes.

"My only question is," he said, putting his reading glasses on, "do you have any other properties in mind to offer to the residents once this neighborhood has been bought out? And you realize that it will have to be somewhere with relatively new homes. Because about the only bargaining chip we have, is the prospect of buying a younger and newer home."

"Aren't you building some middle-income developments in Chatham County?"

"Yeah, but I hadn't planned on making the developments all-black," he answered.

"And what if they are all-black? There are plenty of all-black neighborhoods in Durham that are good places to live."

"True, but I am not in the business of housing black people. I build houses to make money—and lots of it."

Charmayne bit her lip. She had to remember that Jethro was still a rich white man with little compassion for hardworking black people like her and members of her family. Sometimes the price tag on success and money was almost too high for her taste.

She said, "So what you're telling me is that we are going to offer this money and nothing more?"

"Well you can always call a black Realtor and put back into your so-called community."

Charmayne got up and gathered her things.

"What time do we meet with the DUDC tomorrow?"

"The official meeting is at nine. But Patty got me some time with them at eight. Be there."

"Aren't I always where I'm supposed to be?"

"Yeah, and you never arrive on CP time. I like that in you, girl."

Charmayne walked off. Jethro took a moment to watch that fat butt swing on out of the bar and then went back to the proposal.

Craig Utley rarely went into the This Ain't Your Carolina Blue Sports Bar and Grill. He worked with what Lamont called "ole-skool dookies" all day long in banking, and had to have a break from them during his off hours. In fact, Craig, who truly loved the Lord and was a powerful man of God, rarely set foot in a bar. But when one of his clients insisted that they meet here for convenience sake, something in his heart urged him to say yes.

His pastor had once told them during Bible study that there were times when the Lord would lead you to go someplace that didn't make a lick of sense at the moment. But if you just trusted Him, you'd understand it by and by. And lo and behold, if he didn't get the absolute fulfillment of understanding when Charmayne Robinson zipped by him, lips tight and obviously mad at Jethro Winters.

He grabbed a seat in an unobtrusive spot, or "the cut" as Lamont would have called it, and studied Jethro. He was deep in thought as he plowed through a stack of papers, chewing on a pen, and glancing up every now and then to look for a waitress. Patty Harmon had insisted that they give Jethro some private time tomorrow morning, which most of the knuckleheads on that committee had agreed to.

Jethro stopped reading and frowned, then pulled a calculator out of his briefcase and punched in some numbers. He looked very worried and pulled out his cell phone and started frantically punching numbers.

Craig was glad that his client was running late. He pulled out his Bible, which he knew looked odd in this setting, and searched for a scripture that would speak to what he was feeling. It seemed so strange to be able to watch Jethro get unraveled. But he was thankful for that small blessing.

He was about to text-message his wife for some help with this, when verses 7, 8, 12, and 13 of Psalm 140 practically jumped off the page. It read:

> *O Sovereign Lord, my strong deliverer, who shields my head in the day of battle—do not grant the wicked their desires, O Lord; do not let their plans succeed, or they will become proud.*
>
> *I know that the Lord secures justice for the poor and upholds the cause of the needy. Surely the righteous will praise your name and the upright will live before you.*

Craig figured that Jethro must have gotten his business in order. He had put the papers away, was sitting back in his chair calmly sipping on his drink, and scoping out a woman he obviously was intent on taking somewhere for something he had no business whatsoever doing. He hoped that whatever Jethro did tonight was good to him. For all of Jethro's maneuvering and machinations, Craig knew that his man-made plans would crumble like a sandcastle swept away by a strong wave when he faced off with a business plan that had been anointed by the Lord.

He started to call Lamont but became obedient to the whisperings in his heart to let go and let the Lord work it out in accordance to His perfect way and perfect will. As soon as Craig put his cell away, he felt tremendous peace and joy. It was going to be something sitting back and watching how the Lord was going to deal with the powerful Jethro Winters and certain members of the DUDC.

Chapter Sixteen

THERESA PULLED HER HAIR UP INTO A HIGH PONYTAIL and secured it with a sparkling black and lavender band. She turned to admire her brand-new, lavender velour athletic suit with black satin piping around the edges of the sleeves and down the length of the pants. Her black, quilted satin house shoes with "Theresa" embroidered on them with lavender silk thread were the perfect complement to this oh-so-stylish outfit.

She twisted and turned in her mirror, making sure that her ponytail had the right amount of bounce in it—didn't want to look too girlish, just perky. But something just wasn't quite right. She peered in the mirror—no makeup. Even though she was at home and wanted to give the appearance of being natural, she still wanted to look good.

Theresa dusted her cheeks with blush, put on mascara, and added a feather-light touch of raisin lip gloss. She checked herself in the mirror one more time and realized that something was still missing—earrings. She went and retrieved a pair of one-carat amethyst studs set in white gold. Only thing left was some perfume—something that everybody said smelled good on her. She pulled the Hanae Mori off her perfume shelf and sprayed her neck, wrists, and clothes. She even put some in her hands and dabbed at her hair.

One more mirror check revealed that she was ready to meet Lamont Green at the door and casually hand him the brand-new cell phone Vanessa insisted she replace after stomping his to pieces. It had been Rhonda, Vanessa, and Lena's idea that she go to the trouble of dressing up in something that was what they called the "down-low knockout" gear. In other words, she was supposed to get all fixed up, while at the same time giving the appearance that she was comfortable and dressed for staying at home. While it sounded simple, pulling it off had been something of an event. It took a lot of work to give the impression that your appearance was natural and effortless.

Theresa did a quick check of the house to make sure everything was in order—fresh-scented towels, milk-and-honey-scented hand soap, hand lotion, and sandalwood-scented potpourri in the guest bathroom; fresh fruit, muffins, and pretty napkins laid out on the kitchen counter; the lighting was soft but not so soft it was suggestive; lights turned on outside; and good music. Vanessa had recommended *The Quiet Storm* show on the radio because, she said, "it gave the impression of being perfectly content to spend a simple and relaxed evening at home."

She ran around the house checking it and making sure all was just right a second time and then stopped cold, right in the middle of the family room floor.

"Why," Theresa asked herself out loud, "am I acting like this man is coming over for a romantic evening with me? He's not my man. We've never been on a date. We haven't even shared a kiss . . ."

She stopped on that one. They had shared a kiss—

the memory of it so poignant, she could still feel his lips and how the entire length of his body felt pressed up against her own. As much as Theresa wished it were not so, she was in love with Lamont Green. She hadn't tried to be in love with him but it just happened and she couldn't help it.

It had been a long time since she had loved a man. That last time she got her feelings hurt. She had moped around for weeks and played Vesta's song about the lady running to the church to verify if her man was marrying somebody else so many times, the CD started melting. She had been just about as stupid as the lady in the song, too—especially when she considered going to the church before the ceremony just like the lady in the song and making a big fool of herself. It was only after talking to her friend Yvonne, who was living in Richmond, Virginia, at the time, that she knew better than to go over there with that mess.

Yvonne had said, "Girl, it's one thing for Vesta to be belting out all of that misery about I thought it woulda been me. And like I wish I could tell the sista in the song, I am telling you—if there was an inkling of a chance the bride coulda, shoulda, woulda been you, don't you think that the brother would have said something before he was standing at the church eagerly waiting to say I Do to someone else?"

All Theresa could do was laugh. Yvonne was right. If that man would have thought anything about her, at the very least, he would have sent her a chain e-mail. Bug always told her that she was blessed to have the good sense to surround herself with friends who were Proverbs-wise and never failed to give good counsel.

He was right, too. Proverbs-wise friends were definitely a blessing. And they could stop you from doing some stupid stuff if you listened to them. She would never forget when Chablis "Table Wine" Jackson ran into the very same problem she had without a posse of wise friends.

Chablis's former man, whom she'd been apart from for three years, met and married a very sweet woman. But for some reason—despite that Chablis only saw this man once a year at the CIAA basketball conference, and shared a few "for ole times' sake" dances to a favorite slow jam at a couple of the tournament's after-parties— she managed against all rational thought to harbor the notion that one day he would woo her back into his arms. So, when she ran into the brother and his new wife at the CIAA, rather than greet them with a respectful hello and congratulations, the knucklehead blurted out, "I heard you got married."

And before the man could say a word, she leaped into, "So, why didn't you call me and tell me and get my permission 'fore you ran off and jumped the broom," right in front of his wife.

But the wife, who Theresa knew for a fact surrounded herself with wise folks, put Chablis in her place. Instead of cutting the fool, Miss Lady took her husband's hand and then looked up into his eyes with the sweetest smile lighting up her face. He was so touched until all he could do was return the favor and lean down to kiss her gently on the lips.

And before Chablis could regroup and make another move, the wife said, "Chablis, my husband is a good man. A good man doesn't desecrate the sanctity of his relationship with the woman he loves, cherishes, and is intent on making his wife by asking an old flame for permission to marry her."

She made the statement with such gentle, firm, and no-nonsense sincerity, the husband immediately apologized for unwittingly putting his "boo" in the line of fire for that insult. Theresa hoped that when she married, she had that kind of dignity and fortitude to set right an errant woman who sought to diminish and put asunder what the good Lord had obviously put together.

She checked the time—it was almost eight. Lamont said that he would stop by after he left the office at seven this evening. She found herself feeling excited, scared, and then kind of silly for getting all in an uproar because Lamont was coming to her house. Theresa took a few deep breaths to calm her nervousness, cupped her hand over her mouth to check her breath, and put three breath strips in her mouth that made her eyes water because they were so strong.

The doorbell rang just as she was about to get some water. She went to the door, resisting the urge to holler out, "Hold on, I'll be right there."

Lamont was standing on the porch, blowing into his gloved hands because it was so cold outside. She turned the knob and then remembered that she hadn't unlocked the top deadbolt and didn't have the key in the lock, either.

"Hold on, I'm coming," Theresa said, hoping she wasn't sounding too loud and country, as she ran into the kitchen and searched for one of the spare keys. Finally, she returned to the door, and fidgeted with the key and the front door just like some little old lady who wasn't sure if she wanted to let in whoever was on the other side.

She pulled the door wide open, hoping that the smile on her face wasn't so big it made her look goofy. Theresa wanted to give the impression that Lamont coming by the house like this wasn't overly special to her—when, in fact, she was so excited to see him, she had to resist the urge to jump into his arms when he walked through the door.

Lamont was still mad at Theresa for throwing that tantrum and stomping his cell phone to bits. He really didn't want to come by her house to get the new phone. As far as he was concerned, she could have just as easily mailed it to him. But he let James convince him to pick it up in person.

As soon as that door opened, and Lamont saw Theresa standing there glowing and all giggly like she was fifteen years old, he felt kind of bad that he couldn't return the favor by smiling back at her. He wondered why it was that men and women could be on different pages like that sometimes. He'd seen the same thing with his parents, and James and Rhonda.

There were times when he'd been at James's house waiting for him and talking to Rhonda. The garage door would lift and Rhonda would get excited at the mere sound of her husband's car rolling up into the garage. By the time the door beeped and James walked in, Rhonda was all lit up like a newly decorated Christmas tree.

But one look at James's face let Lamont know that his brother and sister-in-law were not on the same page. And this became evident when James barked out his concerns over what on the surface were legitimate everyday matters—like Rhonda not checking the status of her checking account before spending money, her forgetting to make a business call, or not getting enough details when she did make the call. And Rhonda, who obviously felt bad, would offer a reasonable explanation, only to get her feelings hurt when James came back with a logical criticism she honestly couldn't dispute.

But as his feelings for Theresa grew and he felt the growing pains of true love, coupled with the tangible results of all the prayers he knew were going up on his behalf, the Lord had blessed him with insight into this problem he knew many men did not have. Recently, when he was privy to one of James and Rhonda's tiffs, the Lord gave him two scriptures from the Amplified Bible.

The first came from Colossians 3:19, where it says, *Husbands love your wives [be affectionate and sympathetic with them] and do not be harsh or bitter or resentful toward them.* And the second was the more detailed Ephesians 5:33, where husbands and wives are instructed in the following way: *However, let each man of you [without exception] love his wife as [being in a sense] his very own self; and let the wife see that she respects and reverences her husband [that she notices him, regards him, honors him, prefers him, venerates and esteems him; and that she defers to him, praises him, and loves and admires him exceedingly].*

Lamont truly believed that if husbands and wives read those two scriptures regularly and adhered to them, they would always find themselves on the same page. When the wife made one of those inevitable girl mistakes, the husband would gently guide her, while at the same time taking the more frustrating aspects of the problem to the Lord— confident that the Lord would help her get it right, protect them while she worked to do it right, and show him the best way to handle these dilemmas for the two of them.

And when the husband made one of those inevitable boy mistakes, the wife would seek out the Lord's guidance for how to get it right, depend on the Lord to give her the words to explain why she had a hard time with those activities to her husband, and open her heart so that the Lord could send love and cherishing through her to her man. And he'd noticed that this last part was real hard for many women, who instead of turning things over to the Lord, tried to teach their husbands valuable lessons by doing the complete opposite of what that second scripture commanded them to do. A wife following those commandments would think twice about punishing her husband by cutting off his love supply like the utility company cut off your water when you failed to pay the bill.

Watching the radiance in Theresa's face dull, snapped Lamont to attention. The Lord had given him two valuable scriptures, and here he was practicing the very thing he'd recently admonished his brother about. He tried to think of something to say that would match what his heart told him was her excitement at seeing him. But all he managed to say was, "Close the door. It's freezing outside."

"Oh, okay," Theresa answered, at a complete loss as to what she should say next.

"You gonna let me get past the foyer? Or am I one of those type of guests?" Lamont inquired, secretly wishing that she would invite him into her kitchen to stay awhile.

"Huh?"

"I want to come in and visit, Theresa."

"You do?" she asked him incredulously.

Lamont nodded and took off his brown suede coat and matching cap, and gave them to Theresa to hang up. He walked into the kitchen, noting with great pleasure what she thought was her quiet perusal of his person. Because he certainly hadn't missed a thing concerning how good she was looking, in her "I took a lot of time putting this outfit together, to look like I walk around the house looking like this all the time" suit. He'd never seen her hair up and liked how cute and perky the ponytail looked on her. And all of that soft lavender up against her beautiful chocolate skin was getting to him.

Theresa loved the way Lamont was dressed tonight—blue jeans, thick oatmeal cable-knit turtleneck sweater, and navy Timberlands. The sweater showed off his broad shoulders and the jeans revealed a round, muscular backside. When she caught herself staring at his behind, she took a deep breath and thought, "Girl, get a grip."

"You gonna offer me some fancy tea and one of these muffins?"

"How you know I have some fancy tea?"

"Girl, pleaz," he said. "All a body gotta do is take one look at this kitchen—has fancy tea written all over it."

Theresa's eyes traveled around the familiar landscape of the kitchen and she chuckled. Lamont was right. The very pale pink-tinted walls, cream tile, pink/lavender/sky blue tiles on the counter and backsplash, coffee mugs that matched the tiles, chrome appliances, and white wooden shutters practically screamed "fancy teas, fancy teas."

"Okay, you win. What do you want?" she asked him, pulling out a lavender, lacquered-wood tea chest that was eighteen by eighteen by three inches. She opened it to reveal what had to be close to one hundred tea bags.

"Dang, girl. You really need this much fancy tea?" he exclaimed and selected one of the plainer teas in the box—Constant Comment.

Theresa reached for one of the pastel mugs.

"Oh . . . no. I ain't drinking tea out of a foo-foo mug. Get me something more substantial than that."

"Okay," Theresa said, and went and got him Bug's favorite one—a huge purple with gold trim mug.

"Thank you," he said as he enjoyed being served a moist pumpkin muffin and the tea, especially when she put the cream and sugar in it for him. "Aren't you going to have something, too?"

"Yep," Theresa answered, as she got her favorite mug out of the dishwasher, and made herself a cup of cinnamon-flavored tea. She selected a chocolate muffin and sat next to Lamont.

"I bet you eat most of your meals here, right?"

"Umm . . . hmmm," she answered with a mouth full of muffin. "It's one of my favorite spots in the house."

Stephanie Mills's "Power of Love" came on the radio. Theresa sipped on her tea and closed her eyes.

"One of my favorite Stephanie Mills songs," Lamont said softly and started snapping his fingers.

"Me, too," was all Theresa said, as she allowed herself to get lost in the pulsating blues beat of the music.

Lamont wished that they weren't sitting here eating and drinking right now. He would have given anything to grab Theresa's hand and hold her tight in his arms on what he thought was one of Stephanie's most sensual songs.

That song ended and was followed by Gerald Levert's "Made to Love You." Theresa loved herself some Gerald Levert—had every CD he'd ever made, going all the way back to when he was singing with the R&B group LeVert.

"They are jamming tonight," Lamont said.

"Yeah, they are," Theresa answered quickly, so as not to interrupt one good note of her boy's song.

That song ended, only to be followed with "You Bring Me Joy," by Lamont's favorite singer, Anita Baker.

"They must be trying to get somebody pregnant tonight," Lamont said laughing.

"Why would you say that?" Theresa asked him.

"Are you listening to all that music on the radio? It's cold outside and this music is so warm and toasty, you can't help but want to snuggle up to somebody, listening to all of that. Anita, Gerald, Stephanie. Shoot, if Marvin and Teddy Pendergrass come on next, I'm taking advantage of the moment and get all snuggled up with you."

"Boy!"

"Don't you boy me," he replied evenly. "I didn't put that music on. And neither did I make that cozy fire, crackling over there in the family room."

Theresa blushed. Her family room, with the lavender suede sofa and oversized chair, soft pale camel-colored walls, big plant in the corner, camel wooden blinds, plush charcoal carpet, and fire casting a warm glow across the room, was practically begging for them to come in there and snuggle up.

"Why did you turn out the light in the kitchen, Lamont?"

"So I could see the light in your eyes better," he whispered and took Theresa's hand and started pulling her toward the family room to sit on the sofa that had been "calling his name" all evening.

At first Theresa pulled back, not sure she wanted to venture into that family room with Lamont Green. But all he did was tug on her hand some more and slowly pull her down onto the couch next to him. He wrapped his arms around her, kissed her cheek, and whispered, "Now isn't this much nicer than a kitchen stool?"

"Uhh . . . I like being in the kitchen," she answered, sounding more like a sixteen-year-old than the smart and sophisticated businesswoman she always presented to the public eye.

"Oh you do, huh," he said and pulled at her ponytail, eyes so full of heat and desire, Theresa could have sworn she saw some flames flickering in them.

"Well . . . you know something, baby," he said seductively, "I prefer being on this cozy sofa with you."

He blew a kiss at her and then proceeded to plant a few on her neck.

At first Theresa was stiff to keep some control over the situation. Then those kisses got hotter and sweeter. And when he moaned, "Ummm," like she was a piece of chocolate candy, the girl forgot all of her common sense and melted right into that man.

Lamont cupped the back of Theresa's head and brought her mouth to his for a soft kiss on the lips.

"Baby, baby, baby. Don't know if I've ever gotten brown sugar this sweet."

He licked her lips, pushing them apart with his tongue before he got himself a big helping of a deeper and hotter kiss.

That kiss was so good, Theresa was dizzy.

"Oooo, I always wondered what Queen Esther felt when King Xerxes had her all up in his private chambers. And now I know. Oooooo," Theresa murmured.

The mentioning of his aunt's name cooled things down faster than hearing her footsteps approaching the living room when he was sneaking and getting all busy with one of his little girlfriends as a teenager.

The shift in Lamont's emotions were so strong, Theresa felt that mounting heat evaporate right into the cold front that passed between the two of them.

"Did I do something wrong?" she asked him. It had been so long since she had the pleasure of kissing and hugging a man on the couch, she feared that she was rusty on "petting etiquette."

"No . . . yes. Why did you have to mention Auntee's name in the middle of all of that good stuff?" he said irritably.

Theresa took a deep breath. She'd forgotten how prickly and snappy a man got when he was in the "I want some" zone and things came to a screeching halt. Only problem, though, she didn't remember mentioning Miss Queen Esther . . .

"Shoot," she thought, *"Queen Esther."* She said, "Lamont, I wasn't talking about your aunt. I was talking about the real Queen Esther, the one in the Bible."

"Baby," he snapped, "that's even worse. You are talking 'bout a Bible lady when I was lovin' up on you. I mean, I may not be Denzel or Morris Chestnut, or Gerald Levert, or somebody or another like that, but I would like to think that I was giving you something you liked."

Theresa laughed and reached for one of the four very beautiful Bibles she kept on the coffee table.

"You sure want to make sure you in good with the Lord, don't you, girl?"

"That's true. But I love the Bible and these four were just so pretty, I didn't want to hide them on a bookshelf."

Lamont picked up the New Living Translation version,

admiring the delicate cream silk moiré cover trimmed
with the palest of pink lace and ribbons.

"I see what you mean. This is very pretty, even if it is
way too prissy and girlie-girlie for my taste."

"That's why I have this one out," Theresa said, taking
the prissy Bible and handing him one she knew he'd like
much better.

"Now that's what I'm talking 'bout," Lamont said,
as he ran his hands over the fine buttery cinnamon-
colored leather with Amplified Bible in dark gold letters
stamped on it.

Theresa opened the cream silk Bible.

"Here, let me read you something," she said, with a
very mischievous grin spreading across her face. "These
are verses twelve through eighteen in chapter two of the
book of Esther."

"I applaud you on your Bible etiquette," Lamont said,
sounding about as excited as somebody waiting to get a
flu shot—knowing it was good for you but wishing you
didn't have to take it.

"Bible etiquette?"

"Yeah," he answered. "I've always thought it a show of
good manners to tell somebody where to find what you're
reading from in the Bible."

Theresa nodded. He had a point. Too many folks
quoted and read Bible verses and passages without giving
the listener any clue as to where it was coming from.

"Listen to this, Lamont."

"I'm all ears," he said dryly and sat back on the sofa,
with his arms stretched across the back of it.

*Before each young woman was taken to the king's
bed, she was given the prescribed twelve months of beauty*

treatments—six months with oil of myrrh, followed by six
months with special perfumes and ointments."

Lamont's ears perked up at that first verse. This was
getting kind of good. He sat up straight and said, "You
mean to tell me that a sister spent a whole year getting
ready for a date with the king, just so he could *hit that*?
And how many sisters did the brother have on hand
anyway?"

"Lamont," Theresa said in what sounded like a middle-
school-teacher voice, "Watch your mouth, boy. This is the
Bible. And to answer your question, I think it says here
what he had."

She flipped through her Bible and found the section
describing the roundup of all the fine women in the land
for the king.

"Well, actually it doesn't give an exact number but it
had to be a lot, if he could wait a year for somebody to get
ready for him."

"Read some more," Lamont said. "I've got to hear the
rest of this."

"When the time came for her to go in to the king . . ."

"You mean the flava of the evening, and not Queen
Esther, right?"

Theresa nodded and finished.

". . . she was given her choice of whatever clothing or
jewelry she wanted to enhance her beauty. That evening she
was taken to the king's private rooms, and the next morning
she was brought to the second harem, where the king's wives
lived. There she would be under the care of Shaashgaz, an-
other of the king's eunuchs. She would live there for the rest
of her life, never going to the king again, unless he had espe-
cially enjoyed her and requested her by name."

"Awe sookie-sookay now," Lamont said laughing. "Sounds to me like ole boy was not the king but the *Kang* with a capital K. The sisters were brought to his *pri-vate* rooms and if one didn't whip it up on him, he did not have to give her some flimsy excuse for not calling the next day. And if she did put some 'whip appeal' on Xerxes or Ahauserus or whatever he was calling himself, then he'd go and request the honey by name. Girl, that was one bad brother."

"Boy, you are so silly," Theresa said, trying hard not to laugh. The story *was* kind of wild when you put it in a modern context. "Let me finish reading."

When it was Esther's turn to go to the king, she accepted the advice of Hegai, the eunuch in charge of the harem. She asked for nothing except what he suggested, and she was admired by everyone who saw her. When Esther was taken to King Xerxes at the royal palace in early winter of the seventh year of his reign, the king loved her more than any of the other young women. He was so delighted with her that he set the royal crown on her head and declared her queen instead of Vashti. To celebrate the occasion, he gave a banquet in Esther's honor for all his princes and servants, giving generous gifts to everyone and declaring a public festival in the provinces.

Theresa put that Bible down and picked up the copy of the Contemporary English Version, a raspberry suede Bible with black leather piping trimming the edges of the book.

"I just want to read this for you because it gives a bit more insight into what happened to the king that night. As much as I love the way the story is told in the first Bible I read from, this one verse just put the icing on the cake for me when I read it: *None of them pleased him as much as she did, and right away he fell in love with her and crowned her queen in place of Vashti.*"

By the time she finished with that last sentence, Lamont was laughing so hard, he rolled right off the couch and lay on the floor holding his sides. He wiped at his eyes and got back up on the couch.

"Whew . . . I love it. That was what the kids would call a crunked story."

Theresa was laughing now. The more she thought about it, the more she laughed. Bible-day folks really were something else.

"You know," she said in between a hearty chuckle, "a li'l ole sweet country girl from the 'hood, went up in the king's, no, correction, the Kang's private chambers and put something on ole boy."

"Yes she did," Lamont agreed.

"And," Theresa added, "it was so good, she was able to appeal to the king to save a whole nation of people. And you know it just occurred to me that in doing all of that, Esther probably helped to save the king, too. I'm sure he was a better man when she came into his life."

"Ain't nothing like a good woman coming into your life to make you a better man, baby," Lamont said softly. "I'm sure he got to know the Lord after that li'l country girl got ahold of him. And you know something, even though the scripture doesn't say it directly, it does give you the impression that Esther was a sweet li'l thing."

"You think she was little?"

"Yeah, tiny, fine, good-looking thing just like my girl Yvonne Fountain," Lamont said matter-of-factly.

"I agree," Theresa said, as she thought about her friend. Yvonne was a little bitty thing, with a big booty and big boobs. She was just so cute and the sweetest person Theresa had ever met.

"You know, this is going to sound so silly. But when you were reading the story, I kept imagining Xerxes looking like Curtis Parker."

"Me, too," Theresa said. "I kept thinking he was just under six-four, chocolate, with a big booming voice, and always telling folks what to do."

"Sounds like my boy."

"And," she added, "if you think of Xerxes as looking like Curtis, you can't help but put Yvonne in the picture. Because ever since she came back from Virginia with the girls after that fool left her, I keep wondering why Curtis won't hook up with her."

"He has a steady girlfriend right now."

"Who?"

"Regina Young."

"Stuck-up, sleep-with-yo'-husband Regina Young?"

"One and the same," Lamont said, wondering what Curtis saw in that woman. But then folks wondered what he saw in Chablis and his other girlfriend, Marsha Hadley. He had been crazy about some Marsha Hadley and his mother and Aunt could not stand her.

Once when he said Marsha was sweet, all Auntee said was, "She ain't trying to make even a brief acquaintance with Jesus, baby. And that sweetness is only reserved for when the two of you are behind closed doors all laid up. 'Cause she ain't sweet enough to figure out what you really need, boy."

"You really think Regina Young is 'the one' for your boy?" Theresa asked.

"No," he said sincerely. "Regina is so full of flair, chic, and confidence that she has out-sophisticated herself. And she has absolutely no interest in coming to church and humbling herself before the Lord. A man doesn't need a woman like that. And if I am remembering the first part of the story in Esther correctly, Queen Vashti was brought down a few notches for being a biblical version of the kind of woman Regina works so hard to be."

"So," Theresa began, "what you're telling me is that give it some time, and the Kang of Eva T. Marshall University basketball is going to find himself pleased with Yvonne more than the others, and then become so delighted with her, he falls deeply in love because she is his yet-to-be-crowned queen?"

"Something like that," Lamont said, scooting closer to Theresa. She smelled so good in that Hanae Mori perfume.

"Speaking of queens, baby," he said in the sexiest voice Theresa had ever heard coming out of a man's mouth. "This Kang wishes he could get you to come to his, uhhh, 'private rooms' sometime."

Theresa tried to think of something sassy to say but couldn't. When she looked into Lamont's eyes, they were smoldering. He was so fine—deep caramel complexion, dark hair with silver running through it, long curly eyelashes, sexy laugh lines around his dark eyes, and that old crooked smile that made him look like he was always up to something.

Lamont cupped her head once more and pulled her lips to his. Only this time, the kiss was hot and demanding. As he caressed her tongue with his, he gently and ever-so-smoothly pressed Theresa back into the couch. When she tried to get up, he slid a hand down the length of one of those long sexy legs, pulled it up near his waist, and whispered, "Uhh, uhh. You are right where I want you, baby."

Theresa wrapped her arms around him tight and returned the passion in that next kiss. Lamont felt wonderful and smelled so good. She loved Chanel's Allure cologne for men.

When he started kissing down her neck, fingers tugging gently at the zipper on her top, she practically purred with delight. It seemed like it had been forever since she had shared something this wonderful with a man. But as good as this man felt, they couldn't take this to the next level.

Theresa looked up at Lamont, whose eyes were almost black they were so dark with passion. She pressed her hand gently on his cheek.

"We'd better cool down before this goes where it can't go."

Lamont kissed her lips tenderly, and whispered, "Okay." Theresa was right. They were both saved and had to act like it. He shifted his body so that they were lying side by side on the oversized sofa.

Theresa blushed and gazed into his eyes with love, respect, and friendship. It was the kind of expression he'd always believed should come from the woman who was to become his wife. While he had always been able to imagine this expression, he'd never been blessed with the opportunity to have a woman look at him in this way. He had seen Rhonda gaze at James that way, his mother with his father, and, of course, Auntee always looked at Uncle Joseph like that.

In fact, Auntee was so prone to gazing at Uncle Joseph, he once overheard him say to his father, "Bill, sometimes Esther gets to looking at me so, it's unnerving. I made her cry once getting on her about that looking. Then I felt terrible when she said, 'Before me, no woman ever loved you enough to have it in her to take pleasure in seeing every inch of you. No woman appreciated how the good Lord formed you. And now you have the nerve to be ugly to me because I truly love you and have the good sense to appreciate every physical quality that you have.'"

He had to agree with Auntee on that one. A man needed to appreciate that kind of look from a woman, even if it did come across as the direct stare that he could imagine Uncle Joseph received from Auntee. He'd never been viewed through the lens of the kind of love reflected in Theresa's eyes until tonight. And he was going to make sure that he could be gazed at like that for the rest of his life.

Lamont kissed Theresa and stroked her cheek.

"Sweetheart, I know who you are. But the important question is do you know who I am?"

The first thing Theresa wanted to say to him was, "I know who you are, hubby-to-be." But she remained quiet, second-guessing herself and not listening to the sweet words being spoken to her heart about Lamont by the Lord.

"I'm going to ask you one more time if you know who

I am. And whatever you are thinking, please share it—no matter how ridiculous it may seem to you."

"You are my husband," she mumbled.

"Say it again," he said, wanting her to fully grasp and accept what the Lord had placed on her heart.

"You are my husband," she said clearly.

"Are you sure?" Lamont asked.

"Positive."

"So, you're going to marry me, right?"

"But we've never even been out on a date," Theresa said, thinking with that so-called limited human "logic" that they couldn't hop up and marry just like that.

"Neither did Xerxes and Esther until they . . . uhhh . . . consummated the marriage."

"Hmmm," Theresa said, biting her bottom lip. "I see what you mean."

Lamont started laughing.

"Girl, you are a trip. Look, when God brings you together, you really don't have to follow the world's so-called protocol. Now don't get me wrong, everybody doesn't need to do this thing like we're going to do it. But then again, nothing is impossible with God, now is it?"

"No," Theresa answered, wondering how she was going to plan the wedding of her dreams in what probably amounted to days.

Lamont sat up and pulled her up with him.

"Theresa, a true dream wedding is marrying the man of your dreams."

"You're right," she said contritely. "When do you want to do this?"

"As soon as we can. So, you just be ready, okay?"

"Okay."

He stood up and started walking toward the foyer.

"You're leaving?"

"Girl, if I stay here a moment longer, I will take your fine self up those stairs and get all *let's become one* with you. Now go and get my telephone, so I can leave."

"You know," she said as she took the bag with the new phone in it off the table in the foyer, "it's absolutely wonderful being with you without that phone ringing."

"Uhh, baby. The phone hasn't rung because it's not working yet."

"Well, it was still nice."

He put on his coat and hat and opened the door. He put his finger under Theresa's chin and kissed her lips so sweetly she almost cried.

"I confess," he whispered, "it was very nice spending time with my baby without that phone ringing."

The door closed, blocking out the frigid cold. But Theresa had barely felt it. All she could think about was that Lamont was marrying her and had called her "my baby."

"God is good all the time. And all the time, God is good," she whispered to herself and then twirled around in that family room giggling like a little girl.

Lamont started up his car and began to back out of the driveway. He stopped and stared at the house for a second. This was his first visit to Theresa's house and as soon as he walked through the front door, it was as if he had just come home. And now it was truly about to become his new home. He loved his townhouse but knew that this was where the Lord wanted the two of them to be for a while.

"Umph," he said. "I came over here mad and wanting to whip Theresa's butt for tearing up my telephone. And for all practical purposes, I'm leaving a married man."

Chapter Seventeen

"IT'S FREEZING OUT HERE, BOSSMAN," NINA RHODES whined as she stomped around the hard, icy ground near the old Meeting House at Cashmere Estates.

"Nina, hush," Nicole admonished.

"Yeah, be quiet," Lauren added. "If you weren't all decked out in hoochie gear, maybe you would be warmer."

"For your information, Big Sister," Nina stated, "my 'hoochie gear' was designed for very cold weather."

"What I want to know, Baby Sis," Nicole said, "is where did you find those boots?"

"They are kinda hot, huh," Nina said smiling. She knew she was clean this morning in that outfit, which really was quite warm, despite how hot and sexy it was.

Nina, who had purchased her entire outfit at Miss Thang's, was wearing a denim miniskirt with cream faux fur around the end of the skirt, a heavy cream turtleneck sweater that hugged her hips, and matching denim, hooded swing coat with fur lining and trim on the sleeves that matched what was on the skirt. She had on thick cream-colored tights that complemented the knit pattern in the sweater, a knitted apple hat on her head, and thick, cream leather gloves. But it was those boots that stole the show. They were two-inch-heeled, knee-high cream leather with blue suede patches all over them.

"You really do have on more clothes than anybody out here," Lamont said. "So, why are you complaining about the cold?"

"She's not cold," Nicole said evenly. "She's just sleepy. Nina hates to get up before seven. And she always complains about being cold when she is sleepy."

"Forget you," Nina said to Nicole.

"Double back to you, Nina," Nicole shot back at her baby sister.

"If y'all don't shut up, I'm going upside somebody's head, and it won't be mine," Lauren said, cranky and sleepy herself.

Nina and Nicole didn't say another word.

"Bossman," Lauren asked, "why did you drag the team out here at seven in the morning? Couldn't it wait and couldn't we do it somewhere inside?"

With the sole exception of Rev. Quincey, the rest of the team members were on the verge of echoing Lauren's sentiments.

"No," Lamont said firmly. "We could not wait, we had to come here, and we couldn't go inside, even if there was an inside to go into. Take a look around."

He spread his arms out to encompass the landscape.

"Nina, can you see what this barren land will become when the first seeds of those beautiful buildings you have designed are planted?"

Nina's eyes filled with tears as they followed Lamont's hands and she "saw" people moving into their brand-new homes. Homes the Lord blessed her with the ability to design. Homes that were beautiful. Homes that hardworking people with less-than-perfect credit scores, big hearts, great faith, and small bank accounts could afford. Homes for people who gladly depended on the Lord to supply their every need.

"Yes," she whispered. "I see it."

"Team, I called us here to pray us to victory. Because this morning at eight o'clock, one hour before the so-called real meeting is to take place, Jethro Winters and his people have been invited to present their plans without the burden of having to defend themselves against the opposition. I cannot fight that. But the Lord sure can do it for me. So, I need y'all to pray with me, to stand with me, as two or more gathered in His name. Okay?"

They all nodded and he continued.

"I have to admit. I had a sleepless night worrying about this. Then I got up, got down on my knees, and turned it over to the Lord, who led me to read Joshua 10: 8–10: *The Lord said to Joshua, Do not be afraid of them; I have given them into your hand. Not one of them will be able to withstand you.*

"*After an all-night march from Gilgal, Joshua took them by surprise. The Lord threw them into confusion before Israel, who defeated them in a great victory at Gibeon . . .*

"That's us, y'all. The Lord has blessed us with the contract. And if not one person on the DUDC—"

"Uhh," Craig Utley said quietly.

"Okay," Lamont continued. "If everybody on the committee but Craig here votes against me and gets on television and all over the radio to say that they want Jethro Winters and his folk, we will still get that contract.

"The Lord told Joshua—"

"Bossman," Nicole said, "you love yourself some Book of Joshua, don't you?"

Lamont sighed and said, "Father, give me strength."

"But I thought that's why you were all up in Joshua," Nina added.

"Can we just find out what else Lamont got out of Joshua so we can finish our business and get out of this cold?" Rev. Quincey asked.

"In Joshua 1:9, the Lord said: . . . *be strong and coura-geous. Do not be terrified; do not be discouraged, for the Lord your God will be with you wherever you go.*

"Team, that was for us. This battle has already been won. And to demonstrate our faith, I dragged all of you out here this morning so that we could pray and bless the wonderful new community that we are going to build."

Rev. Quincey stepped forward and was about to in-struct them to join hands. But they were a step ahead of him. Members of the Green Pastures team, including the new folks, were holding hands and waiting to start pray-ing: the Rhodes sisters, Craig Utley, Uncle Joseph, and the Lacys, who had collected so much useful information on the down-low that Lamont had decided to have both Baby Doll and her husband come work for him.

"Father," Rev. Quincey began, "thank You for this in-credible group of folk who have humbled themselves be-fore You and can't wait to do Your will in this community. Lord, there are so many families who want to live in the kind of neighborhood You will lead them to build here. Let the team see whatever it is You want them to see and show them how to bring Your will to life on this plot of land. And Lord protect the neighborhoods that surround this place and keep them in good standing—too many people have worked too hard and too long to be uprooted and displaced like refugees in their own land.

"Lord, the devil is a liar. And anybody who thinks that Green Pastures will not be building up in here is a fool and one who loves a lie. So, we rebuke the devil in the name of Jesus. And we claim the victory in the name of our precious Savior, Jesus Christ, that this land is Your land, and this time next year a whole bunch of folks who love You will live here. Let all that are standing here and gathered in the name of the Lord say . . ."

"Amen!"

"Now," Rev. Quincey said. "Let's get going. I'm hungry, I'm sleepy, and I am freezing my butt off."

"Not yet," Uncle Joseph said. "My Queen made me promise to bless this place and anoint it. So, here, Rev. Do that so we can go."

Rev. Quincey took the small bottle of Queen Esther's anointing oil and poured a tiny bit out on the ground. He said, "In the name of Jesus Christ our Lord and Savior, we ask Thee, Lord, to bless and sanctify the entire complex and the surrounding neighborhood. Make it the kind of community that is filled with the blessings and anointing of Your Holy Spirit. Make it a place where people come to buy a home and end up finding Salvation and eternal life. Make it a place filled with people who are saved, sanctified, and full of the Holy Ghost. Amen."

"Now we can go," Uncle Joseph said. Even though he was glad to get out of the cold, he knew this place needed to be blessed so that it would not risk becoming spiritually depleted, demoralized, and abandoned again. The old

Cashmere had been a great place to live. But it hadn't been blessed and dedicated to the Lord the first go-round.

Maybe that is what happened to a lot of good affordable communities that fell on hard times and became abandoned or a den of iniquity like the Cashmere. It's very likely that those neighborhoods had not been anointed and blessed, leaving an opening for all of the wrong things and people to creep up in them and ruin the landscape of community life, chasing away all who were capable of making it a decent place to live. Therefore, they had to anoint and bless this new community, so that by God's grace folk could have a wonderful, safe, and beautiful place to live.

Craig glanced down at his watch and tugged at Lamont's sleeve.

"I'm going over to the meeting. I think I need to get there before you."

Lamont agreed. They shouldn't walk in together.

"Me and the Mrs. coming, too—if that's all right with you, Mr. Craig. 'Cause Lamont here will need some extra eyes 'n' ears when he's in there."

"That's fine," Craig answered, trying not to stare at Mr. Lacy, who he could have sworn was blind.

"Extra eyes 'n' ears don't always have to be the natural ones you sighted folks rely so heavily on all the time. I can 'see' a whole lot, you know. And my wife here don't miss a thang. Do you, Baby?"

Baby Doll started blushing and said, "Naw, I don't miss much. And I'll make sure I catch everything going on in that room to protect Lamont."

"Well, that's settled then," Craig said. "Do you two need a ride?"

"No," Mr. Lacy said, "we has some transportation."

Craig looked around to see how they had gotten here, realizing that the two of them had arrived before everybody else.

"Don't try and figure that one out, man," Lamont said. "It'll give you a headache. I know 'cause I've tried and failed."

Craig pulled into a parking space at the Washington Duke Inn and hurried in to get out of that freezing cold—which was far below the normal temperatures for Durham this time of year. He took the elevator up to one of the meeting rooms and headed down the hall. The first people he laid eyes on were Jethro Winters and Patty Harmon coming off another elevator. He didn't miss that their elevator had come down to this floor instead of coming up from the lobby.

His wife always said that "the devil makes people so stupid." And she was right. Because thinking folk would have taken separate elevators down to the lobby and then back up. But then, clear-thinking folk wouldn't have a need for that strategy because they would be too busy thinking on how to live right, and not need to think on how to get by with wrong.

Craig honestly wondered what Jethro saw in Patty Harmon. He had met Bailey on several occasions and thought that she was a very beautiful and sophisticated woman. Patty, on the other hand, always made him wonder if she had ever worked as a stripper, or tried to get into the college shoot for *Playboy* magazine back in the day. She had a decent education, a bit of power and influence, and about as much class as the resident round-the-way girl at the honky-tonk bar—the one who was dressed in undersized clothes, had big, brassy blond hair, and wore harsh, dark eye makeup that did absolutely nothing for her pale skin.

Craig gathered from this location that many of the DUDC's members wanted to make sure that Jethro had sufficient time to use his charm and his wallet to sway the undecided committee members in his direction without having to answer to anybody. Because if they were in the official offices downtown, anybody from the opposing team would have a right to sit in on Winters's presentation if they happened to drop by. And if that happened, the committee would be forced to give the opposition—in this case members of the Green Pastures team—equal time and attention.

He found the room and took a seat amongst the rest of the committee, and Jethro's people. There were only three black people present—Rev. Parvell Sykes, Charmayne Robinson, and the lone black voice on the DUDC, an up-tight businessman whose name Craig could never remember. He found it interesting that Sykes and Charmayne were not sitting together. But then that should not have been surprising. Winters was the master of the divide-and-conquer war strategy.

Patty and Jethro finally came into the room. She was grinning like a cat and putting all of her business in the street—especially when she took a seat next to Jethro and sat there with her hand on his thigh. But in a matter of seconds that grin, along with Jethro's smug expression, were wiped clean off their faces when the next person waltzed through that door.

Even Craig was caught off guard when Bailey Catherine Winters walked in wearing a dark brown mink coat over a beige V-neck cashmere sweater, chocolate suede pants, and matching suede ankle boots. Her thick dark hair was swept up into an elegant chignon, and held in place by a lovely sterling silver and topaz clip. But what set this ensemble off were the diamonds. Bailey had three-carat studs in her ears, a four-carat solitaire hanging off a delicate platinum chain around her neck, and a ten-carat platinum wedding ring.

By this time, the folks huddled in the doorway behind her—Lamont, the Lacys, and the company's legal representative, Nicole Rhodes—had taken a seat to watch the show. Even though it was still early morning, Craig kept getting a craving for some hot-buttered popcorn and an ice-cold Pepsi-Cola.

Bailey ignored her husband's silent request for her to sit down, and walked right over to where Patty was sitting. She stared at Patty like she was the cheapest and nastiest thing she'd ever laid eyes on.

At this point, Patty decided that she was not going to kowtow to this high-siddity woman. If Bailey couldn't hold on to her man, then that was Bailey Catherine's problem and not hers. So, in that moment of low-class insanity, Patty put the hand that Jethro had quickly removed, back on his thigh and slid it higher.

Bailey's eyes narrowed and Jethro started sweating.

Charmayne, who had never seen him anything but arrogant and cool, eased out of the chair she was sitting in to one that gave a better view. She never did like that Patty Harmon and couldn't wait for the show to begin. How often did some black folk get to see some uppity white folks cut the monkey fool with each other?

"I never quite understood what the black colloquial expression 'skank' meant until now," Bailey said in her cool, deep alto and refined Southern lady voice.

"Sugar darling," Jethro began and then shut his mouth when Bailey's eyes sliced right through him.

"You want me to hold your coat, Mrs. Winters?" Charmayne asked sweetly.

"No, but thank you for offering, Ms. Robinson," she answered, glad to have a chance to finally see this Charmayne that Jethro was always mumbling and moaning over in his sleep. She thought her a very pretty black woman and was relieved to discover that Charmayne did not want her husband.

Charmayne didn't say another word. She knew when Bailey, who had never laid eyes on her, called her by name that this white woman was not one to be messed with.

Patty had heard the word "skank," too, but never gave it much thought. Now she wished one of the blacks in the room would say something that would shed some light on the specifics of what Bailey had just called her.

"I bet a host of men in this community have paid you to give them a lap dance," Bailey said, delighted when she saw pure rage burning in Patty's eyes. She took boxing lessons from a former statewide middleweight champion, Mr. Z. T. Thomas, who had also taught her how to pick a fight.

Mr. Thomas, a tough white farm boy from Hillsborough, North Carolina, had once told her, "Bailey Catherine, the best thing you can do to an opponent is to get them so mad they lose their heads and hop up swinging. All you got to do at that point is stay cool and calculate where you need to throw your first punch."

"Fake-boob, skank," Bailey said, satisfied that she had accomplished her first line of offense when Patty jumped up and got in her face.

"You better take that back."

"Skank."

"I'm warning you."

"Your mother is a skank, too. And so is your overly oiled grandmother."

The black folks in the room—that is with the exception of the wannabe on the committee—hollered with laughter. They could not believe that this classy white woman had called another white woman a "skank," and then went on to say in classy white woman dialect, "Yo' mama is a skank and yo' greasy granmama, too."

Patty was fit to be tied—especially when the black folks started laughing. She raised her hand and gave Bailey that quick, sharp white woman slap.

Bailey raised her fist and punched Patty so hard she fell out cold on the floor. Then Bailey got the pitcher of water and poured it on Patty's face.

When she was sure she had come to, Bailey squatted down and said, "You stay away from my man. 'Cause the next time you sneak yourself a ride on my husband, I am going to beat your behind like you just sneaked and tried on my fur coat."

Bailey glared at her husband and then started walking out the door. Jethro hopped up and hurried to follow his wife out of the room. Last thing he needed was one of her male relatives showing up at his office suite ready to fight and cuss and act crazy. He had too much riding on this deal to have to cope with any more family drama. And

Bailey's family, as snooty as they acted in public, loved to fight and they loved drama.

Parvell Sykes hurried over to help Patty up off the floor. Even though he was seriously thinking about marrying Roxanne Daye, she was too dull and churchy for his behind-closed-doors taste. Charmayne refused to speak to him. And now, Patty Harmon had just been forced to end what he suspected was a very hot and torrid affair with Jethro. Bailey was right, Patty was a skank. But Lawd, if a skank wasn't what the doctor ordered when nobody was around.

He dipped his handkerchief in a glass of ice water and dabbed at the bruising and swelling that was covering half of Patty's head.

When the rest of the black folk in the room saw her head, they started laughing all over again.

Patty started to cry and Parvell, her new knight, gently led her from the room.

Craig, who was just praying that he would not collapse into the same hollering laughter, stood and said, "Well, I guess this ends this meeting that wasn't really a meeting, even if it was worthy of being shown as a pay-per-view boxing match."

"Yes, Lawd," Mr. Lacy said. "Now, that is something I really wished I coulda seent with some natural eyes. Woulda paid good money to see that thang go down."

The white folks in the room, along with their lone black wannabe, quietly gathered their things and walked out in a daze. They had come to give someone they considered a Durham mover and shaker a contract that they hoped would signal the beginning of transforming a community that had many of them concerned as to what it would

become over time. But now they weren't so sure they
wanted somebody whose personal life was this tacky and
messy to get that contract.

On the way out, two members stole a few glances at
Lamont. Maybe it was time for a change. Maybe they
needed to be more concerned about helping some of the
good, working people in Durham get a chance at a better
life. Maybe Cashmere Estates really did need to be rebuilt
to honor and carry out what had begun as a very noble
and beautiful dream. If truth be told, those two pondered
on what for them was a radical concept—that good housing and good neighborhoods should not have such a high
price tag on them that good people were robbed of the
chance of having them.

Chapter Eighteen

YOU GOT EVERYTHING?"

"Yeesss . . ." Vanessa answered slowly for the fourth time. "I have it all, Theresa. It's in the trunk of my car. And the alarm is on. And I am going to get it all as soon as we are finished here."

"I'm being a pain in the butt, huh?"

"Uhh . . . kinda . . . sorta . . . something like that, girl," Vanessa said. "But it's okay. We understand. Don't we, Rhonda?"

"Yep," Rhonda said. "That we do. Now, how 'bout us going on in and getting this party rolling? 'Cause we don't have a lot of time left before the Christmas Festival starts. And frankly, my booty's cold. It's freezing out here."

"Amen," Vanessa said.

Rhonda pulled out her cell phone and spoke, "Lena." She waited a few seconds and then said, "Where is your behind?"

Theresa ran into the building. It was cold outside and she was anxious to get started herself. A large group of children and parents had already arrived. Miss Queen Esther and Mr. Joseph were serving homemade hot chocolate, sugar cookies, and punch in the lobby, hoping these treats would temporarily pacify the children running around in the lobby and being chased out of the sanctuary because they were about to lose their minds over seeing Santa. And some of those parents were not helping matters, either, with their own demands for the children to see Santa, coupled with their lenient approaches to discipline.

Plus, if the truth were to be told, Theresa couldn't wait to see Santa herself. She'd caught a blurred glimpse of Lamont when he rushed into the church to get dressed before any children came. She examined her new Mrs. Claus suit. It was even cuter on than it was off. The bright red pants were stretch velvet and hugged her hips in all the right places. The matching velvet top was soft and sassy with white faux fur around the cuffs and the scooped neckline that came so low on her shoulders she looked more like a sexy snow bunny instead of Mrs. Claus.

She adjusted her hat, which was made out of the same material as the pants.

"Ho, ho, ooooo, girl," Lamont said, coming up behind Theresa and grabbing her by the waist. "Now that's what I'm talking 'bout, Mrs. Claus. And those black high-heeled pumps are calling my name. Umph, umph, umph."

He planted a kiss on an exposed shoulder and whispered, "Ho, ho, ho baby bubba," in mock imitation of the funk band Parliament and Funkadelic.

"Look! It's Santa. And he is hugging all on Miss Theresa like she is his girlfriend," said the pastor's youngest son, eight-year-old Derrick Quincey.

Derrick started jumping up and down and pulling on Lena's hand, hoping he could guide her in the same direction that Santa was walking.

"Boy, stop that," Lena said. "Santa doesn't have a

girlfriend, he's married. That's Mrs. Claus, his wife," Lena said.

"Really, Mama?" Derrick's seven-year-old sister, Jasmine, asked incredulously. "I thought Miss Theresa was single. I didn't know that she had gotten married, and to Santa. Man, some ladies are really lucky. Her husband has a house full of toys. You think she'll tell Santa to bring me a fully furnished Barbie house with an alarm system, three-car garage, intercom, swimming pool, pretend wireless Internet connection, and basketball court?"

"I think that," Rhonda whispered to Lena, "Santa better go down in the 'hood and find one of those old-school hoodlums and play the numbers. 'Cause that's a tall order."

Vanessa started laughing and said, "You know that little Jasmine is on some different stuff. I haven't even seen what she is talking about and you know I've been all over the Internet pricing Barbie and Bratz stuff."

"Looka here, baby," Lamont whispered in Theresa's ear and sucked on the side of his tooth all mannish-like, "I better go get situated before Santa gets jacked by Jasmine Quincey."

Theresa laughed softly and said, "You do that because I don't think Jasmine is the only little girl in here thinking about accosting Santa and getting her stuff. I'll meet you down there in a few minutes."

"Now that I know where you'll be in a few minutes, what I want to know is where you gone be later, Mrs. Claus. 'Cause," Lamont said, sucking on his tooth, eyes sparkling pure "bad boy" through all of the Santa gear on his face, "I was thinking 'bout giving the elves the night off, so you could come and warm Santa up a bit.

You know it's mighty cold back at my crib in the North Pole and I need you to take care of that."

"You are bad, Santa."

"Nahh, baby. I'm just a merry old elf who is looking to get his freak on," Lamont said low so that no one could hear him.

"Oooo, Santa, you are so nasty. And in church, too."

"Ho, ho, ho, baby," he said in a low seductive voice that made Theresa blush.

"Can we get some hot chocolate?" Derrick asked his mother.

"Yes," Lena said. "You and your sister get some chocolate and stay over there by Miss Queen Esther while you're drinking it."

"Okay, Mama," they both said and skipped over to the table.

"Hey, Mrs. Claus," Lena said grinning. "What you doing to make Santa so frisky?" Her eyes traveled over Theresa's outfit, and then landed on her shoes. "Hmmm, I see, I see. I bet those," her eyes practically pointed at the shoes, "are making for ole boy to be a real, real, real jolly old elf."

"I know you are not messing with me, when you just ordered some more of those first lady hoochie PJs. I take it that somebody who will remain unnamed, even though he is walking in the building, liked them—*a lot*," Theresa said with a low laugh.

Lena looked out of the glass door and smiled at her husband. He rushed inside shivering and blowing on his hands.

"Man! It's so cold out there, I could barely stand it."

"And hello to you, too," Lena told him with a smile.

"Hey, baby," he told his wife and gave her a kiss on the cheek. Lena jumped. "Boy, your mouth is ice-cold."

Obadiah raised up his eyebrows and just shook his head, as if to say, "What did you expect, I just said it was cold." He turned to Theresa. "Well, well, Miss Lady, how are you today? Glowing and working that Mrs. Claus suit I see. Where's Santa?"

"Down in the dining room getting situated. I better hurry on down so that I can help him."

"Just what is your job?" Obadiah asked.

"Getting the names straight and making sure the kids don't sit on Santa's lap too long. You know how that is when one of them has a list yay long." She held her arms out about two feet.

"I know," Obadiah said. "'Cause those two have lists that look like dissertations. Jasmine almost got her little butt whipped for trying to argue with me when I told her that she couldn't bring it with her."

"Yeah," Lena said laughing. "Missy was determined to give poor Santa everything on that list."

"That's 'cause she *your* child," Obadiah said.

"My child? Obadi, that girl has Quincey stamped all over her. Doesn't she, Theresa?"

Theresa glanced over at Jasmine, and decided to stay out of it. She was standing at the table drinking hot chocolate and watching a little boy fuss with his mother. When the little boy got mad and dropped his hot chocolate on the floor, Jasmine raised her eyebrows and shook her head. In that moment, she was the spitting image of Rev. Quincey, who was also watching that little boy, raising his eyebrows, and shaking his head.

"Now, if that were one of mine," he said, "I'd take

him right outside in that frigid cold and beat his tail like Christmas Day ain't coming."

Theresa was cracking up with laughter. Obadiah Quincey was just as crazy when he wasn't doing "preacher stuff." And if truth be told, both Derrick and Jasmine knew that their daddy would tear their little behinds up if they cut the fool like that. And drop some hot chocolate on the floor? They wouldn't ever sit down again.

"Well, I'm glad that Lamont wasn't out here to see that," Rev. Quincey said. "'Cause I know that he would have told that bad-tail boy that he wasn't getting jack for Christmas acting like that."

The pastor started walking over to the hot chocolate table, and paused for a moment.

"Miss Theresa, I hope you plan on keeping a plentiful supply of those PJs your first lady bought from your store. That chiffon getup was just what this preacher needed. Ain't that right, First Lady?"

"Boy, stop," Lena said, cheeks all pink and rosy.

"That ain't what you said last night," he replied laughing, before urging the kids to finish the chocolate so that they could go and visit with Santa before the other children realized what was going on.

Queen Esther watched Rev. Quincey pimp off. She remembered when that boy was a toddler, running around with a stuffed Lassie dog toy, talking about "woof, woof." "And now, he thinking he show nuff grown, 'cause he way over forty. Mannish thang. Just like her nephews—smellin' themselves big-time and still thinking they grown.

"Grown," she thought. "Folks treat it like it's a sacred word. And 'bout all it really means is that some of God's children are older than others and have acquired

some rights and privileges that goes with being what
we call *grown*."

"You all need to move on down to the dining hall,"
she said, "before I have to *lay hands* on some of these
bad-tailed children running around this church. 'Cause
as soon as Joseph gets back here, we gonna take this table
down and head there ourselves."

Theresa and Lena started moving toward the dining
hall. Rhonda and Vanessa, who had finished changing
into their elf costumes, tried to hurry after them but
poor Rhonda was having a time walking in those long,
narrow shoes.

"Girl, these curled-up toes are killing my feet," Rhonda
complained. "Now, Lena, you know I must love your man
a whole lot to put this mess on my feet. I hope I don't have
to stand up too long, else I'm going to hurt somebody before the evening is over with."

Lena looked down at Rhonda's feet and laughed. Those
shoes made her feet look like they belonged to some crea-
ture in a Dr. Seuss book.

"Shut up," Rhonda said and tried to look mean. But it
didn't work. As soon as she glanced down at her feet, she
started laughing.

"Lookie, looka here," a low, sexy voice said, "if it ain't
Santa's helpers."

They stopped walking and turned to face the voice,
and did a double take. It was Charmayne Robinson and
Table Wine, followed by a very pretty and well-dressed
white woman none of them had ever met before.

"Ladies," Charmayne began, "this is Mrs. Bailey
Catherine Winters. She asked me to bring her over here,
so that she could make a donation."

Not one person said a word. It was one thing for Jethro Winters to send some chump change over to the church in a cheap effort to garner support from a black pulpit. But for his wife, whom they all knew had KO'd her husband's mistress in public, to come here was something else.

Bailey, who knew she had just walked into her husband's enemy's territory, wondered if she had done the right thing. But when she noticed a young couple with two little boys jumping up and down over seeing Santa, Bailey knew she was right to come here. For she imagined that family represented who Lamont Green was working so hard to build homes for. She reached into her purse and pulled out a cashier's check.

"Which one of you is the first lady of this church?"

Lena raised her hand like they were in class.

"Then I want to put this in your care."

Bailey gave Lena the check.

"Look, I am not going to stand in the House of the Lord and try to play any games with you. I know you have all heard what happened. And yes, I came here to get back at my husband.

"I stayed up all night after that encounter trying to figure out what would be the best way to get him, when it occurred to me that I needed to get rid of some money for tax reasons before the end of the year. I hope using it gives you as much pleasure as it did me to give it. And please, by all means, use my name on your donor list."

Bailey turned to Charmayne and Chablis, whom she had just recently persuaded to come and work for her new company.

"Ladies, we need to leave."

As the three of them were walking out of the building,

Lena, who had minded her manners and not looked at the folded check, couldn't stand it any longer. She read it once, then twice, and then a third time to make sure her eyes were not playing tricks on her.

"If you don't tell us what is on that check, I'm gonna cut you with my church knife," Queen Esther said.

"Here, Miss Queen Esther," Lena said and put the check in her hand. "You tell them what's on the check."

Queen Esther, too, read the amount once, then twice, and then one more time to make sure her eyes were focused right.

"Y'all are driving us crazy!"

"Well, if we are driving you crazy, Rhonda, you are going to lose all of your mind when I tell you that this check is for two and a half million dollars," Queen Esther said.

"Di . . . di . . . di . . . did you just say two . . . twoooo million dollars?" Theresa managed to ask.

"NO! I said two and a half million, girl."

"How much money does Jethro Winters have?" Theresa asked. "I never placed him with that kind of money."

"That ain't his money, baby," Queen Esther told her. "That's Bailey Catherine's money. Girl, her family is loaded."

"Umph," Vanessa, who had been very quiet, said. "Kinda makes you wish ole boy will make her mad again."

"You are crazy," Lena said.

"But you know something," Queen Esther said solemnly. "This money is gonna do a lot of good. But my heart goes out to a woman who is so hurt, she'd do this to make a point. We've been trying to raise this money for a

while, and she always has money on hand. She could have
given it to us long before now."

"Yeah," Lena added. "We need to pray for her. 'Cause
that's a deep hurtin' she's going through. And revenge is
not going to heal it."

"That may be true," Rhonda said. "But it sure is going
to heal a whole lot over on our end."

"As Romans 8:28 says . . ." Lena began . . .

*"And we know that all things work together for good
to them that love God, to them who are the called according to His purpose,"* they all said together and started
laughing.

"Here, Theresa," Lena said and put the check in her
hand. "You are the one who needs to give this to Lamont.
And the Lord will tell you when to give it to him."

"Leave all of that alone," Queen Esther exclaimed, frustrated that it was taking them so long to finish cleaning up
the dining hall so they could go into the sanctuary.

It had been a long morning. But it had been a very
good morning. Besides that surprise check from Bailey
Winters, the festival had raised an additional half a million dollars. They started out hoping to raise $325,000
and walked away with a whopping three million. And
she couldn't wait to see the expression on her nephew's
face when he learned just how much money the Lord has
blessed him with. Because at this moment, he was still
praising God over the $500,000.

"Vanessa doesn't have time to run to the car and get
your things, and you don't have time to change, Theresa,"
her mother told her as she put the last of the table decora-

tions in a box. "Rev. Quincey has a meeting in Atlanta tomorrow and has to be at the airport in two hours."

"I'm still in my Mrs. Claus suit!"

"Come on, baby," Lamont said, pulling off his white beard. "We don't have much time and too much time has been wasted already."

"Amen," Queen Esther said and pushed Theresa, who was looking down at her clothes and then back up at everybody frowning, out of the dining room and in the direction of the sanctuary, where everyone sat waiting on them.

"Where is Yvonne?" Queen Esther asked.

"I'm right here at the piano, where you told me to wait," Yvonne said.

"Then where is Baby Doll? I thought you and Baby Doll were doing this together?"

"We are, Queen," Baby Doll said as she hurried down to the front of the sanctuary, completely unaware that her church members were trying not to stare at her red and green plaid corduroy culottes with the matching vest.

"Where," Rhonda tried to sneak a whisper, so that she wouldn't get in trouble with Mr. Lacy, "did Miss Baby Doll find a brand-new culottes suit? And in plaid? I didn't even know that they were still selling culottes until now."

"You think she goes on the Internet and finds that stuff on eBay," Lena whispered back, being careful not to get caught by her husband.

"That or Big Lots," Vanessa put in and then got quiet when she noticed Mr. Lacy's head tilted in their direction.

"Lamont, Theresa. Come on up here," Rev. Quincey said.

Lamont quickly removed the padding from his Santa suit, which made it hang off him. Theresa had a point about them changing clothes.

Watching Lamont in that ill-fitting Santa suit made Lena glad that she'd called her mother to come and get the kids. They would have given her a fit (and Lamont, too) if they discovered that he was the one hiding under that big red suit. As it was, Derrick had asked her three times why Santa was so "tall."

"Take off the jacket, Lamont," James said. "Don't you have on a T-shirt or something?"

"Yeah," he said and gave James the coat. He was wearing a white T-shirt with Green Pastures printed on the back with letters made to look like blades of grass.

Rev. Quincey nodded at Yvonne Fountain, who began playing, while Baby Doll sang the end of the Darwin Hobbs praise melody, causing Vanessa to cry as soon as she heard the words "For you are worthy . . ."

James and Vanessa took their places at the altar. Both were still dressed in elf clothes, including the long green, curled-up-at-the-toe shoes. Rhonda almost tripped over her own elf shoes as she hurried over to Theresa to get her Santa hat and fluff out her hair a bit.

"Wouldn't do getting married and your hair is all over your head," Rhonda said. "Bad enough you're standing here dressed as Mrs. Claus in a pair of hoochie-mama shoes."

Theresa laughed. Her wedding day, and she looked like she had just escaped from a bad Christmas special on TV—the ones where people grinned too much and seemed to forget why they were singing about Christmas in the first place.

"The rings? Y'all got some rings?" Rev. Quincey asked, and started laughing.

This was the funniest wedding he had ever officiated over. But it had to be the sweetest and most anointed one, too. He had prayed for this moment. But never had he imagined that the Lord would answer his prayer with such a humorous twist.

"Yeah," James said, and produced two boxes—one for Theresa and one for Lamont. They had given him the rings, and neither had seen what the other had purchased. James handed Lamont the lavender velvet box with Theresa's ring, and gave her the green leather box with the ring she'd selected for Lamont.

"Y'all haven't seen them, have you?" Rev. Quincey asked.

They shook their heads and resisted the urge to examine their rings.

"Go on. Ain't nothing regular about this wedding anyway. So take a moment to look at your rings. You go first, Lamont."

Lamont smiled at Theresa and opened the box. Tears formed in her eyes. It was a beautiful three-carat marquise diamond, with the finest cut amethyst stones surrounding it, and set in platinum. The platinum wedding band was encircled with diamonds and amethysts. He slid the engagement ring on her finger and waited for her to open his.

Theresa wiped at her eyes and eagerly displayed Lamont's ring. It was platinum with five emeralds and five diamond chips spread across the band. On the inside was the inscription "Green Pastures."

"Thank you, baby," he whispered and fought to hold back his own tears.

"Y'all ready?"

They nodded at Rev. Quincey, who looked up at Yvonne and said, "Hit it."

Immediately, Yvonne started playing "Spinning Around," and doing it some serious justice, with her beautiful, mellow contralto voice, when she got to "Spinning around, spinning around . . . I must be falling in love . . ."

At that point, neither Theresa nor Lamont could contain their tears. They tried to help the other stop crying, and ended up crying and laughing in each other's arms.

Rev. Quincey began reading from Ephesians 5: 22–33:

Wives submit yourselves unto your own husbands, as unto the Lord. For the husband is the head of the wife, even as Christ is the head of the church: and He is the savior of the body. Therefore as the church is subject unto Christ, so let the wives be to their own husbands in every thing.

Husbands, love your wives, even as Christ also loved the church, and gave Himself for it; that he might sanctify and cleanse it with the washing of water by the word, that He might present it to Himself a glorious church, not having spot, or wrinkle, or any such thing; but that it should be holy and without blemish. So ought men to love their wives as their own bodies. He that loveth his wife, loveth himself. For no man ever yet hated his own flesh; but nourisheth and cherisheth it,

even as the Lord the church: For we are members of His
body, of His flesh, and of His bones.

For this cause shall a man leave his father and mother,
and shall be joined unto his wife, and they shall be one
flesh. This is a great mystery: but I speak concerning
Christ and the church. Nevertheless let everyone of you
in particular so love his wife even as himself; and the
wife see that she reverence her husband.

When he finished reading, he said to the two of them, "Do you both understand the importance of what I just read?"

"Yes," they answered in unison.

"Well, let me elaborate for a quick moment anyway. Theresa, Lamont is your anointed husband. Submit to him in love, and know that the Lord will always want to lead him to cherish, honor, and love you right and in the way that you need for him to love you.

"Lamont, you do understand the seriousness of loving your wife like Christ loved the church. It means that she is flesh of your flesh. She is just as much a part of you as you are a part of you. It means that if you hurt her, you hurt yourself. Remember that and trust in the Lord when He guides you about how you are to be with Theresa. And trust that He will show her how to love you right.

"You two got that part, right?"

"We do."

"Good," Rev. Quincey said and launched into the traditional wedding ceremony.

Despite the informality of this service, there wasn't a dry eye in the sanctuary when he finished. This wedding, for all of the wacky-tacky costumes they were wearing, was a testimony to how the Lord moved and worked in the lives of His children when they turned to Him for help, learned to trust and depend on Him, as well as sought to do God's will with all their heart.

". . . I now pronounce you husband and wife. You may kiss your bride."

Lamont took Theresa back in his arms. He looked into her eyes, ran his fingertips along her cheeks, caressed her hair, and whispered, "I love you, baby," before touching his lips to hers and holding them there, savoring the warmth and love that flowed through him from her.

When the kiss ended, Theresa reached into her pants pocket and put the check in Lamont's hand.

"What's this?"

"Your wedding gift from the Lord," she answered him.

Lamont unfolded the checked and tears streamed down his cheeks. He raised up his hands and said:

"Thank you, Jesus. Praise you, Father. Thank you, Lord! Hallelujah!"

Lamont grabbed his wife and held her tight. Today he knew what it meant when Rev. Quincey once told him, "Lamont, just keep praying and hold on to your faith. Because you are about to receive blessings beyond belief."

Rev. Quincey, who had been told about the check by his wife, pulled out a handkerchief and wiped his eyes. He counted it a blessing to be able to witness answered prayer like this, and raised his hand up in thanksgiving to the Lord before he said, "Ladies and gentlemen, I present to you, Lamont and Theresa Green."

"Amen!"

"Praise the Lord!"

"God is good all the time," Theresa and Lamont's parents said in unison.

"All the time God is good," claimed every single person, from the youngest to the oldest.

"Queen," Cousin Buddy whispered, pulling on Queen Esther's sleeve, "I don't know what's going on."

He hit the side of his helmet a few times.

"What you mean, Buddy?" she asked gently.

"Is Lamont really Santa Claus? Or, is Santa Claus really Lamont? And why didn't he take my list?"

Queen Esther sighed. She and Joseph really needed to tell Buddy the truth about Santa before next Christmas. Because at fifty-one, he deserved a bit more information about this business.

Chapter Nineteen

FEBRUARY 14 AND IT WAS FREEZING OUTSIDE. THE wind had blown and howled all night, and it continued on like that into the wee hours of the morning. Theresa considered it a good thing that North Carolina didn't have winters like this every year, or else last Valentine's Day would have been spent wrapped in every blanket in the house to keep warm. But this year, despite the bitter cold, she didn't have to spend it alone.

Theresa had spent many a winter's night on her knees, asking the Lord to send her a husband. Sometimes she had waited patiently and faithfully. And at other times throughout the years, she did just like Peter, when he hopped in the water with Jesus on faith, and as soon as those strong sea waves got to whipping up around him, faltered and started to sink. But praise God, just like Peter, each time she faltered, the Lord reached out and grabbed her hand, putting this question in her heart: *"O thou of little faith, why didst thou doubt?"*

She discovered that waiting on the Lord to answer a prayer, especially when you believed it was an inordinately long wait, was hard. It was during this time of waiting on God to bring her husband into her life that

Theresa truly understood how much faith was needed to have faith the size of a tiny mustard seed. She didn't even know just how little faith most folk—including the ones who were saved—actually had until she found herself waiting on the Lord to send Lamont.

But praise be to God, she had persevered to the point where she could snuggle up to her new hubby on this cold Valentine's morning.

"Why are your feet so cold, Mrs. Green?" Lamont whispered.

"I got up to get some water . . ."

"And go to the bathroom?"

"Yeah. That, too."

"I see," Lamont said as he rolled over and wrapped his arms around his wife. His fingertips toyed with her pajamas. They felt silky and not like the flannel he remembered her wearing when they went to sleep last night. He pulled back the covers to investigate the matter further.

"Lamont, it's cold," Theresa complained.

"I know that from your feet, woman. But what I don't know is what you have on."

He grinned at her in the flickering light coming from the fireplace. Theresa was wearing a pair of red, sheer silk chiffon pajamas with "Lamont's" embroidered all over them with black silk thread. It didn't take much light to see the black lace bra and matching thong peeking at him through that sizzling red chiffon. Her dark brown skin glistened against all of that red—making him glad it was so cold. Otherwise, he would have been burning up.

"Lamont's huh?" he asked in a mannish voice.

He smacked Theresa on the behind.

"Is this Lamont's, too?"

"Uhh, yeah," Theresa said kind of sheepishly.

"You don't sound too sure about that, baby," he said and placed a hot kiss on her collarbone—one of her *spots*. And it was his mission to hit all the *spots* that would get his bride as hot as she was looking in all of the "Umm, baby-baby Valentine's Day red."

Theresa gave a soft moan and Lamont kissed that spot one more time, taking an extra moment to lick her collarbone.

"You are so bad, Lamont."

"Not as bad as I plan on getting."

"Oooo, Lamont," Theresa said.

"That good, huh . . . and I ain't even got started good."

Lamont slipped out of his boxers and T-shirt and eased the pajama top off Theresa's shoulders.

"We don't need these, either," he murmured and slid the bottoms off, snapping the waist of the thongs, and then cupping her behind in his hands before sliding his fingers up to that bra and removing that, too.

Theresa got as close to her husband as she could and purred with pure delight when he took the "scenic route" getting her out of those fancy thongs.

The first part of his mission accomplished, Lamont came back up to kiss his wife's lips and whispered, "I love you, girl."

"I love you, boy," she answered him back.

"This is sure turning out to be a *very* happy Valentine's Day," he said in a hot and sexy voice, as he rolled over on top of Theresa. She felt so good to him. He had never felt such completeness with a woman before. He had to wonder what had taken him so long to recognize and claim this blessing the Lord had been holding in escrow for him all these years.

"You ain't never lied about that one, Lamont," Theresa said softly, as her hands began to travel all over him, giving extra special attention to those *spots* that caused him to moan when her fingertips brushed up against them.

He gazed down into her eyes and said, "You know you something else, girl."

"You are, too, boy."

"I know." He laughed and gave her a good sample of "something else."

"Ooooo, Lamont."

"That's my name, baby. Say it again . . ."

"Big Daddy."

"Now you talkin'."

"Big Daddy . . ."

"I think I need my hard hat, girl," he said and then became quite diligent at finishing the job he had started.

The Greens hurried and hopped into Lamont's car. Neither remembered Valentine's Day ever being so cold. Lamont turned the temperature up and then flipped the radio to The Lite gospel station. This was one of those mornings when he wanted to get as full in the Lord as he could. This morning the DUDC would review the presentations from the Winters Development Corporation and Green Pastures, and then make their final decision. As Craig had told him last night, they were tired of this war and wanted to end it as soon as possible.

Lamont didn't feel nervous. He knew that if the Lord wanted him to have the contract, He'd bless him with it. As he grew in his faith and walk with the Lord, he was discovering what the "peace that passeth understanding" truly meant. That thing about learning not to lean on your own understanding was a powerful concept, and it was helping him avoid a whole lot of worry and stress. If Lamont had gone to this meeting just six months ago, he would've been a wreck and made everybody else on his team crazy, too.

So, despite this morning's frigid temperature, and that he was getting ready to face a devious, powerful, and fierce adversary, Lamont was happy and about ready to shout. He couldn't wait to see how the Lord was going to show up and show out at this meeting, which was being held at his church. How Craig and Rev. Quincey managed to pull that one off was a mystery to him. But some mysteries didn't need time wasted on being solved. Sometimes you accepted it as the blessing it was and kept stepping.

Lamont squeezed his wife's hand.

"You're looking good enough to make me late for this meeting, Mrs. Green."

"Thank you, Mr. Green," she answered him grinning.

Lamont gave his wife the once-over and sucked on his side tooth. The girl was so sharp he feared her outfit would cut up his leather seats. She was wearing a lavender St. John's pantsuit with black trimming, black suede ankle boots, and black sapphire stud earrings trimmed with diamonds and set in platinum. It was a simple yet elegant outfit that signified class and good taste—

especially when she added her finishing touch of that lavender leather swing coat and matching hat and gloves he loved so much. Theresa was wearing that coat the first time he acknowledged that she was capable of pulling at his heartstrings.

"You know, you not looking so bad yourself, Mr. Green."

"Hey, we put on the spiritual armor of God when we prayed this morning. And I didn't think the Lord would mind too much if I added the right outer garment to go with that inner gear."

"I don't think he would, either, hubby. Because the angels assigned to help you with all of that heavenly armor, looking at you, boy, and saying, 'He know he is big-pimpin' today.'"

"Girl, you crazy," Lamont said with a hearty laugh. "But I do look awfully good, don't I?"

"Umm . . . hmm," Theresa answered as she surveyed his charcoal wool slacks, lavender-tinted, gray silk mock turtleneck sweater, and gray, black and pale purple tweed sports jacket. His charcoal cashmere overcoat, a Christmas present from Theresa, was lying on the back seat. And he had the smoothest "Big Daddy" charcoal fedora sitting on his head, as well as a pair of new black leather lace-up boots on his feet. If looking good could get Lamont that contract, then the meeting might as well be canceled.

He backed the car out and blew a kiss at Theresa before pulling off.

"Baby, you put it on me this morning. Umph! I am *ready* to do battle."

"Just trying to be a good helpmeet, baby," Theresa added grinning, winking at him.

"Grown, fast-tailed gal," Lamont said, in mock imitation of his aunt.

"You like it, boy," she answered.

"God is good . . ."

When they pulled into the church parking lot, Rev. Quincey was standing outside waiting for him, blowing on his hands and stomping his feet in a feeble effort to keep warm. They got out of the car and he took them in through a side door, so that they didn't have to be bothered with any of the folks eating the breakfast prepared by Roxanne Daye's missionary group in the lobby.

"I thought you two would prefer waiting for the meeting to start in the comfort of my study," Rev. Quincey said as he opened the door, ushered them in, and locked it.

As soon as they got back in the inner office, there lined up against the wall was family and friends. The first person Lamont saw was his son, Montavous. He hadn't seen his baby boy in months. Monty had been down in New Orleans working on the Gospel United Church's task force to rebuild some of the churches that were destroyed by Hurricane Katrina.

"Dad," Monty said and grabbed his father in a big hug. "Sorry couldn't make the wedding. Mama said that it was kind of impromptu and you would understand. But she—"

"I also said," Gwen stated, coming out of her seat way back in the corner of the office, "That he had better be here today. He flew into Durham late last night."

"Thank you, Gwen," Lamont said.

"It's our wedding present to you and Theresa. Just wanted the two of you to know that we love you and think you make the best couple."

"Thank you, Gwen," Theresa said and went to hug her and Monty.

"Now that that's been taken care of, can we get down to business?" James asked. "Because it's 'bout time you two newlyweds made it to your own meeting."

"They still on their honeymoon, baby," Rhonda said. "And judging from that great big hickey on your sister-in-law's neck, we better be glad they even made it to this meeting."

Theresa blushed and put her hand up to her neck.

"Wrong side," Vanessa said and laughed.

"Yeah, baby," Lamont said, grinning because he just knew he was the man. "It's right here." He kissed the spot and whispered, "Still as sweet as it was when I first laid down my mark."

"Boy!" Theresa said, all embarrassed.

"I bet that's just what you said earlier," Lena stated. "That's why your neck all hickeyed up."

"We need to quit teasing Mrs. Green and do what we are all up in here on top of each other for—pray," Rev. Quincey said.

"Now grab somebody's hand and bow your heads. Miss Queen Esther, will you lead us in prayer?"

Queen Esther poured some anointing oil on her hands and held them out so that everybody could get some of it. When everybody had oil on their palms, they rejoined hands and she began.

"Lord, we come together in agreement that You are going to bless Lamont with the opportunity to rebuild

Cashmere Estates, and that You will give him all the money and support he will need to do it and do it right. We bind up anyone and anything who will try to stop this in the name of Jesus. And when he enters the sanctuary and gives his presentation, we claim in Jesus' name that somebody on that committee is going to award our Lamont with the contract. Let us all say . . ."

"Amen," they finished, and then added as one voice, "In Jesus' name."

"Let's go, y'all," Lauren Rhodes told them.

The meeting wasn't scheduled to begin for another twenty minutes. But when they entered the lobby, it was clear of all of those people who were there just fifteen minutes ago. They walked up to the main doors of the sanctuary and found them closed.

Rev. Quincey pulled at the door, and was stopped by a member of Jethro Winters's team, who said, "You will have to wait until Mr. Winters finishes his presentation."

"But this meeting wasn't even scheduled to start yet," Rev. Quincey stated, and had to be held back by Joseph, James, Bug, Monty, *and* Cousin Buddy when that man closed the door to the sanctuary of *his* church in his face.

"Oh, I know that white boy didn't try and clown you like that, Rev.," Rhonda protested, ready to snatch that door open and hurt somebody.

Baby Doll and Mr. Lacy, who more and more were becoming integral parts of the church's spiritual life, started laughing because they knew they were getting ready to engage in a good fight. And if there was one thing both of them enjoyed, it was a good fight for all the right reasons.

"Oh, we are going to turn this meeting out," Baby Doll said, wondering why everybody was staring so hard at her clothes.

"Uhh, Miss Baby Doll," Bug said, "I kinda like your suit."

"Thank you, baby," she said. "It was a Valentine's Day present from my sweet husband."

"It's nice," everybody said, in awe of the pretty pink corduroy pantsuit she was wearing with a white turtle-neck sweater. It was kind of unnerving to see her dressed so regular. And then somebody thought to check her feet.

"Whew. I was worried that a whole bunch of things were going to be out of whack until I glanced down," Rhonda leaned over and whispered to Theresa, who took note of Miss Baby Doll's pink jelly shoes and said, "Yeah, talking about being thankful for small miracles."

"Come on," Mr. Lacy said as he started walking away. "We are going up in that meeting and turning it out."

They walked outside and around to the side door that gave access to the choir loft. Rev. Quincey opened the door with his key and they all walked right in and took their seats in the choir loft, with the exception of Rev. Quincey and Lamont. They went and sat in the pulpit chairs.

Jethro Winters was giving a detailed report of his plans to a large audience from a podium that had been placed on the floor near the center of the altar. He stopped talking when he heard the doors opening and turned around to find out what all of the commotion was about. When he saw all of those black folk sitting up in the choir loft behind Lamont Green he was "fit to be tied." And he became spitting mad when he saw his wife and her new employees, Charmayne and another high-maintenance-looking black woman, sitting in the back of the church laughing.

"I believe," he said through tight lips and clenched teeth, "that you people have violated protocol and need to move to a more suitable location until I am through with my business."

Rev. Quincey glanced over at his audio man and nodded. When Jethro started back into his report, all everybody heard was that annoying squeaking sound no one could stand to listen to.

Nina Rhodes, who was in charge of Green Pastures' presentation, nodded over at Yvonne Fountain and a small ensemble of musicians to start playing. She smiled at the audio man, who immediately slipped her DVD into place and turned the lights down.

Yvonne, heedless of Jethro's angry posturing and sputtering, joyfully struck up one of those good-ole country gospel songs by North Carolina's own Luther Barnes. Almost everybody in the sanctuary got up out of their seats and started swaying and clapping like they were at a church service.

When Jethro Winters, along with a few members of his team, made to protest, Rev. Quincey pulled a cordless microphone from out of nowhere and said, "You broke the rules when you started the meeting early and without your competition present. Then you and your

people came up in *my* church and attempted to bar me
and my members from entering the sanctuary. Now,
when I last checked the list of folks who tithe to keep
this church running, I did not see a one of your names.
So, you sit down before I forget that I am a preacher and
come out of this pulpit to deal with you like the brother-
man that I am."

Unless he wanted another fight on his hands, and this
time in front of television cameras, Jethro realized that
it was in his best interest to sit down for the moment.
He reasoned that Green couldn't do too much, if he had
to rely on some old country Negro church music to get
his point across. Black people killed him with always
having to play music, sing a song, and give a testimony
when they had to deal with some serious business.

The musicians resumed playing, and the audio man
turned Nina's clever and classy DVD presentation back
on. It began with a brief history of the old Cashmere Estates with pictures of the homes, the landscape, and the
people who once lived there. Then it showed how the
community had deteriorated over the years and fallen
into the wasteland that it was today. There were inter-
views with former residents, footage of the surrounding
neighborhoods, and Green Pastures' trump card—
Nina's virtual creation of the new Cashmere Estates. It
was so incredible, so warm and inviting, and so beautiful that folks— black and white, old and young, rich
and poor—got up out of their seats and gave Lamont's
company a standing ovation.

The television and newspaper people went crazy with
excitement over what they were seeing. They had been
invited to the meeting by the Winters Development Cor-

poration. But the true news-breaking story was coming from what one reporter would coin "the little company that did."

Jethro tried to ease out before the media saw him. But Bailey, who knew many of the members of the press, smoothly guided their attention to him and his team members as they were walking out of the very door Lamont, Theresa, and the rest had been forced to walk in.

Craig Utley ran up to Lamont and almost knocked him down when he grabbed him in a powerful bear hug. Others affiliated with the DUDC, with the sole exception of Patty Harmon, Parvell Sykes, and that lone black man whose name so few people could remember, were now running up to Lamont to congratulate him on receiving the contract.

Lamont looked back at his wife and blew her a kiss. When he turned to answer a barrage of questions from the media, he saw Jethro's wife, Charmayne, and Chablis. All three smiled at him before they left. Bailey had recently started a company that would rebuild individual homes and small-business sites that had fallen into disrepair. She was quite aware that they would need to partner with Green Pastures from time to time on various business ventures, and wanted its CEO and president, Lamont Green, on her side.

Lamont knew the Lord had given him the contract ever since he got the check from Bailey Winters. But to see how it all played out and manifested was nothing short of incredible. There really was nobody like the King of Glory. God was all that, a bag of chips and more, as the teens at the church always said.

"Kinda makes you wonder why more folks haven't wanted to get saved and know Jesus, don't it pastor?" Queen Esther said to Rev. Quincey.

"Uhh huh," was all he said, as he held his fist out for her to give him some "dap."

Epilogue

March, One Year Later

LAMONT AND THERESA WERE SO TIRED, THEY WERE seeing cross-eyed. They had been a part of three move-ins today, and it didn't seem like they were done. James and Rhonda needed help with putting dishes away in the kitchen and dining room. Nina Rhodes wanted Lamont to help her with placing her new sofa at her cottage around the corner from James and Rhonda. And Theresa's parents, who'd been talking about downsizing for years, would not leave them alone until they stopped by to see how the unpacking at their new row house was coming along.

As much faith as he had in his project, seeing it come to life was a miracle. When Lamont and Theresa first drove into the new development, he got out of the car when he saw the entry sign. Tears streamed down his cheeks as he ran his hands over the smooth blue limestone with large black lettering that read, "Cashmere Estates: A Green Pastures Community."

He and Theresa had walked the entire property hand in

hand, praising God when the first set of homes went up. When they reached what was to become the new Meeting House, Theresa started to cry when she saw the street sign, "Holy Ghost Corner." It was on that very spot that she and Lamont shared their first kiss. And it was on that same corner that the Green Pastures team prayed for this to come to be.

But today, moving day for the first set of residents, was beyond anything that either Lamont or Theresa could imagine. Cashmere Estates was finished and it was something to see.

There were four different types of homes in the development. The first had been built with young families, single-parent families, and empty nesters in mind. The units were one- and two-story red-brick row houses with anywhere from 1,300 to 1,700 square feet. Every home had a small front yard, with a slightly larger backyard, which included a deck and storage unit. A park was nearby with a pavilion, clubhouse, picnic tables, tennis and basketball courts, and Olympic-sized indoor and outdoor pools. The walking/biking trail, which started at the park, wrapped around the entire community.

The second set of homes, which were larger, consisted of one-story stucco cottages in Caribbean colors of yellow, peach, pale green, turquoise, and light blue. The homes started at 1,600 square feet and could get as large as 2,000. The yards were about the same size as the first set of units. And about the only difference concerning the yards were the screened-in back porches attached to the decks. To complete the Caribbean theme of the landscaping, there was a wonderful garden square set in the midst of this section that would display all manner of bright flowers and foliage during the summer months.

The third section of homes was the most expensive and distinctive. The elegant gold and pink brick townhouses ranged from 1,900 all the way up to 3,200 square feet. They had the same amount of yard space as the homes in the other sections, with one added feature—a second-floor screened-in porch that opened from the sitting room off the master bedroom.

These homes were so nice, Theresa and Lamont snatched up one of the larger units and immediately put both of their homes on the market. They were like two little kids when they worked out all of the building details with Lauren Rhodes-Ramirez, who never failed to check on their home when conducting her routine site visits to make sure that each house in Cashmere Estates was being built to perfection.

Every day during construction, Lauren could be seen walking around in jeans, Green Pastures work shirt, green Timberlands, and a pretty green hard hat with "Lauren" painted on it in a soft yellow. And sometimes trailing behind her were those three bad little boys running around in their own hard hats and Bob the Builder tools, driving everybody but their mama crazy.

But the award-winning section in this already highly praised community was built especially for the seniors. It consisted of three single-story gold-brick buildings. Two buildings housed senior citizens who were healthy or had minor health and mobility concerns. And the middle building provided nursing care for those needing it on a permanent and temporary basis. The middle building also contained a senior clubhouse, a cafeteria that served some of the best food in town, and an urgent care clinic.

The press loved Cashmere Estates, the public officials loved Cashmere Estates, real estate agents loved Cashmere Estates, and mortgage companies loved Cashmere Estates. But most importantly, the residents loved Cashmere Estates.

When the press came to interview the brand-new manager of the janitorial team, Mrs. Baby Doll Lacy, she told them, "You peoples is walking round this place oohing and ahhing about how good it look, how warm it feels, how affordable each level of the different houses is, how caring the developer is, and being all in awe over how Lamont Green was able to get something like this done. Well, Lamont Green didn't get this done—God did. And since nothing is impossible with God, the awe should be over getting a good whiff of His wondrous working power."

Theresa and Lamont left her parents' house and headed toward the car. It was getting late and she had to go by the store to place some orders. Lamont was about to open the door for Theresa, when he paused and said, "Did you hear that?"

"What?"

"That," he said and then sniffed the air.

"What you sniffing at and listening to?"

"Theresa," Lamont said grinning. "Can't you hear the Delfonics on the radio? It's coming out of somebody's open window. Imagine that—an open window with a radio in it."

She tilted her head, and sure enough, "La La Means I Love You" was sounding so good in the window of a house several feet away from them. Then she sniffed and laughed.

"Lawd, the houses ain't even up good and somebody out here cooking barbecue."

Several little boys ran past dribbling basketballs, followed by somebody's sister on a fancy scooter calling out, "I'm tellin' Mama. She said you had to let me come with you."

Their church's van passed by, going in the direction of the seniors' section.

"Senior singles night meeting," Lamont said.

"Then that explains why I saw Mother Clydetta Overton sitting in the front seat of the van," Theresa told him. "I didn't realize that she had joined Fayetteville Street."

"She didn't," Lamont told her. "I just said that it's senior singles night."

The only ice cream truck Green Pastures allowed in the neighborhood turned into the development just as the church van made its way out.

"Why is the ice cream man out here? It's still kinda chilly outside."

"He lives here and sells his homemade ice cream all year round."

The truck stopped and a few mothers went over to get a gallon from Mr. Lacy, who thankfully was sitting on the passenger side.

"Baby," Theresa asked, "who is driving the truck?"

"Mr. Lacy's brother."

"The one who can't walk?"

"Don't ask or try to figure it out, Theresa. I've tried it. And you'll only give yourself a headache."

Lamont leaned on his car.

"Come here, Miss Thang of the legendary Miss Thang's Holy Ghost Corner and Church Woman's Boutique," he said and grabbed Theresa around the waist, pulling her close to him.

"You do realize that you started your first business here, when you had that cart of 'Assorted Church Lady Items' back in the day," Lamont said.

Theresa had almost forgotten about that cart. Her husband was absolutely right. What was to become Miss Thang's got its start almost on the exact spot where she had just planted her feet. She turned back and smiled at Lamont, who returned the favor with a soft kiss on the lips.

He tightened his hold on his wife as they watched the sun setting in a pink and purple and blue Carolina sky, basking in the sights, sounds, and delicious smells of home.

Reading Group Guide

Discussion Questions

1.) Theresa Hopson is described in the book as a black woman who has it all. She is saved, loves the Lord, is well educated, owns a lovely home, is blessed with family and friends, and is the sole proprietor of a thriving business she built from the ground up. Yet Miss Lady is not happy—not really. What is the source of Theresa's hidden unhappiness, and what does faith in God have to do with addressing her dilemma?

2.) Lamont Green has it all—or so he thinks. Unlike Theresa, Mr. Man is very happy and is actually content with his life. Even his desire to win that contract to rebuild his old community, Cashmere Estates, doesn't make him unhappy, even though there are times when the problem weighs heavily on his heart. What do you think about someone like Lamont, who allegedly has everything but Jesus, and doesn't have a clue that is what he needs for things to work out?

3.) Why are the characters Baby Doll Henderson and Mr. Lacy important to what happens to the main characters in the story?

4.) When the Saints encounter people like Parvell Sykes and Jethro Winters, what do they learn from these troublemaking blessing blockers?

5.) Ephesians 6:12 states: *"For we are not fighting against people made of flesh and blood, but against the evil rulers and authorities of the unseen world, against those mighty powers of darkness who rule this world, and against wicked spirits in the heavenly realms"(New Life Bible)*. How did this scripture play out in the lives of the characters in the book? And who represented those "mighty powers of darkness who rule this world"?

6.) Queen Esther Green is a no-nonsense, bible-toting, oil-carrying, and scripture-speaking kind of woman. The "folk" in *Holy Ghost Corner* look to her for a Word from the Lord and Holy Ghost–inspired guidance. Why do they need her? And why do we need the Queen Esther Greens of the world in our lives?

7.) Look up Romans 8:31 in your Bible, where it states, *"What can we say about such wonderful things? If God is for us, who can ever be against us?" (NLB)* How did you see this scripture come to life in the lives of the characters?

8.) What made Cashmere Estates such a wonderful place in which to live, and why was it so important that Lamont Green be the one to rebuild it?

9.) Why is it so important that God be in the midst of building affordable housing in our cities? How did Cashmere Estates reflect this?

10.) Who were your favorite and least favorite characters in the book?

Author's Note

I had a great time writing *Holy Ghost Corner*. I live in Durham, North Carolina, and I relished the opportunity to create some folks who would traverse my daily stomping grounds. For example, the Kroger's where the character Dayeesha works really exists, and many of my friends and family members shop there.

I hope that you, the reader, enjoyed this story, the first of three interconnected tales of contemporary Kingdom living in the Bull City. It is in this story that I take my "church folk" outside the traditional confines of the church building, to explore what life is like for the Saints when they pull out of the church parking lot. But even more so, I wanted to tell a story of how God blesses us with the desires of our hearts when we put Him first in our lives.

Theresa Hopson had all kinds of blessings, and the one thing she needed to do was trust that the Lord was listening to the nuances of the beat of her heart when it came to blessing her with the love of her life—a man only God could choose. And then there was Lamont, who needed to understand that all that he was, and could ever hope to be, was due to making Jesus Lord of his life.

It gave me great joy to write a story that demonstrated all the miraculous ways in which God works in the lives of those who love Him with all their hearts, with all their minds, and with all their might, only to discover how to love their neighbors as themselves. Words from the Word upon which hang all the laws of the prophets.

God bless you readers—each and every one. May you prosper as your soul propers in Jesus' Name.

Michele Andrea Bowen

MICHELE ANDREA BOWEN

RETURNS TO THE WORLD OF

CHURCH FOLK!

Please turn this page
for a preview of

MORE CHURCH FOLK

Available in hardcover in July 2010

"When the godly are in authority, the people rejoice. But when the wicked are in power, they groan."

PROVERBS 29: 2

Chapter One

REV. THEOPHILUS HENRY SIMMONS, SR., WAS SENT TO serve as the Senior Pastor of Freedom Temple Gospel United Church in St. Louis, Missouri at the conclusion of one of the denomination's most corrupt and volatile Triennial General Conferences. Only one other conference made it to the "Crazy Triennial Conference Hall of Fame," and most of the folk responsible for that meeting had gone on to their just rewards. But back in 1963, good, stalwart, saved, and sanctified church folk feared that the devil had managed to get such a firm foothold in the church, God was going to strike each and every one of them dead for just being listed on the church roll.

At that conference, folks were shocked and dismayed to discover that some of their top leaders had the unmitigated gall to run a brothel right in the midst of the conference, as if it were the first in a chain of franchised "ho houses"—and in a funeral home of all places. Whoever heard of a bunch of black people, no back then,

Negroes, wanting to party at a place where dead people were in "escrow" en route to their final destination? Black people didn't make it a habit of hanging out in funeral homes. And anybody foolish enough to differ from this norm, were clearly either crazy, or corrupt and without a lick of sense.

There were a lot of mad church folk, who were ready to throw down on those preachers with "membership" at the "ho house." When that "blue book" hit the conference floor, with the names of the "members," folks bombarded the conference floor platform in Virginia Union's gymnasium, and found out who was wrong and who was right. That information led to some much needed changes in the Gospel United Church—changes that led to Rev. Murcheson James being elected to an Episcopal seat, and Theophilus's appointment to Freedom Temple.

Twenty-two years later, Freedom Temple had grown from a respectable congregation of five hundred members, to one of the major players in St. Louis's black church community, boasting three thousand dedicated and tithing members under the leadership of their senior pastor, Rev. Theophilus Simmons, Sr. Shortly after Theophilus took over the helm, the church bought up all of the property within a ten block radius. They rebuilt the church into an impressive structure with a beautiful, state-of-the-art sanctuary, a suite for the pastor which included a full bath, library, kitchenette, and conference room. There was a small book store, and two more libraries—one for the youth, and another one for the adults.

The First Lady's mother, Lee Allie Lane Hawkins, had worked alongside her husband, Pompey, to design the new church kitchen and cafeteria that was large enough to host the Annual Conference and most wedding receptions. There was also a nursery, teen room with video games, a gymnasium, first aid room, and several good sized education rooms. There was also a large conference room, where big meetings and workshops could be held.

The actual grounds of the church had been landscaped by Dannilynn Meeting, a well respected architect coming out of Evangeline T. Marshall University in Durham, North Carolina. Dannilynn was the granddaughter of the premier black architect in the country, Daniel Meeting, who had been responsible for designing most of Eva T. Marshall University.

There were flower gardens to walk through, sitting areas, a playground that was so much fun, many of the teens and adults loved to share in the fun with the younger children, and the best basketball court in the area. And that was a good thing because Freedom Temple Gospel United Church had the best teen basketball teams for boys and girls in the St. Louis metropolitan area.

Freedom Temple was a happening place, and if you listened to any of the members talk, you found out that it was a great church to attend, with a wonderful pastor and first lady. The women admired Essie Simmons's style, they shopped at her boutique, and they all came to her whenever they needed a one-of-a-kind designer outfit—be it a handcrafted wedding gown, debutante gown, or a trousseau for the bride's honeymoon wardrobe. Essie received so many requests for her designs that she had to hire a second designer, two seamstresses, and a tailor to keep up with the volume of requests.

As far as Theophilus and Essie were concerned, it was an even better church to pastor than it was to attend. They loved Freedom Temple and felt so blessed that the good Lord had seen fit to let them serve in the capacity of senior pastor and first lady. Their members were warm and loving people. They were also people who loved the Lord, were hungry for his Word, and were determined that they would not stay baby Christians once they turned their lives over to Christ. The folks at Freedom Temple kept their pastor on his toes. Since taking over the pastorship at Freedom Temple, Theophilus had found himself needing to study Greek, Hebrew, Latin, and Arabic, just so he would be able to continue to inspire and educate his members about the Word and the goodness of the Lord.

Today was the third Sunday, and Theophilus had been at church since six a.m. Every third Sunday he met with his ministerial staff so that they could pray together, cover each other in prayer, and encourage one another in their walks with the Lord. Preaching was hard work. Pastoring was harder. Folks just didn't know—they didn't even have a clue of what it took to be a good pastor and a great preacher.

Rev. Simmons was both—and that was saying something. Some ministers could preach Lazarus out of the grave. And some could pastor a whole city to the Pearly Gates of heaven. But to be able to do both? Man-oh-man! Now, that took some doing.

Theophilus knew that he was both, just like the young brother sitting next to him—Rev. Obadiah Quincey, from Durham, North Carolina—was well on his way to becoming. Obadiah was a graduate of the school of divinity at Evangeline T. Marshall University, and he had been selected by Theophilus to do his requisite two-year apprenticeship under him at Freedom Temple. Obadiah was sharp, well read, and had a great sense of humor. He had done well here. About the only problem Theophilus could discern, was that the young man, his wife Lena, and their baby boy, were all homesick for Durham.

Theophilus was so sleepy this morning, he could barely keep his eyes open while the announcements were being read by Mrs. Tommie Ann Jenkins, who at eighty-three, was one of the meanest members in the church. He couldn't stand the way that old woman abused the status of her age. Mrs. Tommie Ann was definitely blessed to have lived this long, and to be as healthy and robust as she was. But she was (and according to some of the other older members had always been) the worse announcement person in the history of "announcement people" at Freedom Temple.

Once, when he felt guilty about wanting to throw Mrs. Tommie Ann up a tree and leave her there, one of his other ninety something year olds told him, "Pastor, don't feel bad about that old heifer. She has always been like that—ain't nothing changed about Tommie Ann in all of the years that I have known her. She was mean and stupid at 25, she was a dumb cow at 40, she made folks want to slap her at 66, and now she's lived to be old enough to make somebody in this church give her a personal invite to go and visit the Lord and never come back.

"I am just amazed that Tommie Ann has lived this long and not been cut or shot by some woman who was mad at her for sleeping with her husband. So, don't you feel bad about that, Pastor. 'Cause that thang is a piece of work. And now she's just old enough to get away with being crazy."

A bunch of folk, mainly his senior members, had begged the pastor to retire Mrs. Tommie Ann from this position. But God had not given him the go-ahead. When Theophilus first took the matter to the Lord in prayer, God touched his heart with these words: *"Wait. Just wait and let her fire herself."*

Theophilus just couldn't even begin to imagine how someone who was so prideful and thought so highly of this particular church job, would find a way to fire themselves. He would have thought that a person like a Mrs. Tommie Ann would be very good at finding a way to keep such a position. But the Word said that God's ways were not our ways, and His thoughts not our thoughts. So, given that biblical truth, Theophilus was obedient and trusted that if God said wait, and he waited, one day Mrs. Tommie Ann would up and fire herself. He just hoped that day was sooner than later.

The only other thing that stopped the church from mutinying against Mrs. Tommie Ann reading the announcements every third Sunday, was because she'd been at Freedom Temple so long, she knew way too much on just about everybody at the church. As one of the members of the "Senior Usher Board" said.

"Don't nam-nobody wanna mess with that evil-tailed heifer and make her mad enough to start giving the morning announcements on who been creepin', who been stealin', who been drinkin', and who sittin' at home from church 'cause they been fired and don't have no money to put gas in they car."

The teens in the congregation—including the three Simmons offspring—secretly hoped Mrs. Tommie would continue to do the third Sunday announcements because she was some of the best entertainment they could expect to have during the morning service. It was wonderful to attend a church that was so on point, it did so much right. But it could be kind of boring if nothing crazy, outlandish, or just blatantly ridiculous happened at your church. You needed these incidents to happen, so that you could go to school on Monday morning and compare notes with teens attending other churches in the city.

Freedom Temple teens frequently bemoaned that they didn't have enough crazy church folk in their congregation to talk about with their friends at school. But this morning, things were getting ready to take a turn for the worse. And as far as the young people in the church were concerned, it wouldn't get any better than this.

Mrs. Tommie Ann steered her walker up to the smaller podium in the pulpit that was to the left of where the pastor sat. She started off with the week's list of birthdays and anniversaries. Then, she went into a lengthy discussion about the members not using up so much toilet tissue in the rest rooms.

That woman held out her hand and waited for the rumored newest old man in her life to place a roll of toilet paper in it. She held it up and said.

"Freedom Temple. This is how we can stop using so much tissue in those bathrooms downstairs. As head of the 'Tissue, Paper Towel, Napkin, and Toilet Paper Ministry' in this church, it is my duty to instruct you properly about the use of such in this church."

"By whose authority," Rev. Quincy leaned over and whispered to his boss very carefully. He did not want to have to deal with Mrs. Tommy Ann if she happened to overhear what he said, and throw a hissy fit on him.

Theophilus whispered, "I don't know because this if the first time I've ever heard of the 'Tissue, Paper Towel, Napkin, and Toilet Paper Ministry.'"

"Rev.," Obadiah whispered, "She's about to do the demonstration."

Mrs. Tommie Ann rolled off three sheets of toilet paper, folded them, and patted the side of her hip like it was her bottom, to show how this was supposed to done by the members of the church.

Essie was sitting in the designated "First Lady" spot, right down from the pulpit. She willed herself away from making eye contact with her husband. She was having a hard enough time keeping it together sitting next to her mother and stepdad. They were passing notes, poking at each other, and trying not to laugh under their breaths.

By now, the teens were riveted to their seats. They could not believe that old woman had a roll of toilet paper, and was showing them how to save on it, by using her hip as her pretend butt.

Mrs. Tommie Ann patted her hip again before giving the usher the toilet paper roll, along with the sheets of tissue she'd used for the demonstration.

"That mean old lady knows good and well that she needs more than a few sheets of toilet paper for her big butt," Linda Simmons, the middle child of the Simmons children whispered, praying that her mama and grand-mother weren't looking up at the balcony, watching her every move with those old Charleston, Mississippi hawk eyes. They could get on your nerves—saw everything. And then, if that wasn't bad enough, they always had a comment—*always*.

"Mama's staring at us," Linda's oldest sister, Sharon whispered.

By now, folks were assuming that Mrs. Tommie Ann Jenkins had gotten enough attention with that toilet paper lecture, to go somewhere and sit down. But as Essie always told her husband, "When did the devil ever become satisfied enough to just go somewhere and sit down."

Mrs. Tommie Ann was not happy with the way her own church members were sitting there looking bored, passing notes, and obviously too spoiled and selfish to take note of what she'd tried to tell them. That is what she hated about spoiled and selfish people—they were always so caught up in themselves and what they wanted to say and do. Never mind the other person. It was always all about them.

Her eyes scanned the balcony where most of the teens and young adults liked to sit. She knew why they were up there instead of on the main floor. They loved that perch—gave them a perfect view of everything going on in church on a Sunday morning. And on top of that, it afforded them the opportunity to whisper, snicker, and pass notes about what was going on during service.

She stared at them for a second, eyes narrowing into slits when they landed on that little red hussy, Linda Simmons. Mrs. Tommie Ann couldn't stand that little girl. It wasn't that Linda had ever done anything to the lady. Mrs. Tommie Ann didn't like Linda because she knew Linda saw straight through her and never tried to act like she didn't.

"She is staring at you, Linda," T. J., or Theophilus, Jr., said to his sister.

"I see her," Linda retorted, and stared back at that mean woman without flinching.

"That Linda is just like her mama," Mrs. Tommie Ann thought, as she picked up the announcement bulletin.

"I don't know why Theophilus has so much trouble with his announcement people," Essie's mother leaned over and whispered to her husband, Pompey Hawkins, who nodded, remembering some past announcement people at Theophilus's old church, Greater Hope in Memphis. As good as a pastor Theophilus was, he always managed to have one fool on his team of folk giving the Sunday morning announcements.

Mrs. Tommie Ann fumbled with the bulletin for a moment. She looked like something else was bothering her. She put the bulletin on the podium and pushed her false teeth at the top of her mouth up and down for a few seconds with her bottom lip. She looked like she was trying to scratch her top gums with the bottom of her mouth. When that didn't work, Mrs. Tommie Ann sucked the teeth up loudly and wiggled her mouth around in a feeble attempt to make the proper adjustments to her teeth. And when that attempt failed, she reached down to the pocketbook anchored on her walker and got something out. Mrs. Tommie Ann hung the pocketbook back on the walker, took her top teeth out of her mouth, put some extra Poligrip on them, put them back in, sucked them into place, slipped the tube of Poligrip in her pocketbook, and said.

"Christian friends, before I finish with the announcements, you all need to get your registration straight for the upcoming Triennial General Conference in Durham, North Carolina, before they run out of hotel rooms, and the prices go up. I keep telling the pastor that he needs to do something about this since he is such a big shot in the Gospel United Church. But Pastor is so hard-headed and thinks he knows everything."

Theophilus couldn't even get upset with that old lady for talking that junk because he was still trying to keep it together through the "Toilet Paper Ministry's" demonstration, and her teeth. Mrs. Tommie Ann had done some crazy stuff while giving the announcements during his tenure as the pastor of Freedom Temple. But she had never fixed her teeth before the entire congregation. It reminded him of the time that old man's teeth shot out of his mouth at an Annual Conference in Memphis, Tennessee, back in the early 1960s. That old man was talking crazy, too—just like Mrs. Tommie Ann. And his teeth shot out and landed right on the altar, looking like they were trying to grin at somebody from outside of his mouth. That teeth mess was funny then, and it was still funny now.

The kids, and especially Theophilus and Essie's three children—Sharon, Linda, and T. J.—were sitting up in the balcony about to lose it, trying not to laugh at that crazy old lady. Their dad knew they had worked hard to keep it together when Mrs. Tommie Ann did the toilet paper thing. But the teeth sent them right over the edge.

The entire balcony row of teens was now ducking down under the pews, trying so hard not to laugh too loud. Linda, who was the splitting image of her mother, got up and tried to sneak out of the sanctuary without her dad seeing her. But she didn't escape the pastor's scrutiny, especially since she was standing in the vestibule laughing loud enough to be heard back in church.

The parents all looked up in that balcony and tried to give their children that age old stare that said, "I'm gone come up there and beat your behind if you don't sit up and act like you got some daggone sense." But it didn't work this time because every time they looked at those children, they fell out with laughter themselves.

Essie leaned over and whispered to Precious Powers, who was a member and good friend, "What possessed that old woman to do that up in that pulpit like that? It ain't like she is senile. She crazy but all of her gray matter is intact. And look, that thang has the nerve to get mad."

Actually, Mrs. Tommie Ann was past mad this morning—she was furious. She picked up that big orange and yellow pocketbook hanging off of her walker, and said, "I can not believe those bad-tailed children of yours is up there laughing in the Lord's house like that. Now, Pastor," she said to Theophilus, "I've been reading the announcements for over sixty years, and nobody ever laughed at me like those children are doing right now. And that lil' red gal of yours owe me an apology."

Theophilus took a deep breath to get a grip on his anger. He looked over at Essie, who was on her way over to the pulpit, and shook his head. This was something that he had to handle as the pastor, even though that old heifer had pushed every single parent button he had in him. He walked up to the large podium in front of the pastor's chair, grabbed each side, tilted his head a bit, and stared at Mrs. Tommie Ann for a few seconds. The church was so quiet you could hear folks holding their breaths in anticipation of what the pastor was going to say to that mean old lady.

Most folk in this congregation had been waiting for the day when the pastor told that crazy Jenkins woman to take her walker-toting, orangey-red-dyed-hair, dyed reddish brown and thickly-drawn-on eyebrows self somewhere and sit the heck down! Today, Mrs. Tommie Ann had finally gone far enough to make the pastor check her, and check her good. It was enough to make some of the Saints get up and start running all over the church, praising God for this mighty miracle in their lives.

Freedom Temple folk loved themselves some Rev. Simmons. Theophilus was a good pastor—superb preacher, astute businessman, exceptional clerical leader, patient, and compassionate. It was his compassion for souls like Mrs. Tommie Ann that stopped him from zooming down on her the first time she showed the rim of her britches to everybody. But this morning, folks knew that she had gone as far as to "tear her draws" with the pastor.

You didn't mess Rev. Simmons—especially over some pure-tee foolishness. You didn't take it upon yourself to roll up on the First Lady. And you definitely didn't get crazy enough to take pot-shots at the Simmons children. If there was one thing their big, fine, chocolate pastor hated, it was "church mess"—particularly when that mess was directed at a member of the church family, or a member of his own family. At some point the pastor would eat you up alive if you didn't stop while the going was good.

"Sister Jenkins," Theophilus said sternly, opting

to forego calling Mrs. Tommie Ann by her pet church name—Mrs. Tommie Ann.

"Yes," she answered, matching his stare, as if to say, "I ain't *scared* of you."

"I just want to take this moment to thank you for your sixty some-odd years of service to this great church as a long-standing member of the Announcement Ministry. And since this is your last Sunday working in this capacity, I would like for the entire congregation to stand and applaud you for such dedicated and constant service. Freedom Temple has never and *never, ever* will experience the way you have handled the relaying of information to this great church each and every third Sunday of the month.

"Thank you, Sister Jenkins, and God bless you as you take a seat and witness the service of the next person who will assume this responsibility. Come on, church. Stand up and give Sister Jenkins the send-off she deserves."

Everybody in church stood up and gave Mrs. Tommie Ann Jenkins a round of applause. She had been mean and hateful to so many of her fellow members, and they were ecstatic to see her go. A couple of folks she'd been especially mean to because she thought her family was better than theirs, started giving out whistles and were cheering. People at Freedom Temple were sick and tired of being sick and tired of this woman.

Mrs. Tommie Ann was outdone. She had been holding this post for decades. She'd been getting away with doing other people in the congregation bad. And frankly, she didn't ever think that all of that would come to an end.

Oh, she knew the pastor wanted to get rid of her, and

she had prepared to fight him down to the ground to keep her position of power in this church. But she wasn't prepared for this. It was hard to cut the fool when folks were up clapping and cheering over you.

Essie caught her husband's eye and winked. She had to hand it to her man, he was good. Few folk, including Essie herself, would have thought of handling that woman like he did. She winked again, and blushed when he winked back. Essie knew that wink, and the promise behind it. She picked up her church bulletin and tried to fan away the heated flush that was spreading across her face.

Theophilus grinned that mannish grin, completely unaware of the church women who suddenly felt an urge to fan themselves with their church bulletins. He walked over to Mrs. Tommie Ann and gave her a big hug and a kiss, trying not to laugh when she rolled her eyes at him. Then he said, "I would like my financial officer on the Steward Board to make sure you have a parting gift of five hundred dollars at the close of today's service."

He turned back towards Obadiah and said.

"I want you to oversee this, Rev. Quincey. Make sure that Mrs. Jenkins receives this gift before she leaves this church."

Obadiah nodded, fighting the urge to blurt out, "Why me, Pastor? Why me?"

Mrs. Tommie Ann Jenkins was the last church member he wanted to be bothered with this morning. Folks just didn't know that preaching was not easy—not by a long shot.

Mrs. Tommie Ann wanted to cuss out the pastor but was stopped dead in her tracks by that unexpected gift of five hundred dollars. Instead, she thanked the pastor, got a good grip on her walker and with the help of one of the ushers standing nearby, came down from the pulpit, and went and sat down.

Theophilus started smiling. It was so good to know the Lord, to be able to hear His voice, and to have sense enough to do what He told you to do. Mrs. Tommie Ann had done exactly what God said she would do—fired herself. All he had to do was wait on the Lord and be of good cheer. And lawd knows he was of good cheer right now!